Saving Graces

by

Alex Charlton

Grosvenor House
Publishing Limited

This book is published by
Grosvenor House Publishing Ltd
Link House
140 The Broadway, Tolworth, Surrey, KT6 7HT.

This book is a work of fiction. Any resemblance to
people or events, past or present, is purely coincidental.

A CIP record for this book
is available from the British Library

ISBN 978-1-83975-610-8

To Laura, the inspiration for
Grace Adams
And so much more in my life!

Acknowledgments

As always to John,
for his infuriatingly searching editing!

Grace Adams
2010

Chapter 1

M25, M3, A303 – the sodden grey landscape whipped by the small black car as it hurtled along the congested, monotonous roads. Grace Adams gripped the steering wheel. She knew she was driving far too fast but, quite frankly, she didn't care. Her mind kept replaying the conversation that she had had with her doctor earlier that week … and the disastrous events that had followed.

The doctor looked intently at his computer screen. He didn't meet her eyes at first, but then slowly lifted his gaze, pushed back his thick dark hair, removed his glasses and said, 'If you do not change your lifestyle Miss Adams, it is unlikely that you will be having a conversation with me – or anyone else – in ten years' time.'

Grace, briefly, stopped fiddling with the strap on her handbag, looked Simon Patterson in the eyes, and really listened. 'What do you mean?'

The young doctor stood up and paced across the room to the window. Outside, incessant rain cloaked windows, the building opposite, the traffic-choked road, battered trees, and the people hunched against the cold, driving wetness.

'To speak frankly, your habits are destroying you. Instead of breathing air, you snort cocaine; instead of drinking liquid that restores your body, you drink alcohol that destroys it. You smoke. Your blood tests are worrying. You are losing weight. A size six may look good on a model, but not coupled with shortness of breath and loss of concentration.' He took a deep breath. 'Don't tempt me to lecture you. You have so many natural advantages that you are wasting.'

'If I had wanted a lecture, I would have gone to my bloody aunt!' retorted Grace. 'Who the hell do you think you are, speaking to me like this?'

'Your doctor. The person you came to because you felt ill. The person who is trying to point out to you that you are destroying yourself.'

'Oh, get lost!' she had shouted as she slung the heavy shoulder bag over her shoulder. 'I've got work to do – even if poncing around giving whiter than white advice is all you have to occupy your time.'

Slamming the surgery door behind her, she strode quickly across the crowded waiting room, her asymmetrical hair, long suede boots and short leather skirt attracting responses that ranged from envy in her contemporaries to a flurry of head-shaking and tutting in the crowd of elderly people who thronged the room, coughing and sharing their latest ailments with relish.

Simon Patterson removed his glasses and for a few moments held his head in his hands. What a waste of a life! Such beauty, obvious intelligence and talent, just being frittered away, whilst outside in the surgery waiting room were people with cancer, diabetes, and all the array of bronchitis, colds and flu that a raw winter incessantly brought into his surgery.

Ah well … Wearily replacing his spectacles, he walked slowly to the door, consciously squaring his shoulders. 'Mrs Patel – good to see you. Do come in and let's see what we can do for you today?'

⊰╫⊱

Grace strode along the pavement, not noticing the dirty puddles or the piles of rubbish in shop doorways.

She was fine. She had just been overdoing things recently. She knew she had – and that had been the reason for doing coke too often, too often even for her. Anyway, so what? Everyone does it – it's London 2010, not 1810! She just needed more energy, more focus, just for one more day – enough to get her latest collection launched and on to the catwalk.

She had gone to the doctor for some medicine or tablets or something, not for a bloody lecture! And she had come away with a swingeing headache, shaking hands – and deep frustration!

She took the staircase two steps at a time to get to her studio.

Her colleague, Tom, looked up wearily from a pile of drawings. 'Hey lovely!' he greeted her automatically, then, seeing her face – chalk-white and dripping wet – 'Grace, sweetie! What's happened?'

She told him. 'Then this tosser of a doctor started telling me I should be living like a nun! No booze, no … anything! And I've got less than twenty-four hours to get this lot out there!' She gestured expansively at the rails of clothes neatly arranged against the wall.

Grace had worked at the small fashion house for two years, still incredulous that she had been head-hunted by the senior designer straight from college because of her edgy autumn/winter collection. Tom had joined at the same time. A couple of years older than Grace, he had just returned from Shanghai with his partner Shu Chiang, whom he had met whilst working in a leading silk-merchant's house. Both men had been exploring new ways in which the feather-light, strong, natural fabric could be coaxed into meeting the needs of the modern market; and in discovering its twenty-first century potential, they had found each other. They shared an immaculate flat on the top floor of a Victorian villa in Notting Hill, where Grace was a frequent visitor.

Grace and Tom had immediately hit it off, and never had Grace been so glad to see her colleague as now. He threw a towel across the studio to her; told her to 'chill'; and got her a strong black coffee.

'Look sweetie, just how much work do you still have to do on these beautiful babies?' he asked, gesturing to the jewel colours of Grace's current collection.

'Oh, God! You know, Tom – the finishing details which can make or break a collection. You *know!*'

'Ssh! Take it easy honey. Can I help?'

'Since it is now seven-thirty and I have precisely eighteen hours before that lot has to appear on stage, you certainly can! Do you have anything with you?'

'Sure.' Slowly Tom took out a twenty-pound note, pulled out a credit card and expertly racked up two thin white lines, rolled up the note and passed it to Grace.

A couple of deep in-breaths later, Grace felt herself relaxing, her spirits rising and her concerns lessening.

'Thanks, Tom. That's so much better! Right, let's get on the case with this lot! Look, I don't want to push you, but do you have any more? I can't see me getting to bed tonight …'

'Grace, you can't live without any sleep at all. You just can't.'

'Oh, sod off, Mr Doctor friend! Have you?'

'OK. Yes, I have,' admitted Tom reluctantly.

By eleven o'clock that evening Grace had given up any idea of returning to her bedsit. It was gloomy and cramped and she had started to use it more like a dumping ground than a home. She felt so much more alive in her minimalist, white design studio, where the only colour was provided by framed vintage copies of *Vogue* covers from the mid-twentieth century and a huge purple and blue poster pronouncing boldly: *Stop avoiding showers; learn to dance in the rain.* Better by far than the peeling paintwork and drab walls of her bedsit.

Surrounded by images which catalogued the changing conceptualisation of style, Grace skilfully coaxed that final magic touch of life and impact into the racks of dresses, shirts and trousers that she had created over the last two months.

Smiling, she held up a vibrant, purple cocktail dress with a deep-red silk sash. It fell perfectly, tulip-shaped, around her slim hips as she held it against her in front of the full-length mirror. Next came a bridal dress, zebra-striped, the veil covered with question marks as it softly cascaded from a black, velvet dunce's cap.

Grace grinned, affirmed that her dystopian take on life was being expressed so clearly in her latest collection. She knew it was risky, but quite frankly people could take it or leave it – and increasingly the public were deciding to take what she offered, embracing her clear, two-fingered statement about marriage, or sexuality, or cocktail parties.

Oh God! Suddenly the room swam. She had forgotten to eat again. Ah well, even the deli on the corner would be closed by now. She rooted around in her chaotic handbag and found a bag of sweets that she had bought a couple of days earlier. Mechanically, she opened one and popped it into her mouth as she walked at her usual fast pace along the corridor to the coffee machine. Black, with sugar: she pressed the slightly grubby buttons and watched the murky, bitter liquid swirl into the cardboard cup.

Hm! Not the Ritz! But she *would* make it one day. She would follow in the footsteps of the people who had inspired her – McQueen, Vivienne Westwood – and would move out of her disastrous bedsit to a place full of sunshine and flowers.

Grace walked quickly back to her design studio. Just eight and a half hours to go before the place opened and everything hit the fan at once. She took a deep breath.

By seven the next morning, her collection was ready. Exquisitely made, innovative, every item making a sharp statement about life, in London, under pressure, where some people made and lost a fortune in a day and others died unnoticed on the streets.

Done.

Chapter 2

Esmé Long, the director of the fashion house, walked slowly and elegantly into Grace's studio. Without speaking, she looked appraisingly along the racks of clothes, pulling out a trouser suit styled as a flak jacket and combats, and the wedding dress.

'Intriguing darling …' Her deep red nails raked the seams and the beading, flicking the gathers of the veil. 'This appeals to me. Let's hope it will appeal to the people who count. We are sold out for this afternoon. Rumour has it that certain *rather influential* people will be here. Time to get this lot downstairs to the dressing rooms. You have Imogen, Kate, Aleysha, Alexsi and Aila to model your collection. They should be arriving in …' consulting her tiny jewelled watch '… about an hour. You haven't got long, Grace.'

Tom drifted into her studio almost as soon as Esmé had left.

'Oooh! I heard that! Who's the favourite girl then?'

Grace tried to grin but felt, almost literally, that she had hit a wall. She was so tired she could hardly move. She couldn't remember when she had last eaten anything but the boiled sweets that she had sucked her way through during the long dark hours while she was putting the last touches to her collection and stood up, swaying slightly.

'You OK?' In an instant, Tom was all concern. 'I can at least carry some of the stuff downstairs for you.'

'Oh, for God's sake Tom, stop fussing around me like an old hen! I can take the lift! You know – that strange modern invention that avoids the stairs?'

Tom was perennially teased for his deep love of all things Victorian. His delicate, swirling, silk creations replicated the style, sound and movement of an earlier and more graceful age.

'Sarcastic!' he pouted. 'Never pays off you know! But I am here if you want me.'

Trying to shrug off her extreme tiredness and short temper, Grace attempted to laugh, 'I'd better not tell Chiang that you go round making those sorts of offers …'

Tom smiled, moving towards the door.

'Tom, have you – you know – do you have anything with you?'

Unusually for him, Tom turned and frowned slightly, checking that no-one was within earshot before he spoke. 'Look darling, I like a line of coke as much as the next person – but just how much have you taken in the last twelve hours or so?'

'Oh, not much. I'm fine. Look at me!'

'I am, honey!'

'Oh, you are turning into a boring old man! Go and try on some of your Victorian party frocks!'

Shaking his head slightly, Tom turned and walked silently away.

Grace realised that her hands were clenched into fists, her purple nails digging viciously into her small palms. She walked deliberately across the scrubbed wooden floorboards to the sash window which overlooked the front entrance of the fashion house four storeys below. It was still bloody raining! Still grey! She leant her hot, tired forehead against the cool, slightly damp glass of the five-metres square work area, which was fast becoming the centre of her life. Her eyes were so tired that she felt as if there was a coating of grit under her eye-lids. She opened them slowly and looked down – down to the pavement far below. Once again, her head swam; she knew her heart was beating far too fast. Already taxis and private cars were arriving and pulling up in front of the immaculate entrance to the fashion house. Standard bay trees had been placed on either side of the imposing Portland stone portico, where two liveried men stood ready to open car doors and welcome the glitterati attending this major fashion event.

Grace was beyond tired. She noted the flock of high-end cars as they arrived, deposited their furred and killer-heeled occupants, and silently left again. It was almost as if she was watching herself watching the cars … this just would not do! Fifty minutes only now to get her collection downstairs and organise the models that had been allocated to her. Aleysha … mm! She could be really tricky. Tall and striking, the word 'diva' could have been coined just for her. Grace had already planned that her signature piece – the anti-wedding dress – would be hers to show off to its very best advantage.

Unbelievably, she got her collection safely down, in the lift, in only another ten minutes. Now she would really have to exercise her patience! Her models were ready: a row of perfectly made-up, perfectly formed – almost doll-like – women who, against all expectations, became vibrantly alive when on the catwalk. They were seductive, funny, quirky, and skilfully created the impression in each member of the audience that they were involved in an intimate dialogue, a nuanced joke, which existed between model and that person alone. They translated ideas and concepts into the stuff of dreams and, in Esmé Long's terms, hard cash.

Lifting her head and consciously trying to take charge, Grace smiled at her models: Imogen, Kate, Alexsi and Aila. 'Where's Aleysha, girls?' she asked.

'Oh, didn't Esmé tell you? She can't make it. Just hanging from last night …'

Grace swallowed, almost in panic. 'No. No she didn't tell me.'

'Well, there is no way we can wear more than our quota!' challenged Aila, hands on child-sized hips. 'We don't want to look ridiculous, or too hot, or … anything.'

Grace bit her lip, turning away slightly and thinking furiously. They were right. Unfortunately, they were absolutely right! They would get flustered and her collection only had a limited time slot. She had fifteen outfits – with Aleysha, that would have been three per girl. She would just have to model herself.

The girls hung around, waiting for direction, looking idly at their nails and whispering quietly behind their hands, for all the world like schoolgirls, thought Grace, irritated beyond measure. She turned to Tom, who was lovingly arranging the delicate folds of cream and rose and lilac that predominated in his hallmark palette. Shu Chiang, skin like gold, dark eyes like almonds, stood smiling by his partner's side.

'Tom, I need your help.'

He was so forgiving, her funny, gay friend.

'Thought so!'

'Tom, Aleysha isn't coming. I have got to model some of my collection. Can Chiang dress the girls?'

'Oh, bless you sweetheart, of course he can!' And seamlessly Tom switched into practical mode, calling over his partner and explaining the help that Grace desperately needed. Shu Chiang often worked with Tom, loving the soft feel and vibrant colours of the clothes that surrounded him. He bowed slightly, smiling, 'My pleasure, Grace.'

Right! She returned to the bored group of young women, still in their underclothes, waiting to be dressed – *just* like dolls, Grace idly thought to herself. Striding swiftly to the clothes rails, she explained what was going to happen and chose three outfits for herself – her particular favourites.

'But you are not properly made up!' Kate pouted. 'You can't go on looking like that!'

'Oh, but I can!' Grace retorted. 'I am following a black and white theme. Black hair. White face. Just watch me!'

The transformation from designer to model was refreshing, thought Grace. In her new adopted role, her whole focus was to demonstrate to the very best advantage every angle, every design point of each outfit. She had watched the models' turns and pauses, the angle of the head, the stance, countless times and felt she could replicate at least some of these. Reaching into her bottomless handbag, which accompanied her everywhere, she pulled out powder and black eyeliner. Soon she had effectively blanked out every vestige of colour from her face. She was monotone: jet-black, sharply angled, asymmetrical haircut dipping to below the right side of her jawline from above her left ear; kohl-black eyes and painted eyebrows; white face.

She turned back to her collection, almost like doing battle.

'My God, Gracie, you look amazing! Here, a tiny reward for your balls – they are certainly bigger than mine,' giggled Tom. He handed her a ten-pound note, carefully rolled into a tube and a half bottle of vodka. 'I reckon you will need this.'

'Oh Tom, thanks – I owe you several – be back in a minute!'

Grace almost ran the short distance to the Ladies loo. She inhaled the line of coke, eyes closed, waiting for the usual kick, which soon came, and took a deep drink of vodka. My God – that was better! The nerves, the vulnerability – all gone. This was a challenge. She was unstoppable. Her clothes were amazing and Shu Chiang was doing a wonderful job. She floated back into the dressing rooms and told him so. 'If you weren't spoken for, Chiang, I would claim you for my own,' she laughed.

'In your dreams, darling!' he retorted, his ageless face expressionless.

Her golden dream just slightly dented, Grace countered, 'Ah well, I know you two are joined at the hip …'

Imogen had just sashayed back into the changing room, the combat trouser suit faultlessly set off by her baby-blond hair and impossibly long legs. Alexsi was on her way. Her lace shorts, thigh-length boots and black-lace sports bra caused a stir amongst the audience.

Alexsi was back. She returned to the dressing room to significant applause. She looked, without comment but with a quiet insolence, at Grace. Almost in slow motion, Grace pulled on the tulip-skirted short evening dress. She loved it. It was one of her best pieces. Her white face expressionless, it was Grace's turn.

The catwalk was impossibly long. It looked like a runway for a jumbo jet. Focussing every ounce of energy that she possibly could on her movement, she glided onto the narrow walkway. She did her best. She turned, stopped, stood, one leg in front of the other. No audience reaction – nothing. This was ridiculous! This dress was much better than the trouser suit. She returned – applause-less – to the dressing room. Almost immediately, she saw the undisguised, patronising smiles, the raised, flawless eyebrows. Swinging her hair deliberately and turning her back on the smirking girls, she put on her next outfit. The peacock-blue, tailored vintage-style suit was received with a similar lack of enthusiasm from the audience. Could it really be that the verve and sexless flirtation of the professional models counted for so much?

All her other outfits had been modelled; and, ironically, she knew that, apart from those which she had worn herself, they had made a real impact. Cameras were flashing as the press eagerly tried to anticipate the next autumn and winter trends. Right! She was going to have to pull something pretty dramatic out of the bag to ensure that the highlight of her collection, the dystopian wedding dress, had the effect it deserved. It fitted her perfectly. She had lost even more weight in the last two days on her diet of boiled sweets, black coffee and cocaine and to say that she looked striking was an understatement. Black and white makeup, black and white outfit – she looked like every fashion designer's dream and every doctor's nightmare.

This was it! Stepping slowly out on to the catwalk, she focussed on the spotlights at the far end. They played onto the small circular area, around which were clustered the fashion house's most influential and wealthy clients. Here she would turn, swirling the train full of question marks in a wide arc before she walked slowly back to the changing rooms.

As she came out there was an audible gasp. This was good! She walked almost in a dream, hardly able to feel her feet as they trod lightly along the carpeted stage. She had the sensation of almost floating along. No, she felt she actually *was* floating along – flying – as she was no longer conscious of her body, just the glorious feel of the silky fabric against her skin. This was what she had been waiting for. This was her moment! As she had planned, at the end of the catwalk, she stopped; then started to spin, faster and faster, the long train billowing out and displaying its hundreds of question marks, of doubts, as to the validity of marriage. She was never sure exactly when it happened, but her last conscious moment was feeling as if she were flying indeed, as she tripped and sailed over the floodlights, straight into the heart of the A-listers, the minor royalty, the fashion buyers.

Chapter 3

The blinding light, as Grace momentarily opened her eyes – only to swiftly shut them again – reminded her instantly of her last conscious minutes. Oh God! What had she done!

'Sister, Ms Adams is awake!'

A large nurse bustled into the room. 'Ah! We are back in the land of the living, are we? Open your eyes. Let me take a look.'

Grace's head was heavy – heavy as lead. Even opening her eyes took a huge amount of energy and effort. She just wanted to sleep, and sleep, and not to remember. She glanced briefly to her left, to see that a drip was attached to her arm.

'Mm!' muttered the nurse. 'Long way to go yet.'

And Grace drifted back into unconsciousness.

She had lost her job, of course. The letter from Esmé Long accused Grace of gross misconduct, through being under the influence of drugs and alcohol. But all the time, Grace knew that really, centrally, it was that she had negated any possibility of the prime group of clients amongst whom she had landed buying any of her collection – or indeed any items designed by her colleagues. The great and the famous, and infamous, had left within minutes of her undignified exit from the stage. Tom told Grace afterwards that the press had swarmed like locusts towards the area where she lay, clicking away frenetically, changing their story from 'Latest A/W trends' to 'Falling from Grace'.

She remained in hospital for two weeks, being rehydrated and her body detoxed. During the long days of inactivity, lying in the sterile hospital environment, she relived again and again the joys of having created her best collection ever – and the misery of having destroyed her chances of being taken seriously again as a designer in twenty-first century London. Most papers featured the story; and it dominated the newsfeeds of social media. To the general public, her name was a five-day wonder; but she knew that in the world of fashion this would never be forgotten. Her career was over. She couldn't really think of anything beyond this.

Tom came to visit, to tell her that the desperately poor salary which all the junior designers were paid was insufficient to retain her dismal bedsit. A black plastic bin sack containing her few belongings had been dumped by her landlady at the reception desk of the fashion house a week after she was admitted to hospital. Tom held it up now. 'Er, what shall I do with this, Gracie?'

'Oh, just leave it here.'

'Is there any other stuff?'

She shook her head painfully. 'No. That's the sum total of my life – all wrapped up in black plastic.' Tears came to her eyes. She had lived so long in the intensely creative world of design and deadlines that being abruptly cut off from it all seemed to have stopped her brain from working.

The morning on which Grace was due to leave hospital, Simon Patterson came to see her.

'Oh God! Why are *you* here? To gloat? To tell me that you were right and that I am a very naughty girl?'

'Whether you like it or not Miss Adams, I am your doctor and I need to talk to you. The hospital contacted me, because they know you have nowhere to go when you are discharged.'

Grace continued to gaze straight up at the ceiling.

She was looking better, much better, thought Simon. Rather a dramatic way to bring about such a transformation in a person but, if it meant that, somehow, she could start again, could take hold of her life and re-assess priorities, maybe this disaster was positive after all. He had visited her whilst she was still unconscious, and sat for some time with Tom and Shu Chiang, who had brought grapes and fruit juice, just in case she was in a fit state to eat and drink.

'Do you know her well?' Simon had asked.

'Not really,' replied Tom, munching a grape. 'Just enough to know she is a brilliant designer – totally wedded to her art. I just don't know what she is going to do now …' He bit his thumb nail thoughtfully.

'Don't spoil that manicure, Tom,' reprimanded Chiang gently, laying his small hand on his partner's.

'Does she have any family … a boyfriend?'

'She doesn't talk about family very often, but I believe so – to a minimal extent. Mother living in Spain with a much younger partner; aunt in the depths of the south-west – Dorset, I believe. No siblings. Few friends. Certainly no boyfriend on the scene. Chiang and I thought she was gay for ages, but I don't think she is. She is just absolutely in love with what she does – or did.'

Simon had glanced down at his unconscious patient. She looked so much younger. Her face was quiet and unexpectedly gentle: bold, black brows defined her eyes; her generous mouth, curved into a semi-smile, was pink as a child's.

But now, fully conscious again and ready to leave this place of temporary security, Grace's mouth was set into a determined line, and her eyes were narrowed defensively against what her doctor was about to say.

'Miss Adams – Grace – what are you going to do? Where are you going to live?' Simon really was at a loss as to what to say next. Silently, Grace drew her knees up to her chest and deliberately turned her back to him, facing the wall. Simon observed the human default position of self-comfort with compassion and patiently waited for some sort of response. After several minutes, she jumped out of bed, swayed only slightly, then walked to the window of the small room in which she had spent the last fortnight.

'Well, I thought I would take a break in the country!' she announced defiantly. 'My aunt is getting on a bit and could do with some help. I can hardly continue here. No job, no money and no fixed address are not the ingredients of a successful London life.' She spoke in a matter-of-fact voice which was brash and sarcastic, but her reflection in the window betrayed her: she quickly dashed away a tear before turning to face Simon again with a somewhat fixed smile. 'Are we going to give advice about country life now? Get your tetanus injections up to date, don't speak to any strange cattle, wear your thermal underwear …'

Despite his irritation, Simon smiled. What a funny, challenging person this complex girl was! 'Yes – all of those – and also remember that if you ever need to talk to me, about medical matters or anything really, here are my contact details.'

Grace took his card and slipped it into the pocket of her jeans, barely glancing at it. 'Thanks. And now I must go, before this overcrowded hospital actually throws me out!'

'Can I give you a lift to the station?'

'No thanks, that's OK. Aunt Annie has hired a car for me, to transport me and my vast number of personal belongings back to her cottage. It's outside apparently.'

Simon extended his hand and enclosed Grace's in a handshake. Inconsequentially he thought how small and delicate her hand was inside his, small and birdlike, with the same fragile grip on life. He left her hand inside his for just a second too long and she blushed, quickly withdrawing from the handclasp. Then, picking up her black plastic bin sack, swinging it over her shoulder, and tossing back her hair, she was gone.

Chapter 4

Soon the tedious main roads gave way to even more tedious, impossibly muddy lanes that twisted their way through the drenched countryside. Would it ever stop raining? By now Grace had a splitting headache, so she pulled into a pot-holed layby and eased her cramped limbs out of the car. She just had to stop and get some fresh air for a few minutes. Despite the rain, still cascading down from the darkening sky, she leant against the post and rail fence enclosing the field which bordered the road and gazed thoughtfully across the sodden grass. It was so unbelievably quiet compared with London. The only sound she could hear was the very occasional swish of a passing vehicle along the wet road and the wind sighing in the branches of some nearby trees. There were no street lights; no comforting eternal background noise of humanity getting on with its complex existence; no skilful visual merchandising to draw her to the work of talented and creative colleagues. The world here was black, saturated and silent. How could she ever bear this!

Her mind danced back into the past and trod warily into the unknown future. Her face and hair were, she knew, becoming impossibly wet, but still she was reluctant to resume her journey – to take up her new and uncertain life, in an unknown village with an almost unknown relative. She could hardly remember her aunt. How long was it since she had seen Annie Adams?

⊰)||(⊱

Grace must have been seventeen when her father took her to Quintin Parva, the village where his elder sister lived. The tall, tanned woman had smiled with genuine warmth at the sulky teenager sitting sullenly in the kitchen, hands thrust into slouchy jeans' pockets. Defiantly, determined to ignore her aunt's attempts at conversation, Grace had gazed fixedly at the lush garden through the open stable door. It was, she recalled, a perfect summer's day. A thrush sang on the top-most branch of a tall conifer and wrapped the deep-green countryside in a web of golden melody.

She remembered how her aunt had gradually penetrated her wall of silence. Grace was still hurting from the loss of her mother. It would have been easier if she had died, Grace had thought on more than one occasion, as she tried to explain to her curious friends why her lively, fun-loving mother had left without warning. The only reasons ever given were in a brief note which Grace had discovered one day on her return from school. Her mother had made it clear that she was 'bored witless' and intended to go travelling, which she had 'never had time to do until now, as she was too busy being a devoted wife and mother.' That was it. No forwarding address; no regrets at leaving her husband and daughter. Nothing.

So, Grace reflected, automatically licking the raindrops as they ran down her face, it had been six years since she had last sat in her aunt's sun-filled kitchen. She recalled that she had eventually been tempted to eat the freshly-baked bread and home-made jam and drink tea poured from a tea pot in the shape of a chicken and, despite herself, become almost happy again in the quiet, calm presence of her aunt.

Before she and her father had left Quintin Parva to return to their suburban semi in Croydon, Annie took Grace into her vegetable garden. 'Your father looks pale, Grace. Can you cook?'

''Course I can! I'm not totally useless you know!'

'Good. In that case, let's pick some useful things which you can give to him over the next few days.'

And they had picked spinach and beans, tomatoes and raspberries, placing the fruit and vegetables in a wicker basket that Annie Adams had slung over her arm.

⋰⊱‖⊰⋰

It was getting dark now. Rain was starting to trickle coldly down Grace's neck and she shivered, consciously tearing herself away from the memories of that happy day. She wondered just how much longer it would be before she reached the remote part of Dorset where her aunt lived and, jeans clinging clammily to her legs, she jumped back into the relative warmth of the car, putting the heater on full blast. She started the engine, indicated, and pulled out once again on to the narrow mud-coated tarmac. Her mind still playing with the past, she remembered only too clearly what had come next – such a short time after that sun-filled visit.

She had been at school, working in a practical textile class, wrestling with an item that she was preparing for her 'A' level exam. She had decided on a piece that she had since re-invented several times during her short design career: lace shorts with a masculine cut, but a feminine finish. If she could just get the balance right, the yin and yang of the design, it would guarantee her an A*.

'Grace Adams! Could you come with me please?' It was the Deputy Headteacher. Quickly Grace reviewed her actions over the past few days. She had smoked with her friends behind the shed which housed games equipment. Could she have been seen? She had been late the day before …

She followed Miss Wright into her office.

'Sit down, Grace. Would you like some tea?'

Tea? What? Just what on earth was going on?

'No thank you, miss.'

'Grace, this is not easy to say. Not easy at all. Your father …'

'What's the matter?' Grace stood up sharply, sensing immediately the news that was about to come.

'I am afraid that your father … he has passed away, Grace. At work this morning. His office phoned me just now. I am so sorry.'

She had sat down again abruptly, her mind whirling.

As the small car raced through the growing dusk, Grace realised that this was the exact moment when she had grown up. From that moment she had been determined not to swerve from her intention: to go to college and to become a fashion designer. Through her success, she would honour her father's memory. She would succeed. And she had, until – swearing under her breath – her irretrievable 'fall from grace'.

Standing at the door of Rose Cottage, Annie Adams was shocked when she saw her niece get out of the hired car. Could anyone be so thin and not be terminally ill? But she concealed her anxiety with her usual monumental calm.

'Grace dear, how lovely to see you again! You get more like your father every day.'

'Hi, Aunt Annie.' Grace stretched, rain dripping from her hair. She was so unutterably relieved to be free at last from the prospect of endless wet tarmac stretching inexorably in front of her.

'Let me show you to your room. You can wash and change if you wish whilst I put the meal on the table.'

'Oh, I am really not hungry. I just fancy a drink. Do you have any wine, or vodka?'

Annie threw back her head and laughed. 'Tea, coffee, cocoa or Horlicks! That's all that the bar menu runs to! And it's soup or scrambled eggs – which would you prefer?'

Flushing, Grace mumbled, 'Soup please, and tea.'

As she came into the stone porch, the old cottage seemed to open its arms to her, offering welcome warmth and light. She stopped to take off her shoes and socks, both sodden, and went into the sitting room. She had forgotten so much about her aunt's home. A fire crackled in the huge inglenook fireplace, banishing the damp and chill of the interminably long and wet spring. Deep, soft armchairs flanked the fireplace. Ceilings were low and beamed. Everywhere was the smell of lavender, and polished oak furniture gleamed in the firelight. Grace climbed the old wooden staircase slowly, uneven treads split and worn through centuries of use, following her aunt who was carrying the black plastic bag of belongings. She was so tired, so incredibly tired! That concussion must have taken more out of her than she realised.

At the top of the stairs, Annie Adams turned right and opened an old pine door. 'This is yours for as long as you need it, Grace,' she said quietly. 'Let me put your stuff on the bed and then you can unpack it after supper. Just give me any washing you have. Those jeans are soaking wet by the look of things.'

The room was small, spotless and very comfortable. Blue roses on the curtains and bedcover contrasted with the pale-gold walls and cream carpet. Thick, fluffy white towels were heaped on an old-fashioned wooden towel rail by the window. A minute en-suite bathroom led off the left of the room. Grace ran a basin of warm water and splashed it over her face again and again, trying to wash away the tide of memories and anxiety that continually threatened to overwhelm her. She slipped on a pair of jogging bottoms and dumped her wet jeans in the dirty-linen basket.

They ate in the kitchen, the dark-blue Aga humming away companionably in the background. Even though her initial, almost automatic, reaction had been rebellion, Grace found herself relaxing in the peace and quiet security of her aunt's home. The soup was probably the best she had ever tasted and, as she ate and drank, she felt her eyelids drooping. Grace had expected a thousand questions to be fired at her, a thousand pressures to be exerted. But Annie smiled and chatted about comfortable generalities: the village; the weekly bus service to the local town; the Women's Institute which met once a month; the knitting group which made clothes for refugees; the garden club. Quintin Parva did not just seem miles away from the fast pace, impossible expectations, noise and action of

London – it seemed to be on a different planet! If she had not been so totally exhausted, Grace would have felt horrified. As it was, she was too tired to generate any extreme emotion and, when her aunt calmly said, 'It is ten-thirty, Grace. Bedtime', unexpectedly she acquiesced and followed Annie upstairs.

Her room was like a nest, she thought sleepily: a soft, pale nest, surrounded by flowers. She showered quickly, slipped on her pyjamas and experienced a novel sensation: of falling asleep, literally, as soon as her head touched the pillow.

Chapter 5

It was the light that woke her, flooding through the curtains and falling across Grace's face. At first, she didn't have a clue where she was. Hospital? On a friend's sofa? And then she remembered.

She yawned and drew back the curtains. The early-spring garden had been rain-washed and sparkled in the bright sunlight and, just as she remembered from her visit shortly before her father's death, a thrush's song filled the scented air. She lifted the sash window and breathed deeply. It was as if she had never breathed before. More and more deeply she inhaled, until the breath filled her lungs and then, ever so slowly, she exhaled luxuriantly, unconsciously ridding herself of the last vestiges of pollution and second-hand air that had surrounded her in London.

For a full minute she sat on the window seat and just looked, and breathed, and listened.

'Grace, would you like tea or coffee?' her aunt's voice drifted up from the kitchen.

'Oh, coffee please! I'll come down.'

Annie Adams looked hard at her niece as she came into the kitchen. She had slept for a full ten hours and looked refreshed, if still painfully thin and pale.

Almost because she was not being questioned closely about her future and her intentions, Grace felt herself wanting to share what was in her mind. 'Auntie, I must get a job! I can't exist on fresh air and I have no money – and I'll need some sort of transport.'

'So the weekly bus is no use to you then?' laughed Annie.

'Er, no!'

'I thought you might like to come with me to the WI. Our meeting starts at two this afternoon.'

'Aunt Annie, I can't tell you how much I appreciate all that you are doing for me, but I'm just not interested in the Women's Institute – sorry, I'm just not!'

Her aunt smiled quietly. 'You might brighten their ideas up a bit, Grace! Some are so terribly stuck in their ways.'

Grace grinned at her aunt. 'Purple dungarees and asymmetrical hair, eh? Just what Quintin Parva has been waiting for!'

'Look Grace, I can't afford to buy a car. The rental people are coming in an hour or so to collect the Fiat you drove home yesterday – but I do have a bike. Would that be any use?'

'Anything, Auntie. I can't stay in the village all day, every day!'

⁂

Although singularly 'un-cool' – being around forty years old, heavy, upright and with a basket set firmly behind the hard seat – Grace was enjoying her new vehicle. The countryside around her aunt's village was renowned for its landmark hills – steep, round and chalky, their summits crowned with trees – and its deep wooded valleys. Standing into the pedals, Grace drove the ancient bicycle up the winding road out of the village.

The day was bright, with a cool breeze that made the daffodils in gardens and hedgerows nod and dance. Half-way up the hill she stopped, her attention caught by a stone trough on the right-hand bank, below the church wall. Water gushed from a spout in the stone wall behind the trough, and the volume was so great that it spilled over the side of the stone container and ran across the road in a steady stream. At the top of the stone surround she read: *Vita nova ex aqua resurgit*. Grace had nominally 'studied' Latin at school, but its relevance had completely escaped her and she had given it up as soon as she could. But there was something about the lettering, the way in which the engraving was done, the flowers and birds that were carved into the stone, that really caught her attention. She knew she had never seen the fountain before, but it filled her with an emotion of utter intensity which had literally stopped her in her tracks. Propping her bicycle against the stone church wall, and tracing the moss-filled letters with her slender fingers, she experienced a mixture of longing, fulfilment and joy. The twisting tendrils of honeysuckle and rose, the feathering on thrush and robin were all so finely done. Wouldn't it be wonderful to capture some of that delicacy in a fabric design – perhaps use feathers themselves on the sleeves to replicate the transient loveliness of these most fragile of animals. She stood gazing for some moments, simply lost in thought. Then, roughly shaking her head, she reminded herself that it was pointless thinking of dress design – pointless! All these ideas that still crowded in her head were unbearable – and what the hell did those stupid words mean anyway? She would ask her aunt; Annie's plants and bushes all seemed to have Latin names.

At the summit of the hill she stopped and caught her breath, before leaping back on the bicycle and freewheeling down the hill, the cool spring air catching her dark hair and making it stream behind her like an uneven pennant. She shot past her aunt's cottage, past the old school, now a private house, and drew level with the village hall.

Women, in twos and threes, were drifting into the low, stone building. Without exception they had obviously dressed in their best and taken time and trouble with hair and makeup. The only jarring note, thought Grace, grinning, was that their clothes, hair and make-up were all decades out of date! Once again, her longing for the excitement, the buzz, of the city hit her and she felt an almost physical pain. How could she ever live in this place with its respectable, predictable, inhabitants? Her aunt was genuinely kind, but she saw the undisguised critical looks as the Women's Institute branch members stopped and openly stared at her windblown, colourful appearance.

In an instant, she had decided: she would go to the meeting after all. These sour old girls were not going to look down their noses at her! 'Is this where the WI meeting is?' Grace asked cheerfully, as she leapt off the bicycle and propped it against the wall.

No-one spoke.

'Sorry – you must be hard of hearing! Is this where the WI meeting is taking place?' repeated Grace, raising the volume of her voice significantly.

'Er, yes. Are you a member?' asked one elderly woman at last, in clipped tones.

'No, but my aunt is.'

'And who, may I ask, is that?' queried the same person. 'I am the Chair.'

Grace was getting pretty tired of this relentless coldness. What had this horrible old woman got against her anyway? She didn't know her! She was just judging by appearances: old people always did that.

'Someone a million times better than you, you unfriendly old cow!' declared Grace, leaping back on her bike and peddling off past her aunt's cottage and up the hill again. She was breathing deeply, really angry, and was surprised to notice that she was physically shaking. What was happening to her? The criticism and bitchiness of the fashion world had never bothered her. She had laughed in the face of the first, and given as good as she got as far as the second was concerned. That stupid fall must have really given her health a knock. As she deliberately put more effort into her uphill pedalling, unbidden the face and voice of Simon Patterson came into her mind as she recalled his words:

'*Your habits are destroying you. Instead of breathing air, you snort cocaine; instead of drinking liquid that restores your body, you drink alcohol that destroys it. You smoke. Your blood tests are worrying. You are losing weight. A size six may look good on a model, but not coupled with shortness of breath and loss of concentration.*'

Maybe it had not just been the stupid fall into the audience …

Chapter 6

A fortnight later, Annie Adams sipped her tea thoughtfully as she watched her niece digging the vegetable garden with unnecessary violence. She had lost that dreadful pinched, pale look and had put on a little weight, but anger and hurt were clearly still filling her mind.

'Lunch, love!' Annie called.

Grace embedded the fork deep into the rich dark soil and shut the little wicket gate to the vegetable garden behind her before trudging up the path to the kitchen. She took off her soil-laden boots, washed her hands and sat down, without a word, at the kitchen table.

They ate silently for some time then, quietly laying down her knife, Annie reached across the table and laid her large capable hand on her niece's small white one.

'Grace, talk to me. Tell me what you are thinking! Clearly you are not happy. You look much, much better, but anyone can see that you are miserable. Please share your thoughts with me. I may be able to help.'

Grace put her head in her hands and, uncharacteristically, started to cry silently.

Annie stood up and put her arm around her niece's shoulders. 'Come on, dear. It's not that bad!'

'Oh but it *is*, Auntie! It is! It's awful! Do you know what actually happened in London?'

'I got the general idea from your friend Tom. When you were completely out of it, he was really supportive. Nothing was too much trouble. He told me what happened, Grace.'

'You will know then, that I've ruined everything. I'm a laughing stock. All those beautiful clothes I made – all gone to waste. All the ideas I still have locked in my head …' She beat her fists against her temples in frustration. 'I can hardly set up as a fashion designer in Quintin Parva, can I? "Personal design consultant to the Chair of the WI!" I can't go back to London. I am regarded as a complete pariah by the world of fashion! I have no other talents – none, Auntie! I am just shrivelling up here. The youngest person is the postman and he is about sixty!'

'What about inviting some of your London friends here, Grace? How about Tom?'

Grace thought of her unconventional, overtly camp, funny, intelligent friend exposed to the scrutiny of the WI, outraging them with his piercings and eye makeup; or in the vegetable garden, tiptoe-ing delicately between the emerging rows of spinach and potatoes.

'Oh Auntie, you don't know what you are talking about – Tom is so London! He polishes his shoes when he gets to the studio if they are even a little bit dusty! How would he cope with the acres of mud here?'

'Well how about this Simon Patterson, then?

'Who?'

'Simon Patterson. I found his card in your jeans before I washed them after you arrived. Is he a friend?'

'No, he bloody well isn't! He is an interfering do-gooder, who dogs my life and thrusts my conscience in my face at every opportunity!'

'Oh, right.'

As her aunt turned quietly towards the Aga and mechanically went through the actions of ladling out the homemade soup, cutting the fresh brown loaf and placing a bowl of fruit on the table, Grace struggled to find the words to say sorry – to apologise for her abrasive words when she knew that all Annie wanted to do was to help her.

Both women were silent over lunch as they fought to articulate their thoughts, but just when Annie had finally managed to make a start, saying softly, 'Grace, I have been thinking ...' her attempt to re-open a conversation was abruptly cut short when there was a light tap on the door.

'Oh hi, Annie. Oops, sorry! I am clearly interrupting your lunch. I just wondered if you could help me out?'

Annie Adams got up with a smile of genuine fondness on her face. 'Hello, Alison! Of course! But first let me introduce my niece. Grace, this is my neighbour Alison Ingram – Ali to her friends.'

'Or even to her enemies,' quipped their visitor.

Painfully aware of her red eyes, Grace struggled to smile and extended her hand. 'Hi, Alison – Ali – pleased to meet you.'

The woman who had just arrived smiled directly into Grace's face, but didn't lift her hand to respond to the younger woman's automatic gesture. This was not the sort of encounter that Grace would have expected with any of the inhabitants of what she had, to this point, taken to be a respectable, wholly Conservative (definitely with a capital C), introverted village. None of these words seemed to apply to Annie's neighbour, who was relatively young, tall and statuesque, with thick, curling blond hair. Her style of dress, Grace thought sardonically, would certainly *not* be approved by the WI mafia, consisting of a full orange, purple and red chaotically-patterned long skirt and a tight black top, revealing a magnificent bosom in keeping with her Amazonian stature. But the most striking thing about her, thought Grace, was her eyes: they were pale-green, still, cool and deep, appearing to be at the same time both appraising and a place of refuge.

'How very interesting to meet you,' murmured Alison softly, after what must have been several seconds' silence. Then, almost as if she were gathering her thoughts together from the remote place to which they had drifted, she turned to Annie, leaving Grace confused and puzzled. 'As you know, Annie, this wisdom tooth has been giving me hell for months. My dentist has just had a last-minute cancellation for this afternoon and I really want to take this appointment – but my hyper-active pooch presents a problem. I have to leave now and Henry needs walking – you know how precious he is about his routine!' Alison raised her eyes and hands in a gesture of humorous exasperation.

Annie laughed. 'Is that all? We'd love to take him out. We'll be around in a few minutes, after we finish our lunch. Go and get yourself sorted!'

Alison gave her friend a quick hug, demonstrating, thought Grace, that she was not averse to physical contact with *some* people. 'Bless you, Annie. I will speak with you later, Grace.' This was a statement, not a question. Then, with a swirl of her long, brightly-patterned skirt, Alison smiled and was gone.

Annie returned to the table. 'I was going to ask you whether you would like to come out with me this afternoon,' she smiled. 'There is a plant sale at the Old Rectory – such a fine building, Grace! It's a private school now, but once it must have been an amazing home. The children have been growing seedlings to raise money for new computer equipment. But one of us needs to take out Hectic Henry. He is a lovely dog, but young and very silly!'

'Oh, I don't mind what I do … digging, dog-walking, going to a plant sale, all fabulous world-changing events. I'll do the dog.'

Grace left her lunch untouched and, still intensely frustrated at her inability to communicate fully with someone who clearly only had her wellbeing at heart, stormed out of the kitchen into the utility room, pulling on her muddy wellingtons and a shapeless waxed jacket of her aunt's.

Annie sighed as she watched the slight, delicate figure. She was swamped by the coat and, as she trudged to the garden gate, she had her head down and thin shoulders hunched against, it seemed, the world. Just when she thought her niece's health was actually improving, when her volatility was becoming less acute … Annie heard her gate crash shut.

'Hi. I'm here to take out Henry.' Grace spoke in a monotone. This woman was marginally more interesting than the other inhabitants of Quintin Parva, but distinctly weird. Why wouldn't she shake hands? Why had Alison looked at her in silence when she came round to her aunt's house? For God's sake – she was doing it again!

'Look, is there something wrong with me? Do I have two heads or something? I have come to take out your bloody dog and all you do is stare at me! Do you want me to walk the mutt or not?'

Alison smiled slightly and shook her head. 'I am sorry, Grace. We need to talk. I really do have to go out now, but when you bring Henry back, can we talk then? I didn't mean to offend you.'

Grace calmed down slightly. 'OK,' she shrugged. 'What time will you be back?'

'Four-ish.'

'See you then.'

Henry was a black Labrador, enthusiastic and very, very strong. As Grace slipped on his lead, he set his powerful shoulders and, right from the start, pulled her towards his favourite walk. She was propelled down the village street – faster than she would have believed possible – and across a small muddy field in front of a stately Georgian house where a blue and gold sign neatly proclaimed its status:

Quintin Parva Preparatory School

The Old Rectory

For children aged 3-8

Headteacher: Dr Matthew Moore

Already people were looking at the clusters of plant pots, arranged in orderly lines on wooden tables outside the front of the classical building, but Grace was whisked swiftly past, towards a meandering footpath that led ultimately to the river. As soon as she possibly could, she took off Henry's lead. He happily galloped across the fields, snapping at daisies, dandelions and bees, taking deep draughts of muddy puddles and eating anything that remotely resembled food. Despite herself, Grace's black mood lifted and she smiled. This dog was so incredibly spontaneous! In the animal world he lived like she had in London: doing what he wanted to do best of all and loving every minute of it! Unconventional enough to drink muddy water and attempting to eat what appeared to be a plastic bottle whilst running around in circles, was this any stranger than her behaviour had been?

She looked at her phone and was surprised to see that it was already a quarter to four. She called Henry to her, but he studiously ignored her, preoccupied with what must have been an overwhelmingly strong scent which followed the course of the river. Half-an-hour later, Grace was getting nowhere. She had tried to run after him, but he had simply picked up pace and easily outstripped her along the river footpath. She threw a stick, but Henry remained motionless, watching the stick incuriously as he returned to his trail. Eventually, flushed, breathless and utterly frustrated, Grace threw herself down on the soft, spring grass. At that, Henry bounded up to her and started to lick her face and her hair, gently nibbling her coat.

'Got you, you beast!' Grace tackled the dog, grabbing his collar and slipping on his lead.

It was half-past four when she returned to the Old School House, Ali Ingram's home, and rang the bell. She noticed casually that there was a small brass plaque to the right of the door – almost hidden by the twisting stems of a white, climbing rose. She idly tried to part the thorny branches to see what the plaque said, but the stems were thick and the thorns vicious. All she could make out were the first words of the inscription:

Grace also noticed a deeply-scored area of brick – an ugly scar, which, presumably, the rose had been planted to cover – before the door opened.

'I am really sorry about being late Alison, and about being rude earlier.'

Alison smiled broadly. 'I see Henry the Hectic has worked his magic! You look, er, slightly less stressed, than you did earlier. Do come in. Tea?'

'Please!'

Alison led the way into her house, through a vaulted entrance hall with a mezzanine floor where her many books were crowded onto old pine shelves, into a tranquil room which ran the length of the back of the school building. Lead-lattice windows overlooked the lush garden, causing Grace to exclaim, 'This is just lovely – what an outlook!'

'I know,' laughed Alison. 'It's like a glorious jungle! The grounds were well-planted years ago when this was still a school. Even the old outside loos are still here! They need renovating really, but will have to remain as they are for the moment. I love this place! I know it's ridiculously big for just Henners and me but, for the time being, it is our resting place.' She looked thoughtful, tracing the lozenge shapes of the lead in the windows and gazing along the flowerbeds to the towering trees at the bottom of the garden and the pond, edged with flag iris, already plump with flower buds. With a sigh, she turned to Grace and visibly gathered her thoughts. 'Do sit down here by the window and make yourself comfortable whilst I go and get the tea. I need to explain a couple of things to you, Grace.'

Grace watched the seemingly tireless young dog splash in and out of the pond, once again drinking copious amounts of pond water. He found a stick, which this time proved to be of interest, and sat chewing it happily under the tall poplars.

'I made this cake yesterday. Would you like some?' smiled Alison.

'Actually, I am starving!' admitted Grace.

'Grace, there is no easy way to say this, so I will say it as it is. I am a psychic medium and when I met you earlier today, I saw that you had two distinct and separate auras. It was as if you were walking alongside another invisible person. I have never seen this before – never – in the whole of my experience. That is why I looked at you, rather rudely I now realise, without speaking to you. I'm sorry, I was just so taken aback. I wanted to take your outstretched hand, but I knew that if I did, it would not be just for a polite greeting. If I take your hand Grace, I will need to look at it, to look at its significance. Do you understand what I am saying?'

'You mean like reading my palm?'

'Sort of.' Alison smiled her calm, gentle smile again.

'OK – let's do it!' Grace agreed, setting aside her cake plate.

Very slowly, Alison also placed her cup and plate on the small table in front of the window. She then sat for some time with her hands clasped in her lap, looking Grace full in the face with her fathomless, green eyes. 'Give me your right hand, Grace,' she said softly at last.

Grace extended her small white hand.

'I thought I would see something like this,' Alison whispered. 'You have two distinct life lines – not a break or divergence, but two entirely separate lives.'

Chapter 7

Grace couldn't stop thinking about her conversation
with her aunt's next-door neighbour. She had slept long
and soundly since arriving in Quintin Parva, but the
night after her conversation with Alison, sleep was
impossible. In London she knew that she would have
dismissed the woman's comments as 'complete
bollocks', but somehow, sitting in Ali's quiet drawing
room, with the gently ticking clock and the fading
daylight – and above all the pensive concern of the
woman who held her hand – such a dismissive response
was impossible. The next morning, she was once again
tired, confused and dispirited.

'Morning, dear! How are you today?'

'Bloody awful!'

In her usual calm and patient way, Annie Adams
looked at her niece. 'Didn't sleep too well?'

'What does it look like?'

Annie poured coffee, made toast and put two eggs to
boil on the Aga. She stirred her drink thoughtfully.
'You need a job, Grace. Any sort of job, but something
that will take you out of the village and allow you to
meet other people, to gain other interests. Also, to be
honest, you don't know everyone in the village. There
are younger people …'

'Oh for God's sake, what do you call young? Thirty is old in London! I am going out.'

'But you haven't had your breakfast …'

'I don't want any bloody breakfast! You are just trying to make me fat – like all the other losers in this god-forsaken hole.' Grace flung out of the kitchen, pulling on her Doc Martens and heaving the bicycle out of the garden shed. Impatiently, she jumped on and cycled off as fast as she could along the winding road that led to the river. She had discovered various circular routes from her aunt's house and intended to ride down the relatively level river road, then to loop round back to the church and down the hill to Rose Cottage.

As she pedalled furiously along, she gradually calmed down. Her aunt had been ace: kind, never prying and consistently serene. Grace knew that she had always had a short fuse and was self-analytical enough to realise that all her energies were now just building up, because they were not being channelled into anything creative and were not being dulled or controlled by alcohol or drugs. She slowed down her pedalling pace as the river fields drifted by. The day was sunny and still: a perfect May day. The water meadows looked like an illustration from a mediaeval manuscript: bright green and dotted with the impossibly vibrant pinks, golds and blues of early summer flowers. She decided that she would pick as many of these as she could and take them back to her aunt. She would say sorry. She really would try to get a job – any sort of job – just as Annie had suggested.

Her good mood restored and the basket on the back of the ancient bike filled with flowers, Grace powered down the steep, narrow winding road from the church. Just because, apart from her aunt, everyone else in

Quintin Parva was a bitch, didn't mean that she had to be too. Something would turn up!

The day was so quiet! All she could hear was birdsong and the wind rushing past her hair, longer now and evened out with a pair of kitchen scissors, when she just could not stand any longer the right side obscuring her vision as she bent to help her aunt in the garden. There seemed to be so many birds in Quintin Parva. This time it was a blackbird that caught her attention, sitting on the churchyard wall, just by the stone fountain and trough. It was singing its heart out in the warm early-summer air and the joy of its song couldn't fail to raise a smile in Grace. Glancing towards it, she recalled how her aunt had told her the story that surrounded the stone fountain head and the trough into which the water poured.

It was part of village history and – whether apocryphal, or holding a core of truth, Grace was unsure – it went like this. The spring had always been there and was associated with the village pond and the settlement that had surrounded the church in early mediaeval times. But the oldest inhabitants of the village recalled how the stone fountain head and trough had appeared at the time of one of the first peacetime weddings to be celebrated at the church – a memorable occasion with the most beautiful bride and handsome groom ever seen at St Michael's church, so villagers said. The work was considered to be some of the finest carving that the local family firm of stone-masons had ever produced, and the details of feather and leaf, wing and petal, were much admired by the entire village. But as to the meaning of the words *Vita nova ex aqua resurgit* – and even the approximate translation *New life rises again from the water* – well, everyone felt they were a bit strange, to say the least! Squinting sideways at the exquisite and timeless decoration, Grace wondered whether it meant that all those birds and flowers, carved around the spout and the trough into which clear spring-water constantly flowed, were kept alive by the water itself. But she just wasn't sure. She applied her brakes to try to get a clearer view. They still squeaked badly and, alarmed by the sudden noise, the blackbird unexpectedly shot off the wall directly in front of her, making its loud alarm call. Automatically, to avoid the bird, she swerved and braked again – this time too hard – and felt the unwieldy vehicle slew heavily to one side as it hit the trickle of water that overflowed across the road from the stone trough. Desperately trying to regain her balance, Grace clung on, but the brakes had locked completely, and she found herself flying through the air for a second time in as many months. But this time it was not into a crowded audience, but into the solid stone of the water trough.

She hit it head-on, the bicycle landing on top of her. The armfuls of flowers she had picked for her aunt were tossed high into the air and landed randomly in a thick pall over her quiet, still body.

In the silence which followed, the blackbird resumed its exquisite, implacable song.

Grace Brabazon
1942

Chapter 8

Grace Brabazon stood in front of the Headmaster's desk with her arms folded and her gaze steady. 'I am sorry sir, but I just cannot agree with what you did to-day with those new evacuees!'

'It is not for you to agree or disagree, Miss Brabazon. You are my junior teacher. Quite simply, you do what I tell you!'

'Yes, sir. But surely to keep them indoors for the entire lunch period just because they couldn't recognise the different trees on the poster was too harsh? Where they come from – east London – what trees do they see? Are there even any left, or have they been all blown to bits, together with these children's homes?'

'You miss the point entirely. They were given the research as homework, and they did nothing.'

'But sir, they arrived only a week ago. They are still settling in!'

'And what good homes they have now! Dr Pedder; the Misses Prendegast; the dairy and bakery, have all opened their homes and their hearts to these poor children.' Pleased with his oratory, Ivan Miles smiled complacently. Grace, however, did not.

'Yes, sir. And my father has told me just how difficult it is for the children to research anything. They can hardly read! He had tea with Elsie and Maud Prendegast yesterday. Maud told him that she was up at three o'clock when one of the little girls – Emily Channing – was crying because of a nightmare. She is only six years old. She has lost her home. Her father is away fighting in the Far East. Her mother is living with her aunt in London, and Emily doesn't know whether she is dead or alive. To research anything in these circumstances, Doctor Miles, is ...' Grace fought to find an appropriate word '... challenging. Challenging in the extreme.'

'Well, they have the opportunity to redeem themselves tonight,' said the Headteacher of Quintin Parva Church of England Primary School. 'I have reset the homework.'

He stood up.

'But sir, let me take them on a nature walk tomorrow. They will learn quite naturally as we see the real trees for ourselves and touch and smell them.'

'Books were all I ever needed when I was their age, Miss Brabazon, and that discipline has stayed with me all my life.'

'But Doctor Miles, you are a classicist and your background is so different from theirs! These children come from families of dockers, shopkeepers, hackney carriage drivers ...'

'Good afternoon, Miss Brabazon. I will see you at eight-thirty sharp in the morning.'

Grace was furious. She walked quickly back to her classroom, hands thrust deep into the pockets of her cardigan. The long, low room had been transformed by Grace into a bright and exciting place, where the youngest children in the village were eager to come.

Grace had attended the school herself, before the current Headteacher had arrived, and still fondly remembered her headmistress, Evelina Dickinson. A mainstay of the community, Evelina was funny, keenly intelligent, and deeply knowledgeable about literature, which she made come alive by constantly referencing it to everyday life. She read to the whole school last thing in the afternoon, taking an extended text, such as *Swallows and Amazons*, and transporting the children to a world of adventure that was just within the reach of their imagination. Grace loved every minute of it. Because she had been enchanted by the magic of accessing different worlds through education, her decision to become a teacher had come as no surprise to her parents or her school.

Miss Dickinson had retired two years earlier and her successor, an elderly academic with a distinguished career in private education behind him, had arrived. He had taken the school governors and the rector of the parish, Grace's father, by storm, explaining that the only reason he would ever consider teaching in a village school of some forty-five children was that he had 'suffered a health setback' – a slight heart attack. This necessitated his taking over the headship of an establishment 'somewhat less demanding' than the five-hundred-place, leading public school of which he had been Headteacher for the past twenty years. Completely taken in by his eloquence and extreme self-confidence, the governors had appointed him.

Back in the sanctuary of her own classroom, Grace shook her thick, black hair free of the clips which her Headmaster had insisted she use to restrain its natural exuberance. She walked past the rows of small desks and gazed out of the leaded lights at the back of the room. The short December day had nearly ended and already the grass was becoming powdered with frost; whilst a thin, sickle-shaped moon had appeared like a sliver of silver in the cold, deep-blue sky. Grace leant her forehead against the chilly glass and closed her eyes, breathing deeply to settle her emotions. After a few minutes she turned again to the neat classroom and walked to her own desk, which she had positioned across one corner, allowing her to access the blackboard, move easily to support her children, and see the familiar and reassuring view across the school grounds. She sat down and, almost automatically, her hand slipped into the bottom left-hand drawer. Here she gently moved aside the loose papers until her fingers closed tenderly around a small rectangle, wrapped in a much folded and re-folded brown paper bag. Carefully undoing the creased wrapping, Grace cradled in her palm a black and white framed photograph and, her face expressionless, she ran her forefinger lightly over its surface.

She could recall Alex's features perfectly, without having recourse to the grainy image that lay in her hand: his thick dark hair, largely covered in the picture she held in her hands by his RAF cap; his blue eyes, direct and full of laughter; his broad shoulders and strong hands. When the telegram had been delivered to the vicarage, announcing that he had been '*lost over the south coast of England, leading his air squadron with valour and skill*', she had thought her life had ended, that there really was no point in going on. But her father's gentle support, his quiet love, the numerous cups of cocoa which he had brought to her room throughout the sleepless nights, his fervent and endless prayer that his daughter should once again find a meaning in life had, in the end, prevailed.

In the weeks after Alex's death, Charles Brabazon watched his pale, silent daughter gradually taking up the reins of her life again. When he had been introduced to Alex Jamieson two years earlier, he had been delighted – which father would not have been – when he realised that his daughter was falling in love with the handsome, charming pilot. But a persistent doubt nagged at the back of his mind. He saw with delight that his daughter smiled, talked and was clearly radiantly happy with Alex, but he saw too that she often set aside her own deepest interests – her passion for improving the lives of the children of Quintin Parva and her absolute belief in equality – and was intent solely on pleasing the man she loved. He knew that people often took Grace's quietness, her seriousness, for lack of character but, because she reflected rather than chattered; because she kept her feelings to herself; this did not mean that she was shallow. Nothing could be further from the truth.

Charles had recalled how, when she had been a little girl, they had acquired a pony that a local farmer had been ill-treating and wanted to dispose of. It had been unkempt, with a rough, dull coat and eyes that held no hope. As it was led into the field in front of the vicarage, the animal had its head down and its steps were slow; it seemed to have lost all interest in a life that was nothing but work and discomfort. Charles had watched with respect as, for several months after its arrival, every day Grace had brushed and washed and stroked – but, above all, talked to the neglected animal. Gradually her patience had coaxed back into the pony's eyes the love of life. He had started to hold his head high again, and whinnied a welcome to the small girl as she ran lightly across the glebe paddock with a carrot, or apple that she had picked up as a treat from the vicarage garden. He had seen the same outcome when his daughter interacted with under-privileged or disengaged children. No – Grace was not lacking in character. He sometimes felt that he hardly knew her, and wondered from where her deep love of knowledge and passionate desire for equality and social justice had stemmed.

Grace had returned to her post as assistant school mistress with a determination to put all her love, care and energy into the education of the children entrusted to her. But how she missed her fiancé! Two years after Alex's death, she still longed to see again his quick, radiant smile; to experience once more the excitement she had felt in his company; and to anticipate their years together. Silently, she wrapped the photograph once more in its worn paper bag, and replaced it in the drawer.

Restless, she moved back to the window. The natural advantages of the school site had been maximised by Miss Dickinson when Grace was still a pupil. She remembered with a smile the long, summer days during which she had worked alongside the other senior children in the school, digging, levelling, sowing grass seed and planting flowers, to make the extensive garden a place of discovery and a sanctuary. There was a small, paved area in front of the school building where the children could play if it was very wet but, for the majority of the time, everyone chose to sit, or walk, or play, in the flowery, grassed, tree-encircled grounds at the back of the Victorian school building.

Grace recalled how they had all learned through experiencing the fascination and inter-connectedness of the natural world at first hand. They had watched bees pollinate the flowers, moving ponderously, laden with pollen, from flower to flower. She had once said to her teacher that she was astonished that such a spherical insect could fly. Miss Dickinson had laughed and told her that, some ten years earlier, German academics had solemnly pronounced that a bee's flight was 'aerodynamically impossible'.

'But clearly, Grace, they can and do fly, and without them what would we have? No flowers, no grain, no bread, no honey – no food chains. "There are more things in Heaven and Earth than are dreamt of in our philosophy …" Can you remember who said that, Grace?'

And this, she reflected, was how she had learned. How she had picked up an insatiable desire to acquire knowledge. From pollination, through biology, to physics, to Hamlet. This, thought Grace, was true learning. But now, Ivan Miles demanded that children should memorise poems with no contextual background; and should know the dates and order of British Monarchs from William the Conqueror to their current king, George VI, who had acceded to the throne some six years earlier. If you were going to become a farm-worker, what use was this, thought Grace impatiently, running her fingers through her abundant black hair.

Whatever her Headmaster said, she *would* apply the same principles of education that had inspired her to those bewildered children who had arrived at her school the previous week. Watching the antics of lambs in the spring, or the grunting satisfaction of pigs wallowing in mud, perhaps some small element of joy could be introduced to young lives which had known little but noise and savagery and loss.

Grace was as sure as she could be that, happily incarcerated in the larger classroom at the front of the school, where learning was defined by rows of dusty books and careful copperplate handwriting on the chalkboard, her Headteacher would never discern or understand what she was doing.

Chapter 9

Grace was shivering when she reached the vicarage. She had sat too long in her unheated classroom and the short walk down the village street and across the field where, years ago, the pony had been kept, had been enough to chill her to the bone. Clearly her mother was still upstairs in her studio. Heat and cold, day and night, passed her by unnoticed, when she was engrossed in her painting.

'I'm home, Mother!' shouted Grace, coming into the stately reception hall of the Georgian vicarage in which she had lived all her life. The dimensions of the building with its high ceilings, rich panelling and even a glass cupola, which allowed extra light to fall onto the staircase, spoke of an elegant era when the church had been wealthy and so too had the incumbents. Now the spacious proportions of the hall just served to emphasise the bitter cold of the December weather. Exquisite tiles, uncarpeted because, according to her mother, 'that was the intention of the architect', made the vast space even chillier.

'Oh hello, dear. What time is it?' came a faint, preoccupied voice from the first floor.

'Nearly five o'clock, Mother, and I'm starving!'

'Give me just one moment, Grace. I need to capture the turbulence of the clouds on this canvas …'

One moment, as Grace well knew, could equate to minutes, or more likely hours, in the timeless, creative world in which her mother existed. Leaving her coat on for the moment, and thrusting her hands deep into her pockets, Grace crossed the hall to the rear of the vicarage and knocked on her father's study door.

'Come in!' The response was warm: one of his parishioners had once said that listening to Charles Brabazon's sermons was like being given a firm, reassuring hug. Grace opened the door and stepped into the only room in the entire house that could remotely be called cosy. Wood-panelled, with a fire roaring in the ornate marble fireplace and thick Turkish rugs on the floor, this room was, without doubt, Grace's favourite.

'Ah, your mother is lost in the World of Art once more I see, my dear!' Charles Brabazon stood up from his desk, eased the stiffness out of his back and crossed the room to embrace his daughter. 'And how was Ivan the Terrible today?' he asked quizzically. Charles had long ago realised the extent to which the school governors and he himself had been duped by the show of erudition and the posturing of the new Headmaster.

'Terrible!' Grace said through gritted teeth. 'Can I make some tea for us, Father? It would be such a relief to talk to you about my day.'

'If you don't produce something for us to eat, I shall be impelled to do so myself – and we all know how dangerous that can be!'

The warmth of Charles Brabazon's personality had worked its magic and, at last, Grace grinned as she linked arms with her father and crossed the hall into the cavernous kitchen. They both remembered how, a month or so earlier, in sheer desperation at his wife's absorption in her latest painting, Charles had tried his hand at baking. Using the last of the flour ration, he had managed, against all expectations, to follow the various stages of the recipe, placing half a dozen rather irregularly shaped teacakes on a baking tray and sliding them into the depths of the huge, cream Aga. Turning to fill the kettle and place it on the hob, he had been disturbed by the front door bell.

''Scuse me sir, can you come? It's me grandad! He's been taken bad – real bad. Mum says he cannot last much longer.'

Selfless, generous with his time as always, Grace's father had immediately reassured the small, grubby boy who stood at the door, turning his shapeless hand-me-down cap this way and that with anxious fingers. 'Of course, Bert. Just stay there. I will get my things.' Picking up the sacrament and placing it in its leather case, then snatching his warmest overcoat, Charles had left the house, his baking completely forgotten. On her return from school, an overpowering smell of burning greeted Grace as she entered the kitchen and she had gingerly disinterred the charred remains of her father's cooking from the Aga.

To avoid any such further disasters, Grace had started to get up even earlier, so that she could make the necessary preparations for tea before leaving for school. Today was no exception and, entering the kitchen, in a series of actions so swift that they almost seemed simultaneous, Grace drew the heavy blackout curtains, switched on the light, slipped off her coat, put the kettle on the Aga and settled her father in a chair close to its comforting warmth. Then taking out the dough from the larder, she dexterously cut, shaped and rounded each teacake and placed them on a greased baking sheet. 'Right, Father. Let's have a cup of tea whilst we are waiting. Are the bantams laying?'

'I haven't a clue, dear! I can go and check!'

'In the pitch-black? No – it will have to wait until the morning. We must be egg-less tonight.'

They sat companionably on either side of the Aga, cradling cups of tea in their hands. As she gradually thawed out, Grace shared her frustrations with her father. 'Those poor children!' she exclaimed. 'They are totally bewildered. How would that academic buffoon get on in the blitz? Would he quote Homer or Ovid as the bombs fell? Honestly, Father, I am so cross!'

'I know, darling. I blame myself. To be taken in like that … I am so sorry.'

'Ah well. I have a plan! And I need something to eat – and so do you!' Jumping up, Grace slid the tray out of the oven and slit open two of the hot teacakes, swiftly putting the smallest scrape of butter on each half. 'I'd better take up something to Mother. Even if she were developing hypothermia, she would just not notice!'

Smiling, her father nodded.

Grace set a small tray, put on her coat again, and crossed the hall to the sweeping staircase. One of the large, north-facing bedrooms had been her mother's studio for as long as Grace could remember. She knocked and waited outside the panelled pine door.

'Mm?'

'It's Grace, Mother. I have brought you some tea.'

'Mm.'

Grace went in. Thick blackout curtains shrouded the floor-to-ceiling windows, but the room itself was bright with as many lights as her mother had been able to muster. A huge canvas, extravagantly splashed, coated and textured with thick layers of paint, defied the crushing grip of war on the country.

'Oh darling, thank you!' Catherine turned her large, violet eyes towards her daughter. Her black hair, threaded now with grey, was twisted into a rough knot, from which tendrils escaped at will. She wore black trousers with a vivid purple overtop – threadbare and shabby, but still proclaiming the wild exotic talent of the much-fêted graduate of the Royal Academy of Arts. Her only jewellery was a large engraved silver locket, containing photographs of Charles and Grace, which she wore always.

Shivering, Grace kissed her mother on her paint-streaked cheek. 'Mother, it's freezing up here!'

'Is it darling? Honestly, I haven't noticed. Do you think this shade of grey is just *too* dark here …?'

'I think this is utterly amazing, Ma! I love it! It's the view over our fields, isn't it?'

'Mm …' The affirmation was, as always, vague, as Catherine Brabazon turned away again from the reality that surrounded her to the intense, visionary beauty that she was intent on creating.

Smiling, shaking her head gently, Grace quietly closed the door on the vibrant, self-contained world which surrounded her mother and went down again to the warmth of the kitchen and the comforting presence of her father.

Chapter 10

'And to-day we are going to see how many animal tracks we can find in the snow. Put on everything you have worn to come to school this morning and please line up, as quietly as you can, by the side entrance.'

There had been a heavy fall of snow overnight and Grace had worn her warmest coat, hat, scarf, gloves and fur boots to walk to school that morning. Watching the children wrap up as warmly as they could, Grace momentarily worried whether her mother was taking sufficient care of herself in the bitterly-cold vicarage. The previous evening, Catherine had eventually left her painting some three hours after Grace had arrived home, to arrive in the kitchen almost blue with cold. Grace had made her mother fresh, very hot, tea and watched as she absent-mindedly ate four more teacakes, before asking, 'Mother, did you have any lunch?'

'I don't think so, Grace. The ideas were coming just too swiftly.'

Firmly pushing to the back of her mind her constant concern for her unworldly parents, Grace stood quietly at the head of the line of fifteen small children. 'Right. We are going to look very carefully at any marks or footprints that we can see in the snow and try to decide what kind of animal made them. It is really important to walk slowly and carefully, so as not to spoil or tread on any footprints we may find.'

And footprints they most certainly did find. The small, round paw-prints of the school cat; the elongated print of a fox; the imprint of a duck's webbed foot and numerous delicate bird footprints – the tiny ones of a wren and the huge ones of the crows that clustered around the tall, brick chimneys of the Headmaster's house.

Grace answered the constant stream of questions as fully as she could, sometimes posing a further question if the ability of the child warranted it. Bending down to the level of the children, she encouraged them to trace with their fingers the outline of the larger prints, noting the indentations of pads and claws. They were outside for nearly an hour, coming back into school just before lunch, with rosy cheeks and eyes sparkling with the excitement of what they had just discovered. They crowded around the big wood-burning stove in the centre of their classroom, rubbing their hands together. One of the smallest of the evacuees, Jim, turned to Grace with a huge grin. 'Miss, that was amazing!'

Grace realised that this was the first time she had ever seen any colour in the child's pinched, grey-white face, but all she said was, 'Good – I thought you were very grown up, Jim! You listened carefully to what I had said to you – well done! But now, let me tell you what we are going to do this afternoon: we are going to start practising for our Christmas play.'

A buzz of excitement flickered around the room and hands shot up.

'Miss, miss, are we doing the 'Tivity again this year?'

There was a universal groan from the children.

'Oh no! Not again! It's so boring.'

'The story never changes …'

'All the soppy girls want to be *Mary,* gazing at a daft doll!'

Grace held up her hand for silence. 'Well, I suspected that you might feel like this, so this year we are going to do something different. Let me explain. Come and sit around the stove and I will tell you a story.'

Putting out the overhead lights and opening the heavy, cast-iron doors of the stove so that the firelight played on the eager features of the children, the soaring ceiling of the Victorian classroom, and the black criss-crosses on the windows overlooking the fast-freezing school grounds, Grace sat in her storyteller's chair. 'Once upon a time, hundreds and hundreds of years ago, there was a brave knight. His name was George and he lived in a castle just up the hill here, by the church.'

'Really miss, did he really? Near to where we live?'

Grace silently put her index finger to her lips. 'One day, news was brought to him that an evil dragon was terrorising the village.'

'Like Hitler, miss? My dad says he is really evil.'

Again, Grace repeated the silent gesture. 'The king asked George to rid the country of this terrible creature, and offered him his lovely daughter to marry if he was successful.' Grace scanned the circle of glowing faces. 'And what do you think happened next?'

Hands shot up again.

'He killed it, miss.'

'He married the princess.'

'Both quite correct,' Grace smiled, 'and this is what our play will be about this year. We will be using a play that was written many hundreds of years ago, after

George had been made a saint. But as well as Saint George there are lots of other important characters too, so each one of you will have a part in our production.'

The rest of the afternoon was spent in deciding on the casting. Without exception, all the boys in the class vied to be the hero of the ancient story; but Grace noticed that one of the evacuee girls, Jean, had also put up her hand to volunteer for the role.

'Put your hands down for a minute, children,' said Grace quietly. 'I thought Saint George would be the favourite part, so I would like you all to think carefully for a minute and those who wish to play the part of the brave knight will take it in turns to explain just why it is so important to them, so that we can all understand and respect their reasons.'

Grace held the minute egg-timer in front of her and the children eagerly watched the pink sand slip away. As soon as the last grain had fallen, immediately there was a clamour of voices.

'Because he is the main character and I am the tallest boy in the class!'

'Because I can fight well.'

'Because my name is George.'

Last of all it was Jean's turn. Quietly she said, 'Because I think Good always wins over Evil. I want to give hope to people that we can beat Hitler.'

Everyone stopped.

'That is a very strong reason indeed, Jean,' Grace affirmed. 'No-one else gave such a thoughtful answer and because of that I have decided that you shall be Saint George.'

'Oh miss, she's a *girl*!'

'And you are all *boys* – not men – and certainly not knights! We have to pretend when we are acting – that's what plays are all about – pretending. And I have decided that Jean should have that part, because of the very good reason that she gave to us all.'

There was much grumbling, as the boys thrust their hands in their pockets and muttered to each other.

'Anyway,' continued Grace, improvising, 'there are other knights, who are friends of Saint George. There is also the King, the Doctor and the Turkish Knight.'

'How about the girls, miss?'

'There are lots of princesses in the story and their ladies-in-waiting,' responded Grace, thinking to herself that it was good that she had such a creative imagination.

By the end of the afternoon, everyone was happy. A tall, fair girl was chosen as *the* princess and there was an array of ancillary princesses and their maids of honour, all equally thrilled to be given the opportunity to dress up and perform in front of their parents and families.

Chapter 11

That night, unusually, Grace and her parents spent the evening together in the warmest room in the house. Grace and her mother sat on either side of the study fire, whilst Charles Brabazon was at his desk, working on his latest parish newsletter. The snow had thickened into a blizzard within the last hour and, always uncertain, the electricity supply had failed once again. The latest great painting was complete and Catherine was looking restlessly for another project. She was flicking through a pre-war catalogue of a Royal Academy exhibition in which she had shown four major works on the changing seasons and she lingered on their images, tracing with her finger the line of trees and rounded hills of her native Dorset, almost as if she was reliving the process of painting them.

'So, Mother, I have to virtually rewrite this Mummers' Play to include the legions of princesses and knights that were the only way to satisfy the children!' Grace grinned.

Catherine snapped shut the much-read catalogue. 'Would you like me to paint the scenery, Grace?'

'Oh yes please, Ma! Are you sure?'

'Well, what else am I to do until the next commission comes in – cook?' Catherine's lack of domesticity was notorious.

Grace stood up and gave her mother a hug. 'I would *so* appreciate that!' Excitedly, she paced the room. 'I think we need just three sets of scenery: a palace, from outside; the interior of one of the rooms; and a wild heath where the dragon lives.'

'Right,' exclaimed Catherine, leaping to her feet. 'I will get started!'

'But you need huge canvases, Mother.'

'I have them, dear. Just waiting to start something like this!'

'You also need light, Mother.'

'I have oil lamps.' She was off without another word and Grace heard her running lightly up the stairs, impatient to get started.

Her father chuckled quietly from his desk. 'So, no Nativity play this year then, Grace?'

'No, Father. I have decided that the children need to become aware of some of their traditional cultural history.'

'Have you discussed this with Ivan Miles?'

'He never has any time, Pa. He is intent on doing a *Festival of Nine Lessons and Carols,* just like his old college does every Christmas. The children don't understand most of the readings – and some are really tricky to explain. How about Mary's question to Gabriel, when he tells her she will become pregnant by the Holy Spirit? "How shall this be, seeing I know not a man?" He sends the children asking awkward questions to me! One ten-year-old asked me whether they were using artificial insemination like his dad uses on his heifers!'

Charles Brabazon burst out laughing. 'Oh, my darling girl – what would I do without you?' he exclaimed, giving her a hug.

⊰⊱||⊰⊱

December continued bitterly cold and almost every day brought fresh flurries of snow. Overnight it froze, so that solid layers of ice and snow built up on the paths, tracks and roads which linked Quintin Parva with the outside world.

In the school the two, very distinct, Christmas productions were being practised. The sonorous verses from the King James Bible rang out every afternoon, punctuated by traditional carols, as Ivan Miles had asked the church organist to accompany the children's singing on the school piano during rehearsals. In the infant classroom, the scene was very different. Almost every available surface was cluttered with cardboard armour, painted with more enthusiasm than skill; extravagant home-made tabards and dresses; and a pantomime-horse costume, borrowed from the nearby town by Grace and embellished with green scales and pointed tail and claws. At the end of each school day, Grace carefully stowed everything away in the storage shed, amongst the lawnmower and garden tools.

In contrast to the amateur costumes, the scenery sets were totally professional. In the first, a many-turreted castle rose on a rocky promontory above a tree-filled valley shrouded in mist, its shadowy depths reminiscent of an Italian renaissance painting. The second depicted a panelled council chamber, with iron wall sconces, the stained-glass windows showing glimpses of the same valley from an elevated angle. The last was filled with dark menace, showing a bleak heathland, its trees and heather blackened by the deadly fire of the dragon. In the foreground was a yawning cave whose entrance was strewn with gnawed fragments of bone.

When Grace had seen these immense works of art taking shape in her mother's studio she had been really touched, 'These are perfect, Mother!' she exclaimed. 'I can't find the words to thank you.'

An abstracted, 'But I was bored, dear!' was the only response.

⊰∣∣⊱

School broke up for the Christmas holidays on Friday 16th December and the Christmas production was to take place in the school hall the next evening. At four o'clock, Doctor Miles called Grace into his office.

'Are we ready, Miss Brabazon? I am sorry that I have not had opportunity to see for myself what you are planning but,' he steepled his fingers, 'the children certainly seem enthusiastic about your production, going by the amount of noise from your classroom!'

'Doctor Miles, the eldest child in my class is not yet eight. It is an exciting time of the year and the rehearsals have taken the children's minds off exactly what Christmas will be like for them this year. Rabbit and carrot cake are all most of the children in my class remember for Christmas dinner!'

'And is your production a version of the Nativity, may I ask?'

'Er, not exactly. It is a traditional play: part of our cultural tradition. My mother has painted the scenery.'

As she had expected, the last piece of information caught Ivan Miles' attention. He rubbed his hands together with evident delight. 'Really? A Royal Academician the painter of scenery in *my school*! I am delighted, Miss Brabazon. Please do give your dear mother my thanks. Most generous!'

⊹⋙‖⋘⊹

Despite the deep snow and biting cold, all parents and members of most families in the village trod carefully along the slippery, ice-packed roads and pathways to the village school. It was a strange sight, thought Grace, waiting in her coat and hat at the school entrance to welcome visitors. She had still not fully got used to the sight of almost silent groups of people walking without torches, relying on the moon or starlight to light their way.

The school hall was warm and became even warmer as it filled with the eager audience, delighted to have some form of entertainment on this bitter December evening. At seven o'clock precisely, Doctor Miles, resplendent in the full academic dress of his university, rose to speak.

'Thank you for venturing out in such inclement weather. We are going to start with the Junior class and their version of Nine Lessons and Carols, as established by my own university in 1918, just after the Great War. After a short interval, when you can partake of tea and mince pies …' there was a general stir amongst the audience at the mention of such traditional and precious food '… the younger children will perform, er, will perform.'

Once in Royal David's City floated to the rafters of the hall, just as carols had at this time of the year since the foundation of the school nearly a century earlier: the Christmas celebrations were once again under way. The older children had clearly been well rehearsed. They spoke and sang well and with clarity, although they did not, for one instant, look as if they were enjoying, or even understanding, the experience. The interval followed some forty-five minutes later and people mingled and chatted, grateful to be in such warmth and relative comfort to share the latest national news – which was not good – and their own personal successes and concerns.

Grace was nervous. Although the children had been infinitely more engaged by the secular play than by the well-known Nativity Story, entering with gusto into the fights and hyperbole, she knew that she was taking a risk departing from tradition. She glanced over to where her Headmaster was chatting confidently to a group of governors. At the end of the hall she had fixed in place the striking scene paintings that her mother had done, and had draped a black curtain over the first, in order to make its appearance more dramatic. It was nearly time. She had dressed her children during the first half of the performance in their colourful and motley costumes, providing a stark contrast to the exquisite stage sets, and they were waiting eagerly behind their classroom door. A stifled giggle or two was occasionally heard.

Grace rang the school bell softly. 'Ladies and Gentlemen! I hope that you enjoyed the first half of our programme tonight. The second item is in complete contrast. There is no need to remind you of the bitter struggle in which our heroic country is currently engaged and in view of this I thought it appropriate to introduce to the children some of the traditional stories and legends which deal with the eternal fight between Good and Evil.'

There was some nodding and muttered affirmation at this, but also some blank looks as to what this could possibly have to do with the traditional re-telling of the Christmas story which they had come to see. Most people in the room had real respect for the serious and dedicated young woman whom their children adored and so they continued to listen attentively as she went on, 'Tonight, therefore, we are performing for you the *Story of Saint George and the Dragon,* a centuries-old Mummers Play traditionally performed at this time of the year.'

The response to this was some desultory clapping – and many puzzled and disappointed looks. When Grace glanced across at Ivan Miles, his face was like thunder.

They had had such fun rehearsing the strange old play. The language was deliberately inflated and Grace had taken pains to explain this to her children. She felt that they had understood and were deliberately over-acting to match the quality of the speech. The curtain shrouding the masterly painting of the exterior of a crumbling stone castle was lifted and a stocky seven-year-old strode onto the stage, hand on hip:

Here am I, brave Slasher, I am a giant knight.
I come to challenge bold Saint George to
see if he will fight.
He fights for Olde England, I'll soon
knock him down.
I'll break his head and tear his limbs
and carry off his crown!

There was an audible stir in the audience. Grace glanced to where the governors were sitting. The Chair, Lady Maud Montgomery, the dowager of the local titled family, sat as if carved in stone. Her face was an expressionless mask; her feet planted side by side with the rigidity and inscrutability of an Egyptian statue.

Saint George swiftly followed his adversary, cardboard breastplate painted with a large red cross. The small girl stood centrally in the middle of the stage, trying to remember everything that her much-loved teacher had advised her to do as she proclaimed her lines:

Stand-off, bold Slasher, and let no more be said,
for if I am to wield my sword, I'm sure to
strike thee dead.
Thou speakest very bold to such a knight as I.
I'll cut thee into eyelet holes and make thy buttons fly.
And send thee overseas to make mince pies.

There was more head-shaking and quiet 'tut-tutting' amongst the audience who had come ready to coo over the tinsel angels and the ageless tableau of Mary and Joseph worshipping a doll Jesus. The freshness and fun of this secular play – with so many obvious roots in the pagan past – was almost totally unappreciated by the war-weary audience, who craved the ordinary, the known, the comfortingly familiar.

It was impossible for Grace not to be aware of the increasingly frosty reception that her bold experiment was receiving, but when the doctor, dressed in over-sized, striped trousers and a top hat that rested firmly on his large ears, spoke his lines, there was an audible gasp.

Five guineas and a loaf of bread I charge to
raise one from the dead.

Grace decided that this was the point of no return – she had to continue or look a complete fool. More importantly, to stop now would bitterly disappoint the children.

At the end of the play there was a shocked pause for what, to Grace, seemed an eternity. Desultory clapping started, which thankfully increased when the children, without exception grinning widely, stepped onto the stage to take their final bow.

With a distinctly heightened colour, Ivan Miles stepped in front of the younger children and their teacher. Completely ignoring the performance that they had just put heart and soul into, he announced in his dry clipped tones, 'And now, please do gather round the wood-burning stove for further tea and cake, kindly provided by our Chair of Governors, Lady Maud. Thank you all once again for coming, and enormous thanks to our village Royal Academician, Mrs Catherine Brabazon, for the exquisite scene paintings! Do please take this opportunity to look more closely at the highly-skilled and detailed work. We are indeed fortunate to have such a patron!'

Grace's mother was too involved in her next commission to attend the school end-of-term concert, whilst Grace and her father were completely preoccupied with the negative reactions that the Mummers' play had produced, and so the impact of the sycophantic words was somewhat lost.

Smiling in a distant way at the parents and grandparents, aunts and uncles who thronged towards the warmth of the huge stove and the precious offer of cake, the Headmaster turned on his heel and hissed at Grace, 'As for you, Miss Brabazon, I will see you in my office when everyone has gone!'

Chapter 12

'I could have disgraced you publicly tonight, Miss Brabazon, but my respect for your father and mother prevented me from doing so. Lady Maud was disgusted – *disgusted!*' Ivan Miles stood up and paced the length of his small office with the controlled ferocity of a caged lion. Ironically, Grace thought she had never seen him so human!

'May I remind you that this is a Church school! Our mission is to uphold Christian values and to promulgate the redemption and salvation of the Christian message. *Not* to indulge in bloodthirsty violence and pagan medicine men who can raise people from the dead in exchange for a payment of five guineas and a loaf of bread! Lady Maud made it absolutely clear that if this sort of thing *ever* happens again, she will suspend you! And you would probably be dismissed without a reference. *Do I make myself clear?*'

Grace flushed and simply nodded. She actually felt that she had overstepped the mark in departing from convention, but the rosy, enrapt faces of her children, thoroughly immersed in the enactment of the ancient story, flickered across her mind, emboldening her to lift her gaze and look directly into her Headteacher's furious white face. 'The children were bored of the Nativity, sir. They …'

'Bored of the Nativity? It is your role to remove their boredom, Miss Brabazon. Not to pander to their frail human nature! That is enough! I have spoken and I hope that your choices are clear to you: either you start to act like a responsible Christian teacher in charge of vulnerable young children; or you reconsider your profession. Good night!'

Grace kicked at the heaps of snow piled along the country lane on her bleak walk back to the rectory. It just could not get any colder, she thought to herself, turning up the collar of her coat and winding her scarf across the bottom of her face to protect it from the biting, easterly wind. She was upset – really upset. She had been convinced that it was right to depart from school tradition and introduce her children to an aspect of their culture that lay outside the rigid dogma of the Church of England. But now, remembering the faces of some of the parents of those same children, she was no longer so sure.

She was shivering, with cold and reaction, when she reached her home. She opened the heavy front door, then shut it behind her with difficulty against the rising wind, before crossing the hall to her father's study.

His usual 'Come in!' was probably the single most welcome sound that she had heard that evening.

'Oh Pa, I think I have made a dreadful mistake!' she groaned, crossing the blue and red Turkish rugs to the warmth of the fire.

'Come here, my darling!' invited her father, standing up from his desk and holding out his arms to her. 'Your production was unusual, but clearly the children loved every minute of their performance! I realise that it caused a stir, but you know this village! It will be a five-day wonder – forgotten by New Year 1943!' Hugging his daughter tightly, Charles Brabazon continued, 'The children will never forget the fun and excitement of that story; and who knows, as life goes on and they come to experience things that we can never imagine, some aspect of that ridiculous old play might come back to them to remind them of their short, precious years in your care.'

'What would I do without you, Father?' asked Grace, blinking back tears. 'You make everything count, everything positive. Thank you. I'd love to spend some time with you, just sitting here chatting, but I'm exhausted. I think I'll go up now if you don't mind.' And, kissing him on his cheek, Grace crossed the study and hall and climbed the stairs to her small back bedroom. Someone – almost certainly her father – had lit a fire in the black, cast-iron grate and had drawn the curtains, so that the tiny flickers of light from the logs could not be seen by enemy aircraft.

Grace pulled up a small slipper chair as close to the fire as she dared and watched the pictures forming and dissolving as wood caught, and burnt, and fell into ashes. She felt calmer now and thought again of her father's words. She was consciously encouraging in her children the enthusiasm for learning and the passion for life that Miss Dickinson had inspired in her, all those long years ago. Gazing deep into the fire and longing to escape from the pain of the moment, Grace recalled an unforgettable lesson during her final term at the village school. It had been a golden day, heavy with the scent of a million flowers, and her face and arms still glowed with the touch of the sun as she sat down for the afternoon session. On each desk lay some seed catalogues. The books contained a combination of black and white photographs and line drawings of flowers and plants and gave much useful information about how best to cultivate them. Her teacher removed these after the children had had time to read through them, and the children were then given cut flowers and branches of flowering shrubs, which were laid on the tables, rather than being placed in water.

'Which do you find the most stimulating?' Miss Dickinson had asked.

'The actual cut flowers, Miss Dickinson – but they are wilting quickly!'

'Right. Let us go out into the school garden now for a few minutes!'

On that flawless summer's day, the roses and delphiniums that Grace had helped to plant in the previous autumn and again earlier that year were in full bloom. Each flower was exquisite and together their sight and scent were overwhelming.

'And, tell me, which do you prefer now? The seed catalogues, the cut plants, or these flowers growing in their natural habitat, visited by bees and filling the garden with their fragrance?'

The point was imprinted forever on her brain: it was life itself, not the written word, that taught the most powerful lessons.

Chapter 13

At long last the intransigent bitterness of that winter softened and dissolved into a perfect spring. The children who had been evacuated to Quintin Parva were now virtually indistinguishable in appearance from their country counterparts. The snow and wind, and the necessity to walk everywhere, had made their cheeks rosy, their eyes brighter and their limbs more sturdy.

Grace was happy. The Christmas play, as her father had predicted, became a faded memory in the minds of villagers – although the Chair of Governors, Lady Maud, still greeted Grace with only a chilly, imperceptible nod of the head. Everywhere the countryside was waking from its long-enchanted sleep and snowdrops and daffodils flowered at the same time, so cold had been the months following Christmas. Pussy willows swelled on the trees by the river, still swollen from the winter snow-melt, and everywhere the grass was rapidly losing its unhealthy, yellowed appearance. Grace took her children out at every available opportunity. They drew, painted, and picked flowers and unfurling leaves, pressing them carefully between pages in school library books. To Grace, it seemed that the books had never been so well used, never so alive.

One day, she decided to walk her little flock down to the river and enlisted the support of her father in shepherding them along the narrow lanes to the footpath that led to the water meadows.

'I'm tired, miss! How much further is there to go?' panted Rosie, the smallest of the reception children.

'Not far now, Rosie. Long ago, when people had to work hard all day or walk for miles, they used to sing songs. It helped them work together and really put a spring in their step! Let's try out an old song now about the coming of warmer weather and see if it takes away your tiredness!'

> *'Summer is a-coming in, Loudly sing cuckoo!*
> *Groweth seed and bloweth mead*
> *And springeth wood anew!*
> *Sing cuckoo!'*

The children soon became familiar with the words and tune and their pace noticeably quickened as they swung along in a double file, older and younger children holding hands. Charles Brabazon smiled as he watched his daughter leading the children, with the occasional light skip in her step; the spring breeze gently blowing back her unruly, black hair; her piercing blue eyes full of life and mischief. What a girl! She was like a spirit of place: a dryad or naiad, completely at home in the trees or river valley of this part of Dorset. How had he and Catherine ever managed to produce a child who combined freedom of spirit with dedication of purpose? He was acutely conscious of his traditional approach to life and of his wife's obsessive eccentricity. He loved deeply the rituals of the Anglican Church, the candles and incense and the solemnity of the Eucharist. There was nothing he liked more than to lead Evensong in his historic church, when the setting sun brought to life the glowing colours in the west window. Song and prayer, candle smoke and incense rose to the arched roof timbers as they had for the best part of a thousand years. The human condition, he mused, did not materially change from generation to generation. People still loved and hated; needed to eat and sleep; still had a longing for beauty and peace. Whether the congregation in his church had come together to pray and seek comfort in the days of the plague; or to support each other as they had over the last few years in the face of the threat of invasion, common humanity linked them all.

'Let's stop here!' Grace called out to the line of children following her across a timber bridge which spanned the river. 'Line up along the sides of the bridge, children – and listen. What can you hear?'

'Water, miss!'

'Reeds being blown by the wind – a sort of rustling dry sound.'

'Birds …'

'Do you know what sort of birds?'

'That there on the top of the big willow, miss, that's a song thrush! Me grandad told me once that he repeats his song trying to teach the other birds – but they just sing their own type of songs.' Bert rubbed a grubby hand across his eyes. He had been inseparable from his grandfather, who had died a couple of months before Christmas.

Charles Brabazon laid a kindly hand on the small boy's shoulder, 'And your grandad was quite right,

Bert. He does sing his song twice over – at least! And he is always at the top of the tallest tree he can find so his song carries further.'

Grace smiled at her father. They both had a particularly soft spot for this small boy. His father was in the army and had been away from home for more than two years, leaving his wife to care for their large family alone. Bert always seemed to be clothed in hand-me-downs: boots far too large for him; huge, battered tweed cap set on his small head.

'We are going to write a sound poem when we get back to school, making a note of all these sounds on a large piece of paper. Then we'll carefully draw pictures around our poem of all the wonderful things we have seen today. So just stand still and listen, and look, and remember.'

The children stood immobile, noting seed-heads, burgeoning leaves, celandines, lambs – all the energy and promise of life to come that surrounded them.

'You have been so quiet and so incredibly grown up!' Grace told the children, 'that I am going to teach you a new game. It's called Pooh sticks and is like a little boat race, but using sticks rather than boats!'

'Pooh sticks, miss?'

'Yes. It comes from a book written by a man called Mr Milne about twenty years ago. Listen to part of the story.' Grace got out her own battered copy of *The House at Pooh Corner*. 'These stories are about a small bear called Winnie the Pooh and his friends – and their adventures. Their game first started with fir cones.'

'Pooh bear "… dropped two in at once, and leant over the bridge to see which of them would come out first; and one of them did; but as they were both the same size, he didn't know if it was the one which he

*wanted to win, or the other one. So the next time he
dropped one big one and one little one, and the big one
came out first, which was what he had said it would do,
and the little one came out last, which was what he had
said it would do ... And that was the beginning of the
game called Pooh-sticks, which Pooh invented, and
which he and his friends used to play on the edge of the
Forest. But they played with sticks instead of fir-cones,
because they were easier to mark."'*

'Miss, miss. Can we play?' asked Bert.

'Well, yes – I thought we could! When I say "Go!"
each of you search for a stick under those trees.' Grace
paused, watching the expectation on the faces of
the children. When she eventually gave the signal, the
children scattered amongst the willows around the
bridge, eagerly picking up sticks that looked
'streamlined' and 'promising'. After a few minutes,
Grace called to them again, 'Back you come! Jack and
Emily, you can be the team leaders. Jack, you stand at
this end of the bridge; Emily, you go down there at the
other end. Now take it in turns to pick your teams!'

Some of the younger children were so excited that
they were jumping up and down, waving their sticks in
the air.

'Concentrate, children!' Grace's raised hand stilled
the cries of excitement. Charles, once again, smiled
incredulously. Such an innocent and simple game – but
the children loved it!

The teams were soon formed and at last it was Bert's
turn. He dropped his carefully-chosen stick into the
river on one side of the bridge, then swiftly crossed to
the other. In order to see more clearly, he climbed onto
the lower rung of the wooden rails flanking each side
of the bridge.

'Mine's winning, look!' he shouted in excitement, gesturing to the rest of the class and jiggling frantically up and down. It was inevitable really: suddenly his foot slipped and his small body slid in between the rails of the bridge and into the deep, grey water of the river.

Without a word, Grace kicked off her shoes and slid down the bank into the water after the small boy. His head bobbed up and down as he was carried along by the current, pathetically small and totally powerless against the deep, cold river. Fortunately, Grace was a strong swimmer. She had learned in that very same stretch of water, during long golden afternoons with her father before this interminable war, on the few days off that he allowed himself. She put every ounce of effort into her crawl, drawing close to the little boy in a matter of seconds.

'Miss, miss! He's gone under!' shouted William, another farmer's son.

Grace was painfully aware that the struggling that she had first seen in the small figure – the raised arms and the natural instinct to keep nose and mouth above water – had now ceased. Bert was no longer visible on the surface of the water, and so Grace dived, furiously pushing aside reed and watergrass, to catch a glimpse of her little charge.

There he was: feet caught in a tree root, his small body being washed in the same direction as the vegetation – but he was still moving, weakly but surely, his hands trying to free himself from the vegetation that held him, Grace tore at the twisting wet roots and, sooner than she could possibly have hoped for, held the limp little body in her arms. She surfaced, gasping for breath.

'Catch my hand, Gracie!' her father shouted, grey flannel trousers saturated and dog collar wildly askew.

He had run alongside the river as she swam and hung onto a willow with one hand whilst reaching out towards his daughter with the other. Grace clasped the firm, warm hand of her father with utter relief. Under her right arm she had tucked Bert, who curled instinctively towards her body.

'Here. Give him to me!' puffed Charles Brabazon. Anxiously, Grace's father tried to recall what he had learned during the St John's Ambulance course which he had arranged for his parishioners, when he had realised that the war was not necessarily going to stop on the far side of the Channel. He lay the child down on his front and pressed firmly and rhythmically on the little boy's back with his hands. Coughing and twitching, Bert brought up the water that he had swallowed and sat up, sobbing and shaking.

'Thank God!' breathed Grace.

'Thank Him indeed,' nodded her father.

Chapter 14

'You are reckless, Miss Brabazon! Reckless indeed!' Ivan Miles sat, grim and unsmiling, on the far side of his desk, looking at his assistant teacher as if she was one of his recalcitrant pupils. 'Mrs. Smithson came to me in tears this morning. She could not believe that you had put the life of her child at risk. Just *what* exactly were you thinking of? She has also been involved in considerable expense, because she had to call out Dr Pedder to attend her son Albert, following his immersion in the river.'

'We were playing a game, Doctor Miles.'

'That says it all, doesn't it, Miss Brabazon: a game! A *game* ! Life is not a game. It is a serious business, and nearly losing one of our children in a river does not form part of this *game!*'

'But we were looking at the diversity of the natural world. Everything is waking up after the interminable winter – it gives us all hope for the future! The children have much to deal with in the course of their young lives. Air raids – even here! Fathers and brothers fighting for our country. No toys. No seaside holidays. Learning and living are part of the same whole – and we all need hope, Doctor Miles.'

'Don't you *dare* lecture me on what constitutes learning – or hope for that matter – young lady!' shouted the Headteacher, rising abruptly to his feet. 'Did *you* attend the foremost university of the land? Can *you* read and write Greek? Are *you* the Headteacher of this school?'

'No, sir! But I *am* appointed to educate the youngest children in this village. And that is what I have been doing! If you have nothing further to say to me, Doctor Miles, I would like to return to my class.' Grace rose, flushed and shaking, but determined to stand her ground.

'There is just one further thing that I need to say to you, Miss Brabazon: you are fired. Fired! You will have no reference. You have no future. You will leave the school at Easter – and you certainly have *no hope* for the future. Have I made myself clear?'

'Totally, Doctor Miles.'

⊰⊱⊰⊱

'I hate him, father!'

'Oh, darling, I know he is difficult, really difficult, but hate is a very strong word indeed!'

'It is a very strong feeling indeed, Pa! Why should so many people have died, why should someone like … like Alex have died for a self-obsessed idiot like Ivan Miles?'

'Only God can answer that question, Grace,' replied Charles Brabazon seriously.

It was one of the things she loved most about her father – his unshakable faith that everything that happened was under divine control. This absolute

88

conviction filled his church every Sunday and kept a stream of parishioners, who found themselves anxious or distraught, coming to the door of the vicarage.

'Well, there is one thing that I will never complain to God about,' Grace said softly, crossing the study floor to join Charles Brabazon where he stood by the fire, and, putting her arms tightly around his ample waist, 'that He made you my father!'

⟡

It was like a death sentence, thought Grace to herself. Each day was one day less in what remained of her life as a teacher. She cherished each one as the term moved swiftly towards Easter.

'Right, children, this week we are going to make a time capsule.'

'Cap … what, miss?'

'Capsule, Doris.'

'Like a sort of hat, miss?'

'No. A capsule is a sort of container. We are going to put in it lots of things that are special to us: newspaper cuttings, maybe a toy or old plate or cup, maybe photos … and seal them really, really tightly, and put them somewhere safe and hidden.'

'But why, miss? What for?'

'Sit down, children.' Grace realised that she had, perhaps, introduced too quickly a concept that was quite advanced for very young children. 'How do we know about what has gone on in the past?' Grace asked.

'My grandad tells us stories about the Great War.'

'My grannie has old recipes that *her* grannie wrote down in an exercise book. But it's a bit smelly because lots of cooking stuff has got stuck on it.'

'Miss, miss, I went to the museum in Dorchester once. There's lots of Roman stuff there that they have dug up, that was buried in the ground!'

Thank goodness for Esme, reflected Grace!

'Exactly, Esme! And we are going to collect together lots of things so that people – maybe boys and girls who are not born yet – will learn about us and about our lives here in Quintin Parva in 1943.'

For the rest of that week, the children brought into school things that were precious to them and their families. The infant classroom was full of toys, medals, spoons, small spades, tiny tin jelly-moulds, photographs and newspapers. It was chaotic!

Gradually, through discussion and reasoning, Grace helped her class to decide on items that would give maximum information about the year in which they were living. Grace had found an old biscuit tin in a deserted corner of the vicarage larder and, on a Friday afternoon in late March, she sat the children in a circle around her and prepared to pack the chosen items snugly into the tin. There was absolute silence as Grace carefully went through the things they had chosen, repeating again the reasons for choosing each item.

'Well, the most important packet to put in is the photographs of all your fathers. They are protecting and caring for our country just as they protect and care for each one of you. *The Times* newspaper explains what is going on in the War at the moment: this may be forgotten in the future. Bert has brought in his empty ration book and we thought, didn't we, that people may not understand that we can only have a certain amount of food during times of war. I still remember when we could buy much more than we can now. We all love carrot cake and here is Annie's grannie's recipe, carefully copied out by Annie – very neat handwriting Annie! Here is Billy's copy of his mother's shopping list – once again, really careful work, Billy! This sheet shows what we learned last week. Who can remember?'

'It was how birds manage to fly, miss,' one of the evacuee children affirmed eagerly. 'I never knew that they have hollow bones, miss!'

'Well done, Jim, well remembered! And finally,' Grace took a deep, steadying breath. 'This tin mug belonged to a friend of mine. He took it with him to France and it is a good way to remember how difficult the past years have been for so many people.' She had curled the photo of Alex inside the mug that was one of the very few personal items saved when he was lost. She had agonised over including both photograph and mug in the time capsule, but somehow felt that the man she had loved would gain a sort of immortality through being remembered in this way. Quickly she placed the last item at the heart of the biscuit tin and pressed the lid tightly on.

The children watched her breathlessly, caught up in the adventure.

'I had thought about burying our time capsule,' Grace explained softly to her children, 'but decided against it. Can anyone think why?'

There was silence for a few moments, and then Esme's hand shot up.

'Well, if it rains the tin will get rusty, miss!'

'That's right, Esme. Well thought out! So what else do you think we could do with our special tin?'

'Seal it in a wall …'

'Hide it in the attic …'

'Yes, and yes! Two excellent suggestions. I have an idea that combines both those ideas, children. Let me describe it to you and you can tell me what you think.'

The model of practical problem solving was working its magic on the children. They were enrapt!

'The toilets in the yard have a really high roof and, to stop the birds nesting there, bricks have been placed against the rafters. They are not stuck together with mortar – just placed in the angle between roof and wall.' Grace angled her hands together to illustrate what she meant to the children. 'I have discovered that there is quite a large space behind these bricks and that is where I think we ought to place our time capsule. What does everyone think?'

'Oh yes, miss!'

'Yes!'

'It would be safe there.'

'The rain wouldn't spoil our things.'

'Decided!' declared Grace.

As she placed the tin carefully on the deep ledge behind the bricks, it felt to Grace almost as if she were physically burying the man she had loved. In common with so many women she had never had closure, as Alex's body had never been found. In this simple ceremony, she felt as if she was at last laying him to rest.

Chapter 15

After tea that evening, Grace sat in her father's study on the rug in front of the fire, leaning back against his knees, and told him how she had felt. Charles Brabazon's heart went out to his daughter. She had been so incredibly strong about losing Alex Jamieson. She was so incredibly strong about almost everything, he reflected: her bully of a Headteacher; the eccentric vagueness of her mother; the lack of stimulus that Quintin Parva provided for a young and attractive woman.

'Was I wrong to feel as if I was laying him to rest, Pa?' Grace asked, looking at the patterns of flames and shadows in the log fire. Her father hesitated for several minutes before answering in very deliberate and measured words.

'No, Grace. As with almost everything you do, I believe that you have reached a sensible conclusion. It is two years since Alex died; your life goes on. This war will end. You will have a future – a future that we cannot possibly imagine.'

'Thank you,' Grace replied quietly. 'Father, do you think we should …'

'Sh! There goes the air raid siren, Grace. Out we go!'

'I'll go and get Mother!'

Grace ran upstairs to her mother's studio two steps at a time. She flung open the door, expecting to see her engrossed in her latest canvas, all lights blazing, blackout curtains closed tightly. But instead, her mother had drawn back the thick curtains, having extinguished the lights. Catherine Brabazon was watching motionless as several enemy bombers droned overhead, either returning from an unsuccessful mission to Bristol, or aiming for the small local airfield. Searchlights swept and danced across the dark, night sky, illuminating the relentless progress of the heavy planes. Then, without warning, the house shook. One plane had dropped a bomb, on farm land which stretched to the river behind the vicarage.

'Mother, you must come. Come quickly! We must get to the air raid shelter!'

'But Grace, the patterns of the lights are fascinating. Just think what I could do with this concept on a canvas.'

'Mother, now is not the time!'

A second bomb shook the old building more strongly and, looking out of the window, fascinated despite herself with the swirling lights in the sky, Grace saw two things. Firstly, the figure of her father running, not towards the air raid shelter in the vicarage orchard, but towards the school. And secondly, that his destination appeared to be the school grounds, where a fire had started – presumably from where the second bomb had fallen.

'Oh no!' In a flash Grace realised what was going on. Ivan Miles was coaching four of the older boys in Greek two evenings per week. She looked at her wristwatch – it was seven o'clock – and tonight's session would just have started. And she realised that the last bomb had dropped very near to where the school was. Without another word, she left her mother and pelted downstairs. Flinging open the front door she tore across the field where her pony had been kept, in an idyllic time that now seemed more like a dream than reality, and into the narrow village street. She soon saw what she had been dreading. Behind the school, in the extensive grounds cherished and coaxed into life by Miss Dickinson, a fire blazed. The stately horse chestnuts and the walnut tree, where she had sat as a pupil and dreamed and learnt, were alight. The air raid shelter had been positioned a sensible distance from the school building, under those very trees. But what she saw next almost stopped her heart. Her father was carrying two of the boys, one under each arm, away from the blaze.

'Father, let me help!' Grace yelled.

'Stay where you are!' panted her father, laying the boys down gently on the grass at Grace's feet. 'I'm going back for the other two.'

Grace was shaking uncontrollably. The boys were breathing, but unconscious. She had no idea what was wrong with them, nor what to do to help them. All her mind was focussed on the corpulent figure of her father running back once again to the place that should have provided safety for the children, but had actually exposed them to the worst of the bomb blast. Unbelievably, Grace saw her father coming towards her once again, with the other two boys held firmly under his arms.

'Father, what do I do? How can I help them?' Grace sobbed.

'Smoke inhalation. Just leave them for the moment. I'm going back for Doctor Miles. I'll help you deal with them when I come back.'

'What! Can't he walk himself?'

'He seems ill, Grace,' gasped her father. 'Maybe he has had another heart attack. I can't leave him.'

Her hands tightly fisted, tears streaming down her face, Grace watched her father go back a third time. He was running no longer, just walking as fast as he could. For God's sake, she thought, he is as old, or older, than the man he is rescuing!

Time seemed to stand still. Seconds seemed endless – and still her father did not reappear. Grace was on the point of going after him when, unbelievably, he emerged from the school grounds, holding the Headteacher under his arm pits and dragging him to safety.

The night was as bright as day, every detail of the chaotic scene brought vividly into focus. The flames illuminated the figures of Charles Brabazon and the unconscious Headteacher and flickered across the ground towards Grace. She felt nothing but fear for her father and ran, heedless of her own safety, towards him until, suddenly, the whole world exploded into white light and she knew no more.

Grace Adams
1943

Chapter 16

Grace Adams opened her eyelids infinitesimally and shut them again. This was like a re-run of a bad play, she thought to herself: same banging headache, same blinding light as when she had woken in the London hospital after her dive into the crowd. She could only see blurred shapes, but she heard, crystal clear, the clipped, precise tones of someone in the room with her.

'Sister, Miss Brabazon has opened her eyes momentarily!'

There was a starchy rustle and Grace felt a cool hand on her forehead and a hard, cold something – presumably a thermometer – being slipped under her tongue.

She tried again, opening her eyes wider this time. But what she could see puzzled her. In the Royal London, where she had been taken after her farcical exit from her one and only high-profile fashion show, there had, she remembered, been no colour. Walls were white, beds were white, instruments cold stainless steel, white window frames, ceilings, and gowns of doctors and nurses. But here there was colour everywhere: some sort of rose-patterned fabric at the window, blue nurses' uniforms, green painted window frames. She thought hard. Probably this was how they did things in Quintin Parva! But was she still in the village? She couldn't recall ever having seen a hospital – but then she hadn't had the time or the inclination to explore every part of the village. As her mind ran on, she recalled fragments of what had happened and then, as she concentrated, she remembered the whole event: the bicycle ride, the flower collection, the blackbird's song, the heavy bicycle slipping sideways and her head-on collision with the stone fountain.

She was fully conscious now. 'Where am I and what day is it?' she croaked. 'I'm also really thirsty, so please could I have some water?'

The cool hand appeared once again, laid firmly but lightly on Grace's forehead. 'You are in the Cottage Hospital, Miss Brabazon. It is April 23rd – exactly one month after your, er, accident.'

'What?' Grace tried to sit up, but seemed to have no energy to lift herself off the high pillows. 'That's crazy! My bike crashed in May! Either I have been unconscious for eleven months or you are lying! And who the hell is Miss Brabazon? I am Grace Adams for God's sake!'

Cool hand looked under her eyelids at her colleague: 'Confusion, shock, lack of acceptance of what happened,' she asserted quietly.

''Scuse me, Nurse Frosty Arse, I am not confused! I know exactly what happened – better obviously than you do! I was cycling down the hill and crashed into the stone fountain – in *May*. End of!'

'You will feel better if you sleep, Miss Brabazon,' the nursing sister said firmly, leaving the sunny room and closing the door behind her.

Grace lay back on the pillows. This was like the worst sort of trip! Why on earth weren't the nurses calling her Miss Adams? Could her medical records have somehow been confused with someone else's? There was one thing sure-fire certain: she was going to get herself out of this place and back to her aunt.

She took a deep breath and sat up, swinging her legs out of bed, but had to pause for a few moments as her head started to swim. When she felt that she could actually stand without falling over, she got to her feet, determined as always, but swaying slightly. After a few tentative steps, becoming acquainted once again with the use of her limbs, Grace gradually felt more in control of her own body. She walked across to a small square mirror on the wall, next to a calendar with a picture of a cow on it in black and white – strange subject! Blinking her eyes, she glanced at herself in the mirror. My God! What had they been feeding her on? Bricks? She must have put on about a stone in weight and her hair seemed to have grown to a ridiculous extent. Perhaps she *had* been unconscious for eleven months! Peering more closely in the mirror, she had to admit that she looked ridiculously healthy for someone who had been in hospital for a month …   or eleven months …

Automatically, she glanced at the calendar, checking dates. She looked harder, then, characteristically, threw back her head and laughed out loud as she read: April 1943. What the …? All her life Grace Adams had danced on the edge – the edge of acceptable behaviour, of respectability, of legality, of fashion. The extraordinary events of the last half-hour were either a very elaborate practical joke, or time travel of some sort! No different really to taking some of the drugs she had used, except that, this time, the dimension was outside her own head, rather than within her own altered mind!

Grace felt a flutter of excitement in her stomach. What was going to happen next? The twilight land that she was used to inhabiting – somewhere between reality and the places that coke, or weed, or, on occasion, ecstasy, had taken her – was as real to her whilst it lasted as this situation in which she now found herself.

How should she play this? Slowly, she walked back to the bed, also covered in a rose-patterned quilt, slipped inside the bedcovers, closed her eyes and thought hard. If she persisted in saying that she was Grace Adams, rather than Grace – what had they called her? Brazier? Brannon? – well, whatever they had called her, they may think she had completely lost the plot. Best to hold her counsel, to observe, to engage with the adventure! What, after all, had she to lose? She had no career, no money, no future in the world of 2010. The risk-taker, always strong in Grace, took control. Once again, she laughed out loud – then quickly tried to stifle her laughter. She must play this game of pretence very carefully. If she had really slipped back in time, then perhaps 1943 would hold more promise for her than her shattered life in 2010.

Chapter 17

'I know how close you were to your father, dear,' murmured Grace Brabazon's mother. 'How are you coping?'

'Er ... OK.'

'OK? Oh, you mean not too bad I suppose. It never ceases to amaze me how we are taking on American phrases ...'

Catherine Brabazon was, predictably, immersed in her latest huge canvas. It was black, splattered with whirling lights and colours.

'That's amazing, Catherine!' exclaimed Grace. It chimed so precisely with her dystopian take on life: black with the occasional flash of colour!

'You like it? I thought you would be horrified ... since it shows what we both looked at the evening Charles lost his life.'

'No, it's cool!'

'Sorry, dear! Is this some latest American idiom? I think the atmosphere it creates is quite hectic – quite hot – actually.'

'Er ... I think it's great, Catherine.'

Sticking a paintbrush in her hair, which she wore coiled thickly in a loose bun, Catherine Brabazon turned thoughtfully to Grace. 'Why have you started calling me Catherine, Grace?'

'Well … because I am getting older now and it is the modern thing to do,' replied Grace, grasping at straws. She found it impossible to call this striking, sophisticated woman 'Mother'. This word was associated firmly with the slight, shallow, hedonistic woman she could only vaguely recall.

'Oh, I see. All right, Grace. Or should I say, OK?' Catherine smiled, retreating into the abstract world of art which was more real to her than the loss of her husband, or the exigencies of war.

⊰⍉⍙⊱

It had seemed so easy at first to take that decision – to stride without a backward glance into the world of 1943 – nearly seventy years before the fast, fascinating, dangerous world that Grace had loved. But as the weeks moved on, Grace became increasingly lost and, as her strength grew, so did her old restlessness.

'I'm going out, Catherine!' she announced at breakfast one morning. It was a hot June day, full of the scent of roses that not even the war could take away. Up until this point, Grace had pottered around the large vicarage garden and slept longer than she had ever slept before. She tried half-heartedly to help run the huge rambling house, but she had not, to date, had the nerve, to put it bluntly, to walk into the village.

Catherine Brabazon munched absent-mindedly on week-old bread, from which she had just cut the areas of mould that had started to grow. She was coaxing the small amount of strawberry jam which she had unearthed from the depths of the stone larder shelves

into overlapping swirls on her white plate. 'Mm …
right, Grace. Do you think I could incorporate layers of
colour on top of painted swirls to suggest movement?
Or would that be too complex?' Catherine had
been used to years of musing out loud without ever
receiving a reply – her husband and daughter neither
understanding the nature of her thoughts, nor being
particularly interested in them.

'I do actually, Catherine,' replied Grace. 'If you
over-light with silver and under-light with a darker
version of the same colour, immediately you will
introduce a dynamic element to the shapes.'

Mildly surprised that, after nearly a quarter of a
century, her practical, pragmatic daughter – so very like
her late husband in character – should actually have
engaged in a conversation about art, and even made a
suggestion that Catherine herself had not thought of,
caused the older woman to stop making circling patterns
in the jam. She looked directly at Grace, a slight
frown creasing her high, broad forehead before she
smiled and said with feeling, 'Thank you, dear. That is
really helpful. I will go and try it out immediately.'

'Don't you want some of this?' Grace asked. 'This'
was several sticks of rhubarb that she had unearthed in
a corner of the vicarage orchard and had attempted to
cook. She stuck a large spoon in the dark-brown,
unappetising heap of fruit. 'It's got some sort of vitamin
stuff in it that's supposed to be good for us …'

Catherine absent-mindedly shook her head,
removing the paint brush she carried almost
permanently in her hair, as she quickly ran up the
classical curving staircase to her studio.

Unenthusiastically, Grace stuck her spoon into the
resisting brown mass.

Before she had tasted Annie Adams' cooking, Grace's staple diet – apart from boiled sweets – had been only takeaways, Subway rolls and burgers – the unappetising, poor food to which her mother had introduced her. Living with Catherine Brabazon was easy. It was like living with a shadow, or more accurately a scintillating rainbow of colour and dynamism, but both women found the practicalities of life impossible. Grace had vaguely watched Annie cut and stew rhubarb from Rose Cottage, so earlier that day had diligently cut the ruby-red and green stalks into neat two-inch pieces which she had put into a large pan on the Aga.

Timing was not Grace Adams' forte. Half-heartedly tidying the kitchen whilst waiting for the pan to come to the boil, she caught sight of a pile of newspapers and a couple of magazines. She saw several copies of the *Church Times*; a few badly-printed, thin, national newspapers; and then, unbelievably, a copy of *Vogue*, with the front cover headline, *Bright Fashion for Dark Days*.

Grace actually gave a whoop of joy and, rhubarb forgotten, curled up in a chair, eagerly turning the pages. At least, she smiled sardonically, she would not read about any 'fall from Grace', since the magazine had been printed some sixty-seven years before the disastrous fashion show that had marked the end of her career in the twenty-first century.

As she turned the pages of the magazine, she realised that, in the world into which she had been catapulted, people used everything to make their clothes: parachutes; maps printed on silk; old curtains; bedspreads; even checked cloth used to wrap cheese. What she read was inspirational!

Eventually, the smell of burnt fruit roused Grace from her greedy devouring of the magazine. 'Oh God, I *hate* being domestic!' she exclaimed as she tried to lift the pan off the Aga, burnt her hand, grabbed a cloth and slammed the pan and its contents down onto the wooden butcher's block.

Grace prodded and poked the dessert that she had tried to produce earlier that day and, reluctantly, took a mouthful. It was *awful:* burnt, bitter, glutinous. What a waste of time! Disgusted, she scraped the contents of the pan into what Catherine called the 'pig bin' and slammed out of the house. Shoving her hands deep into the pockets of the long, navy skirt that she had been told was hers, Grace realised that, already, she was almost back to the size she had been in her London days. The total lack of ability to produce anything edible was making sure of that! As the shapeless skirt drooped over her hip bones, she glanced up at the pleasing symmetry of the Georgian vicarage and remembered, poignantly, her walk with Alison's dog, Henry. The 'adventure' that she anticipated back in the Cottage Hospital had been much more complex than she had imagined. She missed Annie – terribly. She was puzzled as to whether the people she was living with were, in some way, ghosts. In 2010, did Catherine Brabazon lie in Quintin Parva churchyard? How had the Old Vicarage become a school? How on earth had she ended up in someone else's body? What had happened to that other person?

She crossed the field in front of the vicarage and made her way to the village street. She looked at the rough grass, at the trees which edged the field on one side, and even at the sky before finally taking a deep breath and looking at what lay before her.

Alison's house was boarded up. Clearly it was still, or had been until recently, a working school. A paved area in front of the building had rough, chalked markings on it – presumably the vestiges of children's games. A wrought iron cross was fixed prominently to the wall underneath a small bell tower and weather vane. Two gates, marked 'Boys' and 'Girls', book-ended the area of playground. Part of the roof had collapsed and rough lines across the brickwork showed where the impact of shrapnel had shattered the silence of the night and left its indelible mark on the fabric of the school when Charles Brabazon had met his death. A notice was fixed to the 'Girls' gate.

This school is shut
Until further notice.

Suddenly, Grace was almost knocked over.

'Miss, miss! When are you coming back to teach us again!' A small, impossibly dirty boy grinned up into Grace's face, pushing back his huge flat cap and grabbing hold of her skirt. 'It's horrible at the big school, miss! Them townies make fun of us. They say we smell like pigs! We never have no nature walks and we just sit all day and if you look out of the window all you can see is buildings and streets, not flowers and trees.'

'Er … well … you can see the school is shut.' Grace said uncertainly, trying politely but firmly to remove the child's filthy hands from her clothes.

'But you are coming back to teach us, miss?'

'I don't think so. I … er … I'm still not very well.'

Grace had tried to think herself into the life that the 'other Grace', as she had started to think of her, had lived and she worked hard to piece together the fragments of information that she could glean. One evening, when Catherine Brabazon had finally finished painting and they were both sitting companionably together in the kitchen, Catherine had quietly opened her silver locket and reflectively traced the features of her late husband in the small photograph crammed into one side of the piece of jewellery. Grace looked over her shoulder at Charles Brabazon's kind, but ordinary-looking, features. But she swallowed hard when she saw the other photograph. The smiling, gentle face of Grace Brabazon, framed with abundant dark hair, bore a strong likeness to Grace herself, although her features were softer, less angular. Grace knew that she had been a teacher and had picked up further fragments of information from conversations with Catherine. She learnt that Catherine's daughter had been thrown against the school wall by the explosion on the night of the air raid whilst running towards Charles Brabazon. She also understood that Catherine's husband had been killed that night, saving the Headmaster from the fire caused by the bombs; and was told that the Headmaster, Ivan Miles, had taken ill-health retirement as a result of the traumatic experience. But concerning any further details of the 'other Grace's' life, she knew nothing.

Bert Smithson frowned. He was puzzled. Miss Brabazon had never turned anyone away before. She was always ready to listen, crouching down to the level of the children, smiling, extending her hands towards them. His whole world had been turned upside down in the last few months. Now, every school day, together with the other children from Quintin Parva, he was taken on the post-bus into the nearest town. Bert missed running across the fields from his farm to the little, warm, safe place that he loved: where the world of learning had been opened to him gently and irresistibly. Instead of being with a small group of children that was more like an extended family than anything else, Bert was now in a class of forty-five. In this town school, the children sat in rows at wooden desks. There was no magical story time around the glowing wood-burning stove; no sitting in a circle to share news and the little surprises and excitements that formed the stuff of his young life. Bert hated his new school. And now – the final blow – his Miss Brabazon just couldn't seem to get away from him quickly enough.

Bert pulled his over-large cap down firmly and surreptitiously wiped his eyes. 'Right you are, miss – but please get better soon.'

Shaken, Grace watched the little boy trudge slowly away, his thin shoulders hunched, it seemed, against the difficulties of the world. Then, thrusting her hands violently into her pockets, she turned and walked past the school – Alison's home in years to come. A straight stretch of village street followed and there it was – Rose Cottage. It looked exactly the same, apart from vegetable beds instead of the rose and herbaceous borders that Annie Adams loved so much.

For someone who had carefully eradicated any emotion from her life after the dual betrayal of her mother leaving and her father dying, Grace was surprised to find tears in her eyes. She remembered that the last time she had cried was on the final morning of her life in the twenty-first century and could almost feel once more her aunt's warm, strong hand reaching out to her over the kitchen table. She recalled the bicycle ride and the flowers that she had collected for Annie, and the strange end of her fragmented, desperate life as Grace Adams. For the first time in her adult life, Grace was lonely.

Chapter 18

It was autumn, five months after that extraordinary morning when she awoke in 1943 and Grace was manoeuvring the heavy mahogany tea-trolley with difficulty across the tiled hall of the vicarage towards the study. She could hear the occasional soft comment from Catherine, but predominantly the clipped, cultured tones of the large woman who had arrived in a swirl of tweed and self-importance fifteen minutes earlier.

'...and we members of the Women's Institute consider it *our duty*, Mrs Brabazon, to lighten the load of the less fortunate people of our village. Just talking about something that is not to do with this wretched war lifts the spirits. Yes – and the *hearts* of the cottager, the ploughman, the farmer and the baker.'

As Grace crashed into the only comfortable room in the house, apart from the kitchen, she saw the large figure of the visitor silhouetted against the window. Hauling on the trolley, she managed to bring it to a halt before it collided either with furniture or the two women engaged in a somewhat unequal conversation. Catherine Brabazon sat beside the fire, whilst the low, afternoon sun illuminated the rigid curls and the determined, wide-footed stance of the woman who was haranguing her.

Almost desperately, Catherine jumped up. 'Oh thank you, dear! You *will* stay, Grace, won't you?'

'Of course. You must taste these!' Grace proudly gestured to the flat, slightly orange, squares which she had placed, as neatly as she could, on a delicate china plate. The few months that she had spent with Annie Adams had influenced her more than she realised: they had, in fact, been her only experience of being mothered in her short, chaotic life. As she ground her way determinedly through the dusty collection of stained cookery books in the vicarage kitchen, a vision of the contentment, warmth and security that Annie had given to her for such a brief period haunted her and she longed to be able to replicate it.

The large visitor strode across the room, hand outstretched. 'And how are you, my dear? Jean Smithson was telling us at the Institute meeting that her son Albert was quite shaken when he met you a few months ago.'

'Really? Why?' Grace asked directly, and with a fair amount of irritation. She had spent ages cooking these wretched carrot-cake squares and had anticipated that she might be able to introduce some of the comfortable domesticity that Annie Adams' cooking had created, into the large, cold house. But now she felt that Catherine's visitor was ignoring her best efforts and, in some obscure way, criticising her behaviour.

'Well, dear, because you just did not seem like the old Miss Brabazon – simple as that!'

'Sorry – what's your name?' Grace stood motionless, furious that even this tiny gesture of trying to be of use, to do something, was being disregarded.

'Ginny Hartley.'

'Well, *Ginny Hartley*, perhaps I am not the same as the old Miss Brabazon! Has that ever occurred to you, sitting in judgement? Do you have any vestige of an idea of what I have been through? Do you? Is it written in the constitution of the Women's Institute that: "Thou shalt sit in judgement on thy neighbours"? Sorry Catherine, excuse me. The atmosphere in here is stultifying!' Grace turned on her heel to walk away, seeing with surprise a ghost of a smile on Catherine Brabazon's lips, whilst Ginny Hartley flushed an unbecoming beetroot-red and patted her immobile curls.

'Well!'

Catherine gave a resigned sigh. 'Oh, do sit down, Ginny – sugar?'

The Chair of the WI took a deep breath. Her visit here was not after all purely social. She most definitely had a purpose.

'I suppose it is the trauma?'

'Mm.' Catherine's habitual, non-committal response allowed her hectoring visitor to blunder on.

'Must be so difficult for you, my dear. Almost like losing both your dear husband and your daughter!'

Catherine gazed absent-mindedly at the setting sun. Soon it would be time to draw the blackout curtains. She was shocked that, since Grace had come back from hospital, she had actually discovered a relationship with her daughter that she had never had before. Until the dreadful night of the air raid, Grace Brabazon had been self-possessed and infinitely closer to her father than to her. Often, although Charles and Grace did not realise this, Catherine saw father and daughter exchange a look which suggested that they were tolerating, almost patronising, her. But, since Grace had regained consciousness after her accident, she now seemed to share her passion for art, and was ready and able to discuss creative ideas and concepts. Bless her, all this on top of trying to cook for them both and dig the garden.

Grace stood motionless in the hall, just outside the study door, hands clenched into fists. What she would give to punch that fat woman in the face! She expected Catherine to make an anodyne reply to Mrs Hartley's false sympathy, which would dismiss Grace's significance with a word. But what she actually heard shook her.

'Well to tell the truth, Ginny, Grace and I have never been closer. She is working so hard to sustain the household and I think that that is admirable. Do have one of these carrot-cake squares. Grace has been baking them most of the afternoon.'

Grace almost gasped. This woman – the vague out-of-the-world woman who forgot to eat, or change her clothes – was actually protecting her!

'Well, I hear what you are saying, Mrs Brabazon, but I am ruffled! Distinctly ruffled.'

Grace took a deep breath and squared her shoulders. If someone was prepared to speak up for her, then she would go back and stick up for them! 'What are they like, then?' she asked, as she opened the study door again and took a seat by Catherine.

'Delicious, dear! Thank you so much.' Catherine smiled as she watched the slight figure impatiently take a plate and two of the carrot-cake squares which, actually, were solid, tasteless and somewhat overcooked. She watched Grace's small hands making quick gestures as she ate and drank her tea, pushed her hair back from her face and played with the lace arm-chair cover. There was so much that was different about her daughter since the night of the air raid. Yes, she looked the same, although much more slender than she had been, but her behaviour had changed. She was quixotic and volatile, rather than quietly passionate: instant light and heat, rather than a slow-burner. Her gestures were quick, rather than measured; her facial expressions much more animated, rather than self-contained. Catherine remembered the weeks of quiet self-control when the telegram had been delivered to the vicarage, announcing in terse terms that Grace's fiancé, Alex, had been *'lost somewhere over the south coast of England.'* During that period of quiet intensity, her daughter and husband had seemed to draw even closer together, if that were possible. Catherine's mind was wandering far from the heavy monotone of her unwelcome visitor, but she was brought back sharply to what Ginny Hartley was saying, when she became aware that she had been asked a question.

'So, what do you think?' asked her visitor.

'Forgive me Ginny, would you mind repeating what you just said?'

After a deep sigh of lightly-cloaked impatience, her visitor repeated what she had obviously just asked. 'It would be marvellous if you could possibly come and give a talk to our branch about your Art, Mrs Brabazon. As I said, this would be inspirational to the villagers, whose spirits, let us face it, are not high. I know how busy you are, I know what a high professional profile you have, but think of *your country,* Mrs Brabazon!'

'All right.' Catherine Brabazon cut across her visitor's indefatigable barrage of talk. 'When is the date of your next meeting?'

'Oh, you are too generous! As I said, November 15th – in about a month's time.'

'I'll put it on the calendar. And now Ginny, you must excuse me. I need to work.' With uncharacteristic firmness, Catherine got to her feet and walked slowly over to her late husband's desk, lightly touching a black and white photograph of her and Charles on their honeymoon in Switzerland. Sadly, she glanced down. She did miss him: his gentle ways, his … well, his goodness she supposed, and his profound care for other people.

Grace saw the sadness cross the older woman's face. 'Let me get your coat, Ginny,' she proposed.

'Thank you, *Miss Brabazon*.'

Grace opened the heavy front door, allowing a swirl of dry leaves to patter across the tiled floor. 'Good bye, *Ginny*!' she called, closing the door firmly behind the square, tweed-suited figure, determined not to be put down by some obscure protocol relating to the use of Christian or Family names.

As Grace skipped across the cavernous hall and into the study to clear away the cups and plates, she saw that Catherine stood there still, eyes looking into a previous time in her life that Grace had no part of. She looked so remote, as motionless as a statue, her thoughts clearly in the past. Grace looked at the silent figure pensively: what was 'the past'; and what does 'the present' mean? Her life over the last year had shaken up any thoughts she had formulated about the concept of Time, never very profound, since she had almost always been concerned only with the punishing schedule of production dates and preparation dates for the shows of her fashion house.

Both women were cool emotionally, but Grace walked over to Catherine and laid her hand lightly on her arm. The older woman started slightly, and came out of her reverie. 'Thank you, Grace,' she smiled, and walked swiftly to the door. Grace heard her light footsteps running up the staircase, followed by the sharp click as the studio door closed. She would not, she knew, see Catherine for the rest of the afternoon, and possibly the rest of the evening too.

Chapter 19

She had washed up. She had scraped – and soaked, and scraped again – the enamel baking tin in which she had cooked the carrot-cake, yet it still looked filthy. Where were the non-stick baking tins that Annie had used so effortlessly? She imagined they were decades away from being discovered.

Eight o'clock. Horrible, thick, black curtains drawn, and dim lights lit. The fiery restlessness of Grace's character had never burnt so bright. She just had to do something. She paced the floor, thinking back to her life in London which already seemed like a book that she had read, rather than something she had experienced. She wondered what she would have been doing there, back in 2010 or, she supposed, forward to 2010! She grinned, realising that, almost certainly, she would have been working. The usual pang – almost a physical pain – hit her as it always did. She knew that her creativity was as powerful as ever. She only had to see the fine fabrics from which some of the curtains in the vicarage were made, or the design concepts in the precious copy of *Vogue* that she had unearthed, for her brain to team with ideas about how to utilise the first, or actualise the second.

Grace ran up the stairs to Catherine's studio and popped her head around the door. As usual, Catherine was totally immersed in her work and Grace was astonished to see that, already, the artist was busily putting into practice what they had talked of a couple of days earlier. Her canvas was huge, as if she needed those dimensions to express the surging grandeur of her artistic imagination. Grace saw that she had painted a tranquil pool – green and blue and gold – the colours of deep summer. But into the pool fell raindrops, which Catherine had painted as swirls of colour underlit with the dark green of pond-weed and over-lit with the silver and gold of the fitful sunshine of that summer day. It was breathtaking!

Grace had intended to ask whether she could get Catherine anything, but instead she stopped short and gazed disbelievingly. 'Wow! This is utterly amazing. You feel as if you can see the bottom of the pond *and* the sky at the same time. It's fantastic!'

Catherine smiled vaguely and returned to her intricate, yet flowing, work.

Quietly, Grace closed the door and walked softly to her bedroom at the back of the house. Earlier in the afternoon, she had optimistically put a few twigs and fir-cones in the black cast-iron fireplace whilst she had been waiting for the carrot cake to cook, and now she set light to these, hoping that somehow, this time, her attempt at fire-lighting would actually work. She sat on the small rug next to the fire, listening to the moaning of the wind around the corner bedroom and the tall vicarage chimneys. It was so cold! She shivered and wrapped a blanket around her shoulders, watching the flames, unbelievably, take hold of the cones and wood. Looking around the room, with its faded wallpaper patterned with pink cabbage-roses, the matching curtains, and the little, battered desk with a litter of her own things, she glanced again at a black and white photo of a rather conventionally good-looking man, in some sort of cap and uniform. She wondered about the life of the person who used to live in this room and what this man had meant to her. Somehow, she had never been able to bring herself to move the photograph from its place at the back of the desk, but now the man's eyes seemed to watch her.

Grace had never been particularly interested in men. Clothes design and creation were her passion. There had been boyfriends, yes, but they had soon grown tired of her lateness, her unreliability, her refusal to sleep with them because she had to meet tight deadlines. Grace hugged her knees to her chest, wrapping the blanket more tightly around her back. To be honest, the men she had known had bored her. They had been too self-obsessed; too conscious of their own masculinity; too pissed or off their heads on ecstasy or coke – or worse. For probably the first time in her life, she wondered what it would be like to be in love with someone, and to want to spend every day of her life with that person. She supposed it was like the longing she felt to bring into being an idea that existed only in her head. She thought of the shocking black and white wedding dress she had designed and how she had been able to express her philosophy through creating that outfit. How she had been able to be more completely herself through that act of creation. Was that what being in love was like: to become more completely oneself through a relationship with another human being?

Grace jumped up. For goodness sake, she was becoming maudlin! She used to be so spontaneous and practical, her mind taken up completely with making her ideas real, not sitting gazing into a fire and *thinking*! Swiftly, she put the dented metal guard in front of the fire. Right! People in this strange world of black, drawn curtains, little sugar and powdered egg, said it was a bad idea to go out at night. All sorts of things might happen. Hitler might be hiding behind a haystack; germ warfare might start at any minute. So, if she couldn't go out, she would explore the parts of this rambling Georgian house that she just had not got to yet.

The ground floor she knew like the proverbial back of her own hand. The symmetrical square rooms on either side of the entrance hall: to the right, the drawing room; to the left, the dining room. Behind these two spacious formal rooms lay, on the right, the study which she and Catherine used when they were not in the kitchen; and, to the left, the kitchen which extended behind the central reception hall and led to a rabbit-warren of smaller rooms: dairy, larder and some sort of storage room with stone shelves. The first floor was similar – the Georgians could not have had much imagination, thought Grace – as the front bedrooms corresponded with the formal rooms on the ground floor. Behind the right-hand bedroom lay a bathroom and behind the left-hand one her own little bolthole was wedged. The big front bedroom on the right was Catherine's studio, filled with her own paintings, huge cushions and rugs. It looked like something from an Eastern bazaar! Dramatic, enticing, exotic – rather like Catherine herself.

As far as the outbuildings which lay behind the vicarage were concerned, Grace had only entered them a couple of times since she had awoken in 1943. They consisted of a row of low stone stables, which were joined to a two-storey substantial coach-house, still with its high arched door.

Above the first floor of the main house, she thought, there must be attics. There was a small oak door, next to the bathroom, which she had only opened once, to see a flight of uncarpeted oak stairs rising and then turning at right angles to disappear into the gloom.

Mind made up, she decided that she would explore the attic floor of the house, which she had so unexpectedly learned to call home.

Chapter 20

The moon was so bright that Grace didn't need a light, which was just as well as the attic windows were un-curtained. She opened the little door and trod softly up the uneven steps. Perhaps the servants used to live up here, Grace thought. Lucky servants! Each separate room was considerably larger than the dingy London bedsit she had reluctantly inhabited during her previous life.

She made her way gingerly across the dusty, wide elm floorboards. In one corner she could make out the angular shape of a broken chair, lying close to which was a Union flag and some triangular bunting, also in red, white and blue. Perhaps these had been displayed when a previous war had ended – the First World War?

She walked quietly into the second of the dim attic rooms and her heart quickened with excitement as she made out the shape of three huge, brass-bound trunks.

At school, Miss Garner, Grace's English teacher, had tried to interest her in literature – any sort of literature – by suggesting alternative forms of fiction. Looking at her student's jet-black hair, her Goth eye makeup, long black skirts and Doc Marten boots, Connie Garner had made a guess that *The Castle of*

Otranto, the prototype Gothic novel; *Northanger Abbey*, its parody; and the *Twilight Saga* might just catch the interest of the stubborn, reckless girl. They did; but not sufficiently to inspire Grace to work any harder towards achieving a respectable grade in English Literature – textiles and art remained her only passions.

Now, in the rambling, shadowy attics of the Georgian vicarage, Grace thought of the ghosts, the bodies, the vampires that she had read about, and laughed out loud. For the first time in months, she felt that she was re-finding herself. She had tried so hard to support Catherine, to meet the expectations of life in that all-pervasively grey, wartime society. But really, she saw that it was hopeless. She was Grace Adams, born in 1987; not Grace Brabazon, born in – unbelievably – 1920, if she too were twenty-three. Being quiet, trying to be domesticated, attempting to produce what was inevitably inedible food, all this was absolutely not her! Living on the edge, creating a fashion statement that made people gasp, giving two fingers – both literally and metaphorically – to conventional society: this was Grace Adams. And whether she had been the subject of time-travel, or weirdly was living in the body of someone else who had lived in the 1940's, she could never, she decided at that moment, be false to her own soul, her own intensely individual and creative nature.

She moved quickly, her heart beating fast with excitement, to the first chest. It was massive and heavy. Even the lid was weighty but, to her surprise, was not locked. With difficulty, her delicate hands managed to click back the brass catches and heave the lid up.

Involuntarily, she gasped. Carefully folded in layers of delicate paper, itself exquisitely patterned with the stylised fruits and flowers of the Arts and Craft era, Grace lifted out dress after dress. Narrow-waisted, with voluminous, swirling skirts of silk and taffeta in rose, cream, crimson, blue and saffron yellow – all the colours that stimulated Grace's mind and engaged her creative intellect – the garments swished and danced before her. There were cashmere shawls; head-dresses of silver wire twisted with silk flowers and feathers; long gloves; capes made of fine wool. It was astonishing!

Hands shaking, Grace moved on to the second chest. This was full of gentleman's clothing, from a scarlet dress uniform to lusciously-embroidered waistcoats, whose silver and gold thread caught the soft light of the moon. Thick army capes and long, fine leather boots lay at the bottom of this chest.

It was like a young girl's dream: the sort of dream which fulfils the longings to be locked in a dress shop when everyone has gone home, trying on everything and finding that everything is perfect.

The third chest, she felt immediately, was different. On top there were two long, plain, cream dresses, each with a rose-coloured sash and matching velvet drawstring bag. Then came two children's dresses, made in the same material and style. Layers and layers of tissue paper were folded underneath these delicate garments, from which rose petals fell. Their colour could still be made out – they were pink – and, unbelievably, the scent lingered: the essence of far-off summer days. Grace let out another gasp of awe as she saw what lay at the bottom of the trunk. It was a silk wedding dress – a fairy-tale dress. A dress that made the harsh dystopian vision of Grace's black and white creation look like a cheap joke. Layers of fine silk stirred and shifted as Grace reverently lifted the exquisite garment from the chest. It was almost as if the dress had a life of its own and was leaping into the moonlight, joyous to escape from its years of incarceration. The neckline was low and edged with rose-coloured silk which, every few inches, was coaxed into tiny flower shapes. A deep-rose, silk sash encircled the tiniest of waists. Underneath the dress lay a pair of pink, heeled shoes, embroidered with summer flowers – peonies, honeysuckle and white daisies. Close by them lay a delicate circlet of silk flowers, matching the shoes exactly.

Grace stood, giving silent homage to the creative genius that had brought dreams of such loveliness alive for the woman who had worn that dress and the girls who had supported her dream of happiness. She just had to find Catherine. Who was the woman who had worn such a stunning garment? What was the history of this? How old was it? Flying down the stairs, she knocked on the door of Catherine's studio, but the lights were off. She shot down from the first floor to the hall and heard vague noises from the kitchen, where she found Catherine absent-mindedly chewing carrot cake and drinking hot milk, which she had warmed on the Aga.

'Catherine! Do you know what I have just found!' cried Grace, her cheeks flushed.

'No, my dear. I cannot read minds!'

'The most amazing things I have seen for … for a very long time. Chests, full of clothes. Beautiful things. And a wedding dress which is utterly indescribable.'

'Ah,' Catherine gave a thoughtful smile. 'My grandmother's chests.' She stirred her hot milk slowly and dunked the dry carrot cake into her drink. 'Alicia was a renowned beauty – but she was also kind and generous and was loved by everyone in the village. My great-grandmother organised her first season, which was beyond successful. The whole of London society was wild for her, hoping to see her at the theatre, or catch her out to dinner with her mother and father. Every eligible beau in town sought her and was desperate to marry her in order to capture this peerless heiress for himself. Viscounts, even a duke, paid court to her. My great-grandmother's letters tell how she was pleasant to them, invariably polite, but would have none of them. And then …' Catherine sighed and stood up, hands on hips, stretching the stiffness out of her back and shoulders '… and then she met Captain James MacIntosh.'

'The clothes in the second trunk belonged to him?'

Catherine nodded. 'Almost from the first moment they met, they fell deeply, passionately, in love and were married within six months. Theirs was the perfect match. Both were strikingly good-looking: tall, with dark hair and vivid blue eyes. They took an extended honeymoon in Venice and returned to the village with Alicia already pregnant with my mother.'

'Did they live here, Catherine?'

'No, my dear. At Manor Court, just by the church. This house came into our family when my mother married my father, who was vicar of the parish at the time and whose family had lived here for generations. As their only child, I inherited the house and your father and I have always lived here. It seems that vicars as husbands run in the family.'

'No chance, Catherine!' Grace interjected sardonically.

'Anyway, they lived in their white house at the top of the hill, idyllically happy. But James' regiment was called to the opium war and, with only a few short weeks to go before their baby was born, Alicia was left alone with her household and her mother.'

'This story doesn't have a happy ending Catherine, does it?'

The older woman shook her head. 'It is almost predictable, isn't it? James was killed in action in China; and Alicia, absolutely destroyed by her loss, died giving birth to my mother. All that is left of their marriage, that brief yet idyllic relationship, is contained in those chests and, I suppose, in you and I.'

Both women sat, silent, lost in their own thoughts.

'Were you in love with Charles, your husband – I mean, my father?' asked Grace softly.

'He was a good man. He adored me, and tolerated my foibles. But 'in love' in the way that Alicia and James were? No – sadly not. My art is my first love, and I think Charles knew and respected that.'

'I so know what you mean. It's the same with me!' Grace declared passionately.

Catherine gave her a quizzical, direct look and continued, choosing her words deliberately and carefully. 'To love someone as much as I love my painting would mean that he had to share that vision, that interpretation of life that I endlessly seek to represent. His passion for art would have to be equal to mine – and somehow in that equal passion there would be an overwhelming meeting of minds and souls. Do you see what I mean?'

Grace nodded, astonished to find that tears had come to her eyes. She had never been able to express her restless dissatisfaction with the fleeting relationships that she had had with men. But this colourful, eccentric woman, with paintbrush still heedlessly stuck in her hair, munching thoughtlessly on dry carrot cake had, somehow, just put into words exactly what Grace herself felt. She thought back to the doctor that she had met in London. She wasn't stupid. She knew that he found her attractive, if challenging. But there wasn't a flicker of interest in him, as far as she was concerned. It was as if he came from a different planet.

Abruptly, Grace stood up. 'Thank you, Catherine. For the story and for the philosophy! But I'm tired, so I'm going to say goodnight.'

As she ran up the wide, shallow steps of the sweeping staircase to her bedroom, Grace felt that she needed time to internalise this conversation. How likely was it that she would ever find someone with the same intense focus on creating clothes that simultaneously both enhanced the wearer and expressed the designer's take on life? As she shrugged out of her dusty skirt and jumper, Grace reflected ironically that if she had been asked this question a year previously, she may well have responded that it was about as likely as travelling in time.

Chapter 21

Rather than drag the clothes chests down into her bedroom, where space was definitely at a premium, Grace decided to leave them in the attic. She carefully brushed and cleaned the dusty wooden floorboards, removed cobwebs from the ceiling and wall timbers, and laid on the floor old dustsheets that she had unearthed in one of the stone outbuildings.

This was such a gift! She felt that just touching the delicate fabrics and running her slender fingers across the tiny, skilful stitching had awoken again the old Grace, the creative Grace. She was unsure how, but was determined to use them in some way in her own life to affirm, to stimulate, to bring vitality and awareness to the dull and limited community in which she found herself.

She started to sketch again, using the reverse side of old sermons that she had found in Charles Brabazon's desk and a precious stub of pencil. She felt slightly guilty but, as she saw her old angular style dominating the yellowing paper, once again expressing the disguise, statement and influence that fashion is able to give to its wearers, the guilt faded. Surely what she was doing was of equal importance to the spiritual solace that

Charles had given his parishioners? He had given food for the soul; her aim was to feed the imagination.

One wet day she had spent hours in the attic, taking a thick blanket to provide some protection against the cold. She was lying on her front, sketching in rapid, sure lines. All day she had been playing around with the idea of role reversal, based upon the neatly-folded clothes that lay secret and powerful in the nearby chests. Why shouldn't a woman wear a tightly-fitted military tunic and tight black pants, whilst a man could relax in a romantic, soft shirt and loose-fitting trousers? She was basing her designs on the exquisite, antique garments she had discovered.

Grace was so totally engaged in her sketching, that she didn't hear the door opening. When she heard a soft exclamation behind her, she jumped and twisted quickly around to face Catherine who had entered the attics.

'Grace, these are amazing! But why are you making these drawings?'

Grace tried to put together a plausible explanation, which remained true to her own passion for design, whilst avoiding any convoluted reference to her previous life in London. As Catherine stood, silently listening, nodding from time to time in affirmation, it struck Grace that her companion had an extraordinary ability to accept without over-questioning. Grace was sure she must be astonished that her 'daughter' should develop a totally new talent after a devastating accident; but if Catherine was astonished, if she did have a thousand questions about Grace's changed behaviour, not one escaped her lips.

'Can you make these?'

'Yes. I can.'

Catherine Brabazon laughed. 'I've just had a wicked idea! Do you remember Ginny Hartley's visit?'

'How can I forget it?' Grace made a pretence of lumbering ponderously to her feet, blowing out her cheeks and making her slender body as wide as she could. *'Now, my dear Mrs Brabazon, can you come, absolutely gratis, to one of my boring meetings and try to wake up the old dears who have fallen asleep through sheer boredom or old age ...'*

Through her laughter, Catherine continued, 'She runs the village branch of the WI like a military campaign, so why don't you make me a military outfit for my talk?'

'Wow! I would *love* to! That will give the old cows – girls – something real to talk about instead of trying to manufacture malicious gossip about the poor inhabitants of Quintin Parva! Leave it to me!' And Grace danced across the attic, then clicked her heels together and saluted sharply.

Chapter 22

Grace and Catherine grew ever closer together over the next couple of weeks. Grace was astonished that, in the unlikely setting of wartime Quintin Parva, she had found another truly free spirit, someone who was ready to kick against convention and prick self-importance.

They met in the attic, like schoolgirls sharing some guilty secret, laughing together as the chic black trousers and bright, soft wool jacket, took shape. Grace had decided to take full advantage of Catherine's tall, slim, almost model proportions and cut the trousers tight and the jacket short. Initially, the greatest challenge faced by Grace was sewing the garments together.

'Do you have a sewing machine, Catherine?' she asked one morning, munching flat, tasteless bread that, for once, she had managed not to burn. But why had it not risen, she asked herself? Oh, she gave up!

'Mm, I think so. My mother used to use one when I was growing up. I think it's somewhere in the outbuildings.'

And it was: dusty, exotically patterned in gold on black, mounted on a sort of trolley. Grace stood and scratched her head. Compared to the digitally-controlled, precise machines that could embroider, overstitch and hem, this was basic indeed.

'Did you find it, dear?' asked Catherine at dinner-time.

'Well, yes, but can you help me get it to work? It's on a type of trolley, and doesn't seem to have a connection for electricity. Is that right?'

'Mother used to sort of pedal the footrest underneath Grace; and we only had gas, for lamps, when I was a girl. We can have a go together.'

The machine was heavy, filthy and rather rusty, and it took the strength of both women to push and haul it back to the house. In a little, stiff drawer Grace had found a mildewed instruction book, curled with damp and fly-spotted, which showed a line-drawing of a tightly-corseted Victorian woman rocking the cast-iron plate under the machine to and fro with her feet.

After much swearing, oiling and cleaning, unbelievably they got it to work and, treadling away, Grace laughed at the absurdity of the situation. But absurd and laborious though the sewing process may have been, gradually, using the precious, perfectly-preserved materials held safe for over a century in the attic chests, the outfit for Catherine was created.

'Do you realise I can run upstairs twice as fast now I have the Dreadful Machine?' Grace asked Catherine, holding out the red and black garments in her arms. 'My leg muscles are like iron!'

Catherine put down her palate and ran her fingers over the perfectly-finished clothes, 'Oh, you clever girl – these are perfect!'

She looked amazing: sleek, reed-thin, the cut of the garments showing her spare figure to its greatest advantage, with the occasional tantalising glimpse of the ever-present silver locket between the tailored edges of the jacket.

'And now,' she grinned, 'I am ready for Mrs Ginny Hartley!'

⧽╫⧼

It could have been a replay of that day in her other life when Grace had tried to join the Women's Institute meeting. The women's attitudes were the same: buttoned up, unfriendly, dressed in their wartime best, walking sedately and with a sense of their own importance towards the village hall.

Grace and Catherine had arrived there early, managing to carry between them two of the enormous canvases that lit up Catherine's studio. Ginny Hartley's eyebrows had nearly disappeared into her rigid curls when she saw the striking figure of Catherine Brabazon stride into the hall. Now Grace, from one of the windows, watched the straggling line of women making their way down the village street, whilst Catherine stood on the slightly raised stage, composed and magnificent. Flanked by her two vivid interpretations of life, she was ready to talk about why she painted as she did and what inspired her.

There were no questions. Most of the women just stared open-mouthed at the vibrant figure, talking with passion about what mattered to her most, and Grace realised sadly that they sought only to criticise, not to learn.

Afterwards, there was the inevitable tea and cake.

'Carrot-cake, dear?' asked Mrs Hartley, with a smirk on her large face, offering a plate of evenly-cooked, uniformly-raised offerings. 'My daughter Marianne baked these earlier this morning.'

Grace bit back a sharp retort. Today was Catherine's after all, and she had withstood the patronising comments about it being 'so good of her to come so soon after her bereavement'; and 'so encouraging to see her facing life in such obviously good spirits.' If Catherine could do it, then, Grace decided, so could she – but couldn't resist the slightest touch of wickedness when she replied, 'Never touch the stuff, Ginny. That's why I am so thin!'

⇥||⇤

Later that evening, Grace and Catherine relived some of the most excruciating moments of that afternoon, laughing together over the narrow-minded bigotry of some of their fellow villagers. Grace felt alive in every fibre of her being. She had made a stunning outfit – maybe not for the rich and privileged to snap up, but something that shook peoples' perceptions of behaviour and attitude. Something she loved to do.

Eventually, her mind still racing, Grace climbed the stairs to the little room that she had come to love so much. She did not switch on the light but, instead, drew back the pink-flowered curtains to let the moonlight flood in. It struck her that it was an entire month since she had discovered the treasure hoard in the attic: once again the moon was full. She leapt into bed, desperately trying to get warm, and hugged her knees to her chest in excitement. How could she do more of this? How could she continue to feel as fully alive as she had over the past weeks, designing, creating and showcasing her work?

Midnight came and went. The inexorable path of the moon across the sky marked the passing of time. It was no use, she just had to get out and go for a walk, before her excess energy made her head explode! She pushed to the back of her mind the dire warnings about going out at night, promulgated vigorously by Ginny Hartley's husband, the local Air Raid Warden. The skies over Quintin Parva had been quiet now for some months and it seemed that the focus of attacks must be somewhere else. Leaping decisively out of bed, Grace decided that she would take advantage of the silver-bright moonlight and explore the countryside at night.

Grace put on some oversize, dark trousers that had belonged to Catherine's daughter and secured them with a tightly-cinched belt. Everything belonging to her namesake was too big and made of fabrics so incredibly dull that they just did not stimulate Grace to remake or remodel them. Stumbling towards her bedroom door, however, she decided that wearing such heavy, bulky clothing was ridiculous. If she blundered out in these she would fall into a ditch, or trip over her own feet or something! The only slim-fitting trousers were those that she had made for Catherine. They had been replaced carefully in the attic and, almost as quick as the thought, Grace was up the attic stairs and slipping them on. They were a delight to wear! The cloth was soft and warm, full of the luxury of an age and class for whom expense was no consideration. She couldn't resist slipping the jacket on too, over her black jumper, and she twisted her hair up and back, grabbing the red and black cap that would just not fit over Catherine's long thick hair.

Grace felt like another person. Self-contained and ready for whatever next her extraordinary life might throw at her, she slipped silently out of the dairy door behind the kitchen and walked quickly and quietly towards the river. She remembered poignantly the ludicrous antics of Henry, as he had dragged her along that same footpath and towards the river in her other life.

From the vicarage, Grace had to follow a short stretch of road. She kept very close to the deep shadow of the high, thick hedge, and then turned with relief into the soft grass of Gypsy Lane. Catherine had told her the origin of the name. It led to a clearing, hidden from view and surrounded by overgrown hedges and tall trees, and it was here, away from the prying eyes of the villagers that, for generations, Romany travellers had pitched their caravans. Catherine had smiled gently in reminiscence, as she told Grace of the skipping game which she had played with her friends at the village school. As the rope turned, the children had chanted:

'My mother said I never should
Play with the gypsies in the wood ...'

Grace marched briskly along the soft, grassy track in time to the rhythm of the old playground chant. It was very cold, and a dusting of frost on grass and hedgerow gleamed softly in the moonlight. The trees were bare of leaves and sighed gently in the imperceptible breeze. Winter was not far off. She stopped – surely that was an owl? She had never heard the sound in London, but during her time with Annie Adams, a tawny owl habitually called from the black walnut tree at the end of her garden. Distinctly freaked out at first by the eerie sound, she had grown to love it, lying safe in her bed whilst feeling a part of the wildlife of the night-time world. Here in the ages-old green lane, Grace closed her eyes and let the timeless light of the moon, and the sound of the owl, wash over her again and again.

She felt even more awake now than when she had left the vicarage and decided to continue, following the deep shade of the hedgerows to the river. But after a few further steps she paused: was that the sound of voices, of music? She crept stealthily on, but soon stopped short. Ahead of her she saw, almost like a stage set, a scene which set her pulse racing.

Tarpaulins had been slung over the high, flexible ash trees at the end of the lane, bending them down to act almost like roof timbers. The tarpaulins nearly reached ground level and, because of the dense bracken and deep, thick grass, any trace of light was very effectively blanketed out. Grace squatted, trying to catch a glimpse of what was going on within the enclosed space but, still not being able to see clearly, she quietly lowered herself to the ground and inched forward silently on her belly.

What she saw utterly amazed her: brightly painted caravans – vardoes – circled a grassy clearing, in the midst of which a wood fire burned. Groups of travellers stood or sat, chatting quietly together, and somewhere someone was playing a plaintive, lilting tune on a violin. It was mesmerising, and totally unreal. Most people would have focussed on the music, or the timelessness of the scene, or the age-old bright roses and stylised scenery which decorated the vardoes, but for Grace it was the staggering beauty of the clothes worn by this reclusive people that drew all her attention.

'My God!' she breathed, taking in the scarlet flounces; the wild, exotic embroidery on the tight black tops of the women; the soft cream, green and gold folds of the flowing shirts worn by the men; the vast, intricately smocked outfits of the old gypsy women; all sitting, nodding together and smoking their clay pipes in the dancing light of the fire.

Without warning, her right arm was whipped tight behind her back in a crippling half-nelson and her head was jerked up and back.

'What a pretty little soldier boy we have here!'

Without thinking, Grace did the only thing left to her to do – she bit hard and deep into the arm that was threatening to break her neck.

'Gesù Cristo!' The man sprang back, and Grace leapt up, losing the red and black cap in the process. Her hair swung thick and black across her face.

'Un gatto … a cat … and a very beautiful one at that!'

Her attacker sucked his arm, where blood was oozing from the marks left by Grace's strong, white teeth. Grace watched him, poised ready for flight, taking in his height, the breadth of his shoulders, his tanned skin showing above the creamy whiteness of his ruffled shirt and the latent strength and grace of his hands.

'And what is the name of this wildcat that creeps on her belly in the dark?'

'My name is Grace. What's yours?'

'Romani – Angelo Romani.'

'Ha! I must say you don't look – or act – much like an angel.'

'And your actions don't carry much grace – so we are, as our American friends say, quits! But I am just known as Romani and I will call you Grazia.'

Grace Brabazon
2010

Chapter 23

'But it's three months now, doctor! Surely there should be some signs of returning consciousness?'

'It's not time to worry yet, Ms Adams. Your niece's brain suffered significant trauma, but the MRI scans, I can assure you, show no lasting damage. We have used the most sophisticated techniques and I have discussed the results at length with the Consultant. Please be patient, we must just give the brain time to heal.'

For some minutes Grace Brabazon had been aware of a strange cacophony of sounds – just noises at first, but then gradually the soft, gentle tones of the woman's voice and the deeper, carefully articulated words of the male voice, came together to make sense. She opened her eyes – just a flicker – but the light was so intense that it was unbearable.

'Dr Patterson – Simon! Did you see that? Grace opened her eyes!'

Annie Adams swiftly came to Grace's bedside and knelt quietly, touching her arm gently.

'Grace … Grace, can you hear me?'

Grace Brabazon opened her eyes again, this time for slightly longer, and saw the evident concern in the eyes of a woman who was a complete stranger to her.

'Who are you?' she whispered, licking her dry lips, 'and where am I?'

Annie Adams took in a sharp breath.

'I am your aunt, dear – Aunt Annie. You had a really bad fall off that stupid old bike of mine and hit your head on a stone fountain and all those lovely flowers that you had picked were scattered all over the place …'

'I just don't know what you are talking about,' whispered Grace, closing her eyes again and wishing that this endless stream of words would stop. Her head had started to ache.

'Ms Adams, please can we have a chat. Let's go and get a coffee.' Simon Patterson stood up, frowning slightly, and opened the door for Annie. She found she was shaking as they walked along the wide corridors, lined with bright paintings in an attempt to alleviate the white and stainless-steel uniformity of the hospital. The months of waiting – of sitting by her niece's bed, as her inert body was tested and scanned and fed and supported – had been hard. Now, in late summer, Annie's garden mirrored the chaos in this previously orderly, competent woman's life. Only when Grace seemed so far away that she would never be able to touch her again, had Annie realised just how fond of her niece she had grown. This random, quirky girl had stirred the sort of affection in Annie that she had previously reserved for animals and roses. Grace was vulnerable and hard to reach, and Annie's warm compassion had reacted to that.

'What's going on?' asked Annie.

'Sometimes, Ms Adams, there is amnesia following brain trauma. It usually lasts only a short period of time – very occasionally, longer. What is absolutely paramount is that the patient is not over-stimulated or stressed in any way.'

Annie rested her hot head in her hands. 'So, Grace can't remember anything?'

'It would appear that this is the case at present.'

'Will she have to stay in hospital?'

'Yes, until she is physically strong enough to go home with you. Her blood pressure needs to be steady, her temperature normal. This could happen quite soon. You will find that home will do its own healing.'

'So I should remain quiet when I go back to Grace?'

'Yes – calm, quiet and positive. She needs these things above all. Ms Adams, she *will* get better – she *is* better. Her body has made a full recovery – it is just that her brain is a little behindhand.'

Simon Patterson sounded more confident than he felt. When Annie Adams had telephoned him following Grace's accident, he had immediately come down to Dorset, taking long overdue leave and leaving his London partners to cover his patient quota. He retained the interest, almost the sense of responsibility, that he had always felt for the quixotic, volatile girl who now lay, seriously ill, in the specialist neurological unit of Southampton hospital. Since she had left London months earlier, defiantly proclaiming that she would be fine in Dorset, he had not been able to get her out of his thoughts. Round and round his concern ran. Was she all right? What was she doing? Could she somehow utilise the considerable design talent that she clearly had in her new rural context? Was she living a life clear of drugs and alcohol, away from the easy temptations of London? It was almost a relief when he heard the warm, anxious, tentative tones of Grace's aunt – even though it was to tell him that, once again, Grace had had a serious accident.

Annie stood up, pale but composed. 'Right, back I go!' she smiled. 'Round 152! Thank you, Simon. You have been such a help – well, more than that – a rock really.'

'All part of the job!' he smiled in return. How good to be praised, he thought ruefully, watching Annie's upright figure leave the coffee shop and turn to go up the stairs to the quiet side ward where Grace lay. Running his fingers through his hair, he removed his glasses and rubbed his tired eyes. How different from the endless stream of addicted, stressed, aggressive patients that inundated his practice in London. Not for the first time, he re-ran a thought that had been coming to him ever more frequently in his half-waking moments, at the start or the end of the day. Why should he stay in London? His parents lived a picture-perfect life in Hampshire and any conversation that he had with them almost invariably centred around bridge parties or golf. Their existence was light-years away from the demanding, never-ending work to which he had decided to devote himself. He had no time for friendships in London, no time for leisure pursuits. He only had time to be a doctor and try to heal people who seemed intent upon self-destruction. The frequent trips that he had made to the South-West over the preceding three months had served only to highlight the contrasts between the life he led in London and the life he could lead in the country.

Chapter 24

It was exactly a week later that Simon drove Annie and Grace back to Quintin Parva. Not a breath of wind stirred the flowers and grasses on this late-summer day and the village basked sleepily in a fragrant dream. Annie was certain that Grace would flinch when Simon's Audi drove slowly past the fountain and stone water-trough with which she had collided back in Spring. But Grace was gazing thoughtfully out of the car window and gave no sign whatsoever that her memory had been stirred by the familiar sights of church, trough, or the steep winding hill down into the village. Simon stopped his car in the little courtyard entrance of Rose Cottage and opened the door for Grace and her aunt, then got out her small case from the boot, which he smilingly handed to her. When, spontaneously, Grace returned his smile, for a second Simon was completely non-plussed. She had never smiled at him before – never! The direct looks that she had sent in his direction when they had met in London were at best challenging, and at worst toxic. But he quickly regained his composure and opened the little wicket gate with a flourish. 'Remember, Miss Adams – rest, fresh air and good food: the best medicine in the world! I will call by again at the weekend.'

'You really are very kind. Thank you. I am just tired now.'

'Tea and rest time, dear! The sun loungers are on the patio. Give me your case and I'll take it indoors.' Her aunt bustled past the rose beds to unlock the heavy, old front door.

Grace walked slowly down to the secluded sitting out area by the stream. She felt exhausted and angry with herself for what she felt was weakness. And she felt so disorientated! People had told her that her name was Grace Adams. This kind woman whose garden she had just entered was, she had also been told, her aunt. The doctor said that he had known her in London – London! She had no mental image of the city at all. She could not recall one single aspect or feature of it. Just trying to untangle all her thoughts was beyond her capability at the moment, so she just sat down in the comfortable steamer chair with the rather stained and battered cushion, closed her eyes and listened to the sound of the stream trickling along its sandy bed.

'Tea, Grace.' The gentle voice of Annie Adams woke her from the light sleep into which she had almost immediately fallen.

'Sorry! I must have dozed off.' Grace sat up and yawned, looking across the garden, past the ancient, mossy apple tree, to the roof of the neighbouring building which showed over the high, overgrown hedge. Grace saw a bell, in its tiny tower in the centre of the roof, and at last something in this confusing new world was intensely familiar.

'Annie, what is that building? Why is there a bell there?' she asked, frowning and trying to pin down the fleeting feeling of familiarity, which had slipped away almost as soon as it had arrived.

'It is Alison Ingram's house, dear – the Old School House. The bell is a relic from the days when it was actually a school. It was closed back in the war they say. Now, I have made this sponge especially for you. I know you love it, so you must have at least one piece. Remember what Dr Patterson said!'

'The school …' Grace shut her eyes, desperately trying to pin down a thought that remained just out of reach, but it was hopeless: the building became just a building again – bricks, tiles, no more.

⇥||⇤

Simon Patterson drove thoughtfully down the village street, trying to analyse his feelings. He was puzzled – and totally confused. Grace's appearance was unchanged: slender, altogether lovely, her thick dark hair and pale blue eyes a striking combination. But her behaviour was fundamentally different: she was softer, more gentle, less edgy. Simon had been intrigued by Grace in London, but she fascinated him now. The aspects of her character that he had deplored – her drug taking, her rudeness – had been replaced by a reserve and a gentleness that he would not have thought possible.

The honey-coloured stone houses of Quintin Parva, their gardens full of roses, lavender and nodding hollyhocks, slipped by. This village was idyllic: golden, remote and restful. What a joy it would be to live here, he thought ruefully. And then, edging cautiously around a tight corner overhung with heavy-leafed trees, he saw a low, stone house on his left, almost hidden in the luxuriant, summer growth of the overgrown garden which encircled it. Leaning at a slight angle by the gate was a sign, reading:

For sale
'Pedders'
An historic and unspoilt property with mediaeval
origins, for renovation
With one acre of gardens and orchards

'Grace, would you like tea or coffee with your breakfast, dear?' Annie Adams called up the steep wooden staircase the next morning.

'Oh tea, please!' Grace replied without hesitation.

Annie shook her head. Simon wasn't the only one who had noticed the changes in Grace. Before her accident, Annie had felt as if she had a truculent teenager in the house, or a whirlwind or, sometimes, a wild cat. But now, the presence of her niece was – she struggled to find a word – peaceful? restful? The sort of words which she had never thought she would apply to Grace in a thousand years.

'Thank you so much, Aunt Annie,' Grace said, smiling, as she sat down at the pine kitchen table, ready to eat the bowl of porridge that had been placed in front of her.

'How are you feeling today, dear?' asked Annie.

Grace put down her spoon and looked seriously at the older woman. 'To be honest, confused,' she replied. 'It is as if I have been parachuted into a ready-made life that I just don't understand! Some things I can recognise, things like most of the contents of this kitchen.' She gestured around the warm room, which always seemed to smell of baking. 'But other things are completely unfamiliar to me, like Doctor Patterson's car. I have never seen anything like that. Or the electric toothbrush in the bathroom, that you say is mine. I just cannot remember it at all!'

'And people?'

Grace reached over the table and placed her hand on top of Annie's. 'Sadly, I recognise no-one. Not even you! But I just don't know where I would be without your kindness.'

Annie was immensely touched and it struck her that the spontaneous gesture of warmth that Grace had just shown had been the first time that she had reached out, either emotionally or physically, to another human being for as long as Annie had known her. Annie patted the small, white hand which rested lightly on her own. 'Eat up, Grace. Remember Doctor Patterson's instructions.'

Surprisingly, she found herself swallowing hard. Was the stressed, volatile young woman who had arrived nearly a year ago, soaking wet and almost skeletally thin, actually softening? She looked hard at Grace. She was thin, yes, but even after a stay in hospital, she looked healthier than when she had first arrived from London.

⊰≫⊪⊰

The months mellowed into a golden autumn. It seemed as if, that year, the world did not want to let go of the warmth and luxuriance of summer. Grace continued to get stronger, to gain colour, as she helped the woman she had gradually come to accept as her aunt in the kitchen and the garden, cutting and tidying the borders and digging over the gaps in the vegetable garden. Annie Adams had followed Simon's advice to the letter, ensuring that Grace set her own pace as she re-found her life. She had shielded the woman she believed to be her niece from almost all social contact, as she didn't want Grace's mind to be over-burdened with struggling to remember. But today, circumstances had presented themselves which prompted Annie to gently encourage Grace to step outside the safe circle of Rose Cottage and their life there together.

'What were you thinking of doing today, Grace?' asked Annie.

'No idea!' Grace responded with a smile. 'Is there a special project in the garden you would like me to tackle, Aunt Annie?'

'Thank you, but no. How about something entirely different? Could you possibly do a spot of dog-sitting, do you think?'

'Dog-sitting?' Grace queried.

Carefully avoiding any disturbing questions or prompts about Grace's memories of her life before her accident, Annie explained, 'Well, our next-door neighbour, Alison, has a hospital appointment this afternoon. She has been feeling pretty rough recently and has been seeing her doctor every couple of weeks. Today she gets the results of further tests at Salisbury hospital.' Annie shook her head, obviously deeply concerned. 'No-one could have a better neighbour, Grace. Anyway, I said I would drive her over to Salisbury in that old VW of hers – she seems to get so tired these days.'

'And the dog?'

'Henry is her irrepressible young labrador. She will have taken him out for a walk first thing this morning, but he needs company. He chews almost anything and loves playing with his toys in the garden. You could stay here – the forecast is for sun – and just let him lollop around. Or Alison said that if you prefer you could sit with him in her garden next door. It would be a change of scene for you, Grace, and you will love it – it's a real 'secret garden' – hidden from the village street by the school building! The trees and some of the flowerbeds are nearly eighty years old apparently, and some of the people in the village remember how they helped to plant and establish the grounds when they went to school there.'

Grace laughed. 'Sounds like an ideal way to spend the day! It's probably best if I go round next door – dogs are sensitive to emotion and change, and he may have picked up on his owner's stress. He will probably be more settled in his own home.'

Straight after lunch, Annie and Grace walked together to the converted school. Annie chatted easily, trying to gently re-awaken some sort of memory in Grace. 'Over there is the village hall – the meetings of the Women's Institute take place there. To the right is the road which leads up past the stone trough where you had your accident, then on past the church and out of the village. To the left are houses that used to be the bakery and a little shop years ago. Both have long since closed, as has the school. They say …' Annie looked at Grace, who had stopped at the school house gate, her hand resting on the stone gatepost.

At that moment Alison appeared in a swirl of scarlet skirt, tight black top and jacket. Simultaneously, bounding out of the front door came Henry, carrying what appeared to be a filthy, headless toy pig.

Grace visibly pulled herself together and stretched out her right hand to Annie's neighbour. Alison smiled, but did not take the proffered hand.

'Lovely to see you looking so well, Grace,' she murmured thoughtfully, her green eyes looking searchingly at the younger woman's face. 'Do come in both of you,' she continued. 'I've put out a sun lounger by the pond, close to Henry's toy basket.' Alison gestured to a chewed, blue, plastic container, brimming with balls, rings and various rubber animals in a wide state of dismemberment. 'Just make yourself at home, Grace.'

'Come on, Ali!' Annie put her hand encouragingly on her friend's arm. 'If we get a move on, we can call in at that interior design shop near the cathedral precinct. Let's get that veteran Beetle of yours cranked up!'

Alison turned and smiled gratefully at her neighbour. 'What would I do without you both?'

The afternoon was still and sunny. But Grace felt odd: distinctly restless and disturbed, as if discovery of her former life hovered on the edge of her consciousness. As she looked around the lush, extensive garden, her memory was stirred by the shapes of the mature trees on the boundary and the sweep of the flowerbeds filled with Michaelmas daisies in blues, purples and whites. Again and again her gaze was drawn to the low, latticed windows at the back of the building, which gave a wide view of garden and pond.

After an hour or so, Grace stood up and stretched. She needed to get some movement back into her limbs and decided to explore further, starting with the front of the building. Making her way along the narrow strip of land at the side of the old school, past the climbing roses and the vine, laden with fruit, she came to the small, enclosed front patio garden. Some features of the building clearly had their origins in the days when it had been the village school. The front area, paved and enclosed with iron railings, and now crowded with pots of colourful dahlias, had obviously once been a small playground. The wording over the two arched doors still marked the separate boys' and girls' entrances; and the iron cross proclaimed the previous church school status of the building.

Cautiously, Grace again rested her hand on the heavy stone gatepost, feeling once more the fear and resentment, held almost within the stone itself, that she had experienced earlier. Her eye was caught by the dull glint of the brass plaque, nearly hidden by the heavily-laden climbing rose which arched over the front door. Using a stick, she carefully moved the thorny branches aside. The words were simple and unemotional:

> *In commemoration of the bravery of*
> *the Rev Charles Brabazon*
> *who gave his life for others.*
> *March 1943*

The plaque had been screwed into the wall underneath an area of brickwork which had been cracked and damaged. Repeatedly Grace's fingers traced the bleak words '*who gave his life for others*'. Almost automatically her eyes moved from the words on the plaque, to the brickwork … and then, she remembered. She remembered everything: the desperate dark night; the threatening drone of the heavy bombers; the searchlights splitting the sky; and the figure of her beloved father, elderly, overweight, but putting every ounce of his energy into saving his fellow human beings. She remembered her reckless, unthinking run towards her father; and her final memory, of an explosion that blew her into oblivion and this confusing new life.

Chapter 25

Simon Patterson smiled broadly to himself as, once again, he drove slowly down the steep, narrow hill into the village of Quintin Parva. He had worked his notice and had finished at his London practice the previous day. There had been no congratulatory card or present, just a farewell handshake from his partners, who were starting to anticipate the additional pressures that the absence of their talented colleague would bring. But, quite frankly, Simon didn't care. He had given ten years of his life to his dream of working with the most difficult-to-reach sectors of humankind, and he felt that he had made not one iota of difference. He was looking firmly to the future, not back to the dismal, frustrating time that he had spent in London.

Simon's solicitor had worked hard to bring about a swift exchange and completion on the historical, but dilapidated, old house that Simon had loved at first sight. It was, apparently, the oldest in the village – and it was serendipitous when Simon's solicitor had discovered that, for generations, the same family of doctors had practised from the building. Their surname had been Pedder and, over the years, this name had been given to the house itself. Originally a hall house, the wide chimneys and two huge, back-to-back inglenooks had been added in the sixteenth century, but in the lofty attic the carved kingpost could still be seen, blackened by the wood smoke of generations who had lived in the shadowy spaces of the mediaeval hall. As with many really ancient properties, its grounds were circular. Mossy apple trees leant at random angles and, in Spring, were surrounded by a golden froth of daffodils. A great creamy-white rambling rose graced the front of the house and yew trees sat as guardians on either side of the arched, oak front door to which Simon now had the key. Heavy and ornate, it was far too large to be accommodated in his pocket and so lay snugly on the passenger seat, on top of the Ordnance Survey map of the village and its local area.

At the bottom of the hill, Simon slowly passed Rose Cottage, consciously slowing down to see whether he could catch a glimpse of the woman who, increasingly, he just could not get out of his mind. He glanced at the Old School House, sprawling next to Annie Adams' neat cottage, and saw Grace, apparently standing immobile, gazing at something that had obviously caught her attention next to the front door. He just could not help it. He had to stop.

'Good afternoon, Miss Adams … Grace. How are you?'

As she turned to him, he realised that she looked different: flushed, excited, more animated than he had seen her since she had awoken from her period of unconsciousness.

'Simon! I have remembered everything! It's incredible! I hardly know how to begin to tell you.'

156

Simon swallowed. Did this mean that, in recollecting her previous life in London, her previous frustrations, Grace would return to being her sarcastic, cutting self?

At that moment, Alison's bright yellow VW Beetle appeared at the corner, with Annie still at the helm, and Simon was just getting out of his Audi as the two older women pulled up. Grace ran to the car as her aunt opened the driver's door. 'Annie, I have remembered everything! I have just got to tell you. I have got to tell all of you.'

The pensive, concerned look on Annie Adams face cleared for a moment and was replaced by a broad smile. She took Grace's hands. 'That's fantastic, dear! But we need to tell you something too: something not quite so joyous.'

Alison got slowly out of her car. 'Let's all go in. Yes, you too Doctor Patterson. I could do with a conversation with you, as a matter of fact.'

The others settled themselves in Alison's comfortable furniture whilst she mechanically flicked on the electric kettle, got out cups and saucers, poured milk into a jug and reached for a plate, on which she carefully arranged slices of home-made fruitcake. Simon looked concerned; Grace was flushed with excitement; but Annie looked distinctly torn. Clearly, she was desperate to hear her niece's news, but equally she wished to support her friend in what she was about to announce.

In contrast, Alison remained monumentally calm. Still not saying a word, she placed the tea tray on a low table and, as if on auto-pilot, handed around tea and cake. Then she sat down and folded her hands on her lap. 'I need to get this over and done with,' she announced with a sad smile. 'I have cancer. I have been attending a clinic for some months, but couldn't bring myself to tell even you, Annie. I'm sorry. My consultant thought that it had been contained and was being dealt with, but sadly the treatment hasn't worked. Today I have been told it is terminal. In fact, the oncologist explained that it is a question of months, rather than years, before I die. They can do nothing, as the cancer has now spread to my lymph glands and almost certainly to my bones. I need to ask Doctor Patterson how best I can manage the time left to me but, since nothing can be done, then weeping and regret are pointless. It is absolutely paramount to make the best of the time left to me – however short that may be. I wanted to get this announcement out of the way, because we need to pay attention to what Grace is so anxious to tell us! Her life is just beginning. My life as an earthly being is ending and the essential Alison – my soul, if you like – is moving to a new, and more exciting, phase. So now, please do share your news with us, Grace.'

To say that the whole room was stunned, was an understatement. To hear that this vibrant woman, apparently in the prime of her life, was dying, was shocking indeed.

'But Alison, don't you want to talk more about the implications for you of what you have just told us?' asked Simon, concerned.

'I will do – but please, not now,' came the firm reply. 'Grace, please share with us what happened this afternoon.'

'As you wish, Ali,' Grace responded softly, 'but Annie and I will talk with you, or just come and keep you company, whenever you wish.'

Grace walked across to the lattice-paned windows through which the low, late October sun was slanting and, looking at the darkening garden, in a clear, steady voice, began her story.

'My name is not Grace Adams. I am Grace Brabazon. I was born in Quintin Parva in 1920, at the Old Vicarage. I was a teacher here when this was still a school and prior to that I was a pupil here. I planted that tree …' she gestured to a tall, stately beech, swaying in the cool October breeze, its leaves turning to bronze. 'My father was Charles Brabazon, the vicar of Quintin Parva, and the brass plaque on the front of this building explains that he died when the village was bombed in 1943. What it does not say is that I believe he died saving the life of the useless Headmaster of this school.' She impatiently wiped tears from her eyes with the back of her hand. 'I was running towards my father when a bomb blast threw me against the stone gatepost at the front of the building, next to what was then the playground. My father must have been killed some time after that – I didn't witness his death.' Grace turned slowly to face the room. 'No wonder I didn't recognise any of you. The people I knew lived long ago … I lived long ago …'

No-one spoke. Annie dazedly got to her feet and walked across the room to put her arm around Grace's shoulders in a caring, protective gesture. She was completely at a loss as to what to think, but her overwhelming instinct was to protect her niece. Simon looked deeply concerned. Everything he had just heard made him suspicious that the woman for whom he had started to feel such overwhelming attraction might have a serious and lasting psychological condition. Only Alison was imperturbable. She gazed directly at Grace, her expression unfathomable, and it was she who broke the intense silence in the room.

'I can see that you both think this is unbelievable,' she said, looking at Annie and Simon, 'but let me share a few things with you. When I met Grace – this Grace – earlier today, I observed a phenomenon that I have seen only once before in my entire life. I saw that she had a double aura. By this I mean that it was as if she was walking with another, invisible, person. The aura which surrounds you is blue, Grace; the second aura is gold. The first and only other time that I have ever come across this was earlier this year, when your niece had recently arrived from London, Annie. Her aura was gold; the second aura with which she walked was blue. I believe that somehow your niece, Grace Adams, has lived, and may still be living, the life started by Grace Brabazon.'

'But this *is* my niece!' exclaimed Annie Adams. 'She looks exactly the same!'

'Does she *behave* in the same way, Annie?' asked her friend gently.

'Yes … yes, of course'

'Are you certain?'

'Well … sorry, Grace … but you do seem gentler, less volatile …'

'Kinder, warmer, happier in her own skin?' added Simon.

'Well, yes,' admitted Annie.

'That's what I feel too,' affirmed Simon.

Alison continued. 'Annie, I know this is hard for you … very hard. I also appreciate that what I'm saying is outside Simon's medical and scientific experience. But it is hardest of all for Grace here. Is the work that I do any more unbelievable than what she has just shared with you? When people come to me for help, to see into the future, or to be healed because of hurt in the past, I have my spirit guides. When I seek their help and direction, they come to me with dead people I have known, from my family and from this village. They stand here in this room, looking as real to me as all of you do now. Who is to say what reality is? Who is to determine what can and what cannot happen? I know that it is unusual, but why can't two women's souls become transposed? Would such a transposition be any stranger than the creation of a soul in the first place? Our destiny is complex and perhaps, just perhaps, in order to fulfil the destiny of two precious human beings, the constraints of time had to be broken in this case. You confided in me that your niece's career in London was over, Annie. Grace, was there an unresolved problem in your young life all those years ago? Was there something intransigent to which there was no apparent solution?'

The colour had drained from Grace's face.

'Yes, Alison, there was. I had lost my position as teacher in this school because of the bigotry and narrow-mindedness of Ivan Miles, the man whose life my father died saving. I loved my work. It was my life. I lost the man I was going to marry in the war and only my teaching was left to me. Ivan Miles took away my future.'

'Ah! But, you see, he didn't. I believe, against all expectations, indeed against all the rules that we believe govern our life here, that you have been given a second chance, a chance to fulfil the destiny that you were born to fulfil. You are so lucky, Grace! Embrace the future. You can do nothing about what has passed, but everything about what is to come.'

Chapter 26

Alison died in the early spring. During the months of her illness, she gave no outward sign of the increasing pain that she felt. Only Simon really knew what she was going through. During the restoration of his dilapidated old house, he had started to undertake some locum work at the surgery which Alison attended and made a point of calling in to see her on his way home every evening. She was as colourful and enigmatic as ever, but only Simon knew at what cost to herself she continued to wear her bright, individual clothes and struggled to maintain at least some order in her rambling garden.

Annie and Grace – especially Grace – were Alison's constant companions, and they comforted each other as they saw the woman they so admired fade before their eyes. Grace and Henry became inseparable, walking for miles together every day. Often they climbed the hill to the churchyard where the young dog would wander, nibbling daisies, whilst Grace put flowers on Charles Brabazon's grave, or sniff the flower arrangements experimentally whilst she polished the commemorative plaque near the altar rail.

Grace's father was buried on rising ground, from where there was a clear view both of the vicarage and the school, the place where he had lived and the place where he had died. As Grace walked up to the churchyard, or sat by her father's headstone, she mulled over what had happened to her and gradually, very gradually, she reached a sort of acceptance. There was no other option, she decided. But one fact that nagged at her constantly was that there was no trace of a grave or memorial to her mother. She painstakingly examined the weather-beaten, worn headstones, carefully parting long grass and flowers to reveal names, but there was nothing. Could her mother still be alive? She would be – Grace did a swift calculation – well, just too old for this to be feasible. Perhaps her ashes had been scattered elsewhere. Maybe one day she might meet a villager who remembered her mother and who could cast some light on this mystery.

When Alison was too tired to talk, Grace recounted her previous life. She painted a verbal picture of her eccentric, brilliant mother and spoke of her father with great love, describing his loving character and his rock-like dependability. She talked of some of the children in her care and, as she recaptured those memories, she became aware that it was becoming very difficult indeed to recall her fiancé with clarity. One bitterly cold night she lay curled in her warm, soft bed in Rose Cottage and tried to conjure up in her imagination Alex's features and his character. She managed a summary sketch: dark hair and eyes; his smile; the RAF uniform; but his personality and the relationship they had shared, these things were becoming elusive.

It was the 1st March. The cold wind sent the clouds scudding across the sky and bent the daffodils on their tall, slender stems. Alison had seemed more tired than usual when Grace had called, directly after breakfast, to take Henry for his morning walk. The older woman sat in her armchair by the window and the room was very warm: it had to be, because now Alison was virtually immobile. Simon called in to check her pain levels at least three times a day – way above the call of duty.

'Grace, I wanted to thank you properly for your love and friendship,' Alison murmured softly, taking Grace's hand lightly in hers.

'But Ali, it's a pleasure! I love being here. I love this house. I love your dog and,' kissing her friend gently, 'I love you. We will have a good chat when I get back. It is bitter out there and Annie has made extra soup today. I'll bring some round for you and we can all eat our lunch together in here – even Henry can have some!'

Alison gave a faint smile, but said nothing except, 'Goodbye Grace, dear Grace.'

When Grace returned, glowing with the cold, she realised that, at last, Alison had lost her battle. She sat, eyes peacefully closed, hands clasped in her lap, clearly in the next world in which she believed so firmly.

⊰)|(⊱

'But that's ridiculous!' protested Grace. 'There must be some mistake – I was just Alison's friend, not a relation!'

'There is no mistake, Miss Adams,' George Jesty, Alison's solicitor, pronounced. 'Ms Ingram specifically says in her Will that she wishes you to have her house, car and furniture, on the single condition that you should care for her dog, Henry, for the rest of his life.'

Grace didn't know whether to laugh or to cry, and actually found that she was managing to do both at once. 'Of course I will look after Henry. He's so funny … and such good company. But what am I going to do with a great big house? I live with my aunt next door. I am not going to move!'

'What you decide to do is down to you, Miss Adams,' George Jesty smiled.

⊰❘❘❦⊱

'There is so much *stuff*, Simon!' sighed Grace, munching on a chocolate digestive and drinking tea from a chipped mug.

Simon's house was chaotic. Plaster had been stripped off the walls because of damp, and mouldering carpets had been ripped up and thrown into a large skip which took up most of the driveway. A cache of old, oddly-shaped blue and green medicine bottles, discarded by the generations of doctors who had previously lived and practised in the house, had been unearthed in a corner of the garden, and these were lined up on the window sill of the old scullery, ready to be washed and displayed. All the windows were open, in spite of the cold spring weather. Simon had a rudimentary bathroom and, currently, no kitchen. His kitchen equipment consisted of a kettle and camping stove.

'And there is no way I want to *live* there! I remember it as a school or as Ali's house. It just wouldn't seem right. Annie, Henry and I are quite cosy next door! Henry loves Annie's Aga. It is his … what do people say now … NBF?'

'Well,' chuckled Simon, 'they might text NBF, but they would probably *say* New Best Friend!'

'Pedant!' grinned Grace.

Simon loved to see Grace like this: vibrant, yet calm, glowing with exercise and full of life. What a contrast to the pale, tortured spectre he had tried so hard to help in London! He still could not clearly differentiate the two women in his own mind. To him there would only ever be one Grace, even though gradually his rational, scientific mind was reluctantly coming to accept the *possibility* that what Alison Ingram had tried to explain could actually have happened.

'Ha – how ironic! You have all this *stuff* and I have bugger-all! Well, only an enormous empty house and the basic essentials to sustain life!'

Grace jumped down from the window sill where she had been perching, choked on her chocolate biscuit and coughed convulsively. 'Simon, I know! You have all the stuff! We can transport it around the corner in a wheelbarrow or something. There is china, loads of really precious things bought in the best of taste – whole tea and dinner services. There are leather chairs and sofas, an oak dining table, beds, bedlinen … everything.'

'No, I can't accept this, Grace. I …'

'Oh, don't be a stuffy old doctor!' Course you can! It is a present from a grateful patient.'

'But you're not my patient.'

'No, but Ali was. And she was so grateful to you, Simon – seriously.' Grace smiled. 'Well, that's the contents of the Old School House sorted. But how about the house itself?' She pushed back her thick black hair and frowned. 'Please can you give it some thought, Simon? I haven't a clue what to do at the moment.'

'I will try my best, Grace.' Watching her lick the chocolate off her fingers, he laughed and asked, 'Would you like another biscuit? Another packet of biscuits?'

'Don't be daft. I must go. Henry needs his usual marathon.'

Simon watched her from his front window walking swiftly past the skip, brushing past his car which was parked at an angle on the verge outside his house. He would have given much to go with Grace, but he was a man in whom duty was a strong driver and so, as soon as her figure had disappeared, he turned resolutely back to the dusty shell of the house which surrounded him. He was determined to do this right. As a doctor he was thorough and methodical, and these were the principles he was applying in order to bring back to life this living piece of history.

Chapter 27

'Grace, have you ever thought of teaching again?' Annie Adams was flicking through the classified advertisements of the local newspaper. 'They are advertising for a supply teacher *"for one term only in the first instance"* at the local prep school which was set up in the Old Vicarage about eight years ago.'

'The Old Vicarage, Annie? That would be terribly difficult for me – it used to be my home, remember. But to answer your question – yes, I have thought about it. In fact, I have been thinking about little else recently. How old am I? Actually, that's a thought! How old *am I?* Ninety? No, let me be serious again. In this particular life, I'm twenty-three. I can't just dig your garden or help Simon with his house renovations for the rest of my days.'

'Why don't you go and speak to the Headteacher?'

'This isn't straightforward, Annie! How can I present myself as a suitable candidate?'

'Do you have teaching qualifications, Grace?'

'Yes, I do. My teacher training was thorough, but my *passion* for teaching developed when I was a pupil at the school next door. Our Headmistress, Miss Dickinson, was a genius and the lessons she taught me when I was a child have stayed with me always. When a position was advertised at her school, I simply couldn't believe it, and I was beyond pleased when I was successful in my application. I worked with Miss Dickinson for far too short a time – she was on the brink of retirement when I was appointed. Then she was succeeded by that travesty of a Headteacher, Ivan Miles …'

'That's a good starting point, Grace!'

'Yes, Annie, but how do I get a reference from someone who probably died half a century ago? How do I account for my teaching experience in a school that closed in World War Two? Could I get copies of my teaching certificate? Maybe, but it would show that I am over ninety!'

'Hm, I can see the difficulties!' Annie got to her feet and paced the length of her small kitchen. 'But there must be a way forward, Grace. Just look at the advertisement …

***Wanted for one term only in the first instance
Teacher for Reception Class
Qualified or Unqualified
Apply to Dr Matthew Moore, Headteacher.
Visits to the school are warmly welcomed.***

'It is generously worded – "qualified or unqualified" shows that the Headteacher has an open mind, I think. Could you ask whether he could give you a trial – a practical trial, I mean?'

Grace read and re-read the advertisement, whilst Annie scanned her face for an indication of emotion, but there was none. Eventually, Grace stood up straight, closed the newspaper and said, 'Right, I'll go. He can only say no'

⊰≫‖≪⊱

'Doctor Moore? My name is Grace Adams. I saw your advertisement for a temporary teacher and wonder if you would consider me for the position.' Grace had decided that the easiest course of action was to retain Annie Adams' surname. Otherwise, how was she to explain her sudden change of name to the gossip-mongers of the village, or rationalise her connections with the Brabazon family?

Matthew Moore looked searchingly at the tall, slender young woman with a particularly determined expression who stood in front of him and drawled, 'Do please sit down, Miss Adams.'

They were in Charles Brabazon's study. The fireplace, window and pine shutters remained – otherwise, all was changed. A fine modern rosewood desk and matching swivel chair dominated the room and faced a large, green leather sofa, whilst a Scandinavian rug in neutral colours sat sleekly on the polished wooden floorboards. The whole was starkly modern and, momentarily, Grace had a flashback to the shabby cosiness of the room, when it had housed her father's worn desk; the glowing Turkish rugs; his battered leather books; and the scrawled sermons which inevitably littered his workspace.

Matthew smiled at Grace, who was sitting very upright, hands folded on her lap. Trying to put her at ease, he said, 'Thank you for coming to see me today. Perhaps you could tell me about yourself and why you wish to apply for this post.'

'Doctor Moore, I cannot be anything but honest with you. For as long as I can remember I have wanted to teach. Whenever possible I have taken the opportunity to work with young children and this experience has strengthened my resolve. Your advertisement says that you are seeking a teacher who is "qualified or unqualified". If you could give me a practical trial, I would do everything I possibly could to fulfil your expectations.'

Matthew Moore sat quietly, considering Grace's direct and candid expression. 'I see. What would your approaches be to teaching very young children, Miss Adams?'

'When I was four, I went to a school that I loved. My Headmistress was a passionate educator and gradually I realised that all I ever wanted to become was a teacher. Everything we learned from our Headmistress was practical and relevant and I know that is how young children learn best. Doctor Moore, if you were to give me a trial in your school, I would not let you down.'

Doctor Moore looked shrewdly at his young visitor.

Oh well, thought Grace, that is the end of that! She started to get up, but was halted by Matthew Moore who said, 'I like your directness, Miss Adams, and I like your honesty. I am actually quite desperate for teaching cover. Would you be prepared to go into the Reception classroom right now? Mrs Jennings is our full-time Nursery Nurse and will remain with you, as I don't expect you have yet had a DBS clearance?'

Grace silently shook her head, unsure of what such a thing was.

'And perhaps I could drop in from time to time during the day and see how you are getting on?'

Grace flushed, and jumped up. This was beyond her wildest hopes. 'Certainly, Doctor Moore, just show me the way!'

The Headteacher led Grace across the hallway. Seventy years of change had not dimmed its classical proportions and Grace had to keep herself firmly in check as memories crowded into her mind. She remembered returning from the school house she now owned, freezing, hungry and frustrated at the unfairness of Ivan Miles. She recalled running upstairs to her mother's studio, taking her tea, and later warning her of the air raid that was to take her father's life and finish her, Grace's, life in 1943 …

Matthew Moore led her into what had been the kitchen, which had been altered beyond recognition in order to accommodate the Early Years class. Part of the rear wall had been removed and a spacious conservatory now overlooked the orchard which lay behind the house at this point. Extensive water and sand play equipment was housed here, together with an array of plants which the children were growing. Fifteen children, aged between four and five sat in a circle, listening to a story being read in a rather stilted fashion by a tall, slender woman. At the back of the classroom an older woman was quietly tidying away art materials and arranging the children's colourful paintings on a drying rack.

'Oh thank God, darling! I was just about tearing my hair out! I am due at the stables this afternoon, you know.'

'Yes, yes, Arabella my dear, I do know, but Miss Adams is here now and she can stay for the rest of the day. She has a passion for active learning, just as dear Miss Frobisher has.'

Grace quickly slipped off her jacket and hung it on the back of the chair recently occupied by Arabella Moore. She sat down and smiled at the circle of rosy faces in front of her, realising with a shock just how much she had missed all this – the innocence, the openness, the spontaneity of the children.

Matthew Moore stood by the door as his wife swept from the room. How would this passionate, quiet woman engage these children? He didn't have to wait long for the answer. Grace took up a pink conch shell that was resting on the low table next to her chair, close to a tape recorder. Alison had listened to taped stories on her ancient machine as she became weaker and Grace had been fascinated at the capabilities of such recorded music and words. A glance told her that a music cassette was already in place in the recorder.

'When I was at school, we played a music game,' she explained. 'I loved it! And there is a rhyme to go with it.

Pass the shell around, in our music game
When the music stops, please give me your name.

It will be a good way for us to get to know each other.'

Within a minute, Grace had the children enrapt. In playing this simple game, Grace learned the children's names; and they learned to take turns and to be patient.

With a smile on his face, Matthew Moore slipped out of the room and left her to it.

Chapter 28

Despite the pile of paperwork on his immaculate desk, Matthew Moore was drawn, again and again, into the Reception classroom, where his unexpected visitor was having such an impact on the children.

After lunch, he arrived just as Grace was asking the children to line up before walking around the grounds of the school in order to collect wild flowers.

'But miss, my nanny says I will get my Ugg boots dirty if I walk on the grass.'

'Well, Olivia, grown up girls look after their own boots ... just see how you will impress your nanny when you tell her you have walked across the lawns of your lovely school *and* cleaned your boots afterwards!'

Matthew Moore smiled to himself, as did Mrs Jennings, who had frequently been at the receiving end of Olivia's remarkably high-handed attitude. Apart from the outline that Grace had given him, Matthew wasn't sure of the background of the young woman who had so effortlessly taken control of the cherished children in his Reception Class, but he admired her directness and the way in which, clearly, she regarded all human beings as equal, whatever their age or social status.

Just half an hour before the upmarket four-wheel drive vehicles started to pour into the wide gravelled courtyard to the side of the Old Vicarage, the children returned, with glowing eyes and faces, holding the flowers that they had picked.

'If we are quick and careful, there is just time to put the flowers into books to press them,' Grace told the children as she shepherded them back into the classroom. Then, seeing their puzzled expressions, she swiftly added, 'Look, I will show you how we can fold tissue paper to both keep the flowers safe and stop the pages of the books from becoming stained. Then I hope that tomorrow we will be able to talk about the flowers and plan what we are going to do with them.'

Matthew smiled reminiscently as he waited with Grace for the Reception children to be met by their parents. 'I used to press flowers with my grandmother, Miss Adams. I loved it! But I have not seen children follow such a simple and satisfying activity for years.'

Grace blushed. Little did he know that the quaint old-fashioned activity had been second nature to her and her peers and their charges, as they made the very best use of natural resources. There had been hardly any paper, crayons or paint in wartime. Smiling her most charming smile to deflect any awkwardness, Grace turned to her Headteacher. 'It's really important that the children learn self-reliance, Doctor Moore. They may not always be in a position where they have large cars to drive around in, or telephones that they can keep in their pockets.'

'You mean mobiles, Miss Adams?'

'I do.'

She needed to be careful. She was learning the vocabulary which had evolved to deal with the complexities of the world in 2010 very quickly indeed, but she knew that sometimes, a slip of her tongue sounded quaint, and distinctly old-fashioned.

'Do you have a few minutes, Miss Adams?'

'Of course.'

They walked across the hall again, back into Doctor Moore's study.

'I have liked what I have observed today, Miss Adams. You relate naturally to the children and communicate clearly with them and I believe that you have the potential to become a skilled and inspiring teacher. Although she tried to hide it, poor Miss Frobisher must have become really very ill indeed before she had to take sick leave for her operation. The children were becoming disaffected, and parents were starting to complain.'

'Is she returning?' asked Grace.

'We hope she will be returning to us at the start of the Autumn term. But, after watching you today, I would like to ask you to take charge of our Reception Class for the Summer term.'

Grace leapt up. 'Oh, but that's amazing, Doctor Moore! Thank you so much!'

'For goodness sake, please call me Matthew! Dr Moore sounds so very last century!'

'And please call me Grace.'

They shook hands.

'So, Grace, I will see you tomorrow morning at eight o'clock sharp? And we will put in train your DBS clearance without delay.'

'You will indeed, Matthew. And thank you once again.' Grace almost ran home, skipping across the field where, nearly eighty years earlier, she had nursed a neglected pony back to health.

The Summer term flew by. For Grace, it was almost like being back in her former life, but in reverse. She spent hours teaching in what had been her family home, and returned in the evenings and at weekends to Rose Cottage – next to her former place of employment, which she now owned.

Just two weeks before the end of term, Grace and Annie were working side by side in the garden of the Old School House. They had opened all the windows of Alison's old home to the warm breeze, for now the house was completely empty, the entire contents having been wheeled round to Pedders just as soon as the renovations there had been completed and it was ready to receive furnishings. Simon had scratched his head, but smiled broadly, as bedlinen, cushions, china and lamps had appeared at odd times of the day on his front doorstep.

'What are you going to do when Pauline Frobisher returns in the autumn, Grace?' asked Annie.

Flushed, Grace wiped a filthy hand across her damp forehead. 'Somehow, Annie, I am going to continue to teach, but goodness knows where or how!'

'Oh bless you, lovely girl! Isn't it funny, you are a talented teacher and own a former school, but ...'

'That's it – you wonderful woman!' cried Grace, dropping her weeding fork and throwing her arms around Annie.

'Strange though it may sound, Grace, I am *not* a mind reader! Could you possibly explain what connection that searching intellect of yours has suddenly made, please?'

Grace grinned. 'Sorry – but what you said was the catalyst! Why don't I open this building as a school again, not for the favoured classes who pay thousands of pounds a year to Matthew Moore and his governors, but for everyone – the children of farmworkers, cleaners and shop assistants? Why shouldn't they be entitled to an education equal to that which is open to the richest people in the district?'

Chapter 29

'Can't you see it, Simon?' Grace challenged him. 'The front two rooms, currently the dining room and kitchen, can be converted back … I mean converted … to a large classroom and a staff room. The back room, the sitting room, will be the early years classroom as it has always been. Oh, for goodness sake, you know what I mean!' Grace was animated, excited, and determined to convey her vision to her friend, whose opinion she had come to respect over the months she had known him.

'Grace, there are so many questions! How much will this cost? Alison didn't leave you any money, just this wonderful building. Will you teach the entire school by yourself? If not, who will you ask to work with you? How about the legalities of the situation?'

'Oh Simon, *I just don't know!* But have you heard of Sybil Marshall?'

'Er, no.'

'She was teaching when I was teaching … back in the nineteen forties.'

'Oh God, Grace, I do find it hard when you talk like this!'

'Hard or not, listen to me! Sybil had no opportunity to go to university. She believed, as do I, that education is 'symphonic': many elements are drawn together to inspire and engage children. They learn best when they are learning many things – all at once! She started to write about her theory of education. I bet she is still teaching today!'

'In her late nineties? Sorry, Grace, but I don't think so.'

'Well, I will look her up! There must be a library near here somewhere, Simon.'

'No need. I will google her on my i-Phone.'

'You sound like a parrot! "Google her on my i-Phone; Google her on my i-Phone" What is that supposed to mean?'

'Grace, you are over-excited.'

'Oh, *Simon!* Excited, yes! *Over* excited, *no!*'

Grace had gradually started to come to terms with the extraordinary experience she had undergone and, most of the time, dealt calmly with the inevitable challenges and anomalies. She usually found Simon easy company and had come to like and respect him because of his enormous kindness and desire to do in medicine what she wanted to achieve in education. But, on occasions like this, when Simon seemed to be patronising her because of factors totally beyond her control, she became frustrated and angrier than she had ever remembered being before.

'Oh, go and plaster something! I'm going home!'

⋙∥⋘

It was the last day of the summer term. A tasteful, hand tied bouquet of cream and pink roses lay on Matthew Moore's desk as he ponderously recited his carefully-rehearsed speech of thanks to Grace. She sat opposite, smiling somewhat vacantly at what her companion was saying since her mind was feverishly replaying what she, Annie and Simon had discussed until the early hours of the morning.

'So, Grace, it is with our deepest thanks that the governors and I present you with this small token of our gratitude for stepping into the breach during the last term. The children, and the school, have benefitted from your dedication and hard work and ...'

Jumping to her feet to accept the expensive flowers, Grace responded, 'It has been entirely my pleasure. You have a lovely school here ... but Matthew, do you have a few minutes? There is something I really need to discuss with you.'

Glancing swiftly at his watch, Matthew Moore grimaced slightly. 'A very few, Grace. Arabella is competing in a point-to-point in Sussex tomorrow and we need to make a swift getaway so we can arrive at our hotel in good time this evening. But clearly this is important to you, so please, do sit down again.'

Grace took a deep breath and consciously attempted to slow down her speech. She wanted what she was about to say to have weight and impact. 'Perhaps you know that Alison Ingram left me her home – the Old School House – in her Will?'

Matthew nodded. 'Yes, I had heard that, Grace. You know what villages are like!'

'Well, I want to make it live again as the village school it once was. I understand that if there is need for a school in an area, a group of dedicated people can establish a free school, which is state-funded and open to all. I am passionate about equality, Matthew, you know that. Your school is wonderful. But it is open only to those who can afford to pay what amounts to the equivalent of some peoples' annual income for their children to attend. I accept that this is part of the freedom of choice in a democratic country like ours, but how about the child of the single mother who works at the Pound Shop? How about the families of the women who live in this village and clean the houses of the people who can afford the luxury of employing them? Why should those children have to catch a bus, at half past seven in the morning, to go to a school several miles away? Some of the youngest children are only four or five years old and have to get up in the cold and dark in the winter to access their education. Quintin Parva is their village, their social context. Why should money be a passport to a good local education? Learning should be local and a right for all, Matthew! Wouldn't you agree with me?' Grace was breathing quickly after her impassioned speech and instinctively expected, at worst, a rebuttal or, at best, a non-committal murmur. But she was completely thrown by the Headteacher's response.

'I do agree with you, Grace – wholeheartedly.'

'You do? So how do I go about setting up a free school in Quintin Parva?'

Matthew Moore frowned slightly, stood up and walked across to the window. Grace did a double-take as she remembered her father doing exactly the same, when stuck for inspiration for one of his sermons. She impatiently shook her head and brought herself back to the present, whatever that meant. After what seemed an eternity, Matthew continued, 'My dear, it is infinitely more complex than you think. I took you on, because you have the clear potential to become a highly-engaging teacher. However, if you determine to set up a school of your own and to lead it as the Headteacher, then you will *have to* have a teaching qualification that is recognised by the government and by society. You would never obtain state funding for the school if you did not. If you had a degree, I would suggest a one-year postgraduate course; but you do not. The standard route open to you would be to follow a four-year educational degree, after which you would have the legal qualification to teach.'

Matthew drummed his fingers on the low windowsill, gazing at the grounds shimmering in the summer heat. He turned and looked again at Grace who, suddenly pale, had sat down again. 'However, you did somewhat cut across my speech of thanks earlier! Although Pauline Frobisher will be returning to school from the Autumn term, I am concerned that the Reception Class will be too much for her to manage physically after her somewhat harrowing operation.'

A glimmer of hope made Grace lift her gaze to the Headteacher again.

'I was about to say to you, Grace, that we would be delighted if you could remain with the school, for the new Reception intake in September. Now that you have shared your vision with me, I suggest that together we take this route into formal teacher-training. I can assess you against the teacher standards whilst you are actually teaching. This may take a little time, but is probably the best route forward for you.'

'You are offering me the opportunity to continue to teach here, *and* become a qualified teacher? How can I ever thank you?'

Matthew smiled quietly. 'What you said earlier – that could have been me twenty years ago: passionate, an advocate of social justice. But …' Matthew glanced again out of the study window at the restless, tweed and cashmere-clad figure of his wife striding towards their Range Rover and horse-box, '... life alters you. The demands of family and of earning a certain level of salary, all these factors distort pure motives. If I can help you bring about the sort of educational revolution you are describing here, in Quintin Parva, I will be happy indeed. That would be more than sufficient thanks for me.'

'Would it be possible for me to give you a hug, Matthew?' asked Grace.

'In the circumstances, I could accept nothing less,' responded the imposing Headteacher of the Quintin Parva Preparatory School, grinning widely.

Grace Adams
1943

Chapter 30

Grace Adams looked intently at the man who had attacked her. Angelo Romani – why was that name, and the way he had pronounced it, familiar to her? He had stressed the second syllable of his surname – Romāni – whereas Grace had always heard travellers referred to as 'Rōmany'. She tried to pin down an elusive thought that evaporated as soon as it had come into her mind.

'Romani … I thought that meant gypsy?'

'It does. But I am not one of the travelling people – at least not by birth. Let us just say that circumstances have forced me to follow the ways of this people. They have been kind to me, have accepted me, and it is almost as if my family name pre-destined me to follow the life of the travellers.' He laughed grimly. 'Are you going to bite me again, Grazia?'

'Are you going to try to break my neck again, Romani?'

'Come, let me introduce you. Sit and share a while in this music. God knows, the world does not hold much joy in these present times.' Angelo Romani frowned, and tied a coloured handkerchief around the bite in his arm, which was still bleeding freely.

They walked from the shadows into the light and warmth of the gathering and almost immediately there was silence. Grace looked at the circle of closed, wary faces, trying to assess their expressions.

'See what I have caught in the night! A beautiful cat, but beware – this cat bites!'

'Ah, 'tis time you had a woman, Romani!'

Angelo Romani threw back his head and laughed. 'Ha! My woman would have to be gentle like Florica here; and fertile like Fifika; not built like a boy and as vicious as a wildcat!'

'I thought you wanted to introduce me to your friends, Romani, not insult me!' Grace challenged, sounding much braver than she felt. She realised that no-one knew where she was. She had heard stories about the lawlessness of the traveller community and, like a warning, the old playground rhyme echoed at the back of her mind:

'My mother said I never should
Play with the gypsies in the wood...'

The travellers stood silent still, closing in slightly around the fire and the place where Grace stood with Romani. Grace braced herself to run and tried to work out whether or not it would be possible to break through this human circle at some point.

'Let it never be said that a guest is not welcome to my family.' Breaking the eerie silence, a tall man, with innate authority, stepped forward from the circle and extended a hand to Grace. 'Jesse Kimber, at your service, lady.'

'Grace … Brabazon, at yours!' Grace still found the use of someone else's surname very difficult indeed. She was much happier being just 'Grace'.

'And now you must eat and drink with us, lady. Romani, see to your guest!'

The tension broken, once again the travellers split into groups and pairs, sitting and standing to chat, and to drink, in the fire-lit glade.

Romani sat on the wooden steps in front of a caravan on which were painted stylised scenes of tall mountains, deep lakes and islands surrounded by clear blue sea. He grinned. 'Come, I am only teasing. You look half-starved!'

'Ha! Better than looking *fertile,* like … what was her name?'

'Fifika. It means "God has given another son". She has seven.'

'And a figure to prove it?'

'Meow! The more I get to know you, the more like the stealthy hunter of the night I think you are.'

'Do you have any gin?' Grace asked. The full impact of the risk that she had taken had unexpectedly hit her and she was shaking slightly – she could do with something alcoholic. It never occurred to Catherine Brabazon to buy alcohol, even if it was available, and Grace was by no means sure that it was. In the vicarage, very strong tea was about as stimulating as it got.

'And It?'

'What do you mean?' asked Grace, frowning.

'And "Italian" – vermouth. "Gin and It" is a very popular drink in polite society, but perhaps you don't mix in polite society …'

Grace ignored the jibe. 'Oh, right! Yes, that'll do. You have gin and vermouth, then?'

'No, and no.

'You are bloody infuriating! What *do* you have to drink?'

'Beer, home brewed, or brandy.'

'I will have brandy, then.'

Romani turned swiftly and disappeared into the caravan, a yellow and blue striped curtain swinging across the entrance.

Grace inhaled slowly to steady herself and scanned the scene. It was like watching a stage set. The figures and their vividly-decorated homes were timeless, as were the trees surrounding and protecting the settlement, the wood smoke, the gentle lilting voices and, once again, very softly, the strains of a violin.

Angelo Romani handed her a small pewter mug, battered but relatively clean, full of brandy. He had one himself and sat companionably by her on the caravan steps. 'Remarkable, isn't it?' he observed, serious now. Grace nodded. 'It grabs you, their way of life. So straightforward, so pure, somehow tapping into the essence of life itself that makes my heart sing!'

Grace took a long drink. Here was another side to her assailant: mocking and carefree one minute, yet articulate and passionate the next. 'Why are you here, if you were not born into this way of life?' she challenged.

'Ah, a long story. Do you have to return to your respectable home before your anxious parents call the police? Or do you have time to listen to the rambling tale of a homeless wanderer?'

Grace sat without speaking for some moments. Then she turned and looked him straight in the eyes. 'Yes, I do have time to listen to your story. Because I know damn well that you are putting on an act, for some of the time at least. I think you are someone who has, or had, a life totally different to this. I do not have to hurry home. I will not be missed.' It would be too complicated to try to explain the abstracted approach to life of the woman with whom she lived; and certainly too complex to explain who her parents really were – or rather would be. Idly, she realised that they had not even been born yet.

⊰∥⊱

'I was born in Naples. My mother was an angel and my father was a pig. He felt that he was fulfilling his duty by constantly making my mother pregnant. I was the eldest of six brothers and sisters. My father drank himself to death, leaving my mother a widow without money.'

Angelo spoke dispassionately. He looked at the firelight, flickering low now, as people drifted off to their caravans. Grace wondered what time it was. She had no way of telling by either the growing morning light, or the waning moonlight, because the tarpaulins effectively sealed off the traveller world from the village and the fields which surrounded it. She watched the impassive, dark profile of the man who sat next to her and realised that she liked looking at him. She got the same satisfaction as she always felt when she had created a perfect dress or jacket: the proportions, the style, the presentation, the embellishment, all came together to create something beautiful and unforgettable.

'Trying to memorise my face, eh, Grazia?' he observed, without turning his gaze to look at her.

'Don't flatter yourself! I was just thinking what a very short life story.'

He turned to look at her then, brown eyes full of laughter. 'You never take a comment without retaliation, do you, Grazia?'

Returning his gaze unflinchingly, Grace retorted, 'Never!'

Romani took another draught of his brandy. 'When my father died, I was fourteen. As the "man of the family" it fell to me to provide for my mother and my brothers and sisters, and so I took any work that was offered. At first, I worked in many kitchens throughout the city, washing up or preparing vegetables, and I loved watching the great chefs creating works of art – masterpieces – even though they threw pasta at me for idling. Then, as I grew older, I learned that much money was to be made from showing visitors the sights of the city. After the first war ended, wealthy people flocked to my country to explore. Italia was part of their "grand tour".'

'Wealthy ladies, no doubt,' Grace sneered.

'Indeed, wealthy ladies learnt much in my company. And I learnt much from them.'

'Bet you did,' muttered Grace, drinking deeply. She was, she realised, distinctly disturbed by the story that her companion was telling so sparely. What had he been – some sort of escort? Did they even have male escorts back in the day? Never had the uncomfortable duality of her life been so tedious. There was so much that she just did not know of behaviour and habits at the time she was now living.

Without smiling this time, Romani looked Grace straight in the eye. 'Not what you think. As I took them to the most expensive designer shops in Naples, and sat watching whilst they chose and tried on exquisite new outfits, I felt, for the first time in my life, real passion. Not, as you have been thinking, for women, but for the design, the cut, the colour of the garments they were wearing. This, I thought to myself, was true creativity:

to be able to make a dream, literally, come true; to make an ordinary-looking woman extraordinary by the perfection of what she wears; to project an idea, a concept. I became determined to be able to do this.'

Unbelievingly, Grace turned to her companion. 'So, in Italy, you were a dress designer?'

Romani shook his head sadly. 'Not yet, but I will be! One day, when this war is ended, I will make dreams of beauty come to life!'

In an instant, Grace made the connection. Angelo Romani – of course! As a design student in London, she had loved the flamboyant, colourful designs of the House of Romani; the ambiguity of male and female fashion; the absolute equality of texture, flow and style which a Romani design offered to men and woman alike.

'But you do!' she exclaimed, leaping to her feet, her face flushed. 'I love your designs!' Grace had not intended to speak so spontaneously. How could she explain what had happened to her to someone who was almost a stranger? She collected herself quickly.

Romani frowned slightly. 'Sit down, Grazia. You will wake the others. You mean the clothes I have made for my Romany family? They are good, yes, but the materials I have are only what my friends have stored in their vardoes, their precious linens and fabrics from generations past. But Grazia, I have such dreams!'

Grace drained her battered mug. 'Please could I have some more, Romani?' Just saying his name gave her a physical frisson of excitement. This dark, enigmatic stranger was one of the most intensely creative geniuses of the twentieth century, and here she was, sitting on the steps of a gypsy caravan drinking brandy with him! Could her life become any more bizarre?

'More? You drink like a man!'

Grace smiled and nodded. 'You nag like a woman! And you haven't finished your story yet.'

He returned, having refilled his mug as well as hers. 'Food?'

'No. I live on fresh air and inspiration.'

'Good for a work of art, not a woman. If you ate more, you would gain more womanly curves.'

'If you patronised less, you would gain more friends!'

He clinked his mug against hers. 'Does anyone ever out-talk you, Grazia?'

'Never!' Grace retaliated once again. 'But I promise that I will be quiet whilst you finish your story. How did you come to live with these people?'

Romani's face, once again, took on a distant expression.

'One of the visitors who kept returning to be accompanied by me around Naples, Pompeii and the surrounding countryside, was a woman called Mrs Genevieve Holden. She was American and very rich. I shared my dreams with her and she listened kindly to them. One day, as we were driving back from Sorrento, she asked me to stop the car to look at the view. "I love your home country, Angelo," she said. "I love its history and culture and the inspiration it gives to the whole world. I don't have children. I don't have a family. So, I have decided to give you enough money to fulfil your ambitions. You will be able to study fashion design wherever you think best. The only condition I make is that you will honour me in your first collection." Well, she gave me more than enough. To someone used to surviving on next to nothing, it was untold riches. I told her she had been too generous, that her gift had enabled me finally to be able to provide for my family, as well as to study fashion design. But she just shrugged her shoulders. "My fortune will be left to charities, Angelo," she explained. "If it makes you feel easier, imagine you are just another charity."

'I went to Milan. It was everything I had dreamt of, and more. People said I lived like a monk, I was so devoted to my art, to the act of creativity. But my lover was a concept I sketched on paper, a mistress I was creating with my every breath, every stroke of my pencil, every stitch I made.'

'What happened?' Grace had never heard anyone talk like this before. Yes, she had *thought* like this, but at last she had met someone whose passion matched, or even surpassed her own. Here was a man – let's face it, she told herself, a legend – who was explaining to her his own creative genius.

'It was late 1938. You will remember Europe at the time? No work and no money. Everywhere people were struggling. I had been working for around a year in a small fashion house in Milan when I launched my first collection, the *Genevieve Holden Collection*. It was well received and just when it seemed that I would be able to start to make the impact on the world of fashion design that was my sole aim, no-one was buying dreams any more. They wanted "Economy", so I asked my directors whether I could visit London to see the designs being produced there, which were stylish, but affordable. The rest of the story is short: war broke out; I was a foreigner in England and was arrested because of my nationality. Everyone believed that I was a spy of some sort, not a designer. I was sent to Kent, to work on a farm there. I hated it. My hands were filthy, torn and became calloused and, although it seems a womanly thing to say, I was worried that my skill with the pencil and the fine pinning and sewing of a garment would be harmed. So eventually I escaped and met up with Jesse, who was travelling back to his own people here in Dorset.'

Grace sat without speaking, looking at the final glow in the embers of the fire. Her mind was in turmoil. Her usual cool, mocking attitude to men had been blown into extinction by her companion and what he had just told her. She thought back with distaste to the slick chat-up lines of men whom she had met in bars, back in the London of 2010 where she had fought to make her mark; and she recalled the posturing of other male designers she had encountered. The opposite sex had bored her rigid. But, in one short night, Romani had shaken her world. She had never heard anyone talk as he had done and recalled her conversation with Catherine, when the older woman had explained that she had respected Charles Brabazon, but had not been in love with him. She recalled Catherine's words almost verbatim: *'to love someone as much as I love my painting would mean that he had to be part of that vision, part of that interpretation of life that I endlessly seek to represent. His passion for art would have to be equal to mine, and somehow in that equal passion there would be an overwhelming meeting of minds and souls.'*

In an earth-shattering instant, Grace wondered whether she had, in a gypsy encampment nearly seventy years before the life into which she had originally been born, finally encountered that 'meeting of minds and souls' that was the foundation of deep, transformational love between a man and a woman.

Chapter 31

Romani stood up, stretched and yawned. 'Struck dumb by my eloquence?' he laughed.

Grace shook herself. 'Certainly not, just tired!' she retorted, and stood up ready to, somehow, make her way back to the vicarage. As she got to her feet, she realised just how much brandy she had consumed, and swayed slightly.

Romani, took her lightly by the elbow. 'Come, you will stay the night with me.'

Grace snatched her arm away. 'Not bloody likely! Do you think I am as gullible as those old women who drooled over you in Naples?'

'Don't be silly, Grazia. I think you are … interesting … with your wildness and independence, but I would need more womanly curves to curl into. I will sleep on the floor.' With that, he disappeared behind the striped curtain.

Grace was really very tired now. The emotional impact of the last six or so hours, together with about a third of a bottle of brandy, was having its effect. Gingerly, she crept to the curtain and opened it a little. Curled on a rug in front of the small wood-burning stove, Romani was breathing deeply, presumably asleep already. As quietly as possible Grace stumbled over to the small bed, built across the back of the caravan and covered with a patchwork quilt. She slipped under the blankets and fell asleep almost instantly.

But Angelo Romani was not asleep. He lay, brain in overdrive, trying to interpret the character of the extraordinary woman he had encountered tonight. His arm was no longer bleeding, but was throbbing regularly with his pulse. Wildcat! Beautiful, dark, passionate wildcat! He loved her spirit, the way she parried whatever he said so skilfully. He was taken aback by her independence, her bravery, her slender body that moved so sinuously. Yes, a wildcat indeed …

⊰⊹⊱

Grace moved tentatively and for a moment wondered where on earth she was. Was she back in her old life, sleeping on someone's sofa, or floor? Whatever it was, it was bloody uncomfortable! She stretched, trying to ease her back, opened her eyes, and remembered the extraordinary night that had, it seemed, only just ended. She had a foul taste in her mouth – too much brandy and no toothpaste, she thought sardonically!

She sat up and looked around the snug, neat caravan. In the morning light she could see that everything was tidy, small-scale and convenient. Of Romani there was no sign. She swung her long legs down from the bed and reached the door curtain in three strides, pulling it aside. Her companion was outside, stripped to the waist and washing in an enamel bowl. Tanned and finely-muscled, his body was as fine as his face, she thought wryly. A gold chain hung around his neck, holding something that glittered in the early morning sunlight.

'Ciao, Grazia!' he called cheerfully, towelling down his wet hair, which he pulled back and twisted into a low ponytail.

'Hi,' she muttered. 'I must be getting home, otherwise Catherine and I will be eating mouldy bread and no eggs. She will have forgotten to collect them.'

'Who is Catherine?' asked Romani, slipping a clean, cream shirt over his head. 'I talked until the fire died last night, but I know nothing of *you*!'

'Catherine is the woman I live with.'

'Your mother?'

'Er, yes.'

'You don't seem too sure, Grazia!'

'Oh, leave it, Romani. I feel too fragile to retaliate this morning.' He shrugged his shoulders and turned to throw away his washing water. Grace felt she had been churlish, to say the least, and so, on an impulse, and fully expecting Romani to decline, she said: 'You can come and meet her if you wish. If you come back with me, I will try to cook something edible. No guarantees though!'

'I will. I never refuse anything on principle. Let me bring some food with me though. I have mushrooms, some herbs and potatoes. I will cook!'

'Ah, a chef as well as a visionary designer!'

'Si. Food for the body as well as the soul!'

⊰⊱|⊰⊱

As Grace had suspected, there were no signs of Catherine having eaten anything at all.

'Are you working, Catherine?' Grace shouted.

'Yes dear…' came the vague answer from the cavernous depths of the vicarage first floor.

'I knew it. She is working already!' declared Grace with a mixture of irritation and respect. 'Look, Romani, I am desperate for a bath and some clean clothes. Can you find your way around the kitchen and produce … oh anything! It can't be worse than the mess I make of trying to feed us both!'

Without speaking, Romani frowned slightly, then nodded.

Running up the stairs two at a time, Grace blessed the vagueness of the woman she lived with. She knew that Catherine would just accept that a stranger – a gypsy, or imprisoned spy, or dress designer, or however one wished to describe him – had taken over her kitchen and was producing breakfast for herself and her supposed daughter. A stranger, moreover, with whom Grace had spent the night.

Grace popped her head around Catherine's studio door. 'I'm back! Just having a quick bath, and then breakfast will be ready for us both in the kitchen.'

'Mm,' came the standard reply. 'Lovely. Thank you dear.'

⇥║╠←

Blowing bubbles idly from under the surface of the bath water, Grace blessed the solid fuel Aga that heated it, knowing that they were one of the few households in the village that had this luxury. Immersed in the silent underwater world, she allowed herself to daydream for a few moments. For as long as she could remember, Grace had scorned emotional involvement, which she deemed a weakness. But now her body was experiencing sensations that were entirely novel to her – primarily a fluttering excitement in her belly, as she thought about the man who had entered her life so dramatically the previous night. She had no doubt that he would have mastered the kitchen environment, just as he had moved effortlessly from the Italian fashion world into the life of the travellers whom he admired so much. Behind her closed eyes she saw again his profile, his long dark hair, waving slightly around the strong line of his jaw, his athletic, tanned body.

'Oh, for God's sake! Just snap out of it, you stupid cow!' Grace spoke out loud, with intense irritation at herself, as she surfaced and jumped lightly out of the bath, pulled the plug viciously and vigorously towelled herself dry. Her first inclination was to long for some of the clothes which she had worn and loved in twenty-first century London – especially some of the clothes that she had designed herself – sexy, attention-demanding clothes. But then, in self-revulsion at actually wanting to dress in order to become more attractive to someone, she decided to wear some of the dowdiest clothes that she could unearth from her namesake's wardrobe. She ran lightly along the landing, wrapped in a towel, to her little, rose-patterned bedroom, flung open the white door of the fitted cupboard and looked along the rack of dark, uninspiring skirts and trousers, all of which were considerably too big for her. Eventually, Grace decided on a calf-length navy skirt, which she had to hold up with a belt, and a shapeless navy cardigan. She finished off towelling her thick, black hair, and then let it fall loosely around her shoulders.

'Breakfast, Catherine!' she called, as she strode purposefully along the landing and descended the classic, curving staircase, only tripping once on the over-long skirt.

The most appetising smells that Grace had encountered since her time with Annie Adams were coming from the kitchen, where Romani was intent on creating a mushroom and herb omelette and fried potatoes. He was engrossed in drawing the liquid egg into the centre of the cast iron pan, tilting it this way and that. Grace was struck once again by the self-containment of the man. He seemed neither to need nor to want the company of other human beings: he was sufficient to himself. Perhaps that is how a genius always worked … she didn't know.

He sensed that she had arrived and turned to speak to her, but then his eyes widened fractionally at her appearance. 'What are you *wearing,* Grazia?' he exclaimed. 'You look like your grandmother!' and he burst out laughing.

'Oh, get lost! I was cold.'

He turned away from her again, but she saw that his shoulders were still shaking with silent mirth, as he finished cooking.

Impatiently, Grace strode to the door, flung it open, and bellowed up the stairs: 'Catherine! Food is ready!'

⇥||⇤

They were washing up after breakfast which, Grace thought, had been the most delicious meal she had eaten since the wonderful home-made soup and casseroles that Annie Adams had produced for her. Romani was washing, Grace was drying, but she was hampered by the skirt, which she had never worn before due to its lack of style and its size. It kept slipping down over her slender hips, in spite of the belt that she had chosen to keep it in place. She knew

201

Romani was fully aware of her struggle, as her drying came in fits and starts. Eventually he could stand it no longer. He let go of the plate he was washing and rested it gently in the sink.

'Grazia, dear independent Grazia, please, I beg of you, let me rescue you from your dowdy self! Do you have a pair of scissors? A needle and cotton? Another huge garment in which you can disguise yourself whilst I try to transform this … this … tent, into something bearable?'

'You patronising bastard! Do you think it is only you who can coax beauty out of inanimate cloth? I can too! Come, I have stuff to show you! Come on!'

Romani stepped back and considered Grace carefully. Although he had known her for less than twenty-four hours, she had consistently matched his challenging comments, had retaliated, teased and goaded him, but he had never seen her angry. Now, she was blazing.

'Come on! Follow me!'

Impatiently holding up the ridiculous skirt, Grace climbed the stairs as swiftly as she could without tripping. Up to the first floor and along the landing to the door which led to the attics. 'Come on! You won't ridicule me when you see this!'

She flung open the door of the attic room which she had made her studio. Covering most of the walls, Grace had stuck her designs, the ideas and concepts, for using and transforming the precious collection of clothes and materials which she had unearthed in the chests. Romani stood, breathing deeply from both the swift ascent of two staircases and the impact of the freshness and sureness of line which he saw displayed in front of him.

For minutes he studied her drawings without speaking. Some of the dresses she had left virtually untouched – they were too exquisite, too perfect. One of the cloaks, she had covered with applique stars, planets, comets and the shapes of sun and moon. She had added a deep hood with a silver lining and it was altogether breath-taking. Another of the military jackets she had adapted for a woman to wear: it was now long, lean and elegant.

At last Romani spoke. 'Grazia, these are stunning! You, too, are a weaver of dreams!'

She blushed, and impatiently dashed away tears of happiness and frustration – happiness that one of the premier designers of the twentieth century should be praising her work in such terms; and frustration that she was unable to continue to bring into being her dreams of beauty.

Chapter 32

Romani sat on the attic floor, silently drinking in the array of colours and the angular, sure strokes of Grace's designs. Grace remained standing, as if defiantly protecting her precious collection.

'Come,' invited Romani gently, 'sit with me. Tell me about yourself, Grazia. There is a story indeed worth telling behind …' he gestured expansively, '… all this.'

Grace sat silently for some moments. Could she explain what had happened to her? She looked at her companion's serious, steady gaze, his intent expression, and decided that, although risky, she would try. Actually, was her story any stranger than his? Apart from the time element, both their stories were of success and loss. She had known Romani for less than a day, yet she felt that she had started to glimpse a character who would regard travelling back in time as being immaterial in the face of what mattered so deeply to them both – bringing into being garments that could transform lives.

And so, there in the shadowy rambling attics of the vicarage, with complete honesty, Grace told Romani everything: her success in London and the farcical end of her career in 2010; her time with her aunt; her accident and her waking in another woman's body in 1943; and finally, the discovery of the chests of exquisite clothes.

Angelo Romani sat watching minutely the woman next to him. She held his gaze throughout her narrative and he knew that she was telling him everything. Never for a second did he doubt her integrity, as no-one so obviously transparent and open could create such a complex and fantastic story. When she had finished, she looked at him challengingly, raising her small, pointed chin slightly and shaking back her mane of black hair.

'So that's it, I suppose? You probably think me delusional, and will stride off into the morning to share my ridiculous story with the travellers with whom you appear to be so very much at home.'

'Is that what you think, Grazia?'

She jumped up, treading on the hem of the dreadful skirt. 'Oh, for God's sake. I'm changing! I just cannot stand this any longer!' From one of the hooks which she had screwed into the ceiling timbers, she grabbed a long, fitted, bright red woollen dress, which she had made from two of the military jackets that she had found in the chests. And also, because she was still cold, she snatched up a black fur shrug – remodelled from a huge and shapeless fur coat. She went into the next attic room and slammed the door shut. Three minutes later, she returned, truly transformed.

Romani was speechless. She looked magnificent – all vibrant energy, the very quintessence of beauty as far as he was concerned. He swallowed hard and fought to get his feelings under control. Grace glared at him.

'Struck dumb by my elegance?' she parodied Romani's challenging words, after he had told his story by the dying embers of the camp fire.

'Almost,' he said quietly. 'You are like a flame, Grazia … a beautiful flame. To thank you for sharing your story with me is too insignificant. I will hold your secret close to my heart.'

He stood up and, eyes almost on a level with her own, took both her hands in his. 'My mother was a good Catholic woman and she believed without question that life is pre-ordained. Have you ever asked yourself this question: "Why did I come back through time?"' Romani turned over her small white hands and carefully, almost devotedly, kissed her right palm, folding her fingers carefully over the place where his lips had touched her skin. 'I believe that I have the answer to that question.' And then he was gone, leaving her flushed and in emotional turmoil, surrounded by the exquisite dreams she was striving to create.

⊰⊹⊱

Days passed and Grace struggled to settle again into her previous routine – struggled because in her heart she knew that her life had been changed irrevocably. Her steely resolve that all men were worthless and that life should never be taken seriously had been shattered on that moonlit night when she had chanced upon the gypsy encampment and a man who had shaken her to the core. She found herself lying awake, remembering each tiny detail of her encounter with Angelo Romani. She remembered his strength as he bent her head backwards; his laughter, but equally, his seriousness. She recalled the exact colour of his eyes – deep brown, flecked with gold near the pupil; his thick, dark hair, the colour of her own. She saw again, in her mind's eye, his tanned body, well-muscled, but not to excess: everything about him was, she thought again, just right. She unfurled her right hand and ran her thumb gently over the palm, feeling again the imprint of his lips there.

But he had gone without suggesting that they should meet again, or that he would return, to talk and share their dreams.

⊰⊹⊱

Catherine Brabazon stirred her tea, thoughtfully watching Grace who was furiously trying to punch some sort of life into a grey, soggy mass that should have been dough and murmured, 'Ginny Hartley will be arriving in a few minutes.'

Grace made a noise that could best be described as a growl. She redoubled her efforts with the dough. 'What the *hell* does she want now, Catherine?' asked Grace, pushing back a strand of hair with her forearm.

Catherine sighed. 'Oh, she is searching for a motivational speaker *again* for one of her interminable meetings, Grace. The theme is still *How to raise morale in wartime,* but this time she wants a practical workshop. I just can't stand the thought of all those women wasting my precious paints, daubing colour here and there and being delighted with a representation of a pumpkin!'

Despite herself, Grace laughed out loud. 'Why a pumpkin, Catherine?'

'Oh, it is the only thing that we have a surfeit of in the village this year. There are so many that we just cannot get rid of them and Ginny's idea is that they should be used as subjects for still life.'

'Well, tell her no, Catherine! She is just a pain in the …' Grace's asperity was cut short by the echoing

2 0 7

ring of the doorbell. 'I'll get it!' she said, glad to leave the sticky mass she had been trying to coax into the shape of small rolls on the marble slab in the kitchen, and ran lightly across the hall. She had flour all over her, including her hair, but in the mood she was in, she didn't care. Wiping her hands on her apron, she flung open the door. Her angry glare, however, was soon replaced by a look of confused surprise, when she saw who their visitor actually was.

'Grazia, I have fruit for you. I can cook it if you wish.'

Romani stood on the doorstep, holding a wicker basket with apples, blackberries and sloes.

'Romani! I was expecting someone else!'

'Looking at the expression that you had on your face when I arrived, I am glad I was not that other person. However, if you are expecting a friend, perhaps I had better leave,' he laughed.

'No, please don't go. You can save us from a fate worse than the Women's Institute!'

'The what?'

'Come in and I will explain.' Grace walked swiftly across the tiled hall, desperately trying to compose herself and to stop her hands from shaking. As she went back into the kitchen, she consciously steadied her voice. 'You remember Angelo Romani, Catherine? He cooked us that delicious omelette a few days ago.'

'Of course, how could I forget,' Catherine replied, feelingly. 'Do please sit down, Romani. Tea?'

'I would love some. Thank you.' Romani smiled broadly.

'So … what is the Women's Institute? An institution for women? It is not an attractive title …'

'Neither are the members!' said Grace with fervour. 'They think far too much of themselves and far too little of others. I detest them! But most of all I detest Mrs Ginny Bloody Hartley, their leader!'

'Chair, dear,' interjected Catherine mildly.

'Leader!'

At that moment, the doorbell sounded again.

'Argh!' cried Grace, 'that will be her!'

'Let me answer the door,' said Romani quietly.

The women heard his firm steps cross the tiles of the hall and the sound of the front door being opened.

'Oh! I am here to see Mrs Catherine Brabazon, my man! Mrs Ginny Hartley. Here is my card.'

Into the kitchen strode the Chair of the Women's Institute looking, as usual, like a ship in full sail. 'You have a butler, Catherine!' she stated. 'Excellent! But you must attend to his uniform – far too lax!'

'Actually, Ginny, he is …'

'Shall we go into the drawing room … or your little snug?' asked their visitor. 'I am not used to being received in a *kitchen*.' Ginny Hartley turned on her heel and stepped briskly back into the hall, followed by Catherine, who raised her eyes to heaven, in an expression of controlled frustration.

'You see what I mean, Romani? She is horrendous!'

'Why is she here, Grazia?'

'From what I understand, she is trying to bully Catherine into running a painting workshop to "raise morale" in the village,' snarled Grace.

Romani stood for a few moments, looking at the grey mass that Grace was still struggling with. He, too, had had sleepless nights because of the woman who stood in front of him now, distracted and covered in flour and dough, but burning with a vibrant life that nothing could eclipse. He had agonised about how he could see her again legitimately, and the best he could come up with had been fruit – and cooking! He felt the banality of the excuse to visit the vicarage compared with the overwhelming attraction that he felt for her, her talent and her spirit. He longed to take her in his arms and to feel again her whipcord strength – bending to him this time, not pulling away. But instead, he made a suggestion so mundane, he nearly choked on it. 'I have an idea, Grazia. Let us, you and me, offer to run a workshop for this institution of women. But let it be a dressmaking workshop. One should never respond to mean-mindedness with words or actions that are similarly negative. I have materials that I have collected in my caravan. If we set the date of our workshop a few weeks ahead, we can search for parachute silk, or anything even remotely suitable. Let us give these small-minded people something to think *about!*'

Grace stopped trying to do anything with the inert mass in front of her and turned towards Romani, meeting his gaze. 'I warn you, I do not like these women! It is a more dangerous suggestion than you realise!'

Seriously, Romani returned her gaze, saying softly 'Oh I realise how dangerous you are, Grazia.'

The back of Romani's right hand lightly brushing Grace's left, shoulder to shoulder they went into Charles Brabazon's study to rescue his widow.

Chapter 33

The strains of *Jerusalem* ground to a halt. Ginny Hartley lifted a small wooden gavel and smartly tapped the table, around which sat Catherine, Grace and Romani and the committee members of the Quintin Parva Women's Institute. The vase of late-summer flowers shook slightly under the blow.

'Today, ladies, we have something … ah … quite different for you. Mrs Brabazon has kindly come along with her daughter and butler to start our very own sewing bee, which we hope will become a regular item in our calendar.'

Grace was resting her head casually on her hand, behind which she turned to mutter to Romani, 'Why do you let her describe you as a butler?'

'How else should she describe me? As a gypsy, or maybe an enemy alien?' he grinned.

Grace grinned back.

An audible ripple of anticipation ran through the fifteen or so women assembled in the village hall. They were, of course, acquainted with Catherine and Grace, but the startling good looks of the only man in their midst had caused a flutter of jumper-adjustment and hair-patting as he had walked in.

Over the last weeks Grace and Romani had collected materials from wherever they could lay their hands upon them. Mr Hartley had, surprisingly, supplied them with an almost entire parachute, whilst Dr Pedder, who lived in, and practised from, his rambling mediaeval house in the village, had given two slightly frayed silk maps. Even Lady Maud Montgomery had provided several out-dated, highly ornate, evening dresses. All in all, a very respectable pile of materials lay folded on a long trestle table at the back of the hall. The ancient black Singer sewing machine had been hauled along the road by Romani and took pride of place next to the table which housed the sewing materials – needles, thread, pins and scissors. Grace could not bring herself to expose the exquisite contents of the chests of clothes to the utilitarian needs of the village. They remained safe in the attic.

'And now I will ask Mr Romani to explain what we are about to do,' finished Mrs Hartley, looking rather doubtfully at her guests.

There was an enthusiastic round of applause as Romani stood and moved in front of the table. The audience, thought Grace, were ready to be delighted. All eyes were fixed intently on his athletic figure, his soft cream shirt, black trousers and supple leather boots.

'When did your husband last take you by the hand and look deep into your eyes?' Angelo modelled the action of what he was saying by looking meltingly at two women who were sitting side by side in the front row of chairs: Marianne Hartley, Ginny's daughter; and the young wife of the vicar who had taken over this 'cure of souls' from Charles Brabazon. 'When did he last say you were the loveliest thing he has ever seen?'

he continued, moving his intense gaze to Ginny Hartley, whose Amazonian figure was seen to subtly straighten and attempt to adopt a more feminine pose.

Grace looked askance at the effect Romani was having on the female audience. Bloody typical! He thought he could turn on his charm and any woman would come running! No wonder he was so successful with the rich women he had escorted around the sights of Italy.

'Today, we are going to help you to achieve your desire, to be even more desirable than you already are. Together we will make these maps into unforgettable garments; we will transform this parachute silk and re-model these evening dresses. Prepare to be transformed!'

Almost as one, the women stood up and flocked to the table at the back of the hall. Angelo flashed a smile to Grace, who gave him a stony glance in return.

'Uber cheesy!' she hissed, drifting past him to join the women.

❖

By the end of the afternoon, two blouses had been made: one of parachute silk, the other a map of Somerset. Catherine and Grace circulated, trying to give practical support where needed, but it was Romani who was most sought after. The vicar's wife had tried to monopolise his attention and had cut from one of the evening dresses a stylish deep-green lace skirt, which was now pinned and ready to stitch. The women just did not want the session to end and it was only when the light was fading that Ginny Hartley took up her gavel again and tapped the table for attention.

'Well, I really have to say that I think that this has been one of the most successful meetings we have ever had.'

A fervent chorus of 'Hear, hear!' echoed around the whitewashed walls and wooden floor of the village hall.

'I invite you to show your appreciation of the time and attention that our guests have given to us this afternoon in the time-honoured way.'

There was thunderous applause, which only stopped when the gavel descended heavily once again.

'I'm sure that you will all be delighted to hear that we plan to repeat this sewing bee again in the very near future; and once again, thanks to Mrs and Miss Brabazon and to Mr Romani.'

⊰⊹⊱

'You bloody creep! How could you make cow's eyes like that at those old women?' Grace panted as she furiously pushed the wheeled, cast-iron frame of the sewing machine back along the village street to the vicarage. She knew that Romani had had to win over his audience, but resented every burning glance he had given, every delicate touch of the hand that had corrected cutting or stitching. Oblivious of Grace's anger or that the wheels of the sewing machine trolley were wobbling dangerously, Catherine followed dreamily behind, looking closely at the shapes of the trees against the cold Winter skies.

'They were not all old, Grazia …'

'Most of their tongues were hanging out, just looking at you, Romani! How could you lead them on like that!'

Romani stopped. 'When you design a dress, a coat, or a skirt, Grazia, the witchcraft begins. You weave a spell that links the mind of the wearer with the mystic power of the garment which they put on like a magic cloak. This spell convinces them that they are the most seductive women in the world *when* they wear our design. And because of that, they will come back for more and more.'

'Who are you kidding?'

'No-one, Grazia. Especially not you. And now I must return to the camp. Tonight we are celebrating the anniversary of Jesse and Lyubitshka's marriage. They have been married for fifty years, a cause indeed for celebration ...'

'Or commiseration! Fifty years of seeing the same old face every day, saying the same old words and doing the same boring things – not for me!'

'You are angry, Grazia.'

'Angry – why should I be?'

'Only you can answer that. Come to the camp again tonight. We can talk more of this afternoon ...'

'What – so you can boast of your devastating attraction?'

'To plan for future meetings, and so that you can experience some of the traditions of the people who have taken me to their hearts. It is tragic that all that most people usually see when they encounter travellers is the difference. They do not seek to learn more of the common humanity which lies under the different customs and the travelling way of life.'

Romani constantly unsettled Grace by his shifts from arrogance, to seriousness, to sparkling humour. She had never been so interested in, or fascinated by, anyone before in her life. Redoubling her efforts to move the sewing machine up the slight incline to the vicarage, Grace muttered, 'I'll see.'

⊰∦⊱

The long summer evenings gave Grace the time to spend in the attic that she had come to love, surrounded by her designs and the clothes that she was enhancing, re-modelling, or just enjoying. It seemed an oasis of beauty in a grey, uncompromising world. Usually, the whole house was alive with creativity: Catherine was occupied with her painting; whilst Grace sketched her ideas for new designs, or started to work on the material to embody her concepts. But tonight, Grace's mind was elsewhere – everywhere. She remembered with anger the interactions between Romani and the doe-like women of the village. She recalled, furiously, the casual invitation to attend the celebrations at the gypsy camp. Clearly Romani believed that he could just crook his finger and she, like all the other women, would just follow him obediently. Well, she would show him!

Carefully, she lifted a soft, rose-pink satin dress from the second chest. It was blatantly feminine, low cut and trimmed with deep-red roses. A red sash encircled the narrow waist, from which the skirt flared out in an opulence that had nothing to do with the mind-numbing 'make do and mend' philosophy of wartime. Nestling under the dress were a pair of dark-red satin shoes. Back in twenty-first century London, Grace would not have been seen dead in a dress like this – it was much more Tom's style than her own. But tonight, she had made up her mind to enchant and fascinate Romani, then to summarily dismiss him. She would show him once and for all that women were not things to be taken up and thrown down at a man's will. She would gain the upper hand!

Shivering slightly – perhaps at the chill that was starting to creep into the attic, or perhaps at the challenge of the night ahead of her – Grace slipped on the dress. She was used to dressing her models and seeing the transformation that a new outfit could bring about but, even so, she looked twice at her reflection in the chipped and foxed mirror that she had rescued from one of the outbuildings. She thought of the woman for whom this dress had originally been made and thought that they must have been a similar shape, size and height. She swayed her hips slightly, making the dress rustle and swirl about her long, slim legs. She would do. She would do nicely

Chapter 34

Grace had found a long, dark overcoat in the boot room, which she wrapped around herself, shrouding the delicate satin of the dress she was wearing. She put on some wellingtons and stuffed the red shoes into her pockets. As soon as it was dark, she slipped quietly out of the vicarage and along the road, making her way to Gypsy Lane and the encampment in the depths of the heavy-leaved copse of trees.

As she neared the circle of vardoes, she heard again the muted, plaintive strains of the violin and the low murmur of voices. It struck her afresh how very much a part of the deep countryside the travellers actually were. They were hidden, like the nocturnal creatures that curled unseen under hedges, or in burrows in the ground. They were quiet and unobtrusive, and the stark contrast with the self-important members of the Quintin Parva WI made her almost laugh out loud.

She stalked nearer and watched for a few minutes as couples circled in front of two carved chairs set on the grass by the steps of the large, centrally-placed caravan. On the chairs sat Jesse, whom she remembered clearly from her last visit, and a slender, upright elderly woman, dressed in an ornate off-white dress. The youthfulness of the dress's style was jarringly at odds with the lines in the woman's face and the whiteness of her hair.

'She remembers her wedding day,' whispered Romani, who had come up silently to stand beside Grace.

'Really?' hissed Grace 'I thought she was wearing one of your latest designs, made to suit the age and status of the wearer!'

Grace saw the glint of Romani's white teeth, as he flashed a sudden grin at her sarcasm.

'Come into the light, Grazia.'

They moved quietly and unobtrusively between the painted caravans until they came to Romani's and, as before, they sat on the steps.

'Brandy?'

Grace nodded.

They sat and sipped thoughtfully.

'What did you think of this afternoon … seriously?' asked Romani.

'Seriously? I thought *you* were an embarrassment, but that some acceptable clothes were made by the matrons of Quintin Parva.'

Grace expected a laughing retort from her companion but, as she glanced sideways, she saw that he was watching the travellers' slow dance meditatively, no trace of a smile on his face.

'I will say this just once more, Grazia. It is a performance, an act, how I make love to my clients. The mistress I serve is Beauty and the transformation of a woman through what she wears. If you believe anything else, you are wrong indeed.' He stood up quickly and, placing his mug on the top step of the caravan, took hold of Grace's right hand.

'Come, we too must dance in the celebration. But take off this long coat because, knowing you, it will trip you up and you will fall headlong into the fire, or head-butt Lyubitshka.'

Once again, Romani had wrong-footed Grace. Just when she felt she had started to be able to gauge his moods, he surprised her with his seriousness, or deflated her irritation with his humour. On this occasion his direct instruction had completely foiled her plan to suddenly reveal her unusually elegant and distinctly feminine appearance, only to withdraw dramatically from the gypsy encampment and Romani himself. Therefore, she slipped out of the shapeless black garment very grudgingly indeed. At first, she could not bring herself to look directly at her quixotic companion. What would his mood be now: challenging, sarcastic, disparaging? But, when she slowly raised her gaze, she saw that it was none of these. Romani's dark eyes held hers and his face was utterly inscrutable until he spoke.

'You are the most beautiful woman I have ever known, Grazia. I love how you look. But I love your wild spirit more. Be my partner tonight.'

They moved as one into the gently circling dancers. The old couple at the heart of the circle quietly acknowledged, and celebrated together with the gypsy community, the life and energy of their extended family. Jesse and Lyubitshka watched the men and women, holding hands and waists and arms, moving in gentle homage to the wisdom and stability that their love had given to this group of people here in the quiet hidden fields of Dorset.

It was the exquisite, remorseless blackbird's song that roused Grace the next morning. She smiled. Exquisite and remorseless, like the man who lay next to her in the impossibly small and narrow bed in the vardo. He was deeply asleep still, his dark hair ruffled, lying on his side, head resting on his arm. She remembered the previous evening, the mesmerising dance, and the way in which Romani's eyes never seemed to leave her own for an instant. When the elderly leader of the travellers had stood with his lady, signalling the end of the celebrations, Romani had touched Grace's shoulder lightly. He said nothing – there was no need. She had followed him back to his caravan, then behind the yellow and blue striped curtain. He had lifted her as if she weighed no more than a flower and laid her with complete gentleness on the narrow bed. Slowly he had removed the layers of satin in which she had clothed herself and had stood, just looking without speaking, at her pale, untouched loveliness. She remembered, with a clarity that made her heart beat faster, how he had then knelt and kissed her hands, her face, her mouth and how, with a heart-stopping inevitability, he had answered with his body all the questions that she had always had about what it means to love and be loved.

Grace Brabazon
2014

Chapter 35

The applause echoed high into the lofty, beamed and decorated ceiling of Salisbury Cathedral. It was June 21st – Midsummer Day – and the weather was perfect. Simon, Annie and Matthew, who had folded his tall frame carefully into the back seat of the ancient VW Beetle, sat beaming at Grace as she received her degree. Over the past four years, Grace's teaching had been observed and assessed and graded highly, and now she was the first student to take the small stage, which had been erected in front of the central altar of the cathedral. Flushing partly with pleasure, but mostly with embarrassment, she heard the Dean say, with a huge smile on his face, that he was 'delighted to award the only first-class honours degree that has been given in over a decade, to a young woman who brings such creativity and energy to the teaching profession.' As he went on to talk of her 'dedication, which will ensure the world-class education for each individual pupil that the twenty-first century educational system demands,' Grace was aware of deep irony as her approaches and methods had actually been learnt over seventy years earlier.

Simon and Annie cringed when he added a rider. 'Gone are the days when the curriculum involved simply following any random and whimsical fancy that appealed, which was the teaching 'model' in this country some half-century ago. This young lady encapsulates all that is best in current educational practice that will equip our children for the challenges of the future.'

Grace inclined her head slightly, as her hands were enclosed by the Dean's plump, damp grasp, and accepted the scroll with relief. She hurried as fast as she was able back to the seats occupied by her friends and whipped off her mortar board.

'Thank God that is over! It was excruciating!'

⊰⍦⍦⊱

Grace was so excited that she could not eat a thing, as she mingled with the ponderous and the pompous, the eager and the untried, in the Cloisters restaurant, which had been closed to the general public and laid with buffet-style food.

She watched her fellow graduates with a sort of fascinated horror. Already, having only just qualified as teachers, they were talking of how they aimed to get rapid promotion; how they longed to become Headteachers, who would control and determine future educational policy and become well-known through their research. All Grace had ever wanted to do was to change individual lives, through leading her children from not knowing to knowing – from ignorance to understanding. A couple of the tutors knew Matthew and were bent on engaging him in conversation.

'Of course, Doctor Moore, your protégée could not fail to succeed, having such a brilliant role model as her mentor!' one small, very overweight, gowned individual declared.

'Ah, Nigel, there you are wrong! It has been one of the greatest joys of my life to have the privilege to work alongside Grace Adams. She has the sort of natural talent that puts degrees and status to shame!'

'Ah yes – er – quite, Matthew. Of course. Good to see you. Please excuse me – I must circulate.'

Looking at Grace's expression, Annie, Simon and Matthew simultaneously decided that they needed to point Alison's former vehicle firmly back in the direction of home.

⊰⊱

Grace laid back luxuriantly in one of the deep, green leather armchairs that flanked Simon's inglenook fireplace and stifled a deep yawn. 'I am utterly exhausted, Simon!'

'I know – what a day!' He swirled the amber-coloured whisky around in his tumbler meditatively. 'You know, Grace, one of the most memorable things I picked up in London was from an elderly homeless man, who came to me, I am convinced, primarily for conversation and company. He consistently ended our consultation with the aphorism, "Ah, Doctor Patterson, always remember that today is the first day of the rest of your life." I think that this is particularly pertinent for you today, Grace.'

Grace smiled sleepily. 'I think it is, Simon. But I am far too tired to even start to make plans. Can I come over tomorrow evening to discuss things?'

'Of course. But let me walk you home now.'

'Don't be silly! It is all of two hundred and fifty yards – I mean metres – and I know this village like the back of my hand. I thought that it is me who is supposed to be an anachronism, not the innovative young doctor. Incidentally, what happened to your patient – he of the homily?'

'He died from alcoholism,' stated Simon bleakly.

Grace bit back an inappropriate giggle and desperately tried to compose her features. 'Oh! I'm … I'm so sorry, Simon.'

She was so fond of this man. His seriousness, his care, his professional excellence, all were qualities that the entire village admired. Three years earlier, Simon had been asked by the Medical Practice which he had joined as an occasional locum, whether he would consider joining them on a permanent basis and opening a branch surgery in Quintin Parva. It had immediately occurred to him that this would directly enhance the quality of life of the elderly residents of the village, who could access medical care – or often just professional reassurance – without the expense and worry of travelling to the nearest town. Simon had suggested that he should convert into a surgery one of the front rooms of his historic home and, after a swift inspection by the senior partners, this had been agreed.

Grace loved the consulting room, and its twin, Simon's drawing room, on the other side of the wide front door. Both were fragrant with the scent of fresh flowers, lavender polish or wood smoke, dependent upon the season. In fact, the whole house was safe, tranquil and so quiet that sometimes elderly villagers would nod off to sleep in the comfortable arm chairs which crowded the snug, now the waiting room of Simon's Practice. Grace often reflected that the peace and reassurance felt in the house could well be the result of the care and healing which had taken place here throughout many generations. In a cavernous, dark-oak corner cupboard in the surgery, Simon had discovered several deep-blue glass bottles, decorated with glowing enamel paints and bearing the names of the unlikely medical remedies which they had originally held: arsenic, phosphorus and white lead. From behind a rotten window shutter, he had unearthed a set of delicately-crafted brass scales with tiny brass weights, specifically designed to measure the minute quantities of ingredients which went into the medicines that generations of doctors had created in Pedders to treat the ailments of Quintin Parva. Washed and polished, jars and scales, together with the most interesting of the glass bottles in the cache unearthed in the garden, were displayed along the oak mantelshelf and on the deep windowsills of the surgery as a kind of homage to the dedicated professionals who had lived and worked under this ancient roof.

At every turn, Grace saw the esteem in which her friend was held. She deeply admired his steadiness, his wisdom and his medical skills, but sometimes a flicker of a traitorous thought crossed her mind. Just sometimes it would be good to be surprised by Simon's actions, by his words, by not knowing *exactly* what these would be.

The next evening was unseasonably cold, so Grace had run along to Simon's house as fast as she could through the pouring rain and was now stretched out comfortably on one of Alison's colourful rugs in front of the substantial log fire. Simon sat with a notebook on his knee as, predictably, his advice had been that they should make an action plan to set out the process of creating a Free School in the village; when each stage should be tackled; and what it would cost.

Restlessly, Grace rolled over onto her back, cupped her hands behind her head, and stared at the carefully restored beams of the ceiling. 'I don't think we need an action plan, Simon – you sound like one of my tutors! Basically, all we need is money! I have explained what modifications need to be made to the Old School House and I know exactly the educational resources we should buy. It's just having the finances to do it all!'

'We could apply for grants,' mused Simon, laying down the pad and pencil on a small side table.

'Which would take how much time and effort?'

'We could ask for sponsors.'

'I like that idea more. Speaking to people face to face, rather than engaging in interminable form-filling, is much more my thing. Do you have anyone in mind?'

'Well, I downloaded the latest advice about setting up Free Schools. It says …'

'Oh, you are such a dear!' laughed Grace, jumping up and giving Simon a hard hug 'What would I do without you?'

It was actions like this that completely threw Simon. For nearly five years he had tried to help, support and encourage Grace. She meant more to him than any other woman he had ever known, but she seemed to regard him like a brother, or good friend, rather than anything closer. Simon watched her as she stood in front of the fire, her hands thrust deeply into the pockets of her long jumper, smiling at him broadly. Her face was flushed, her hair curled about her oval face in natural abundance and Simon thought she was one of the loveliest women he had ever seen. Her passion for equality, for doing the best for absolutely everyone who crossed her path, touched him deeply and stood out from the ambition and materialism of almost everyone else he could think of. One of Simon's constant irritations with himself was that, when he was with her, he seemed incapable of speaking or acting naturally. He consistently took cover behind the medical persona which he had built up over the years: solid, dependable, pedantic. Now was a case in point. All he really wanted to do was to take Grace in his arms, to smell the sweetness of her hair and skin, and to feel the curves of her body next to his. What he did, however, was merely to say, 'Let me get the information. I think there are opportunities in the formation of the governing body.'

'Oh, for goodness sake! All I want to do is teach, Simon! Has all spontaneity died in this driven twenty-first century world? I don't often talk about my mother, but she was amazing – passion and spontaneity personified! She was one of the very few female members of the Royal Academy in the early years of the twentieth century. She even forgot to eat unless I fed her, so enrapt was she in creating enormous paintings which she invested with her vivid interpretation of life. She created huge, vibrant canvases … she went round with a paint brush stuck in her hair … she lived for her art.'

Grace turned and gazed into the flickering wood fire. She sighed deeply, seeing in the flames the scarlets and ambers and buttercup yellows of her mother's paintings. 'I would love to know where she was laid to rest, Simon. It is so strange that she is not mentioned either in the churchyard or the church. She deserves some huge, eccentric monument, not a grey grave-stone – but I can't even find one of those!'

'Grace, sit down – please. All I have ever wanted to do is to help and to heal people, but I had to spend years of my life learning about aspects of medicine that do not interest me. We live in a blame culture. If we do not follow the rules in order to gain credibility, then we become vulnerable. I'll make some tea and we can look at the guidelines together.'

Cursing himself under his breath, Simon walked briskly into the spacious kitchen that he had created from a warren of small, dark rooms at the back of the house. The resulting space was light, warm and welcoming. Why was he so utterly incapable of letting go? For God's sake, Grace had been talking about her mother and all he could talk about was the blame culture of 2014 and making tea! He slammed the heavy metal kettle onto the cream Aga in sheer frustration at himself.

Whilst he was gone, Grace impatiently crossed the flag-stoned drawing room and leant her forehead against the cool glass of the window, gazing at the rain sweeping across the flower borders that she and Simon had created on each side of the front path. Her mind was in turmoil. She had waited four years to qualify as a teacher and be able to put her vision into practice, but now the practical difficulties threatened to obliterate the joy of the moment.

As she looked out past the clipped yew bushes and the water-laden flowers to the narrow lane beyond the garden, Grace idly thought back to her previous life – something she did less and less frequently. It was one night, also in June, that Alex had told her he loved her.

She tried to recall how she had felt and remembered excitement, and a sort of desperation that she should be with Alex forever. Life was so fragile in those far-off days. Undoubtedly there had been passion and longing in their relationship, but she remembered, too, how he teased her often, almost cruelly. How he would consistently relegate her to the ranks of the other women in the village, whose major role, according to him, was to support the brave men who were fighting for the free world. In the light of the values of the world into which she had been catapulted, with its striving for complete equality between women and men, Alex's attitudes were outmoded indeed. For instance – and she thought with sudden affection of Simon – Alex would never, ever, have made her tea or downloaded the document that her friend was now carrying carefully in his left hand.

Impulsively, Grace crossed the room, took the tray and set it down on the table, returned to Simon, and kissed him lightly on the lips. He was warm and entirely safe, but she regretted her action immediately. Simon flushed and appeared to ignore what had just happened: he just took up the stapled pages of the government guidance and sat again in his seat to the side of the huge fireplace.

'Right. This is what it says.'

Grace once again took up her place on the rug in front of the fire, lowering her gaze, so that her black hair fell around her face, obscuring her deep blush. Clearly Simon did not appreciate the sort of physical contact that she had just shown. She would have to be more careful in future.

Chapter 36

'So, what you are saying is that we should think carefully about the members of the governing body, perhaps seeking their sponsorship?' Grace reiterated hesitantly, when she had managed to come to grips with the pseudo-legal educational jargon of the document that Simon had downloaded from the Internet.

Simon nodded. 'Perhaps Matthew Moore would consider being one of the sponsors?'

'Oh, Simon, he has done so much for me already. I'm just not sure …' Grace drew her knees up to her chest and hugged them tightly. 'Do you know, when I first started to teach in the 1940's, funding was never an issue. Everything was paid for – in the case of my school, by the Church, for the good of the children. We weren't running a business, we were teaching – just teaching. It wasn't a political football – it was so *right*.'

There was a long pause. Grace gazed at the flickering fire, lost in her thoughts of long ago; and Simon looked at her composed and enigmatic profile, longing more than ever to be able, somehow, to show how he felt about her.

'Grace, would you allow me to be a sponsor? My practice has grown substantially during the last three years, and I would be honoured if you would. I would love to help you in any way I can.'

'Simon, of *course* I would! I too would be honoured. Thank you! But we still need more money! I am sorry that I sound like a broken record, but we need tens of thousands of pounds.'

They had been talking for hours and the heavy skies were leaden, even though it was a mid-summer evening. Grace jumped up, and stretched sleepily, feeling that their conversation was circling and not reaching helpful conclusions. 'I need to go home, Simon. Annie is making shepherd's pie and it's my favourite. But, I wonder, are you free tomorrow evening? Something positive I *can* do is to start decorating seriously. I can, at least, afford paint!'

'Of course, Grace. I will be with you straight after surgery – about six thirty?'

'Perfect!'

⋊║╠⋉

'I don't think that the walls behind the units have been painted since it was the territory of Ivan the Terrible!' Grace puffed, as she vigorously rubbed down the patches of discoloured and flaking woodwork in the room that had been Alison's kitchen. Over the preceding few weeks, whilst Grace had been subjected to her final teaching assessment, Simon had stripped out the kitchen units and managed to recycle them via the village magazine. The exposed stretches of wall were brown, discoloured and peeling – presumably the colour that they had been before the kitchen had been installed. Grace gazed at the walls thoughtfully. 'I remember that awful colour! The dismal brown suited the dismal curriculum that Doctor Miles forced his poor children to follow,' she told Simon.

He was perched on a high ladder, only half taking-in what she was saying, trying to decide just how to tackle the cracks and gaps in the wooden panelling. He tentatively pushed the top of the section of wall nearest to him, which appeared to be several centimetres away from the ceiling. 'Do you know, Grace, this section of the wall is actually moving,' he frowned.

'What! Are you sure?'

'Absolutely. Look … if I hold the top of this wooden panel, and move it back and forward gently, you will see exactly what I mean.'

He slipped his fingers into the deep crevice at the top of the panel and pulled it carefully towards him. Sure enough, a section approximately three metres wide and almost the full height of the wall, visibly shifted.

'Oh my God, Simon, this is terrible. The whole place is falling down!'

'It's not, Grace. Just watch. I think this panel has been inserted here for some reason. The rest of the wall isn't moving. Could you hand me my phone, please? I need the torchlight to see how it is fixed, so we can decide what to do.' Simon was silent for several minutes, shining the light behind the wooden panel and looking increasingly puzzled. 'Grace, come and have a look here. I can see colour and some sort of design.'

Grace took his place on the ladder as quickly as she could and held the torch at an angle, tilting her head and craning her neck to see what lay hidden. After gazing silently into the gap for several minutes, she slowly came down to floor level again. Still silent, and very pale, she sat down on the floor.

'It is the scenery that my mother painted,' she whispered. 'I can see the castle.'

⊰)I(⊱

During the long summer holidays, the three massive panels that Catherine Brabazon had painted for the Mummer's play were gently released from the walls against which they had been fixed and very effectively hidden. Simon had insisted that they should enlist the expert help of a firm of art specialists to release the paintings, and he and Grace had watched, spellbound, as the brilliant colours and exquisite compositions were freed from almost a century of imprisonment.

It was the evening before the paintings were being taken to London to feature in an auction that had already attracted world-wide interest. Simon had insisted that all communications should be directed to him, rather than to Grace, after the art historian who had originally assessed the importance of the paintings had looked distinctly taken aback at Grace's referring to them as 'her mother's work'. Earlier that day, Simon had been told that bids placed from the States and from the Middle East had already run well into seven figures.

'Why do you think they were hidden like this?' Simon asked.

Grace hesitated. 'I'm not sure. The school was closed after the bombing. We had stacked the panels with their painted surfaces against the wall so as not to distract the children from their learning. Perhaps, in the years that followed, people did not realise their significance and just used them to repair or reconstruct the walls.'

Simon realised that she was close to tears as she traced the misty outline of the castle, perched on a sheer rocky outcrop, and gazed at the same view, framed by a lancet window from within a panelled room in the castle. Grace was reliving the bleak, snowy evening when her mother had supported her in the only way she understood – by offering to paint the scenery for the ill-fated Christmas performance. Always closer to her father than to her mother, it was only now, looking at the brilliance of the works of art before her, that Grace realised how little effort she had actually made to understand Catherine Brabazon's world. What she would do to be able to have a conversation with her mother now – to explain, and to apologise.

❧⊫⊰❦

The three paintings were sold for a sum in excess of four million pounds and the future of the school was secure. A firm of local builders was appointed to convert the Old School House back to its original design, with the addition of indoor toilets, a small modern kitchen and a comfortable staffroom. The need for significant financial sponsorship was no longer an issue, and so it was decided that Matthew Moore, Simon, and Joseph Smithson – grandson of Albert, whose family now farmed most of the land around Quintin Parva – should become the founding members of the governing body. Their first meeting took place on a quiet August evening in the lofty space that was to double, once again, as the senior classroom and the school hall. The routine administration of establishing the governance of the school was quickly dealt with, but the final item on the agenda – what the name of the new school should be – caused lengthy discussion.

'Well, it's a village school, so why not just call it "Quintin Parva Village School"?' suggested Joseph. 'What was good enough for my grandfather should be good enough for his great-grandchildren.'

'Strictly speaking, the status of the school should be reflected in the name,' asserted Matthew. 'Something like: "Quintin Parva Free School"'

Simon could see that Grace was becoming increasingly agitated and was not surprised when she stood suddenly, resting her hands on the back of her chair.

'Has it occurred to anyone that this school would not exist if we hadn't discovered the painted panels?' she declared passionately. 'And how about the man who died so that the last Headteacher of this school could live out the rest of his life in some sort of useless retirement …'

'Grace!' Simon spoke softly, but urgently.

Grace breathed deeply and continued more calmly, 'So, let us remember the part that those two people played in ensuring that we can actually open a school for the children of this village! I don't really think that there is any question as to what the school should be called.'

'You are right, Grace,' interjected Simon. 'I propose that our new school should be called "The Charles and Catherine Brabazon Memorial School"'.

'Seconded,' pronounced Matthew, in a tone that brooked no contradiction.

Chapter 37

'It feels so odd not to be teaching at the start of a new school year,' Grace mused. 'Are you sure I shouldn't, Simon? Matthew still hasn't appointed. I could teach his Reception Class for just one more term …'

They were sorting through a selection of objects which the builders had brought to Pedders earlier that day. A writing slate had been unearthed from under the floorboards in the main classroom – the room where Catherine Brabazon's paintings had been found – still with faded chalk calculations scrawled over its surface. Grace had commented sourly that she imagined some poor child, bullied by Ivan Miles, deciding to hide his incorrect calculations permanently from his teacher, by slipping his slate through the gap between two floorboards.

Simon smiled absently and shook his head. 'It's impossible for you to teach at the moment, Grace. You need to appoint at least one additional teacher; you need to recruit your children; to write your policies; order the furniture and equipment, including computers. How about providing the children with a nutritious meal in the middle of the day? What about …'

'Simon!' Grace held her head in her hands. 'I know you are the Chair of Governors, but please don't drive the Headteacher to a nervous breakdown before the school opens! I will do all this! I have a year. Anyway, I have anticipated your nagging. Look!' she pulled a sheet of paper from her handbag. 'What do you think?' Simon read:

A New School for Quintin Parva!
Come and find out about
Our Vision for Your Children
At the School
17th December 2014 at 7.00 pm
Refreshments provided

'Why 17th December?' he asked.

'Ah, 17th December 1942 was the date of the infamous Mummers' play,' Grace grinned. 'Seventy-two years to the day! It is a way of honouring my mother and father; of linking past and present; of remembering and looking forward. Does that make sense?'

⊰⊹⊱

Grace stood by herself in the room that she had worked so hard to prepare for the Open Evening. Ivan Miles' former classroom had been transformed by the team of decorators, who were working their way steadily through the building. Freed from its dismal paintwork and network of cracks, it had become a bright and attractive space, well-lit by the tall, latticed windows that stretched from floor to ceiling. A modern central-heating system warmed the whole building at the flick of a switch and Grace smiled as she remembered the limited heat given by the enormous cast-iron stove, which had been their only source of warmth during the war years. Her mind was full of memories tonight. It seemed to her that, if she opened the door into the long, low room that had been her classroom in 1942, she would see again the excited children, dressed in their cardboard armour and hand-me-down 'princess' dresses. It was at times like this when her extraordinary experience could catch her out, completely and utterly, and she felt deep nostalgia for a simpler and infinitely less demanding age, where people still believed in wholesome ideals and were prepared to die for them. Strange how she could look back with poignancy to a time when life was so easily lost, and was lived always on a knife edge. She lowered her gaze thoughtfully to the object that she cradled in her hands.

The day before, she had gone quietly to the corner of the outside toilets where, in 1943, she and her class had hidden the time capsule, for discovery by someone 'in the future'. Well, she shook herself briskly, she was the future now, safeguarding the future of the children in the village of Quintin Parva in 2014. Those rosy faces and eager hands, giving into her safekeeping what was most precious to them, belonged to the grandparents of children that she hoped to teach again. She took a deep breath and, one by one, took out the contents of the battered tin. There were the faces of the fathers who had fought for their families and for the village, and she reflected sadly that too many of their names were commemorated on the war memorial opposite the school building. She carefully unfolded the ration book, the newspaper and the recipe for carrot cake, copied in a child's spidery 'best' handwriting. It was remarkable how well-preserved the paper was. The years had not faded the print or writing in the least. Last of all, she held again the tin mug that had belonged to Alex – dented, battered, the last resting place of the photograph of the man she had hoped to marry. She waited some minutes before slipping out the photo; and held it, without looking at the black and white image, for some time. At last, she uncurled the photo and gazed again on the face of Alex McIntosh.

He seemed so distant, so alien, a person from another life in another age in which she no longer played any part. Unbidden, Simon's face came into her mind – warm, gentle, clever, and caring. His dark hair was always tousled, his eyes tired from computer work or research for the good of his patients. She glanced back to Alex's face: it was so handsome, yet so unreal, so completely unrelated to the context in which she now lived.

It came to her like a revelation that Simon, her faithful friend, her adviser, her constant default position when upset or uncertain, had surely and comprehensively replaced Alex in her life and her heart. She lightly kissed the photograph and placed it on the display shelves with the other pictures of young men, whose faces had become fading memories of long ago.

⊰⊱

Half an hour before the meeting opened, Simon flung open the door of the school. A flurry of snow entered with him. He was pale with cold.

'This looks great, Grace. Well done!' he started to say, but was cut short by Grace walking swiftly across the room to him. She reached up and held his face in her hands.

'Simon, I have never properly said thank you. I want to do that now. Ever since I have come to know you, you have supported and helped me. Such friends, such men, are hard to find. You mean more to me than you can realise. Thank you, Simon.' And for the second time, Grace kissed him, her warm lips shocking against his cold ones.

For once, Simon did not attempt to withdraw, or recoil. He stood looking down at Grace's open, lovely face, and the gentle smile curving her lips.

'Grace, I …'

Again, the door was briskly opened and shut, as Annie and Matthew arrived together. Annie went straight to the staff-room, where she had been busy for much of the day, whilst Matthew strode to the nearest radiator.

'It is utterly freezing out there!' he exclaimed.

'Must be something to do with it being the 17th December,' Grace smiled.

Gradually the room started to fill. The posters had been placed around the village and within a radius of five miles. Probably less than five hundred people lived in the scattered farms and small hamlets which comprised the potential catchment area of the school, but soon the fifty or so chairs that Grace had placed around the room were filled, and still people arrived.

Shortly after seven o'clock, Grace stood up and smiled warmly at the assembled people.

'Good evening and thank you all for coming,' she said. 'Welcome to the Charles and Catherine Brabazon Memorial School, so called because, after much discussion, the governors wished to commemorate two extraordinary people: Charles Brabazon, who gave his life saving the lives of others on this very spot; and his wife, Catherine, whose paintings have funded the foundation and equipping of our school. Both these people lived at the heart of this community and served it according to the individual skills and talents that each had.'

Grace had steeled herself to talk of the parents who had meant so much to her – in very different ways – but even so, she was finding it difficult to continue. She coughed and took a sip of water from the glass which Simon had thoughtfully placed on the table in front of her. Once again, she smiled at her prospective parents and grandparents and continued, 'And this is what the school will be about: community. Our vision is that we should serve the village and surrounding district to the best of our ability. We want our pupils to grow up being aware of their history.' Here Grace gestured to the display she had created on the deep shelves that the builders had fitted in an alcove. 'Those brave fathers of this village who fought to protect its identity and the equally brave women who worked and fed their families whilst their husbands were away – all deserve to be honoured through the education of their grandchildren. I am determined that not one child in my care should be disappointed or disaffected by the education that she or he receives. I can promise that all will be respected, and all will love the life that they have in this very special place.'

There was a stunned silence in the room. The farmers, shop workers, health workers, carers and cleaners had never heard anything like this. They heard politicians on the news, who all appeared to be saying things that did not, somehow, apply to their own children or to Quintin Parva. Here, out of the blue, was a young woman who was clearly passionate about what they themselves valued: village life and getting the best for their children.

Slowly one old man stood up. He was bent and leant heavily on a stick.

'My name is Albert Smithson, ma'am,' he said, raising his battered cap in an old-fashioned gesture of respect. 'I would like to say that I have not heard such sensible stuff for many a long year. Not since my teacher, Miss Brabazon's, day. She were a wonderful woman. She led us about the village and we learnt all the time – not just in class, like – until she had her accident and then left us altogether. Why, she even looked like you too, miss, if you don't mind my saying so. It could be her, standing there just now … Without doubt my Joseph's children will come to your school. I hope that they will have memories like what I have of my time at this school. I still remember that Christmas play we did on today's date in the middle of the war. I were a knight and felt six foot tall! Anyhow,' he finished, embarrassed, 'that's what I think!'

There was a chorus of 'Aye's' and 'That were just what I were going to say' around the room. Grace was shaking slightly, with emotion and, she supposed, relief. She wanted to say more, but her mouth was dry and she was not quite sure how to respond.

Swiftly, Simon stood up and smiled before starting to speak. 'It is my privilege to be the Chair of Governors of our new village school, but I think that Miss Adams has said all that it is necessary concerning our vision and our aims. May I now invite you to join me for a short tour of our classrooms and other facilities, after which we can all enjoy the refreshments that Miss Adam's aunt has produced for us on this cold winter's evening. We have mulled wine, or tea; and sandwiches, sausage rolls and mince pies. Just one final point: Dr Moore, our educational partner, has a stock of registration forms if you would like to indicate your interest in our new school. He will be delighted to answer any questions that you may have. It remains only for me to thank you all for coming, and express my hope that you will enjoy the rest of the evening!'

Simon had produced sixty registration forms, a number optimistically chosen on the basis of the school having two classes of thirty children each. All the forms were completed that evening.

Chapter 38

By New Year's Eve, much of the main structural work on the school had been completed. And, what was more, sixty-five children in all had registered to start at the school in September 2015.

Several weeks earlier, Matthew had delivered invitations to Grace, Simon and Annie, to attend one of the major social events of the year in the village's limited calendar. Annually, on New Year's Eve, Matthew and his governing body opened the Old Vicarage to invited guests for the *Snow Ball*. Usually the title was completely inappropriate and guests hurried through the rain from their vehicles to the warm, brightly-lit building. But this year, thick snow continued to fall and blanket the quiet Dorset countryside, so the Ball was well-named indeed. Annie had declined the invitation. 'It's just not my scene,' she told Matthew quietly. 'I don't even *own* an evening dress and I've never seen delicate evening shoes for women with size eight feet!'

Grace and Simon had decided to walk to the Old Vicarage and Simon arrived at Rose Cottage in his waxed jacket and wellingtons, carrying a large umbrella and a rucksack for their indoor shoes. Matthew made it clear that he had invited them not just because they were his friends, but because the *Snow Ball* was an occasion when they could make influential contacts. Grace had, therefore, taken a lot of trouble with her appearance. Usually, she simply brushed her hair and wore little, or no, make-up, but tonight she had, with Annie's help, swept her thick, black hair up and back, twisting it into a loose cascade of curls. She had bought new make-up and had carefully matched her lipstick to the deep wine-red colour of a long, velvet evening dress that she had bought in Salisbury before the snow made such a journey difficult.

Simon loved Grace just as she was, whether in jeans, wellingtons, shorts or faded summer-dresses. Superficialities did not matter one jot to him but, when he arrived on the doorstep of Annie's cottage and rang the little metal bell, he was astonished at how beautiful Grace looked. Her body had softened and showed once again the gentle curves that she had naturally developed when she had lived seventy years earlier.

'Do I look all right?' she asked, making a half turn, so that Simon could see the full effect of her hair and the deep V of the neckline at the back of the dress. She was genuinely concerned that, despite her best efforts, her appearance would not match the expensive dresses and hairstyles of the great and the good who were to attend the Ball that evening.

'You look breathtaking,' Simon whispered, holding out Annie's warm black cloak for Grace.

Walking across the snow which covered the paddock in front of the Old Vicarage, Grace thought that she had never seen the gracious old house look so inviting. All the curtains were drawn back from the windows and golden light flooded out, making the snow crystals sparkle like tiny gems. She imagined that this was how her old home would have looked in the days shortly after it had been built, when the Anglican Church was prosperous and the position of Parish Priest respected and financially secure.

Matthew and his Chair of Governors, Sir Ralph Fleming, a prominent QC, greeted the guests as they entered the elegant hall. Matthew welcomed them both warmly, kissing Grace's cheek and saying, 'Grace, I have something I want to talk to you about. Can we have a word before you leave, do you think?' Sir Ralph knew Simon already, as his reputation was becoming very well established in the county. But when introduced to Grace, he bowed and kissed her hand, declaiming that 'with such a Headteacher, the new village school was a real threat to the future of the establishment in which they now stood.'

Grace moved away as soon as she could, muttering to Simon under her breath, 'I hate that sort of stupid flattery, Simon. I never know what to say, so say nothing and people think I am slow and stupid!'

'It wasn't flattery, Grace,' Simon replied, holding her gaze with his own.

The evening was exhausting. Grace just wanted to sit and chat to Simon and Matthew about ideas that she was developing for the curriculum in her school but, constantly, she was being introduced to new people, who simpered or ogled and generally, in Grace's opinion, made fools of themselves. Shortly before midnight, she whispered to Simon, 'Can we get out of here? I just can't stand much more of this …'

'I know what you mean! But don't forget that Matthew said he wanted to speak to you about something before we go. Let's slip out into the orchard for a while. The coats are piled up at the back of the kitchen, so we can retrieve ours and go out through the conservatory. When midnight has passed and the guests have started to leave, we can just drift quietly back in.'

'Good idea.'

The television had been turned up so that guests could hear the count-down to the start of 2015. 'Ten, nine, eight, seven, six, five, four, three, two, one … Happy New Year!' bellowed the voice of the presenter.

'Happy New Year, Simon!'

Simon didn't speak. He just stood looking through the gently falling snowflakes at the face of the woman who meant so much to him. Then, instead of repeating the conventional words, he took Grace in his arms, pulled her to him, and kissed her. 'There is no other way of saying this, Grace, because I know you hate people who beat about the bush. So, I will say this simply and from my heart. I love you. I have loved you for years, and I want to be with you always. Will you marry me?'

'Oh Simon, of course I will!' Grace reached up and pulled him to her, wiping the snowflakes from his glasses. 'You have, literally, been with me from the start of my life in the twenty-first century and I can't imagine living without you. There's just one thing, though …'

Simon released his hold on her slightly, so that he could see her expression. She was smiling wickedly.

'Do you think you can be happy with a wife who is nearly a hundred years older than you?'

His reply – 'Don't be silly!' – was muffled by her hair as, once again, he pulled her into his arms.

⊰⧸⧹⊱

'I don't mind telling Matthew and Annie, Simon, but let's not make a fuss just yet about what has just happened.' With sparkling eyes and glowing cheeks, Grace led Simon back into the fast-emptying vicarage.

'Ah, I wondered where you two had got to!' exclaimed Matthew. 'Come and have some cocoa. I need to tell you some interesting news.'

'Well, actually, Matthew, we need to tell *you* some exciting news!' declared Grace, linking her arm through his.

Matthew stopped and looked for a few moments into Grace's joyful face. 'I think I can guess!' he grinned. 'Are congratulations in order?'

Simon and Grace both nodded.

'Well, all I can say is *about time!'*

'So, this woman – what did you say her name was, Matthew?'

'Mrs Deniston.'

'This Mrs Deniston bought this house from my … from Catherine Brabazon?'

'Not exactly,' Matthew frowned, stirring his cocoa. 'She bought it in the 1970's – some considerable time after Mrs Brabazon had died.'

'And?' Grace prompted gently.

'And, when she was renovating the place – apparently it was in a terrible state, because Mrs Brabazon had let it go to rack and ruin and it had then lain empty for years – she discovered these.'

Matthew walked quickly across the modern kitchen, which he had created from the old laundry room, to a pine dresser and picked up a thick sheaf of papers. They were tied together with string in a dusty roll.

'Mrs Deniston brought these to me this morning and told me how she had discovered them scattered over the floor by the range. She attended the meeting at your school, as she has grandchildren in the village, and thought that you would be interested in reading them, Grace, since they belonged to the woman whose paintings have made your new school possible.'

'So, what are they? A diary, lists, notes?'

'They are letters.'

'To whom?'

'No, Grace – sorry, I have not made myself clear. They are letters written *to* Catherine Brabazon, from her daughter.'

'What?' Grace jumped up, a convulsive gesture sending the mug of cocoa spinning across the granite work surface. 'From her *daughter?*'

Matthew frowned. 'Yes … are you all right, Grace?'

Simon swiftly stepped in, clumsily attempting to gloss over Grace's reaction, and saying the first thing that came to his mind: 'The prospect of becoming Mrs Patterson must suddenly have become overwhelming, Matthew! Thank you for thinking of Grace and letting us borrow these letters.'

'Not borrow, Simon, you can have them. Mrs Deniston has no need of them. She had been thinking for some time about donating them to a museum, but there is not an appropriate one, really. If, as you assumed, Catherine Brabazon had *written* the letters, then almost certainly they would have been of historical importance, and considerable value. But her daughter is quite a mystery.'

Grace sat down abruptly.

'Apparently,' Matthew continued, 'she was a teacher at your school. But, on the night of the air raid when her father, Catherine's husband, lost his life, she had a serious accident and was unconscious for months. When she regained consciousness, she felt unable to teach, and the school, which had been closed after the air raid, was never re-opened as a school – until now. Exactly what happened to Grace Brabazon is not clear. So her letters, having no provenance, as it were, have no historical significance.'

Grace's head was whirling. Assimilating what Matthew had just told them required mental gymnastics which, at the moment, she was incapable of performing. With a huge effort, she stood up and said, 'Thank you, Matthew. Reading them will be absolutely fascinating. But now we must go. Thanks again for a truly memorable evening!' She kissed her host lightly on the cheek, gave the heavy roll of letters to Simon, who slipped them into an inner pocket of his waxed jacket, and they left the light and warmth of the building to trudge again through the winter landscape.

The snow had stopped falling and it was bitterly cold. As they walked across the field in front of the Old Vicarage, Grace looked up at the stars, which seemed larger and brighter and more implacable than she had ever seen them before. Those same stars had shone on the trees and hills, lanes and houses of this remote part of Dorset when the gracious house that she had just left had been her home. They would have shed that same cold light when the rectory had been built, centuries earlier; and they would have illuminated the lives and deaths of the countless generations of villagers who had lived in this place for over a thousand years. Suddenly Grace felt flat, anticlimactic. 'So Alison was right, Simon,' she murmured quietly. 'Someone else did live, or is still living, the rest of my life …'

Grace Adams
1943 – 1950

Chapter 39

Catherine knew the moment she saw them that Grace and Romani had become lovers. It was just after dawn and the sun shone softly on the dewy grass and leaves. Catherine had been awakened by the dawn chorus and, rather than lie in bed, sleepless, decided that she would go down to the orchard and sit under her favourite apple tree. She was just about to leave the house when she saw the couple come into the garden. They were not touching each other, but there was an almost palpable magnetism linking them. Overnight, Grace had opened, from a tightly-furled flower-bud to a flower in its full and dazzling perfection; and Romani was, at last, fulfilled and at peace. Every atom of his vitality was focussed on Grace. They stood, just looking at each other, as the minutes slid by. It seemed to Catherine that it was almost impossible for each to let the other out of their sight.

Unbidden, tears came to Catherine's eyes. She had never loved or been loved like this. She had never been looked at by a man as if he wished to draw her own life into his very own. She was lost, consistently, in her painting, but had never been lost in another, like Grace and Romani were now.

Romani reached gently towards Grace and held her face in his hands, brushing back her dark hair, and tracing the sharp contours of her cheekbones, her chin, her eyebrows with his long expressive fingers, as if he would look at her forever. And then, without a word, he kissed her mouth, her eyes and finally each hand, curling the fingers securely over the place where his lips had touched her palms. Then he turned swiftly and was gone.

For once, Grace entered the house quietly. She seemed almost in a daze. 'What an incredible morning, Catherine!' she said, smiling radiantly. 'I am going to have a bath. Is there any tea?'

'Yes, dear, I've just made some. It's on the Aga. I'm taking mine outside. This golden light is too precious to waste.'

Catherine sat in the garden on the ramshackle wooden seat that Charles Brabazon had erected around the trunk of the oldest apple tree in the orchard. The tree was bent and had lost limbs over the years, but the apples that it produced were still the sweetest in the vicarage garden. Catherine remembered sitting there with her husband when she was expecting Grace, thinking of the years of happy promise that then seemed to stretch for ever before her. How quickly life passed! How soon dawn turned to evening. Perhaps, she mused, that was what intoxicated her about painting. Committing an image to canvas meant that it was never lost, it never changed – in a way, an ephemeral concept became eternal. She sipped her tea, gazing towards the gate where, minutes earlier she had seen a moment that her artist's eye just *had* to capture on canvas, just had to immortalise. She had not painted a portrait since her Art School days, because she felt that human beings were too transient, too fleeting, and lacked that indescribable tension between stillness and movement that the landscape offered. Clouds brush across the face of the unmoving sun; rain slants across hills and fields which are themselves eternally still. But, Catherine reflected, this morning she had seen two human souls which had found stillness and fulfilment in each other; and, across this stillness, love had moved, creating a powerful and memorable tension.

Grace immersed herself in the huge, cast-iron bath, lying back in the hot water and feeling still the imprint of Romani's body on her own: she felt again his weight, the hard muscles under his tanned skin and the clean outdoor scent of him. It was as if he were with her still, so vivid the impression, so real the sensation. In London, Grace had always laughed sardonically at her friends if they talked of their dates, their boyfriends or their one-night stands. Love was seldom mentioned. Relationships always seemed so mundane and time-consuming and, quite honestly, not worth the effort, and because of this, Grace had never fully given herself to a man – until last night. Now, she felt alive as never before: every atom of her being was alight with sensation and longing. And, as she lay there, looking abstractedly at the antique lamp that hung over the bath, it struck her that now she too had found the reason for the bizarre transposition of her life with that of another woman: only in this way could she have met Romani.

As always, Grace was acutely aware that if she and Catherine were going to eat anything, it would be due to her, Grace's, efforts in the kitchen. After her bath, she decided to walk to the village shop to see whether there was anything remotely edible that she could buy and prepare for lunch. She knew that meat was unlikely and she hated rabbit, which was most frequently offered on the meat counter of the little shop. She and Catherine found it totally impossible to grow vegetables. Earlier in the year, in a flush of optimism, Grace had planted some parsnip seeds given to Catherine by a neighbour. She had carefully scattered them in a shallow trench and covered them with the sticky, black soil, but they never appeared above ground. Even the potatoes that she had put in the vegetable garden had only made a dismal show of shoots, and were full of tiny brown slugs when she had finally dug them up. So, vegetables had to be bought, rather than grown.

It took a huge effort, when Grace left the vicarage gate, not to head towards Gypsy Lane and the circle of caravans. She just could not get Romani out of her mind. What was he doing? Was he there? Who was he talking to? She curled her fingers around her palms, just as Romani had done earlier and thrust them deep in her pockets, as she forced herself to concentrate on the matter in hand: finding food.

She turned the corner, just before the village shop, and groaned. Coming steadily towards her on her bicycle was Ginny Hartley, large feet rhythmically propelling the heavy machine along the road. In a basket on the front of the bicycle was a paper bag, from which spilled carrots and onions.

'Good morning, Grace. How are you?' Oh no, thought Grace, she is actually going to stop!

'I was just speaking to Mrs Pedder about our next sewing bee. I am sure that you will agree with me that yesterday was altogether memorable!'

'It most certainly was, Mrs Hartley!' acknowledged Grace. If only the large arrogant woman who had cumbersomely alighted from her bicycle could appreciate exactly *how* memorable!

'Would you and your butler be prepared to attend another of our little meetings next month?'

'Yes – probably. Don't see why not,' muttered Grace.

'*What* a talented man Mr Romani is!' declared Mrs Hartley girlishly, patting her rigid curls.' He seems so passionate about life!'

'Mm,' Grace agreed, not trusting herself to speak.

'Where on earth did your mother find him? He is a treasure indeed – once one gets past his slightly outlandish appearance. Long hair and a gold necklace are not what my Ernest would *ever* wear!'

'Since your husband is bald and built like a bull, I should think not! Are there any more vegetables in the shop?' Grace snapped.

'Really, Grace! I know you have had a serious head injury, but there is no need for rudeness.'

'Indeed, *Ginny,* perhaps it would be good for you to remember that too!' Grace retorted.

'Oh. And, incidentally, I purchased the last of the vegetables that Mr. Skinner has for sale today,' Ginny Hartley added smugly, before launching her heavy frame again on to the grey metal bicycle.

Grace was in a foul mood as she banged her way back into the Old Vicarage kitchen. She shot up the stairs two at a time, before coming to a halt in front of Catherine's studio door.

'Can I come in before I explode, Catherine?' she called.

'Mm, of course, dear.'

The scathing words that were on the tip of Grace's tongue were instantly forgotten as she entered the elder woman's studio. Catherine never attempted to hide her paintings from visitors and the large, portrait-style, canvas was fully visible from the door. 'My God, it's Romani and me!'

'Yes. It is how you looked this morning.'

As always, her work was enormous. It was as if a smaller canvas just could not have contained the extent of the vision that Catherine was communicating. Although abstract, the two figures were clear: much of a height, the woman slender and all light and energy; the man broad-shouldered and narrow-hipped with a controlled vitality.

'The concept is beginning to take shape, but it is not clear enough yet – there is not enough emotional tension between both of you ...'

'I had come to complain about Ginny Hartley and about not having any food for lunch – and you show me this! It really doesn't matter, Catherine, does it?'

'No, my dear, it really doesn't.'

⟡

'Does Romani want to move in here, Grace, do you think?' mused Catherine, as they drank tea after a strange lunch of boiled bantam eggs and sour early apples from the orchard.

'I don't think he would, permanently,' replied Grace. 'He loves the traveller life. It is as if he was born to it. He loves to be free and unconfined by narrow-minded idiots like Ginny Bloody Hartley. But I think he will visit us often here – I hope he does …'

'And you, Grace. Would you go to live with him as a traveller?'

'If that were the only way forward, Catherine, then yes I would!'

Catherine looked at Grace thoughtfully and smiled. 'I need to go and paint, Grace!' she said.

'Catherine – that painting! I have never seen anything like it.'

'And I have never painted anything like it, Grace.'

Chapter 40

Grace was intensely irritated at herself, because of what she interpreted as weakness. Although she longed to see Romani again, ambivalently she was dreading seeing him too. She wondered whether she would feel the same; whether he would have changed; whether the extraordinary and intense emotion that had flowed between them would remain. In the event, it was only three days before she and Romani met again, but it seemed more like three months to her.

Once again, it was early morning and she awoke with the dawn. Since it was summer, Grace slept with her window open as she loved to hear the sounds of the night: owls calling; the rustle of a fox through the long grass of the orchard; the snuffle of a badger below the vicarage windows. The memories of her life in London had grown very distant but, lying in her small bedroom on that summer morning, full of the fresh scents of a new dawn, Grace could not help but recall the unremitting stress of her former life. There was never an escape from the incessant hum of the traffic, the constant sirens of police or ambulance, and the ubiquitous, aggressive human voices, fuelled by alcohol or drugs.

But here in Quintin Parva in 1943, her life had been truly transformed. Instead of dragging herself out of bed and immediately heading for strong black coffee to counteract the over-indulgence of the previous evening, Grace hugged her knees in tight to her chest, trying to contain the familiar flicker of excitement at the thought of her lover. Life now seemed so welcoming, so urgent, and she jumped out of bed to greet the day properly. She looked at the slim arc of the rising sun behind the hills that surrounded the village, the fecund fruit trees – and the motionless figure that stood silhouetted dark against the brightening sky. In minutes, Grace was down the stairs and in his arms.

'I didn't know whether I would see you again,' she whispered against his soft, cream shirt.

'Grazia, why not? How could I not see you again?'

'Because that's what men do – take what they want and move on.'

'Where would I move to? My home is here.' He placed his right hand on her heart.

'Romani, I have so much to tell you!'

'And I you, Grazia. I have been thinking!'

They walked together into the warm kitchen.

'Catherine has painted the most incredible picture of us both, Romani! You must see it. She has captured how we *feel* about each other, rather than just how we look. Oh, and I met that awful Ginny Hartley the other day. I am sure she fancies you. You should have seen her prancing and primping at the mention of your name – ugh!'

'It is about that person that I have been thinking,' laughed Romani.

'Ah, so she is your secret passion! She of the enormous feet and ego,' teased Grace.

'If you are not careful, I will prove to you here, in this respectable kitchen, just how wrong you are.'

'Let me make you breakfast – that will calm you down!'

'I have eaten. But I do need to talk to you.'

Grace understood Romani in this mood. In an instant he had become reflective and serious. She put the kettle on the Aga and sat opposite him at the large, pine table. 'Go on then.'

He steepled his fingers and paused for several seconds before starting to speak. 'Grazia, I am here illegally. I cannot live for ever with the gypsies, even though they have told me that they would like me to. I must return to Italy …'

'Ah, so this is the brush-off Romani, is it? I thought you were just too good to be true.'

'Grazia, stop it! Listen to me. I must return to Italy *after the war* and the only way in which I can do that is to create some sort of respectable identity here in this country. Many of my countrymen and women have lost their passports and any means of identification so, for them, returning to their home country will be difficult indeed. It is not such a ridiculous idea that Angelo Romani should become cook and butler at the respectable home of a member of the Royal Academy. Think about it! I could help your mother – I can help you both! I don't know how long this war will last, but I could use this time by remaining here, establishing a new identity and becoming accepted by this narrow-minded rural community. We could continue those "sewing bees" that seem to mean so much to the ladies of the village – why "bee" by the way?'

'Maybe "busy as – a bee",' Grace snarled, arms folded, ready to disagree with whatever Romani was trying to explain. All she could hear was that he was making use of her and Catherine, in order to leave her and return to his native country.

'You are not making this easy, Grazia. So, if it is possible, maybe I can move here?'

'So I can be available for you whenever you fancy me? I suppose you think I should be kissing your feet, to thank you for your generosity? Well, as far as I know there is no vacancy for a *butler* here! Try Ginny Amazon Hartley! I am sure she would welcome you with open beefy arms!'

Romani stopped speaking and looked at Grace. She was flushed and angry and, he could see, near to tears. He walked round to her side of the table and gently took hold of her hands, pulling her to her feet. 'This is the voice of rejection, of hurt,' he said softly. 'In your unique life, you have been constantly deserted by people you love. Your mother left you and your father; and then your father died. Your profession was ripped away from you – perhaps the worst betrayal of all …'

At this, Grace started to sob in earnest. She could not remember the last time she had cried – in her present life or her past one – and once the tears had started to fall, it was impossible to stop them.

Romani continued, implacably. 'Your father's sister cared for you and tried to give you security and well-being, the things that your mother could not give you and, once again, you were parted from her. Grazia, you told me of Catherine's grandparents, who loved as soon as they met. They loved completely and forever. This is how I feel for you; and this, I believe, is how you feel for me.' He opened the neck of his shirt and unclasped the gold chain around his neck, allowing a worn gold ring to slip into the palm of his hand. 'Grazia, this was my mother's. She never had any valuable thing, but this was a symbol of love, initially for my father and always for her children. When she died, she gave it to me for the woman who would be my wife in the future. It is now yours. I could not go to Italy without you. You need to come with me to the country that will fulfil you like no other. It will strengthen your creativity, your passion. It is hot and fragrant and utterly beautiful – like you are.'

Grace pulled away from Romani and looked at him directly. 'You *are* being honest with me, Romani, aren't you?'

'Yes. I cannot be anything else with you! When you doubt, look at this.' He slipped the fragile gold band onto her left hand and neither was surprised when it fitted. 'Take the chain too, and wear the ring as I have worn it for all these years, around your neck. When we are able to be married, then you will wear it where it should be worn.'

Tears rose again in Grace's eyes. 'I am utterly pissed-off with all this crying,' she sobbed impatiently. 'And anyway, you haven't properly asked me to marry you yet. I might say no!'

Romani kept hold of her hands, in which the ring and chain nestled, but sank to his knees before her. 'Grace, until I met you, I was never fully alive. You have transformed me with your spirit and your loveliness and I want to be with you forever. Will you marry me?'

Grace nodded, but her voice was so choked with emotion that she found it impossible to speak for several minutes. But, eventually, she managed to croak, 'Yes, you bloody idiot. I adore you!'

Chapter 41

Catherine had welcomed the suggestion that Romani should move permanently into the Old Vicarage. Smiling absent-mindedly, she commented that it was wonderful that she and Grace would be free to pursue their 'art', whilst the boring business of cooking could be handed over to someone who actually seemed to enjoy it.

'And where would you like to live, dear?' she asked Romani. 'In the main house, or above the stables? I believe that there is still a flat above the coach house portion of the building – where the carriage was kept that took my late husband's predecessors around the parish. Someone told me that the groom used to live there when the church was wealthy enough to fund such positions. I don't recall ever having been in it, but the building is made of stone and seems strong enough and watertight. But it's up to you …'

'I think that it would be more proper if I were to live in the flat,' Romani replied, after some thought. 'The eyes of the villagers are constantly trained upon each other, and upon us – they are the best spies of all in this war!'

He moved in at the start of autumn, giving himself time to deal with any necessary repairs and sweep the chimneys before the really cold weather set in. He and Grace worked side by side during the endless golden days of September and October, brushing and cleaning and hauling over from the main house the few items of furniture that Romani insisted were all he needed.

Finally, Grace had relaxed and had started to trust Romani. She woke each morning feeling a lightness and a freedom that she had never suspected could exist for her during her narrow, driven, substance-fuelled existence in London.

Romani was more serious than Grace, who found joy in the little things of life. He took his responsibilities extremely earnestly, she discovered, whereas she was always ready to laugh and to dismiss attempts at profound conversation with a throw-away comment. Grace had always believed that she was totally focussed on her work, but she couldn't help but notice that, when Romani was designing, which he had started to do again during the long evenings when they sat, or lay, on the Turkish carpets poached from Charles Brabazon's study, his concentration was fierce and his passion for his work intense. She felt that, at last, she had met someone whose creativity infinitely outstripped her own and, she mused ironically, since he would become one of the foremost designers of the twentieth century, who could be surprised?

By December, the little flat over the coach house had been made into a spartan, but reasonably comfortable, home. No kitchen or bathroom had been installed – such complexities were far beyond the means or abilities of either Romani or Grace, and so Romani cooked for them all in the big, warm vicarage kitchen and used the outside toilets opposite the stable on the far side of the yard. When Catherine expressed concern at this, Romani merely laughed and said, 'It is preferable to a bush, Catherine.'

Grace loved the honesty and lack of affectation shown by both Catherine and Romani. She imagined the raised eyebrows and false coyness that the other villagers – especially the members of the 'Women's Institution' as they now called Ginny Hartley's beloved organisation – would have shown when discussing toilet facilities.

⊰∭⊱

Gradually, the extended household at the Old Vicarage settled into its new routine. Although Romani still visited his traveller friends, it was clear that he had now made it his prime responsibility to care for Grace and Catherine. Catherine was grateful, but constantly abstracted, looking at the world around her with the eye of a painter first and a human being second. She ate the delicious food that Romani prepared for them automatically, whilst thinking of the effect of light through storm clouds, or sunshine through rain. One December evening, Catherine's insouciance really irritated Grace and, as soon as she had slipped off to her studio, Grace said impatiently, 'That was delicious, Romani. But, as far as Catherine was concerned, it could have been my tasteless rhubarb, or my flat, grey bread! Don't you mind that Catherine never praises your cooking?'

Romani shrugged and grinned at her. 'Such is the price of genius!' he laughed softly, pulling her towards him. 'In years to come, people will hold up their hands in horror that Angelo Romani, founder of the House of Romani, used an outside lavatory in the depths of winter!'

'Oh, you idiot, come here!' And Grace slipped her hands inside his warm jumper and stroked the hard, smooth body that she had come to know so well.

Christmas approached and the whole of the country was locked in an icy grip. Romani had lived in his stable flat for three months and gradually the village gossip, which he knew would feed on the situation, had faded away. Snow fell from an unchanging, leaden sky and froze each night, building up layers of impenetrable ice. If food had been short before, it had now become desperate. Romani taught Grace all the skills that he had learned from the travellers. Together they collected rosehips from the ice-covered hedges, which he boiled with honey and then sieved to make a sweet, vitamin-filled purée. He made soufflés from the few eggs that the chickens still managed to lay at this desolate time of the year, and foraged for herbs, showing Grace how, under the layers of snow, wild marjoram and fennel still lingered. From the flour ration, Romani conjured pasta, which he shaped and boiled expertly, and served with a herb sauce.

Discussing what to have for their Christmas meal, Romani had become mysterious and had asked both Grace and Catherine to stop worrying and leave it to him. Gradually Grace discovered that, instead of bristling at the hinted male superiority, she was willing to act in partnership and hand over some responsibility to a person in whom she had complete trust. As each day passed, she came to love even more intensely this man whose character was a complex mix of creative genius and practicality.

During the morning of the last sewing bee before the New Year, Grace and Romani were working together companionably in the kitchen. Outside, the snow was blowing into flurries across the vicarage's frozen lawns. The electricity was flickering badly, which it had been doing since the onset of the severe winter weather. Romani had already bought as many candles as he could and had collected together and cleaned all the oil lamps, past and present, that he could find. Fortunately, the Aga ran on solid fuel independently of electricity and so they were assured of hot food and water but, almost inevitably, the single electric lamp that they had in a corner of the kitchen, flickered and went out.

'Ah, I rather expected this,' sighed Romani. 'We will have to work swiftly with the women of the institution this afternoon to complete their garments. They hope to enchant, to cast spells over the Christmas period, Grazia. Do you know that?'

Grace grunted.

'So ...' Romani left his chopping of the wild mushrooms which he had managed to find in the depths of a sheltered wood and held Grace hard around the waist, pulling her to him, '... let us be *kind* and *compassionate* towards these women who do not experience the sort of love that we have with one another.'

⊰⫶⊱

It was half-past two. Most of the women who eagerly attended the sewing sessions had arrived and were sitting, expectantly, in the rows of chairs which Grace and Romani had placed opposite the table usually presided over by the ample presence of the Chair. But of Ginny Hartley, there was no sign. Romani had lit nightlights in old glass jam-jars, so that the gathering looked warm and welcoming. The women started to fidget, expressing their surprise, in hushed voices, that their leader was not amongst them. They waited. Three o'clock came and went and, at ten-past-three Romani stood up and asked, 'Where does Mrs Hartley live?'

Mrs Pedder, the doctor's wife, cleared her throat and pronounced, in bell-like tones, 'In the white cottage next to the Old Cider House.'

'I will go and see if she is all right,' Romani announced. 'She is a very punctual lady and something must have happened, I think, to delay her.'

'Oh for God's sake, Romani, maybe her bicycle has buckled under her weight. Let's just get on!'

'No, Grazia. I must go. Mr Hartley is in Bristol with the other area air raid wardens for several days' training. She is alone and may be hurt.'

'I'll come with you. I just don't know what to do or say with this lot!'

Grace and Romani trudged through the deep snow that lay on fields and road and verges. A few icy flakes started to fall gently, melting on their hair and faces, but steadily augmenting the thick, white blanket in which the Dorset countryside was covered. The couple passed the bakery and shop and the ancient cob-and-thatch Cider House. Nestling next to this traditional meeting place, and set slightly back from the road, was the timber-framed cottage that was the home of Ginny Hartley. There was no sign of life in the house or garden, so Romani called Ginny's name, but there was no response. He continued to shout at regular intervals, whilst Grace explored the rambling garden. She walked under a trellis arch, which held roses in summer, along a path beaten in the snow towards a chicken coop and outbuilding, where grunts indicated the presence of a house pig, then passed into a small orchard, its snow-laden trees like frozen spectres in the winter landscape. Grace looped to the right, slipping and sliding through the vegetable garden as she headed back towards the outbuildings and cottage. Romani's call, clear as a bell, punctuated her search, regularly marking out the minutes.

Grace was convinced that they were wasting their time and was about to suggest to Romani that they should return to the village hall when, in the most distant corner of the vegetable garden, she saw what at first appeared to be a heap of clothes, partially covered by snow. Almost instantly, Grace realised that it was Ginny, her leg twisted awkwardly under her, lying in a pool of blood which stained the snow. She was muttering to herself, semi-conscious.

'Romani!' Grace yelled, 'Romani! She is here – badly hurt I think.'

Almost soundlessly Romani appeared, swiftly kneeling by the injured woman's side. 'She has trodden on a cold frame that was hidden by the snow. Look, here is the broken glass.' Without another word, he hefted Ginny up and over his shoulder in a fireman's lift, steadying himself under her considerable weight and grinning at Grace. 'There is no way I can carry Mrs Hartley to the hospital – can you pull over that barrow?'

Grace did as he asked and, as gently as he could, Romani lowered the injured woman into the wheel barrow.

'Now push!' he exhorted Grace, as they both leaned their weight into the ancient barrow, to propel it along the snow-covered path of the vegetable garden, round the cottage and then to the road that snaked its icy way to the Quintin Parva Cottage Hospital.

Chapter 42

It was a month later, and could have been a re-run of the December meeting, dramatically abandoned after the discovery and rescue of the Chair, and her ignominious arrival at the small village hospital in a wheelbarrow. Ginny Hartley stood stoically, her left leg heavily bandaged, looking suitably brave and self-effacing as the dedicated lady pianist pounded her way heavily through the last notes of *Jerusalem*.

'Ladies,' began Ginny, 'it is my pleasure to announce a most unusual event!' The members sat alert, waiting for the announcement. 'Today, the Quintin Parva branch of the Women's Institute has decided to bestow a most rare award: honorary membership of the Institute to a *man!*'

There was a loud ripple of exclamations across the room.

'It will be no surprise to you that the man in question is Mr Romani, who selflessly rescued myself from a most difficult situation. But, equally importantly, he has accompanied Miss Brabazon, and on occasion her mother when her busy schedule permits, in establishing and regularly running our popular sewing bees. Never has the directive, which we received from our General

Secretary shortly after the commencement of this bitter war, been better met.' Mrs Hartley carefully placed her large horn-rimmed spectacles on her prominent nose to read a note which she had in front of her on the table. 'She urged us then to ensure that our glorious institution should "provide for our members a centre of tranquillity and cheerfulness in a sadly troubled world." And this we have done, as we have sewn, and talked …'

'And leched after you …' hissed Grace to Romani, thinking of the pink cheeks, bright eyes and flustered attitudes of the women, who flocked around the man she loved like moths around a candle flame.

'… and learnt. We have found tranquillity and cheerfulness indeed!'

'More like palpitations and sleepless nights …' muttered Grace to her lover again.

Ginny Hartley continued to stand awkwardly, and clapped loudly as Angelo Romani came forward, and bowed to kiss her hand. Grace winced. She still could not get her head around the way in which the man she adored could work situations to his advantage by a word or gesture.

'Mrs Hartley, or may I call you Ginny?' Romani gave the elderly lady the full benefit of his intense dark gaze. 'Thank you from the bottom of my heart for this honour. But I have done no more than any man would have done for a woman who carries such influence and …' he looked her up and down boldly, causing her to blush fiercely '… such presence. It has been, and will continue to be, my pleasure to work with such talented and dedicated students for as long as I am needed.' He inclined his head slightly before the assembled ladies, who unconsciously patted their hair and smiled coyly at the compliment.

Ginny went on to deal with other routine matters on the agenda as Romani returned to his seat next to Grace.

'Ugh!' In a swift, hidden gesture, Grace pretended to vomit behind the curtain. 'You sound like a bad film! Why do these women fall for your corny chat-up lines?'

'Why did you, Grazia?'

'I only want to marry you for your money!' she whispered, smiling wickedly.

Romani lightly touched her hand, where it rested on the seat between them. 'One day, my love, you will remember those words which now you speak in jest. One day we will live in a house surrounded by flowers. Your senses will open fully in the sunshine and your talent will reach perfection. You think these things impossible – but have faith, in me and in our future life together.'

❧❦

This seemingly trivial award sealed Romani's acceptance in Quintin Parva. To the inhabitants of the hard-pressed, utterly respectable little village, Angelo Romani was endlessly helpful, patient and good-natured. With Grace and Catherine – but Grace especially – he could be his passionate, fiercely intelligent, creative self. The anodyne persona which he adopted in the village was firmly left at the door of the vicarage, where he and Grace laughed and loved, cooked and created together.

One night, Grace lay curled in Romani's arms. They never put the light on in their bedroom when they were together – either in Grace's snug nest, or Romani's minimalist loft. They knew each other's bodies so well now that light was unnecessary. The feel, the scent of each other, the absolute rightness of their love, had no need to be enhanced. It was an intensely cold night and the light of the stars was sharpened by a heavy frost. Grace lay, looking meditatively at the ageless constellations moving in a stately dance across the inky-black sky, and shivered suddenly, turning to her lover. 'I can't ever imagine being without you, Romani. I don't know what I would do.'

He pulled her closer, kissing her hair. 'One day, my love, you will have to face life without me. I am older than you – you know that. But I will find a way of being with you always. Trust in me. I will never leave you.'

Chapter 43

It was dawn on Midsummer's Day 1950. Grace knelt on the window seat of her bedroom and watched the sun rise, red and golden and altogether glorious. The morning chorus was in full voice and the whole world seemed to be celebrating with her. In just six hours – at half-past ten – she would marry the man who had become her whole world. She was now thirty and it struck her that she had lived just over a quarter of her life with Romani, back in this unspoilt, frustrating world of mid-twentieth century rural England. She watched, entranced, as the sun rose higher into a cloudless sky. The birds were quieter now, already about the business of their day and, like an effect from the most perfect fashion week ever, she watched the sun's rays gradually illuminate her exquisite wedding dress.

Several months earlier, she had called to Catherine from her studio in the attic. Both women were working intensively on their respective projects. Catherine had been commissioned to produce four paintings depicting 'Liberty' for a major hotel in London, which was nearing the end of its post-war re-building programme. Grace had been agonising about what she was going to wear for her wedding. She revisited her previous designs for wedding outfits and remembered – almost incredulously – the dystopian, black and white dress with its dunce's cap and multitude of question marks which had been, literally, the cause of her fall. How bitter and naïve she had been! She closed her eyes and ran swiftly over the years of discovery, of falling ever more deeply in love with the complex, charismatic man who was about to become her husband. This time, for *this* wedding, no-one was the fool. There were no question marks over the utter joy of her union with Romani.

Grace had once more lifted out of the trunk the cherished, ivory-coloured wedding dress which had belonged to Catherine's grandmother. Not for the first time, the similarities of her and Romani's story with that of Alicia and James McIntosh struck her forcibly. They had loved each other almost instantly. They were much of a build – tall, dark and slim. As before, the dress moved and shifted as if with a life of its own. The fabric was so delicate that the gentlest of air movement caused the layers of silk to stir.

Grace slipped the dress over her head and opened her eyes, knowing instinctively what she would see. It could have been made for her, so closely did it fit her slender figure and encircle her narrow waist. She placed the circlet of silk, summer flowers on her thick, dark hair, which seemed to reflect the deep red of the peonies, the gold of the honeysuckle and the ghostly, white daisies. Her mind was made up: they would be married on Midsummer's Day and she would carry a bunch of these flowers – all of which grew in, or near, the vicarage.

Catherine had eventually arrived at the door of Grace's studio and stopped. 'You look beautiful, my dear! Romani's love has completed you.'

⊰╫⊱

Once again, the church bells, silent for so long during the interminable years of the war, rang out joyfully over the wide river valley beneath the hill on which the church stood. Grace and Catherine had walked companionably together across the dry summer grass and slowly climbed the hill towards the church.

'Charles and I were married here,' Catherine sighed, looking out across the fields, shimmering in the heat haze. 'We were happy in our way.' She paused, then added as a statement rather than a question: 'You and Romani will leave now.'

Grace nodded. 'Eventually, yes, we must return to Italy – but not yet. That is where Romani's heart and our future together lie, Catherine.'

Both women stood silently outside the church, absorbing the sunlit peace of the day and listening to the age-old sound of the church bells.

'I understand,' said Catherine quietly, lost in thought for some minutes. 'Grace, are you my daughter?'

For some seconds, Grace was wrong-footed, but then she knew how she had to answer.

'No. I don't know what happened, Catherine. I used to live in London in 2010 and then one day I woke up here in 1943. I don't understand why or how, but …' and here Grace faced the older woman and took hold of both her hands in her own, '… you have been the most perfect mother to me and I want to thank you, Catherine.

Thank you for your friendship and inspiration over the past years.'

Quietly, Catherine Brabazon did something she hardly ever did. She kissed Grace lightly on the forehead and murmured quietly, 'And you have been my perfect daughter.'

Silently the two tall, slender women walked together into the church as the organ started to play the rapid, regal notes of Handel's *Arrival of the Queen of Sheba*. And, thought the members of the congregation in the packed, sun-filled church, never had that music been so appropriate.

⊰◈⊱

For weeks, Ginny Hartley had been haranguing the members of the Women's Institute to pool their ration coupons and raid the larders of the village to honour the unconventional couple who had come to mean so much to them all. As the wedding ceremony was taking place, the members of the WI were loading the tables in the village hall with the very best that they could produce. The wild flowers of the Dorset countryside were everywhere: on windowsills, tables and hanging in garlands from hooks in the ceiling. Their abundance compensated for the inescapably limited wedding breakfast.

It was done. Grace walked out of the great west doors of the church as Grazia Romani, feeling as if never again could she be as completely and utterly happy as she was at this moment. Romani looked – there was no other word for it – exalted, and both smiled and shook the hands of the villagers, equally eager to give their congratulations and to hurry to the village hall where, rumour had it, an unprecedented feast awaited them. Romani, however, showed no haste to leave the flower-filled church, almost deliberately lingering by the door when the last of the congregation had left.

'Grazia, you haven't asked what my wedding present to you is yet?'

'*This* is everything I could ever want,' replied Grace, lightly kissing Romani's mother's ring, which she now wore on the third finger of her left hand.

'Ah, but no. There is something else,' he smiled. 'Come with me.'

He led her along the twisting path to the north-west of the church, out onto the road leading down to the village hall and Rose Cottage.

'Close your eyes,' he teased, leading her carefully down the stone steps to the road. 'Now open them, my love.'

Grace was speechless. In front of her was a stone trough into which water gushed from a spring, deep in the earth. The most exquisite carving ran across the top of the stone and spilled down each side, representing the flowers that she held in her wedding bouquet, twisting and spiralling to provide a resting place for the robin and the thrush that nestled next to their stone beauty. Surmounting the trough were the words: *Vita nova ex aqua resurgit.*

The full impact of the words and their translation, given to her in a life that now seemed so distant, so unreal, that she felt it was a dream, hit her so hard that it took away her breath: *New life rises again from the water.*

Grace Brabazon
2015

Grazia Romani
1957 – 1960

Chapter 44

Never had Grace Brabazon appreciated more acutely the fact that her place of work was local and involved no travel, except on foot. The freezing temperatures continued unremittingly through January and February 2015 and the workmen, who had yet to complete the painting and decoration of the newly-converted school building, were seldom able to navigate the treacherous roads to Quintin Parva. Grace was astonished that the council had not cleared the packed ice and snow, and spoke to Annie about it.

'It's the government cutbacks, dear,' she had explained, when Grace had frivolously suggested that they should buy a sleigh and a team of huskies.

'But it's years after the war ended!' Grace protested. 'Haven't they got things sorted out yet?'

'They did. It's complex to explain, but basically, a few years ago, bankers speculated and lost so much money that the country was almost ruined.'

'But my father's bank manager was such a sensible man! He was always speaking to my parents about *not* overspending. Have things changed so much?'

Annie shook her head sadly. 'People are so selfish nowadays, Grace. That is why the whole village is behind you and what you are doing. You could have kept Alison's house, you know, or sold it – so too with the paintings, which would have made you a very wealthy woman. But no, you insisted that you should sell the paintings to fund the conversion of the school for the good of the children in the village. People just don't do things like that nowadays.'

'Well, they should! What's the point of having so much money that you don't know exactly how much you have got? It's pointless!'

'I know it's frustrating not being able to press on with the school, dear. What is there left to do now? It looks nearly ready to me.'

'It's the small things that are so important, Annie. We need high-quality paint – the sort that you can wipe clean without removing the paint itself. I have ordered blinds and flooring but we still have all the equipment to purchase. We need to consider storage. Toilets and washbasins must be installed and we have decided to put bright, attractive tiling in the washrooms, to encourage the children to take care of what they have – to be good custodians. There are shrubs and perennials to be planted outside and raised beds to build – so much Annie! I know seven months seems ages, but I will need every day.'

'Mm, I can see that,' Annie mused, 'but you also need to conserve your energy, Grace. Everything depends upon you and if you are exhausted, well, that won't be good for everyone else, will it? Winter won't last forever. Give yourself a project to occupy your energies until all these things can be seen to.'

In one of those spontaneous gestures of affection that Annie Adams had come to love, Grace crossed the warm kitchen and gave her a hug. 'As always, Wise

Woman of Quintin Parva, I listen and obey!' Mockingly, she gave a little bow and sat down again with her second mug of tea. She stirred the milk thoughtfully into the swirling brown liquid. 'Actually, there is something that I really must do, but I have been almost afraid of starting it.'

'Tell me more!'

Grace told Annie about the thick roll of letters which Matthew Moore had given to her and Simon on New Year's Eve. 'One of the things that has always concerned me, since my arrival in the twenty-first century, is what happened to my mother. She seems to have disappeared without a mention, and without a memorial. Perhaps these letters will give more information about her life after my accident. I hope too that they will explain more about the writer – the woman who took my place here and lived my life. I have so many questions, Annie. What was she like? What did she do? Did she and my mother live happily together? It is all so *bizarre*! I don't know how many of these letters there are, but they have been burning a hole in my desk drawer ever since I got them.'

Annie Adams was quiet for some time, but then she said quietly, 'Grace, of course you must read them! It is an ideal opportunity to complete part of the complex puzzle that is your life. I don't know how you have exercised such self-control about *not* reading them! This weather, which has put everything on hold, is a gift – take it!'

Chapter 45

Casa di Limoni, Meta,

May 1957

Dear Catherine,

Are you all right? I was really concerned when we left, you looked so sad. But I know that you understand that this is something that we have to do – there is no choice! I am determined that I will let you know exactly what is going on. You have always been so supportive of Romani and me, and I will never forget this.

Our train arrived in Italy yesterday evening at about ten o'clock. It was dark and all I could see was an untidy sprawl of buildings clustered around the railway station. The first impressions of Meta did not, I have to say, live up to the Italian dream that my Romani has been presenting to me ever since I met him! I was so tired. We had been travelling for over forty-eight hours and I was practically asleep on my feet as we climbed the hill from the station into the 'Centro Storico' of Meta. I registered nothing more than walking through a double gate in a high wall, into a garden filled with lemon trees, and then

*into a high-ceilinged, white-painted room, where I,
literally, fell into the huge, soft four-poster bed.*

*But Catherine, this morning, what a revelation!
I had slept for twelve hours without stirring when
Romani woke me with the largest cup of coffee that
I have ever seen. He laughed at me as I woke with a
start, completely confused as to whether I was in
Quintin Parva, London, on the train, or in his caravan
– all those precious years ago.*

*He led me to the double windows leading onto the
balcony which overlooked the densely-planted lemon
trees below, and encircled me tightly with his arms,
saying, 'Look, Grazia, this is Italy!'*

*I looked – across the garden, fragrant in the early-
morning sunshine, to the high, stone wall and the gate
through which we had entered last night; then, over
pitched, terracotta rooftops, which angled sharply
down to the sapphire-blue sea. The morning mist was
still lifting over the expanse of water and Romani
pointed out the islands of Capri and Ischia, rising like
part of a mythical, ancient past.*

Catherine, you would love it here!
With love
Grace x

Casa di Limoni

July 1957

Dear Catherine,
*I am so pleased that your 'Liberty' series is causing
such a stir! Did anyone ever ask who the models were
for your 'Free to Love' canvas? When we return to
England, we must all go for tea at that hotel and see if*

anyone recognises Romani and me as the subjects of the painting.

I haven't been feeling too well recently, but probably think it is the change of food and climate. I feel sick almost all the time – but especially in the morning. As you know, I hate fuss and haven't mentioned it yet to Romani. He would only worry and I don't want to bother him, because he is working so hard to liaise with the fashion house in Milan that he worked for before the war. He spends days away and leaves me to my frustration! I know that we are on the brink of a creative revolution – fashion in the 1960's was an area that fascinated me at College – and I am determined that we will get in on the ground floor, but the timing has to be exactly right. The transition from the very feminine, full-skirted, long dresses which everyone is wearing at the moment, to short, tight clothes which reveal the female body in all its glorious sexuality, needs to be handled delicately – otherwise we would be laughed out of the fashion houses of Italy and back to the sewing bees of Quintin Parva!

I am a bit tired at the moment Catherine. Write soon. Love,
Grace x

Casa di Limoni

August 1957

Dear Catherine,

Catherine, I have the most amazing news for you: I am expecting our baby! I eventually told Romani how I had been feeling, because I can't stand anything unspoken to be between us, and he whisked me off *immediately to the local doctor, who asked him a few questions in Italian and then nodded sagely, gesturing to his examination couch. He asked Romani to leave the room, but my husband shook his head and turned his back firmly. After being prodded for a while, the doctor smiled and said, 'Signor Romani, complimenti!' There then followed a rapid conversation in Italian, which I just could not understand. I really must learn this language!*

Romani looked absolutely stunned. He shook the doctor's hand and led me back, without a word, to our lemon-scented villa. We sat in the shade on the terrace and Romani held me in his arms and spoke softly to me, saying that he had never expected this. This was not quite the reaction I had expected from him as he looked so worried and I have always thought husbands were delighted when their wives become pregnant! I became more and more cross until I told him he could look a bit happier as it takes two to tango!

He still sat in silence – until I completely lost patience with him and jumped to my feet. But in one of those heart-stopping manoeuvres, where he always catches me from left-hand field, he told me that the doctor was concerned about my age (is thirty-six really too old to have a baby?) and the narrowness of my hips. And – this is where he really caught me off-balance – that if he lost me, he would lose the whole world. He just doesn't fit into any mould I have ever encountered.

How did your husband react when you told him you were pregnant, Catherine?

Write soon.

Love

Grace x

Casa di Limoni

October 1957

Dear Catherine,

Romani knew, didn't he? Almost predictably, I lost the baby two weeks ago. I was rather expecting to see a little person when I miscarried, but there was nothing, only lots of blood and strangely, very little pain. So, that's that.

Romani just held me and whispered that we can create together a fashion house that will be our legacy to the world. He also repeated again that as long as he has me, his happiness is complete.

I am glad that Charles was so pleased for you when you were expecting your daughter. As I said back in Quintin Parva, you are a unique and special person and gave me more than you will ever realise. I am fine. I really am. I think in a funny sort of way, the last few months have cleared our way for the future – does that make sense?

Sorry this is so short, Catherine, but I have work to do!

With love
Grace x

Casa di Limoni

1st January 1958

Happy New Year, Catherine!

We had a wonderful Christmas – and I hope that you did too. How is Quintin Parva? Still buried in snow and tradition? Do you know, the only thing I miss about

QP is you! My Romani was – as usual – quite correct when he said that Italy was what I needed to bring out the more unusual (don't say anything!) aspects of my character. I feel so at home here.

Of course, we saw no snow. December is the lemon gathering time and the person who owns the villa came to harvest his lemons and to bring us gifts of the products that he and his family make: limoncello, which is a sort of liqueur; and a box of lemon biscuits. He is very young and apparently inherited our villa from his uncle. He is renting it out until he and his wife-to-be can move in and make it their home. From the amount that Romani is paying, I imagine that they are stashing money away and will be able to move in soon!

We took some time off our designing for Romani to show me some of the area around Meta and Sorrento.

I am so proud of him, Catherine! I sometimes almost have to kick myself when I remember that, at college, one of my style icons of the twentieth century was Angelo Romani! Now I can see him in action, I understand why. He is tireless in putting on to paper his design vision for both men and women. He feels that men are crushed by a stereotype which leaves no opportunity for them to show their individuality in how they dress. I saw the impact that he had on the dress style of the travellers with whom he lived in Dorset. But it is when he turns his attention to women that I see his true genius. He has started to ask me to model his prototype designs. He strokes the lines and angles that he creates over my, very minimal, curves and amends his designs according to how they look on me. It is so exciting, Catherine!

Next week, Romani is travelling to Milan again, with our portfolio of designs – yes, our portfolio! He has decided that we should be known as Angelo and Grazia Romani, founders of The House of Romani. I am so unbelievably excited!

On Christmas Eve, Romani took me to Herculaneum. I'm not sure whether you know or not, but this was an old city that was destroyed when Mount Vesuvius erupted in 79 AD. Catherine, it is shocking that so many people died and their homes were destroyed! Vesuvius looks evil! Wherever you go along the coast here you see this mountain – dark, brooding, dominating the whole of the bay. It makes me shiver, and now that I have seen Herculaneum for myself, it makes me shiver even more!

We walked around the streets, looking through the windows out of which people gazed, centuries ago, on a landscape that has now changed forever. Towards the end of our visit, a small, wizened man appeared from a side alley and started to speak rapidly and at length with Romani, gesturing towards what used to be the sea shore, but is now just a bank – the sea line having moved nearly half a mile away after the eruption.

Romani looked thoughtful and eventually came over to me, explaining that the man had told him that an important new discovery had just been made, and that, for a price, he would lead us to it.

I couldn't imagine anything more moving than the devastated city where we were standing and asked Romani what could possibly be more important than the heart-breaking ruins with which we were surrounded. Romani frowned slightly and explained that the man wouldn't say precisely. He had just asked us to follow him.

Well, Catherine, the man led us rapidly back towards the boat sheds where dozens of people had died, trying to take refuge from the devastating eruption. We zigzagged down from these poignant huddles of human remains, where skeletons jostled together, trapped here forever when looking out on who knows what unimaginable horror. Probably twenty feet lower than the boat sheds, our guide turned sharply left, back towards the modern town of Herculaneum and gestured to a circular shaft in the centre of which a ladder led down to whatever he wanted to show us.

I wondered what on earth could be down the dark and distinctly uninviting hole and asked Romani whether he thought it was safe to blindly follow a stranger in this way. Romani, true to character as always, threw back his head and laughed, asking me whether my boldness had become blunted with age and I took risks no longer. I didn't deign to reply, Catherine!

Well, down the shaft we went. Strangely, the deeper we descended, the lighter the shaft became as it was lit with natural light which entered through cracks in the rock that had occurred, presumably, during the cataclysm. I felt my heart beating much faster than usual because I just did not know where we were heading. Eventually we reached the bottom of the ladder and saw a sizeable, roughly circular, entrance in front of us.

'Cos'è questo?' asked my husband. 'What is this?' Fortunately I am starting to learn some of the standard Italian phrases, otherwise I would have been completely at a loss.

'Guarda! Just look!' responded our unprepossessing guide.

So we stood, and looked.

We were at the entrance of a cave, in the centre of which was what I first took for a statue but, chillingly, soon realised was far more than that. We were looking at two people, frozen in time. A tall, muscular man encircled a slender woman with his arms and his body, trying to protect her, presumably, from the river of gas and ash which was advancing so swiftly upon their city. She was pressed close into his side – so close that it was impossible to distinguish her body from his body. Their heads lay together, cheek against cheek. It was so unspeakably sad and when I glanced at Romani I saw that he was quietly wiping away tears.

Although I could by no means understand all the guide was saying, I knew that he was explaining the story of the hidden figures. Romani listened patiently, not taking his eyes off the figures, and then curtly nodded to the guide, thanking him for showing us this discovery. He handed over some notes and clearly asked the man to leave us.

Standing in the dim grey light, gazing at the silent and tragic testimony to love, Romani asked me whether I understood what had happened to the lovers. I nodded, feeling too uncertain of my emotions to speak. But I shall remember forever what my husband said to me next. 'They died together. They are together forever – fused into one. Now I know how I shall remain with you forever, my love.' Of course I asked him what he meant, but all he would say as he pulled me closely to him was, 'You will see – pray God in the distant future.'

You see what I have married, Catherine? An enigmatic genius, to be sure!

Write soon!

Love

Grace x

Casa di Limoni

April 11th 1958

Dear Catherine,

I am so sorry to hear that you have had a bad cold. Are you sure that it was just a cold or was it actually flu? Did you call out Dr Pedder or just try to battle on alone as you always do. If you are not careful I will have to come home and boss you around and you would then feel guilty that you are stopping me from continuing to create some of the most exciting new trends that are about to hit the fashion houses of Europe! (Aren't I modest?)

My Italian is coming along really well. Romani says it is the language of love and we laughed last night at the extent of my vocabulary, which is centred around how we feel for each other and how we spend our time together. Instead of being able to say, in Italian, 'Good Morning, please may I have a loaf of bread, some cheese and half a kilo of tomatoes', I can more easily say, 'Come to bed, I love you to distraction!' What would the leader – sorry, Chair – of the Women's Institution think about that, I wonder?

On a serious note, I can now ask for food items and greet people as we walk through the town or along the coastal path to Sorrento – as well as enticing Romani to bed!

Just as well I am starting to understand the language, because Romani asked me to go with him to Milan last week to meet his contact there, Gino Franchi. What a suave, smooth operator this person is: tall and thin with slicked-back hair, black suit and the most highly-polished pair of shoes I have ever seen.

Compared with my Romani's broad shoulders and his long, naturally-styled hair and casual clothes, he looked like a shop dummy.

When Romani presented me to this character as co-founder of our fashion house – his design partner as well as his life partner – Gino regarded me arrogantly, his gaze sweeping from my hair to the hem of my gloriously full, riotously-coloured long skirt. Insolently, he asked me where exactly I had designed and showcased my work. You would have been proud of me, Catherine, when I told him that I had exhibited in London and that my first exhibition had dominated the headlines for weeks. Exactly what those headlines were, I did not detail! Then, when he went on to query my design concepts, I really went to town, telling him cooly that before I met my husband, my experience of the world in general – and of men in particular – had led to a consciously dystopian view of society, which was embodied in my unconventional, deliberately provocative, designs. But, having discovered Romani, I now see the world afresh, in all its creative richness. I ended by saying definitively that no other man I have ever encountered can hold a candle to him – either as a man, or as a designer.

After this exchange, Gino Franci started to regard me in a different light and we started to talk sensibly about how we could start to establish our presence in Milan, whilst retaining our home on, or near to, the Amalfi coast.

Travelling back to Meta, my husband kissed me lingeringly, likening me to a tigress, both beautiful and deadly. Then he took my hand in his and, as he has always done, kissed the palm, folding my fingers gently but firmly over the kiss.

I am so happy, Catherine. I love him so much.
... and I am very fond of you too!
Grace
X

Chapter 46

Grace Brabazon stood up, carefully replacing the letters she was reading in an orderly pile on the table next to her. She frequently walked over to Pedders, enjoying both the peace of the old house and the company of her fiancé. That morning, seeing once again the snow-laden sky, she had decided to take the long-awaited cache of correspondence with her to read in the seclusion and cosiness of Simon's spacious sitting room. Already she felt as if she was gradually coming to know the fiery, outspoken woman who had taken over her life, but it was the love that shone undimmed from the dusty, faded correspondence that had moved her profoundly. She was certain now that she loved Simon, but it was with a quieter, more companionable, day-to-day emotion – wildly different from the passion which blazed from the letters. Grace knelt in front of the roaring fire and poked the logs, sending a shower of sparks up the wide chimney. For the first time that year she was actively glad of the snow which still fell steadily outside, serving to isolate her from the everyday world of twenty-first century Quintin Parva, and send her back to her discovery of the other Grace who had so faithfully corresponded with Catherine Brabazon, her own mother.

Simon was seeing patients in his surgery – surely the most delightful consulting room ever, thought Grace for the hundredth time, thinking of the heavy beams, the mellow oak cupboard and doors, and the quiet, safe space in which Simon's patients shared their worries and anxieties. The oldest residents in the village had nodded and affirmed Simon's choice of surgery, assuring him that when they were children, before the foundation of the National Health Service, their parents had taken them to see Dr. Pedder in that very room. The sporadic ring of the doorbell, as villagers came and went with their typical winter complaints, had become a reassuringly mundane background to the extraordinary story which she was gradually uncovering.

Grace curled up once again in the deep, leather armchair and, with the keenest anticipation, picked up the next letter.

Casa di Limoni

13 October 1958

Dear Catherine,

I am so sorry not to have replied sooner to your last letter, but we have been so involved in the autumn/ winter fashion week that I have hardly slept – let alone written a letter.

Do you remember I explained to you that I was determined that we should be at the forefront of the mid-twentieth century fashion revolution, when women's long, full skirts were superseded by short, tight mini skirts and dresses? Well, I have news for you about this!

As I told you several letters ago, Romani and I have fallen into the habit of working together on our portfolio of designs for the next season, bouncing ideas off each other as we always do. One night in June – very near to Midsummer Day, our Wedding Anniversary – we had been working since early morning, and it was nearly midnight when Romani turned to me and held both my hands in his, spreading out my fingers as if unfurling the petals of a flower.

It is at times like this that I most wonder at my husband. I was exhausted, but he seemed to be fuelled by his creative genius. I looked back to the desperate days of my life in London when, as I have explained to you, all that kept me going was a diet of alcohol and drugs. What a contrast to the controlled energy that Romani shows. He eats, he exercises and he works, quietly but with ferocious concentration. Where my designs are still angular, almost expressing my old desire to wound and jab into attention the people who come to see my clothes, Romani's are flowing, billowing, utterly superb – embracing and enchanting the whole world, just like my husband does.

He interlaced my white fingers with his strong brown ones, remarking at the contrast. 'Such small, delicate hands, Grazia, but so full of endless creativity! See! You complete me. Two halves of the creative balance: Yin and Yang, Male and Female.' He paused for some moments, looking intently at our clasped hands, then kissed my forehead, telling me to go to bed as he had an idea that he wished to explore. Holding me close, he said, 'As always you have inspired me.'

I was so tired that, for once, I could hardly speak. I made my way upstairs to our bedroom, with windows wide open to the scent-laden night air, and slipped between the cool, white cotton sheets.

The light awoke me the next morning and I automatically turned to the space next to me, but it was empty. Yawning widely, I made my way down the uncarpeted wooden stairs to our studio which was now covered in interpretations of the hand clasp that Romani had remarked upon the previous evening. A full-skirted evening dress swirled with brown and white clasped hands, and this design formed the scalloped square neckline and hem. A suit with a pencil skirt and short jacket bore the same design, this time controlled and spare, the only softness being a snug, velvet hat which echoed the brown and white theme. It was spectacular! But what excited me most of all was the design that he was working on as I entered the room: a very short, two-toned skirt. The yin and yang of brown and white were now on a much larger scale – each representing half the front and back aspects of the skirt. At last, quite spontaneously, the revolution I had been waiting for had started. I smiled and slipped my arms around Romani's waist, tracing the outline of the design with my forefinger and whispering, 'I have been waiting for this!'

'And I have been waiting for you!' declared Romani, lifting me into his arms.

If you really were my mother, would I ever write to you like this, Catherine? I bet I wouldn't, but I am glad that I can.

With love,

Grazia X   Oops! I mean Grace! X

Casa di Limoni

28th December 1958

Dear Catherine,

I have such news for you! But first of all, are you all right? Your last letter was so short, and didn't seem to contain much news. But above all, dear Catherine, your usual energy and sense of fun just did not come across to me. Please write soon and, if you need me, I am totally serious about coming back to QP for a visit. I will never forget your kindness. We had such fun together didn't we? Painting and designing and trying to cook and going to those awful WI meetings and Mrs Busybody Hartley's sewing bees ...

Well, the main news is that our – yes, our – designs absolutely wiped the floor with those of our rival fashion houses! The newpapers and magazines have been full of the 'fresh and sensuous designs of Angelo and Grazia Romani, the dynamic founders of the new fashion house.' The short skirt which delighted me was acclaimed as a 'fashion revolution for which post-war Europe is abundantly ready' and my darling Romani was praised for having started the revolution in Italy, rather than leaving the innovation to designers in Paris or London. I am sending you a cutting from 'Vogue', which has some photographs and a long article about our 'impact on the world of fashion'.

But for me, personally, the high-spot was my latest wedding dress design. Sensuous, full, flowing and made of gossamer silk, it finally laid to rest the ghost of the jarring, aggressive concept that brought about my downfall in 2010.

On the back of this success, Romani has given me the most wonderful of surprises. When last week he announced that we deserved a day off from our hard work and media triumph, I wickedly asked if he was ill, as he never, ever, takes a rest from the passion which drives him. He laughed and simply told me to follow him down the hill to Alimuri Beach, where there is a small jetty built against the black rock of the cliffside. A boat was moored there and, smiling mysteriously, Romani jumped in and attempted to hand me down into the vessel. Of course I just ignored his proferred hand and jumped down into the small boat. I told him that I should be helping him down into the boat, as he is the senior partner in our relationship!

Well, the boat chugged steadily out from the bay towards the headland which shelters the harbour at Sorrento. We passed the town and then made our way further out to sea. Fortunately, the day was calm – I certainly would not have fancied a trip this long on a rough sea.

We sailed for about an hour and I realised that we were nearing Capri. Everyone in Meta talks about the island, calling it 'bellissima', but because we had been working so hard, I had not yet had time to visit. When we pulled into Capri harbour, Catherine, I thought immediately of you! It is so picturesque and I am sure you would love to paint it. The cliffs are steep, and little, coloured houses are perched at impossible angles on the slopes which lead down towards the shore.

Still maintaining his enigmatic silence, my husband took my hand and led me to some steps which seemed to climb vertically up the cliff. As we made our way along the worn, steep track I realised that we were surrounded by flowers and shrubs which I had not

*seen on the mainland. I stopped to smell one opulent
pink flower and, typically, Romani picked it and
threaded it into my hair which, incidentally, I am
wearing much longer – twisted up on days as hot as
the one I am writing about. After about ten minutes,
Romani untied his silk scarf and knotted it around my
eyes. He led me on, holding my hand tightly. I was
really very excited indeed by this time, but couldn't
have Romani suspecting the impact that he was having
on me, so made one of my caustic comments, asking
whether he had arranged life insurance on me because
of a sinister intention to push me off the cliff!
Infuriatingly, he said nothing but just continued to
lead me by the hand.*

*A few minutes later we stopped. Romani untied the
scarf from my eyes and, standing behind me, whispered,
'Look my love. It is ours.'*

*I read a painted, green sign, saying 'Casa degli
Fiori' – House of Flowers – and, Catherine, never was
a house so aptly named. It is a small, centuries-old,
white-painted villa, with a walled garden absolutely
brimming with flowers and an old vine which has been
trained to cover a pergola to provide shade. The house
is situated high above Capri harbour and the view
across the Bay of Naples is spectacular. As always,
Vesuvius dominates, but the speckled settlements of
Sorrento, Meta, and Naples itself break up the
undulating, green coastline, and mitigate the threat of
the volcano to a certain extent. It is utterly delightful.*

*I looked at my husband, who was smiling at me with
his usual quiet intensity, and recalled the words he had
spoken to me on our wedding day: 'One day we will
live in a house surrounded by flowers. Your senses will
open fully in the sunshine and your talent will reach*

perfection. You think these things impossible – but have faith, in me and in our future life together.'

What a magician Romani is! Conjuring beauty from out of nowhere, making dreams come true but, most improbably, causing me to fall in love with him!

Remember what I said, Catherine. Please take care and write soon!

With love
Grazia x

Chapter 47

Catherine Brabazon gazed slowly around the kitchen. The house had felt so empty since Grace and Romani had gone. The large rooms looked faded and tired – like she felt! The range was out. It had broken and she did not have any idea how it could be fixed. She recalled Grace's well-intentioned attempts at cooking, so many years ago now – the disastrous, stewed rhubarb; the grey, unappetising dough – and felt her heart constrict with loneliness. How she missed Grace's eccentric loudness and Romani's acerbic humour. Although the day was bitterly cold, she filled a glass with water from the tap and opened the larder door. She found some biscuits that looked reasonably edible and, putting them in the pocket of her long, painting overall, went upstairs and into her studio. There was, of course, no longer any need to curtain the windows as she had had to do during wartime, and the grey light shone in on the canvas on which she was working. She was painting another version of her only portrait – ever – which now was the focus of such attention in London. The inspiration for the painting was as fresh as the moment it was conceived: she recalled that pearly summer dawn when she had watched Grace, alive as never before, looking levelly at Romani, and Romani looking with an intense tenderness at Grace. In the version on which she was working, she had sublimated the emotion so that the painting was now even more abstract, more vibrant. The canvas quite simply sang with the utter absorption that the two figures had in each other.

Catherine sat down, tired by these intense memories, tired beyond imagining. She opened a drawer and took out a bundle of papers, which she had carelessly tied with string. She took out from her overall pocket the letter that she had received from Grace that morning and smoothed it carefully before adding it to the considerable number before her. She unfolded the cutting from the magazine that Grace had enclosed with her last letter and traced slowly with her paint-stained finger the beautiful laughing features of the woman who had taken her daughter's place and become infinitely dear to her. Romani was as staggeringly handsome as ever, standing with his arm lightly around Grace's shoulders. With quiet precision, she folded the paper again, slipped it into its place, and slowly tied up the bundle. She must work on the canvas in front of her again. She felt less lonely when she sought to capture the two people who had filled her big, echoing house with such love and energy. But she was so tired. Perhaps she would just rest her head on her hands for a few moments. Catherine folded her painfully thin arms, unconsciously caressing with her right hand the silver locket that she invariably wore, and rested her head on her left arm.

Slowly, Catherine's life faded. Her slender fingers lost hold on the paint brush, and the letters from Grace slipped without a sound onto the floor – the last precious connection with the woman whom Catherine had loved most in the world. The magnificent canvas stood unfinished, incomplete forever.

Chapter 48

Breathing deeply, conscious that her heart was beating much faster than usual, Grace Brabazon started to unfold the article that had been enclosed with the last letter in the bundle. Her hands were shaking so much that, at first, she dropped the fragile, much-creased fragment onto the rug.

Carefully, Grace opened the old magazine article and looked at the face of the woman who had taken over her life. She was shocked at the initial similarity between her own face and that of her namesake: oval, pale, with thick dark hair, a straight nose and a wide mouth. But whereas she was familiar with her own level gaze that shone back when she looked in a mirror – a gaze which always seemed to hold something in reserve – the woman in the black and white photograph looked at the world with a fearless challenge that, even seventy years after the picture was taken, almost made Grace recoil. She was much thinner than Grace, the angles of her face and shoulders were prominent and her small hands, enclosed by those of the man next to her, appeared fragile, almost the size of a child's. As to her partner, he was, Grace thought, utterly beautiful. With classic, finely-formed features, long curling hair, a sensuous mouth and dark eyes, none of his charisma was lost in the old, grainy print. Grace Brabazon smiled to herself as she realised that, in the Quintin Parva world of 1943 which she had inhabited, this astonishingly talented man had lived less than a mile from her own home, his life running parallel to hers.

'I'm starving, Grace!' Simon declared, throwing open the door of the drawing room. 'If I see one more QP resident demanding antibiotics for a virus, I will not be responsible for my actions!' He kissed his fiancée lightly on the forehead and stepped in front of the log fire, rubbing his hands to warm himself. When she remained immobile and silent, he asked, concerned, 'Are you all right, Grace?'

'Oh, Simon,' Grace exclaimed, impatient with herself, 'I completely forgot about lunch! I've been so involved in reading these,' she gestured to the pile of letters, 'that I completely lost track of time. Would a sandwich do?'

'Well,' laughed Simon, 'it will have to!'

Over lunch, Grace told Simon the story she had uncovered in the letters, and finally unfolded the battered *Vogue* article and handed it across the table to her fiancé.

Simon looked at it without speaking for some moments, then smiled thoughtfully. 'She looks so utterly different from the tortured girl I met in London! When I knew her, she was bent upon self-destruction, but in this picture she is utterly fulfilled.'

'So you didn't just fall in love with me because I look like her, Simon?'

Simon shook his head firmly. 'No. I've never made a secret of the fact that I was attracted to the Grace Adams I met in London, but she had a wild – almost untamed – aspect to her character that made me feel unsure and uncomfortable. I love you for your personality as well as your appearance, Grace. I love *you*, completely and comprehensively.' He came round to Grace's side of the kitchen table and put his arms around her in a warm, protective hug. 'Anyway, I look nothing like this character in the photograph! No wonder she didn't fancy me!'

Chapter 49

After lunch Simon had to make several home visits which, fortunately, he was able to do on foot as they were all local. Loading the plates and cups from lunch into the dishwasher, Grace tried hard to ground herself in the moment before making a cup of tea and curling up once again in front of the fire to complete her uncovering of the poignant story held by the bundle of faded letters.

There were just two more letters, but these were unopened, in brittle brown envelopes, curved to the shape of the bundle in which they had been wrapped for nearly seventy years. Grace looked at the date stamps. The first was dated March 1959 and the second January 1960. She hesitated before opening them, because it seemed a sort of violation to open a letter addressed to another person that had remained hidden for a lifetime. But, staring at the dusty envelopes and faded handwriting until the letters blurred, she eventually decided that it was pointless to leave them sealed and unread. Walking into the kitchen, she took a small kitchen knife from the knife block, returned to her deep leather chair and slit open the first letter.

Casa degli Fiori

5ᵗʰ March 1959

Dear Catherine,

I am really worried that I have not heard from you. I may resort to writing to Führer Hartley! Seriously, though, don't worry. I know how busy you must be, and understand how difficult it is sometimes just to find the time to stop working and to make contact with people you care for. I am guilty of that! Just look at how long it is since I wrote my last letter to you.

Well, our life is moving at the speed of light – I can't remember what that is, but I know it is fast. Romani has decided to open an atelier in Rome, rather than continue with our little design studio in Milan. Gino Franchi has not been particularly helpful. I thought he was spiteful when I first met him and he has been spreading negative rumours about our inspiration being second-hand. As if anyone could think that of Romani! So, my risk-taking, decisive husband returned last week from Milan with the words: 'That is finished!'

'A design, your journey, or February?' I quipped.

'No – our presence in Milan. We will be based in Rome from now on, Grazia.'

I told him that I thought it a lot more stimulating than Milan, but warned that I might waste good designing time visiting the Colosseum or a museum for inspiration for my next designs. Romani laughed and pulled me to him, hard. He told me that he had found the perfect place, overlooking the Parthenon and needing repair and repainting, but fitting for the foundation of the House of Romani in the city that echoes our name.

So you see, Catherine, the next months will be taken not only with designing but with decorating, so I don't think I will be able to return to QP just yet.

Take great care – and eat your rhubarb!!!
With love
Grazia X

Casa Degli Fiori

1st January 1960

Dear Catherine,

Still nothing from you. Something must be wrong!

Today is the start of a new decade – one of my favourites in terms of fashion design. In your country Mary Quant will go from strength to strength; Twiggy will become the icon of all things cool. But no-one knows this yet – only you, Romani and me!

We just have not stopped, Catherine, over the last nine months. Our studio in Rome is breathtaking! It occupies the top two stories of a Renaissance palace and there is carving and moulding and painted ceilings galore! You would love it – but I bet you would find all the cherubs as nauseating as I do!

Romani and I did all the painting ourselves – not the cherubs! – whilst at the same time pressing on with our Autumn/Winter collection for this year. Very provocative! I can just see you in some of the clothes. They are elegant and timeless – just like you! Why don't you take a holiday and come here? You could paint and Romani could feed us both – it would be just like old times.

I do miss you, Catherine.
With much love
Grazia
X

For Grace, reading the letters had raised almost as many questions as they had answered. She felt as if, to a certain extent, she had got to know the Grace who had taken her place. She had certainly become aware of the intense relationship between this woman and Romani. But concerning her mother, she had learnt only how close she and *Grazia* had become. It was a mystery who had wrapped the unopened letters with the original bundle: had it been Mrs Deniston; or Catherine herself who had not bothered to open them; or some entirely unknown third party? Had her mother answered some, or most of the letters? Why hadn't she responded to the final two?

Her head aching, Grace watched the flecks of white falling from the darkening sky.

Grace Brabazon
2015

Chapter 50

It was March and at last the snow had started to melt, so that the work on the Charles and Catherine Brabazon Memorial School could start again.

Simon's role in the community continued to develop. A vacancy on the Parish Council had arisen, as the previous Chair had found himself increasingly struggling with both his advancing age and the complexity of the issues that were laid before him. Simon was approached by the Parish Clerk as to whether he would consider applying to fill the vacancy and was unanimously voted on to the committee by the other members. At the same meeting he was asked whether he could possibly take on the role of Chair, to which he rather unwillingly agreed.

One sunny, late-March day, shortly before Easter, Grace was busy organising the delivery of tables and drawer units which had just arrived at the school. She had chosen bright primary colours – red, blue and yellow – and had bought a variety of shapes so that she could arrange the units in different formations, according to the learning taking place. In the Early Years classroom, there were just two circular arrangements of tables and a couple of dozen soft floor-cushions where the children could settle themselves comfortably to read, or talk, or sit together for 'Circle Time'. Grace was delighted with this room. It had all the softness and colour that she had yearned for in those grey wartime years when, even though she had done her best, her children still had to sit on the hard, wooden floor in a classroom painted in neutral colours.

Ever since the snow had melted, she had been busy with Annie in the school garden, which swept down to the belt of fine, mature trees on its boundary. Henry, although now five years old, had returned to some of his old puppy habits, drinking quantities of pond water and burying toys in the newly-dug earth. But despite the dog's best efforts, they had created four raised beds for vegetables and Grace had put an ornamental, wrought-iron plant support at the centre of each for climbing vegetables, such as runner beans or squash.

Grace stood up, stretching the stiffness out of her back from having knelt on the floor for longer than she had realised, arranging books and play equipment in the storage units. She smiled as she looked out over the restored school garden, remembering Alison's vibrant energy which had disappeared all too soon, as her illness took increasing hold on her. In the last months of her life, the garden had become choked with weeds, the clean edges of the flowerbeds disappearing into the untidy lawn. Grace felt as if she and Annie were honouring their friend in their thorough restoration of the garden.

Her reflections were disturbed by the chime of her mobile. It was Matthew Moore.

'Hi, Matthew. How's things?'

'Grace, are you with Simon?'

'No, sorry, he has just started afternoon surgery. Do you need him?' There was a pause, and then Grace heard Matthew take a deep and steadying breath. 'Actually, I could do with speaking to both of you together. Is there any chance of you coming over after surgery?'

'About six o'clock?'

'Yes, that will be fine.'

'Man of mystery! Can you give me a clue what this is all about?'

'Not really, Grace. Sorry. See you both about six.'

Grace frowned slightly – she had never heard Matthew so curt and business-like. Thoughtfully, she resumed her arrangement of the books and equipment in the classroom that, within six short months, would be enjoyed once again by her and the children she taught.

⊰╬⊱

'Would you like a drink?' asked Matthew Moore, more serious than Grace and Simon had ever seen him.

'I would love some tea, Matthew,' Grace responded.

'You may prefer something stronger!'

'Matthew, you are a very dear friend, but I am not in the mood for playing games,' Simon declared. 'We will have red wine if you have any, and then please could you tell us what is going on?'

Matthew turned to the old pine cupboard to the left of the fireplace and thoughtfully poured two glasses of wine from a recently-opened bottle. He handed them to his friends, then removed his glasses and rubbed his hands wearily across his eyes.

'Of course. I'm sorry.' He walked slowly over to the window, looking out at the spring dusk.

'We started work today on digging the footings in the old orchard for the extension at the back of the Early Years classroom. Unfortunately we had to fell the old apple tree – you'll remember the one which, over the years, had sunk almost to the ground – and dig up its roots. This was our poignant starting point. Poignant, because clearly it had meant a lot to someone in the past: it was the only tree to be surrounded by a seat, even though it was green with moss and too unsafe to sit upon.'

'I know about your excavations, Matthew,' laughed Simon. 'I have heard of little else from the stream of patients I have seen today. "That Doctor Moore can't be short of a pound or two! Extending that school *again!*" was one of the politest comments I have heard. What did you discover? Buried treasure?'

Matthew said nothing for several seconds. 'Something buried, certainly ... but not treasure. We found a body.'

'What!' gasped Grace and Simon, almost simultaneously.

'I phoned the police immediately, of course, and they told me that all work on the extension must cease until they have held an investigation. It was so sad,' continued Matthew, rubbing his forehead, 'the body was wrapped in a sort of canvas sheet, not even a proper wooden coffin. The workmen didn't know what they had unearthed at first – it could have been rubbish, or anything really – and so they pulled back the material quite carelessly at first. As they opened the shroud, this fell out.' He opened his desk drawer and took out a heavy, silver locket which, clearly, he had gone to some effort to clean.

All colour drained from Grace's face.

Matthew slipped open the tiny catch on the side of the engraved silver oval and opened the locket to reveal the two photogrphs that it contained: one, the kind features of a middle-aged man, the other the dark hair, straight nose and wide mouth of Grace herself.

'I just had to speak to you two about this, rather than handing this over to the police. The resemblance between you and this photograph is remarkable, Grace, and it would have seemed a sort of betrayal not to speak to you first. Is this a picture of a relation of yours? Could the body that we discovered under that ancient apple tree be a member of your family?'

Grace swallowed with difficulty, before replying quietly: 'The photograph is of me; and the body, I believe, could be that of my mother.'

Chapter 51

There was no choice: they had to share Grace's strange history with Matthew. At first he thought they were joking – although such a jest would have been in very bad taste and totally at odds with his friends' characters. He then became incredulous, even though the details of the story started to make more sense of the way in which Grace had first introduced herself to him. As an academic, Matthew checked and revisited points of detail until, in the early hours of the morning, he was finally satisfied that the whole thing was not some bizarre and elaborate fiction.

Gazing at the last embers of the log fire in his study fireplace, Matthew finally gave his advice, carefully avoiding any direct reference to the body as being that of Catherine Brabazon. 'We must wait whilst the police complete their investigations. Why on earth anyone should be buried here, in non-consecrated ground, is a mystery indeed. But whilst the police grind through their lines of enquiry, perhaps there are discoveries that we can make here in the village. Old memories linger long in village lore. Surely some of the oldest residents of Quintin Parva must remember the post-war years – Catherine Brabazon was a public figure, as well as a resident of the village.'

Grace had been silent for much of the evening. She had experienced a series of flashbacks of her time with her mother, and recalled events that she had not consciously thought of for years. She remembered Catherine's kindness towards the pony that they had rescued; her unfailing acceptance of anything and everything that she and her father had done together; her complete lack of jealousy concerning the close, intuitive relationship that Grace had had with Charles Brabazon; and, above all, her mother's extraordinary talent and her self-containment. Without articulating the need to do so, she had handed over most of the conversation to Simon and Matthew.

At Matthew's suggestion, Simon sat and rapidly reviewed his most elderly patients. By this time, almost everyone in the village had decided that they would sign on at his practice, as Simon was knowledgeable, had a sense of humour and, above all, was easily available. After some time he said: 'One of the oldest patients I have, who still lives in the village, is Bert Smithson who is seventy-eight. You will remember how supportive he was at our first public meeting concerning our school. Then there is Marianne Hartley whom I visit in the retirement home. She is very elderly – ninety-four, I believe, but in remarkable health.'

'Well, try those two first of all, Simon,' urged Matthew. 'Just gently introduce the subject of Mrs Brabazon and see if either of these people can throw any light on her last resting place.'

Grace looked levelly at the two men. 'You know, one of the things that I have found so unutterably sad since I awoke in the twenty-first century is that, although my father is well-commemorated in the village, both in the church and on the plaque by our entrance door, my mother seemingly disappeared without trace. There is no mention of her anywhere. That is one of the reasons I have called our school "The Charles *and Catherine* Brabazon Memorial School". It seemed as if it was the only way to keep her memory alive – apart from her professional reputation as a painter, of course, but that has always seemed so impersonal.'

'Is there any sort of clue in the letters written by her daughter, or rather the person who took your place, Grace?' asked Matthew.

'Not really,' refleced Grace. 'The letter-writer was concerned about my mother's health, but there is nothing definite.'

'Well, it looks as if the first port of call is to talk to Bert and Marianne, Simon. And I will check the parish records to see whether there is any clue there. What is the date of the last letter written to Catherine?' Matthew asked Grace.

'Well, the last letter that had been opened was dated 28th December 1958. But there were two further letters, both still in their envelopes.'

'Right. At least that gives us a starting point. And now, bedtime for all of us! I feel as if my brain has been turned inside out by our conversation tonight. I have always thought that research, that discovering historical precedents, could solve most mysteries, but tonight all my preconceptions have been blown wide open.'

⊰⊱⊱

It was freezing in the vestry. Matthew had telephoned the vicar on the pretext that he needed access to the post-war church records of the baptisms, marriages and burials in the village as part of a local history project he was undertaking with his oldest children.

The Reverend David Tullimore rubbed his plump, white hands together to ease the numbness in his fingers. He had unearthed the records relating to the rites of passage of Quintin Parva residents from 1945 until 1970, and arranged the dusty, faded-blue volumes on the vestry table. 'Here we are, Doctor Moore: hatches, matches and dispatches! As I am sure you will appreciate, I can't let these records leave the church premises, so I'm afraid that you will have to peruse them here – despite the cold!'

'Is there any chance of a heater of some description?' queried Matthew, shivering slightly.

'Well, with the parish share being the size it is, every penny counts, I'm afraid.'

'I will, of course, be making a donation to parish funds for the privilege of accessing these historical records,' Matthew assured him.

Sitting as close as he dared to the ancient single-bar electric fire that the vicar had unearthed from the undercroft, it wasn't long before Matthew had reached December 1957. With great anticipation, he opened the register to start the New Year: 1958. It had not been a good year for the residents of Quintin Parva. Matthew had noted that, on average, only two or three people passed away every year but, flicking to the total at the end of 1958, he noted that eight people had died during that year. Each entry gave the name, date of birth and date of death of each deceased person, but no cause of death.

Matthew methodically turned the pages. He was finding it increasingly difficult to decipher the small, crabbed writing of the incumbent of the time in the fading light of the bitterly cold March day. He could see no mention of Catherine Brabazon and was just turning the final page relating to 1958 when he felt, rather than saw, a difference in the texture of the musty page he was turning. One entry for a 'Jemima Carr' born in 1880, who had died on 30th December 1958, seemed to be written on a double thickness of paper. Matthew took out his phone and switched on its torch-light. Sure enough, a sliver of paper, exactly the same size as the rectangular box in which the details of the deceased person were recorded, had been stuck into the register.

Matthew heard the vicar moving around outside the vestry. It was clear that he didn't entirely trust Matthew with his parish records and was occupying himself in the cold, shadowy church by straightening hymn books and hassocks, and removing dead flowers from the displays, whilst humming fragments of hymn tunes under his breath. Gingerly, Matthew opened his penknife and slipped the finest blade under one corner of the rectangle of thick paper. As he had hoped, the glue had lost some of its adhesive properties over the last sixty years and had become brittle, so it was a relatively easy task to loosen, and then lift, the tiny piece of paper from the Register.

Hardly daring to look, Matthew took a deep breath and read:

Catherine Brabazon	3rd December 1895	28th December 1958

He replaced the slip of paper in the Register, placing it lightly over the entry it had concealed and leaving the book open at that page. 'David, I think I will have to call it a day,' he called. 'I really can't see very clearly anymore.'

'Oh, right you are, Doctor Moore, I trust … Oh, thank you for your generosity!' Matthew slipped two twenty-pound notes into his hand and deliberately nudged the open register on the table, causing the slip of paper which he had loosened to move.

As Matthew had intended, David Tullimore saw the movement immediately. 'What have we here?' he frowned, picking up the small rectangle of paper and pedantically examining the register.

'It appears to have been stuck over this entry,' replied Matthew, indicating the line relating to Catherine Brabazon. 'Why would anyone have done this, David?'

The vicar shook his head, causing his double-chin to wobble slightly. 'I really don't know,' he admitted. 'Let me find the burial and cremation certificates. Perhaps we can find a clue there.' He went over to a filing cabinet and unlocked it, flicking through the section in the third drawer which appeared to relate to the deaths of the village residents. '1958. There should be – he flicked to the total recorded in the register at the end of the year – eight certificates in all. Here we are.'

David Tullimore returned to the vestry table with a large brown envelope and laid out, in a very orderly manner, the certificates which it contained. 'What a mystery: just eight, and no mention of Catherine Brabazon, which would have made the total nine, of course.' He thoughtfully stroked his chin, gazing at the musty, faded certificates, as if somehow he could solve the problem by sheer concentration. 'I just cannot understand this, Doctor Moore. I will pray about what we have discovered this evening. I do not like mysteries like this!' The young vicar carefully gathered up the certificates and opened the brown envelope to return them to their resting place.

Matthew was disappointed. He had felt as if he were on the verge of discovering something, at least, about the circumstances surrounding the death of his friend's mother and was just turning away, his shoulders hunched in resignation, when he heard a sharp exclamation.

'Wait a minute – there is another envelope in here!' declared the vicar dramatically. 'And it has the diocesan seal.' Carefully, David Tullimore opened the envelope, with the broken seal of the then Bishop of Salisbury, took out a sheet of thick cream paper and smoothed it open.

Both men read the bleak contents of the note in silence:

It is the final decision of the Bishop of Salisbury
that the mortal remains of Catherine Brabazon
may not be buried in consecrated ground
within the purlieu of the church at
Quintin Parva
for the reason that
she took her own life.

+

1st February 1959

Chapter 52

'There we are, Miss Hartley, bet that didn't hurt at all.' Simon put the syringe which had contained the flu vaccine into the medical waste compartment of his bag and carefully rolled down the old lady's sleeve.

'When you get to my age, a little prick on the arm isn't worth worrying about,' retorted Marianne Hartley. 'Whilst you are here, would you care for some tea?'

Simon automatically looked at his wristwatch, seeing which his patient sighed and sat down again resignedly.

'Don't worry. I know how busy you are,' said the old lady, reaching for her reading glasses and book.

'Miss Hartley, I'm sorry, it was purely an automatic gesture. We medics are governed by time: surgery opening times; the time it takes to travel for home visits; the time I can allocate for each patient I see. I would love some tea!'

'Excellent,' remarked Ginny Hartley's formidable daughter. 'I hate this novel anyway! All to do with a young woman whose imagination is stronger than her virtue, and a 'hero' who is utterly insipid! Rubbish!'

Simon laughed and chatted about village matters, whilst his companion carefully made tea and opened a box of chocolate biscuits. After several minutes had passed, he felt that there was an opportunity to try to move the conversation around to Catherine Brabazon. 'Quintin Parva really does have its share of the most interesting characters,' he observed, munching on a biscuit.

Marianne Hartley nodded. 'My mother was one of the most notable, you know.'

Simon raised an inquisitive eyebrow without speaking.

'She established a branch of the Women's Institute in the village just before the war and remained its Chair until her death.'

'Remarkable!' commented Simon. 'And when was that?'

'In 1963,' Marianne responded philosophically. 'I took over then.'

Of course you did, thought Simon to himself, diligently eating another biscuit and wondering how on earth he could move the review of memorable people smoothly around to his fiancée's mother. And then, unbelievably, Marianne Hartley gave him the opening he needed.

'Another interesting couple were the Brabazons, you know.'

'Really?'

'Yes.' The old lady stopped stirring sugar into her second cup of tea and looked into the middle distance. 'I am so glad that your young lady has decided to call her school "The Charles and Catherine Brabazon Memorial School." It keeps the old memories alive in an increasingly vapid world.' She was almost talking to herself now, reminiscing about times that were, Simon suspected, more real to her than the stultifying existence that she now led in the nursing home.

'They were an oddly-matched couple. The Reverend was kindness itself, always involved in the village and the school, and loved by everyone. His wife was aloof, remote. The only time she really mixed with the rest of us was when she, her daughter and Mr Romani got involved in teaching us how to sew and make our own clothes. Mr Romani – ah, now *he* would have been a perfect hero for a novel! It was quite a mystery where he came from ... but he soon became the best thing that the village had known since the start of the war. He became Mrs Brabazon's butler – for years. The village thought that something distinctly fishy was going on, but he lived in a flat above the old stables and then, when the war was over, he and Miss Brabazon got married. Now *she* was a difficult person ...'

Simon hardly dared breathe, and was certainly not going to interrupt the flow of memories that the old lady was sharing with him.

'She was one of the best teachers our village school had ever known, but then, after her father, Reverend Brabazon, was killed and she had her accident, she changed completely! My mother found her very difficult. Rude and lacking in respect for her elders – that's how my mother described her.'

Simon nodded gently, but inside his feelings were in turmoil. If he had needed any additional proof of the unaccountable transposition of souls, or character, or identity – however one wished to describe it – between the woman he loved and the tortured individual he had known in London, this eye-witness account gave it in abundance. The words that the old lady had just used were an exact description of the young woman he had

334

known in London. She had been almost invariably rude and nearly always lacking in respect for the whole world, young and old alike. Once again, Simon wondered at the alchemy that Angelo Romani had worked in her life, shown so clearly in the faded photograph unearthed in the bundle of letters. Where there had been aggression, hurt and distrust, Romani's love had created tranquillity, trust and fulfilment. A miracle indeed!

The old lady was now completely lost in her memories, as she continued her story. 'Before my mother persuaded her to support the village through the activities of the Women's Institute, Mrs Brabazon spent most of her time in the vicarage, in that studio of hers, painting great big pictures that people still pay a fortune for. She went very private again when her daughter and Mr Romani went off to Italy!'

She fell silent again, and this time Simon interjected gently, 'How do you mean, private?'

'We hardly ever saw her. She only came down to the shop every few weeks – I just don't know what she lived on. She didn't have milk or bread delivered ...'

'Did she go to live in Italy with her daughter?' asked Simon disingenuously.

The old lady shook her head vehemently. 'No. She died. The authorities reckoned she deliberately starved herself to death, but most of us villagers believed that she died of a broken heart – either that, or had simply forgotten to eat. Criminal it was, that she wasn't buried next to her husband. They just dug a hole in the orchard, under the apple tree that was her favourite. Her daughter did come back, but only after her mother had died. The whole thing had been a disgrace for the village and people were either too embarrassed or too ashamed to discuss the matter. No-one had ever been buried outside the churchyard before and the vicar wouldn't even *see* Miss Brabazon – or rather Mrs Romani as she then was. She didn't stay long.'

So that was it! Only sixty-five years ago, thought Simon, and yet the way in which 'the authorities' had treated the remains of this talented, lonely woman after her death was almost mediaeval in its barbarity. Unable to force down any further food, because what he had just heard had really moved him, he gradually turned the subject to the mundane again and, ten minutes later, made his departure.

⊰⊹⊱

As he had expected, his news – although broken very carefully to Grace – brought about the uncontrollable tears that, as a doctor, he was almost relieved to see.

'That's terrible, Simon,' sobbed Grace. 'My mother never thought about food. She became so immersed in her painting that nothing else existed for her. My father used to call it being "Lost in the World of Art". At least your glamorous friend from your London days did eventually come home to see her – although it was a bit late then, wasn't it? Why didn't she come earlier, when she suspected that things weren't right with my mother?'

'Grace, you don't know the circumstances of her life in Italy. You can't possibly criticise her for something you don't fully understand.' Simon hugged her closer to him and gently kissed her hair. He brought out the second, white, ironed handkerchief of the day and started to try to wipe away her tears.

'You are the only man I know who still uses proper hankies!' Grace spluttered, half a laugh and half a sob. 'I just don't know what I would do without you, you lovely, old-fashioned, silly man.'

Grazia Romani
2015

Chapter 53

Grace – Grazia as she now invariably thought of herself – turned her gaze from the view that she knew almost as well as the features of her beloved husband to her iPad and flicked on the news stream. The glossy world of the super-rich, enticingly displayed in *Vogue, Elle* and *Harper's Bazaar* e-magazines stood in curious juxtaposition with the monotone banality of the *Dorset Echo*. Grazia had never quite been able to forget the limited expectations and narrow horizons of Quintin Parva. After all, it was there that she had met the man who had filled her life. She idly opened the latest edition of the newspaper, expecting to see a report on some prize-winning produce or village show success. Instead, she saw something that set her heart racing: the timeless beauty of Catherine Brabazon's unforgettable painting, *Free to Love*. Once again, she saw Romani as he had been when she had first met and loved him: spare, intense, beautiful. Her hand quickly went to the ring finger of her left hand and pressed the rings there into her right palm until they hurt. Tears filled her eyes as she read the article that followed.

Body of Famous Artist found in Orchard

The body exhumed from the orchard of The Old Vicarage Preparatory School, Quintin Parva, was last week confirmed by Dorset Police to be that of Catherine Brabazon, acclaimed mid-twentieth century artist. Decades after the Church's refusal to allow her body to be buried in consecrated ground, her remains were today finally laid to rest in the churchyard next to those of her husband, Charles Brabazon. The painting shown above is one of her most famous, painted towards the end of the war, and now in a private collection in London. The artist was renowned for her huge, semi-abstract canvasses.

Dr Matthew Moore, who discovered the body during works to dig the footings for an extension to his successful private school, commented: 'It's all terribly tragic. This poor lady was one of the foremost artists of her day and, quite literally, faded away following the death of her husband and her daughter's subsequent marriage and relocation abroad. How the Church, less than seventy years ago, could deal in such a barbaric way with someone so obviously vulnerable, is astonishing.'

The Rev David Tullimore conducted the service, which was attended by a small group of elderly villagers, together with Dr Moore, Ms Annie Adams and her niece, Grace Adams, soon to be the Headteacher of the new village school. Dr Simon Patterson, Miss Adams' fiancé and Chair of Governors of the new village school, also attended. Refreshments were served in the village hall following the interment.

Grazia sighed and looked again at the rings on her left hand. Her wedding ring was now a mere sliver of gold: she had worn it for sixty-five years without ever having removed it and Romani's mother had worn it for who knew how many years before that. But above the wedding ring was a more recent band of heavy gold which held a stone of deep brown, flecked with gold. Automatically, Grazia kissed the stone and turned the ring to settle it again on her slender finger, before impatiently brushing away the tears that stubbornly insisted upon filling her eyes – for the man she had adored and the woman to whom she had probably been the closest on earth. Slowly, she re-read the article.

Grace Brabazon
2015

Chapter 54

It was the 1st May. For once the weather lived up to the layers of tradition that have built up around the day since pagan times. Grace and Simon sat together in the orchard of Pedders. A thrush was singing its gentle, evening song and Grace had drawn her knees up tightly to her chest, leaning her back against the heavily blossomed apple tree just outside the kitchen window. She had sat silently ever since they had come out into the fragrant, early-summer evening.

Quietly, Simon moved closer to Grace and pulled her to him. 'What are you thinking?' he asked.

'Well, pretty obviously, about our wedding. It is only seven weeks away, after all. But I was actually also thinking about the interviews tomorrow for the teacher of the junior class. I should really have done something about the advertisement earlier in the year, but with one thing and another ...' Grace gazed up into the pink and white laden branches, remembering that other apple tree under which her mother had lain, forgotten, for over sixty years. She gently extricated herself from Simon's arms and stood up, stretching hard, as if to rid herself of the almost unbearable thought.

They had received only five applications for the post, which had been advertised four weeks earlier, and had dismissed three almost immediately. One was from a highly-qualified male teacher, who had taught in the private sector all his life, but was suffering from increasing ill-health. Reading his application, which was the first that Grace opened after the closing date, she groaned and passed the CV and letter to Simon. 'He sounds like a reincarnation of Ivan Miles! Everything he says is stale, second-hand and pompous,' she declared in despair. 'I hope they are not all like this!'

The second and third discarded applications were from middle-aged women teachers, who wanted to return to their profession after having raised their families. Both were local, and stressed the convenience of the post to their domestic situations, rather than embracing the vision of the new school which Grace and Simon had carefully set out, both in the advertisement and the information which they had sent to candidates. This vision was to *actively engage the children at all times and lead them to see learning in everything around them*. Grace just could not see in these lacklustre applications the innovation and passion that she believed were essential for her school to thrive.

Hope was fading fast that there would be anyone suitable to invite for interview, but then she had opened the remaining two applications. The first was from a newly-qualified teacher who had just successfully completed her probationary year. Her energy exploded from her letter of application. She expressed her belief in active, relevant learning that was at the heart of the school vision and hoped that she *'would be able to discuss her educational beliefs further at interview.'*

Grace had leapt up and whooped with joy, dancing around the other side of the table at which she and Simon were seated and giving him a hard hug. 'This is more like it – phew!'

The final application was intriguing. It was measured, almost understated, and came from a woman in her early thirties who had '*partially completed her newly-qualified teacher year*'. Grace read and re-read the covering letter which ended: '*... teaching is my life. The natural world holds fascination and learning in its every aspect: a single flower can lead the enquiring mind from the contemplation of beauty to pollination, and on to poetry. It would be a privilege to be allowed to engage the minds of the older children in the Brabazon Memorial School in order to ensure that, whatever the future holds, they have self-esteem, respect for themselves and others and engage in the community to make it a better place for themselves and their peers.*'

'Right, Simon,' she announced decisively, 'I think that we should interview Natasha King, who has just completed her first year of teaching; and Tania Martin, who clearly regards teaching as a vocation and, quite frankly, intrigues me. I am certain that a story lies behind why she has only "partially completed" her probationary year.'

⊰║▷

'And I have seen for myself just what an impact the government initiatives have had upon raising attainment,' pronounced Natasha King.

'So,' continued Grace, trying to draw out the candidate's approach to the rural context of the school, 'if you have in your care the children of farmers, of domestic workers and people who run shops in the towns nearby, what would you expect of them when they leave the school, and your class, at the end of Year Six?'

Almost without hesitation, Natasha replied, 'Well, they would have to be performing highly in numeracy and literacy, but that goes without saying. In my last class, a straight Year Six group of children, I managed to get ninety-five percent of my children to attain level four and above. It was the best results that the school had ever achieved.'

'And was it not possible for you to stay on at your last school?'

With only a flicker of hesitation, Natasha responded, 'No – and actually, I think that if one is ambitious in the teaching profession, one needs to have planned moves early in one's career.'

'Could you give us more details about how you would devise a balanced and appropriate curriculum for our children here in Quintin Parva?'

'Well, I *could,* Miss Adams, but if one wishes to ensure that one's school leads in the field of attainment, then the consistent emphasis must be on literacy and numeracy.'

'Thank you, Natasha, you have given us much to think about. I will telephone you with our decision this evening.' Grace stood up and extended her hand to the well-groomed young woman.

'If you do decide to appoint me, you won't regret it,' was the candidate's parting comment.

'Oh Simon!' moaned Grace, holding her head in her hands. 'What a product of the modern teacher training system! She can't see beyond levels of attainment. She would be running her class like a production line if we were to appoint her.'

Simon looked up from the references for Natasha King that he was perusing again.

'I wholeheartedly agree,' he affirmed. 'Just listen to this: "*Miss King has an unremitting zeal for driving her children to go above and beyond expectations ... her ambition and focus are relentless.*" How could we possibly invite such a force into the heart of Quintin Parva?'

'How indeed! Not much in the reference about empathy, gentleness, or her understanding of children who have additional needs! And her parting shot – that we would not regret appointing her – was almost like a veiled threat, wasn't it? The implicit corollary being if we *don't* appoint her, we *will* regret it!' Grace shuddered.

⊰⊱⊰

'Before we start, Miss Adams, may I clarify something for you?' Tania Martin, small, neat and composed, had just taken her seat opposite Grace and Simon. Grace had not even had time to ask her first question. 'The reason I was unable to complete my probationary year of teaching was that I had a breakdown. The school I was working in was under very considerable pressure to improve and all the energies of the senior leadership team were directed towards this. They ... were unable to give me the support I needed in my first year of teaching, so I would quite understand if you do not wish to continue the interview in the light of what I have just told you.'

Miss Martin looked to be on the point of standing up in order to leave, but Grace hastily gestured for her to sit down again. 'Tania, I really appreciate your honesty and openness and thank you for explaining this to us both. I'm so sorry to hear about your unhappy experience, but this sort of thing is much more common than perhaps you realise, so please do not feel at a disadvantage. I'm very interested to hear more about the approaches to teaching and learning which you outlined in your letter. Could you explain why this particular post appealed to you, please?'

'Of course, Miss Adams – and thank you.'

Tania Martin visibly relaxed, smiled, and in doing so her whole demeanour changed. Instead of being taut and immobile, her features softened and her eyes shone, as she began to talk animatedly of what clearly meant so much to her. 'The opportunity of working in the heart of a community, at the very beginning of a venture such as this, which aims to bring the highest quality education to all learners, is simply irresistible to me. My father was a miner in South Wales and, when the pit closed, he was unable to find alternative employment. He had given his all to his work and, when that ceased, he was unequipped to move on in his life. It was at that point that I decided that there was only one job I wanted to do – to teach, in order to open doors to young people who, otherwise, would be as lost as my father was. Teaching is my life. I am not interested in management opportunities, I just long to have the opportunity to change lives through education.'

Grace found that tears had come to her eyes at the frank and heartfelt answer which Tania Martin had given. Her honesty threw into stark relief the staleness of the attainment-centred responses of the previous candidate.

The rest of the interview continued in similar vein and, after shaking hands with the small, unassuming figure and closing the door of the classroom in which she and Simon had conducted the interviews, Grace could not contain her joy. 'She is *perfect,* Simon! She sounds like me seventy years ago, before this unbelievable government made education a political pawn. She …'

'Shh, Grace, she is only just outside the door!' Simon laughed. 'If she hears you making comments like that, she will demand that you re-write our salary scale!'

'Are we unanimous then?'

'We are unanimous.'

Chapter 55

The phone calls were made and the letter offering Tania Martin the post of Junior teacher had been sent. Tania had been almost speechless as she stammered her thanks, whereas Natasha King had curtly dismissed the carefully-prepared feedback from Grace, telling her abruptly that she had another interview at a 'highly-regarded town school, which recognised considerable early talent through a firmly-established promotion structure.'

Grace leant back at her desk and closed her eyes. She felt the low, late beams of the sun striking through the wide-open windows, caressing her face with light and warmth, and breathed in deeply the sweet scent of the flowers and shrubs that she and Annie had planted and pruned and cultivated with such love and care. She felt that here, at this moment, she was poised between past and present, able to reflect and to anticipate in equal measure.

She thought of herself in wartime, working in this very room, the unwilling colleague of a man for whom she had no respect, and shook her head slightly as she relived the hollow feeling of desperation when he had sacked her. She went on to run through the tragic and extraordinary events which had followed: her father's death and her head injury which, unaccountably, had catapulted her nearly seventy years forward into Grace Adams' life in the twenty-first century. She smiled gently as she thought of Simon, his patient faithfulness and his unfailing support and love for her, as she had gradually realised her dream of once again establishing a primary school in the village.

All was still and immensely peaceful. She had worked late, aiming to tidy the paperwork and complete the administrative tasks that had already landed on her desk, so that she and Annie could spend the following day in Salisbury, trying on their wedding outfits – hopefully for the final time before the day itself. She was tired, but so very happy and fulfilled, anticipating the quiet, village wedding that she and Simon had planned, for they had both decided that everything should be as simple as possible. Annie had insisted that she should do the catering as Grace and Simon's wedding present, adding that it was either that or organic vegetable boxes for the rest of the year. Matthew was adamant that he should provide the champagne for the wedding breakfast, but Grace was absolutely firm that the venue had to be the village hall, rather than anywhere more upmarket. Flowers were to be chosen from what was in season and growing in the gardens of Rose Cottage or the school, or along the hedgerows of Quintin Parva.

Gradually, Grace became aware of a noise that was intruding upon the silence of the quiet summer evening. It was almost like the drone of a bee, and soon Grace realised that it must be one of the light aircraft that flew from the small local airfield, where air traffic had recently shown a sharp increase. Simon, as Chair of the

Parish Council, had received a steadily increasing trickle of complaints from people who lived in and around the village concerning the noise pollution and potential danger from the small, unstable planes. Then another sound cut across her reverie – a light rap on the door of the school, which she ran to answer. It was Annie.

'Come along, dear, tea is ready. We can eat it in the garden, I thought, and then take Henry out for his last walk of the day. He has been bringing me every available toy in his toy basket and dropping them enticingly at my feet in order to galvanise me into action! Let me help you shut up shop – it's seven o'clock and you surely must have finished by now.'

Both women walked companionably through the school, closing windows, checking doors and chatting about their shopping trip on the following day.

'Could we possibly spare five minutes before tea to double-check on the number of vases in the village hall, Annie?' asked Grace. 'I really need to start having definite numbers in mind for the quantity of flowers that we need and it's skittles night tonight, so we can just sneak in quietly and check the storage cupboard.'

'If you insist, dear!' sighed Annie, with mock resignation.

Grace locked the school and set the alarm before they walked across the road and down the slight incline to the village hall. They were just about to enter the building when the background hum of the light aircraft increased and became insistent, then intermittent. Both Annie and Grace turned swiftly to identify where the noise was coming from and saw a small plane spiralling inexorably down towards the village. Grace gasped, as she realised that it was heading almost directly towards the school and instantly recoiled as she remembered the damage inflicted on the same building two generations ago, and the incredible bravery of her father as he puffed his way to rescue Ivan Miles.

Grace was unable to move, so horribly clear was the parallel between the past tragedy which she held in her mind and the present accident which she felt was about to happen. The skittles players had left their game and were lined up behind Grace and Annie, horrified onlookers, as the small plane bucketed and dipped over the school roof and past Rose Cottage. Grace assumed that the pilot had some measure of control over the aircraft and was trying to avoid hitting either building, but, fulfilling her worst nightmare, some seconds later there was a sickening crash.

⊰)|(⊱

Simon Patterson had just finished his late surgery. He yawned and took off his spectacles, rubbing his tired eyes, before heading across the central hall of his rambling old house into the kitchen, intending to make some tea. He thought he would just have a sandwich and then drop round to Rose Cottage to chat to Grace and Annie about the subject which inevitably dominated every conversation at the moment: the wedding. Simon, too, had opened all windows possible on this glorious June day and the old house was flooded with sweet, fresh air and the fragrance of summer flowers. Consequently, he too became aware of the drone of the light aircraft engine, becoming louder, then faltering, then stalling altogether. Concerned as always about anything that could possibly imply tragedy for the human race which, as a doctor, he had sworn to protect and nurture, he looked out of his kitchen window to ascertain exactly what was happening. Gazing across the intervening gardens towards the direction from which the sound was coming, he realised, with a weight like lead descending to his stomach, that it was coming from the direction of the school. He narrowed his eyes as he saw the small light aircraft spiralling down towards the building, where he knew Grace had been working late. Without further coherent thought, he ran out of his front door and along the street, past the village hall, just in time to see a spiral of black smoke erupting from the school garden.

In an agonising replay of the incident that had killed her father, Grace saw Simon racing along the road towards the school and instantly her shocked inaction disappeared. 'Simon,' she shouted, 'Simon! I'm here.'

'Oh Grace, thank God!' exclaimed her fiancé, hugging her close to him. 'But tell me, did the pilot escape – bail out in some way?'

Wordlessly, Grace shook her head.

'Then I must go, my darling. He may still be in the plane.' And with that Simon gave her one last kiss and sprinted over the road and down the passage at the side of the school to the site of the crashed plane.

Grace felt that she just couldn't bear it. To see her father run, all those years ago, to save another and now to see the man she loved and was to marry in a few short weeks' time, taking an almost identical path, was terrible. Annie put her arms firmly around Grace, who was shivering uncontrollably. The volume of smoke increased and suddenly a loud explosion shook the silence of the sleepy village. The only differences between the scene that was unfolding so horrifically before Grace on that June evening and the desperate, explosion and light-filled winter evening which took her father's life, were the season and the absence of shrapnel shattering the brick on the school wall and the peace of the village. Grace was beside herself.

'You stay here,' Annie commanded, uncharacteristically firm, holding her tightly as the skittle players ran towards the school.

Grazia Romani
2015

Chapter 56

Grazia Romani was restless. The heat always made her long for change. Fundamentally, the essence of her character had remained the same as she had aged, and she was as unconventional and outspoken as she had been at thirty. Grazia had just returned to Capri from a visit to the Romani atelier in Rome, where she rigorously scrutinised the quality of the designers' work and discussed the latest trends with her CEO. The designers and staff of the House of Romani wondered at the tall, elegant ninety-four-year-old, whose energy seemed relentless and creativity inexhaustible. Grazia's thick hair was now snow-white and she wore it coiled up and back, away from her face. Far from ageing her, the colour of her hair gave her appearance even more impact. Her features were still delicate and chiselled, although fine lines showed the pattern of her lifelong emotions. Her generous mouth almost always held a half-smile, the result of having been adored by someone who had filled her life with joy for nearly seventy years.

It was hot, and she sipped an aperitif made from a mixture of chilled prosecco and limoncello, a drink that she and Romani had made their own on the long summer evenings when they had laughed and talked and loved in the House of Flowers. On more than one occasion, Romani had recalled her sarcastic comments in the early days of their relationship, and this had made their wit sharper and their interaction more acute.

Memories of her life with Romani were never very far from her mind, especially when she was alone. She sipped her drink and smiled, remembering, remembering …

'Do you recall, my love, when I was penniless and you cruelly told me that you only wanted to marry me for my money?'

'Well, you always thought you were God's gift to women! That had to stop!'

'And do you remember my response?'

'Yes. You said "One day, my love, you will remember those words which you now speak in jest. One day we will live in a house surrounded by flowers."'

Reluctantly, Grazia pulled herself back to the present – the lonely, hot, restless present.

What on earth was going on in Dorset, she wondered to herself. Decades of sleepy nothingness, and then huge drama! First of all, the shocking discovery of Catherine Brabazon's body in the vicarage orchard; then a plane crash that had nearly destroyed the village school, only a few short weeks before it was due to reopen, and the heroic rescue of the unconscious pilot by the Chair of Governors. Perhaps, somehow, she ought to arrange to visit Quintin Parva once again. It would be hard, she thought, to see once more the places where she and Romani had met, so long ago; to relive the intensity of feeling that she had experienced – still experienced – for her unique and charismatic husband. Yes, it would be very hard.

In a gesture that had already become habitual, she turned the thick, gold band on her left hand, kissed the stone, and cradled it in her palm.

Grace Brabazon
2015

Chapter 57

It was exactly sixty-five years since the Midsummer Day when Grace Adams and Angelo Romani had walked together out of the west door of Quintin Parva church and surveyed the golden tranquillity of the Dorset landscape. Today – the 21st June 2015 – it was the turn of Grace Brabazon and Simon Patterson to unconsciously retrace their footsteps and actions. Simon had been treated for smoke inhalation and moderate burns at Salisbury hospital, in the bed next to the pilot he had rescued and, on the day following the plane crash, Grace and Annie had sat together at his bedside, rather than trying on their wedding outfits as intended. Now, on their wedding day, apart from a bandaged right hand and new glasses, Simon was the same as ever – calm, capable and kind – but Grace was radiant.

Grace had known for some time that she loved Simon, but it was only when she saw him, selflessly running into danger in order to save someone else, that she had realised just how much he meant to her. When he had emerged from the school grounds, covered in oily, black, smoke residue, retching and coughing, she realised that she had been fulfilled by the bizarre transposition of lives with another woman, not only because of the fresh opportunity to succeed professionally, but because she had met a man whom she loved deeply and steadily.

⊰╫╫⊱

There was no question of having a honeymoon. Although the opening of the school was two full months away, Grace and Tania had arranged to meet at regular intervals throughout July and August to work together on the curriculum and policies that needed to be in place. Simon was busier than ever in his Surgery, and in his capacities as Chair of School Governors and of the Parish Council.

Simon and Matthew also met regularly and had drafted the Governor policies of the school. They had by that time recruited a full complement of governors which they felt was representative of the different sectors of the community – something they both, with Grace, believed to be of paramount importance. David Tullimore had proved a valuable colleague, working with them closely on the provision of Religious Education and Assemblies in school; and Andrew Duncan, who represented the current generation in the long line of village stone-masons, joined as Community Governor.

Over dinner each evening, Grace and Simon shared the successes and frustrations of their respective days as time ticked steadily away, getting ever nearer to 4th September, the day on which the Charles and Catherine Brabazon Memorial School would finally open its doors to the children of Quintin Parva and their families.

⊰╫╫⊱

One particularly hot July evening Simon and Matthew had decided to meet at the Old Cider House, now a smart village pub, which had a small, but first-class, menu and just four, spectacularly chic, en-suite bedrooms.

'Have you any ideas about how we should mark the opening of the school?' asked Matthew. 'When we opened the Prep School, we had the local MP – Conservative, of course!'

Simon was in a particularly serious mood, because he genuinely had no idea about how to suitably mark the opening of the school which meant so much to his wife, and so failed to respond to Matthew's gentle humour, commenting simply, 'Not really. Grace just wants to get on with the pressing business of educating the children! She hates fuss as you know, Matthew. To invite some sort of local celebrity – Martin Clunes or Sarah Challis, for example – would just make her curl up in embarrassment.'

'I wasn't thinking of a celebrity of that sort, Simon.' Matthew paused and took a long draught of his locally-brewed ale. 'I was thinking of Grace Romani – Grazia Romani as she is now known …'

'What!' Simon cut across Matthew's words. 'Are you mad? This is the woman who used to *be* the person who is now my wife – if you see what I mean.'

'I know it's complex, Simon – it's more than complex! But, as far as the community is concerned, Grazia Romani used to live here; her mother painted the works of art that made it possible for the new school to be funded; and she is now one of the leading "grandes dames" of European fashion. Think about it.'

In the days that followed Simon did think about it. He thought of little else. If they were going to invite this international figure to formally open the school, they needed to act quickly. But how could he ever, he agonised, approach the subject with his wife?

Taking a deep breath one warm, still evening, when he and Grace were relaxing in the deep shade of the ancient orchard which lay behind Pedders, he tentatively broached the subject, expecting a firm refusal. For several minutes Grace said absolutely nothing, but then looked at him with her direct and candid gaze and said, 'I think it is a good idea. I would like to meet the woman who lived the rest of my life, whom you fancied and who deserted my mother. Yes, I would like to meet her very much.'

'Grace, do I detect potential trouble here?'

'I am curious, Simon, that's all.'

After a particularly busy Wednesday in late August, Simon was sitting on the flagstone patio behind his beloved old house which seemed to bask, like a cat, in the sunshine. Eyes closed, he savoured the lingering warmth of the late-summer sun. Gradually his semi-doze was interrupted by the sound of the old VW Beetle that had been Alison Ingram's chugging into the drive and the ensuing laughter as Grace said goodbye to Annie.

'Honestly Annie, I could have walked, you know!' Simon heard Grace protest. The reply was muffled, as clearly Annie had remained in the car, but caused his wife to chuckle again.

'Simon!' she called. 'Where is the Chair of the entire village?'

'Stop teasing,' he replied. 'Someone has to do it! How about being my successor?'

Grace ran lightly through the French windows that led from the breakfast room into the garden and gave Simon a quick hug. 'No way!' she laughed, and then, after an imperceptible pause, added, 'How about becoming Chair of the Parent Teacher Association of the school as well?'

'Don't be daft,' laughed her husband. 'A – I am not a Parent; and B – I am not a teacher!'

'Well, guess what,' declared Grace, 'although B might not be on the cards, you will meet the essential condition to become A in, erm, approximately seven months!'

'Sorry,' muttered Simon, sleepily, 'What on earth are you on about?'

'Simon, wake up!' laughed Grace, giving him a hug. 'I am expecting our baby – perfectly timed of course – to arrive in the Easter holidays!'

'Oh, Grace,' cried Simon, leaping up from his chair and enveloping her in his arms. 'Are you sure?'

'Annie and I have been at the hospital in Salisbury for a scan to confirm it. Baby is about the size of a cherry, but is most definitely there!'

'This is amazing news! Sit down. Put your feet up. Do you have morning sickness?'

'Simon, for goodness sake, stop it! I am disgustingly symptom-free. I am fit and healthy and you need to save your bedside manner for your patients, who actually need it. Annie and I have been discussing child-care, and I will only need to be away from school for the first half of the summer term. As I said, perfect timing! Annie will be delighted to look after baby when neither you nor I are free. She actually said that she has always wanted a child of her own without the bother of having a husband, and that this is the ideal solution to her dilemma!'

'You are, without doubt, the most capable *and bossy* Headteacher I have ever come across,' he laughed.

'Yep!' responded Grace, grinning.

Grazia Romani
2015

Chapter 58

'Signora Romani?' Matthew had been revising his Italian intensively. The sort of man who could never do anything less than one hundred-per-cent professionally, he was satisfied that he could conduct a relatively straightforward conversation in Italian, inviting the head of the House of Romani to open their village school.

'Si,' the cool, well-modulated voice responded.

'Sono un governatore della scuola del villaggio Quintin Parva …'

'Ah,' the precise, clear tones cut across his carefully prepared words. 'Let us speak in English. Continue, please.'

Matthew noted that she had a distinct Italian accent, which softened and extended the ending of her words. Of course, he thought, she has lived in Italy for much longer than I have been alive!

Matthew explained the reason for his phone call, thinking himself hard into the fiction that he had to maintain, that the woman to whom he was speaking was actually the daughter of Charles and Catherine Brabazon.

'Signora Romani, we would consider it an honour if you would formally open our new village school.

Quintin Parva still remembers your parents fondly and with honour …'

'Ha! Now that Catherine has been properly buried, not thrown into a hole in her own orchard – si?'

'Ah, you heard about that?'

'I did.'

'It was nothing to do with the village as it is now, Signora Romani. That decision was made generations ago and has happily now been remedied.'

There was a long pause.

'And the Headteacher of your village school is?'

'Mrs Grace Patterson – Grace Adams that was.'

There was a clear, melodious laugh at the other end of the phone.

'Then I will come. And what is the date for the opening of the school?'

'We are planning for the 4th September.'

'I will be there. Ciao.' And there was a distinct click as she replaced the receiver in its cradle.

Matthew found he was perspiring freely with the effort of maintaining the distinction between reality and fiction. He breathed deeply to calm himself as he, too, replaced the receiver of his phone and, for once, loosened the knot of his immaculate navy silk tie.

Grazia Romani
&
Grace Patterson
2015

Chapter 59

4th September 2015 was a quiet, scent-laden autumn day. Morning mist lay like a light, white blanket across the fields and gardens of Quintin Parva and dispersed slowly as the sun rose across the tranquil countryside. Grace and Simon had been in the school since seven o'clock, ensuring that everything was as perfect as they could make it. Simon continued to marvel at the trouble-free pregnancy that his wife was experiencing. She looked, if possible, even lovelier, with a golden tan and a bloom of good health which enhanced her mobile and expressive features. Tania Martin arrived at a quarter to eight, almost as excited as they were about the start of this new chapter in village life.

The plan for the formal opening of the school was that there should be a special Assembly at ten-thirty, conducted by David Tullimore, who would lead prayers to bless the school. Grazia Romani would then say a few words and unveil the brass plaque, dedicating the school to the memory of Charles and Catherine Brabazon.

To say that Simon was nervous about the meeting between the two Graces was a monumental understatement. The obvious challenge was the surreal situation whereby, in a few hours, he would be meeting an ex-patient who had been some eight years his junior only five years previously, but was now a nonagenarian. But, for Simon, more pressingly difficult was that the woman who would be opening the school once 'inhabited' the body of his wife. Simon was no philosopher and could, quite simply, not find the terminology to begin to describe the transposition which had occurred between the two women.

Grazia had arrived the previous evening by taxi from Gatwick. She had asked her Executive Assistant to book her into the Old Cider House and had reserved the suite of rooms on the second floor. No-one in the village had yet seen her – quite simply because they had not been up early enough – because at five o'clock that morning she had slipped quietly out of the inn and walked through the mist, past the curtained and shuttered windows of the village, to Gypsy Lane. She had never ventured to this part of the village when she had lived with Annie Adams, and so she now compared the present to what she had known in the 1940's. It was so different. She had known that it would be, but the extent of the change shocked her and caused her to stop and catch her breath. A huge, modern barn had been erected at the end of the lane, on the site where the hidden traveller camp had been. Sheet metal and the latest modern cattle crushes replaced the timeless painted vardoes and the camp fire where she had met Romani. She walked carefully down the lane – metalled now – and stopped by the gnarled hawthorn tree where she had been pushed unceremoniously to the ground by the man who had become everything to her. She smiled as she remembered the way in which he had pulled back her long hair, and how she had bitten him, hard and deeply.

She knew that coming back to Quintin Parva would be difficult, but hadn't anticipated that a little of her life would be drawn out of her at the bitter-sweetness of each memory she encountered.

⊰))∥((⊱

All the children who had enrolled at the school had arrived and were settled in their two classes. Grace had decided to use some of the songs and rhymes that she knew her children loved – whether in 1943 or 2015 – and because they loved them, they remembered the words and the point of the songs. So, on this first day in the new life of the school, she started her registration with a song she had used on her first day of teaching seventy-three years earlier.

> *'Abbie Holmes, Abbie Holmes, where are you?'*
> *'Here I am, here I am, how do you do?'*

And so on, through the whole register of her twenty-nine children. She then moved on to the days of the week, with the similar principle of enjoyment being the route to learning.

> *'Sunday, Monday, Tuesday, Wednesday, Thursday,*
> *Friday and Saturday too,*
> *One, two, three, four, five, six, seven days, each day*
> *different and every day new.*
> *And today is???'*

1943 or 2015 – Grace was in her element. The joy on the glowing faces of her children was timeless.

All too soon ten-thirty arrived and Grace took a deep breath. She had told her children what was to happen and lined them up at the arched door leading into the senior classroom, which also doubled as a hall. Focussing deliberately on the well-being and behaviour of her children, in order to manage her own nervousness, she shepherded them into the high, light room. Tania had already organised her class to clear away the tables and chairs which they used during lessons, and they were now sitting on the floor in front of the benches and chairs which held their parents and families.

At last, all was still. Grace walked to the front of the room and said in a voice that was much stronger than she felt, 'Welcome! Welcome children, parents, friends and guests to this important day. Today the village school opens again, and will support and nurture its members to meet the challenges of the twenty-first century. I am delighted to welcome the Reverend David Tullimore, who will lead the first Assembly in our school; but I am especially delighted to welcome our guest of honour today, Signora Grazia Romani, who has travelled all the way from Italy to say a few words on this important occasion. For those of you who do not know …' Grace levelled a wide smile towards her children, '… Signora Romani is the daughter of Catherine Brabazon, who painted the wonderful paintings which we discovered here and sold in order to establish this school.'

Grace took a deep breath and looked steadily across the room to where Matthew sat next to an incredibly slender and elegant figure. She was all angles, thought Grace: angular cheekbones, asymmetrical jacket and a sharp, jagged side fringe below a sophisticated, upswept hair style. It was unbelievable that this woman was nearly one hundred years old. She sat quiet and composed, as if she was preserving every ounce of her energy. And she was looking at Grace directly, her blue eyes still vivid despite her age, almost without blinking. Grace tore her gaze away from this striking, immaculately-presented woman and returned to her role as Headmistress of a new school, who was introducing her speakers.

'So firstly, David, over to you.'

Chapter 60

The prayers had been said and the songs sung which the children had learnt during the 'introduction days' when they had spent time familiarising themselves with school routines before the official start of term. The children, teachers and governors sat down and an expectant hush fell upon the bright, newly-painted school hall. Simon struggled to equate the calm sophistication of Grazia Romani with the raw, troubled young woman he had tried to counsel in London – but it was simply impossible. And so, with an enormous effort, he pushed aside the maelstrom of emotions that he was experiencing, graciously inviting their guest speaker to address her audience. Taking his seat once again, he smiled wryly to himself, realising that where medical science had failed, a lifetime of love had succeeded.

With a smile, Grazia stood up and moved to the left of the brass plaque, standing next to a small table upon which was balanced a vase of late-summer flowers. Matthew had suggested that placing a table here would be a practical measure in case their guest had notes she wished to speak from.

But Grazia had no notes. Although she looked poised and the epitome of elegance, she was really very nervous indeed and had given much thought to what she should say to the village which had irritated her beyond measure, but had been the setting for some of the most sublime experiences of her life. She had no experience of children, but had cast her mind back to some of the earliest memories in her own life. One of her most precious possessions had been a battered book of fairy stories that her father used to read to her when he was able to get home before she was asleep, and she had decided that this would be a good place to start. So she began, 'Do you believe in fairy stories?' Several of the youngest children nodded vigorously.

'Well, I want to tell you one today. Once upon a time, a long, long time ago, there lived a girl who was very unhappy. She felt that she had no friends and that no-one understood her. But, because she thought a lot about happiness, she wanted to make everyone happy through making clothes for them – beautiful clothes that everyone would love. Everything was going well for her, but still she was miserable, because she felt really lonely, and so she started to take a potion that she thought would make her cheerful and successful. But instead, she found that this potion was poison and because of this she could no longer make the wonderful clothes.'

Grace had not expected this, neither had Simon. They both looked at the children, who were utterly spellbound by this 'fairy story'.

Grazia continued. 'Then, like the *Sleeping Beauty*, this girl fell asleep and woke up in a different time. She met a wonderful woman there, who became a real friend to her and soon she met a handsome prince. This prince also wanted to make everyone happy by making clothes for them, but this time the clothes he made were magic and people were completely altered and became good and very happy through wearing them.

'One day, the handsome prince said to the girl, "I have fallen in love with you and would like you to share my magic with me. We can make our enchanted clothes together and change the way that everyone feels about themselves." The girl had fallen deeply in love with the handsome prince too.' Grazia's voice faltered a little, but she gave a slight cough and continued. 'Together the handsome prince and the girl changed the whole world, because they followed their dream. They lived perfectly happily together, almost ever after, because they loved and respected each other.'

Grazia paused, then smiled again. 'The reason I have told you this story is that all of you …' she made an expansive gesture to include the children first and then their parents and friends, '… from today have the opportunity to become like that girl and her handsome prince. Follow your dream, whatever that dream may be. If you want to become a doctor, become one; a gardener, become one; a teacher, the same again – become one. If you want to design the sort of clothes that make people feel they are beautiful, then design them.

'Charles Brabazon believed in this community and he died serving it. Catherine Brabazon had a dream of beauty that she consistently captured on canvas. She created the sort of paintings that people with unimaginable wealth are delighted to buy, even today, many years after she passed away. Both these people followed their dreams and, because of that, this school has been established and is dedicated to their memory.'

A little flushed and somewhat out of breath, Grazia Romani pulled the tasselled cord which swept back the curtain to reveal the plaque. There was a stunned silence, before tumultuous applause erupted in the school hall. Grazia's speech had reached all members of her audience: the children accepted the moral of the fairy story, whereas the adults appreciated the accolade to the Brabazons. Grace was emotionally in shreds. The full impact, the many layers of meaning that the address had held for her and Simon, had hit her almost physically and she fought to gain control of her voice in order to thank the guest of honour for such a memorable and moving address. Simon, deeply affected himself, smiled at Grace and shook his head imperceptibly then rose, taking the responsibility of giving a vote of thanks for the powerful speech which they had just heard.

'Signora Romani, as Chair of Governors, I would like to thank you for such a fascinating and unforgettable address. I am sure that all the children will remember this fairy story and its moral all their lives. If one is determined enough, one *can* make dreams come true. Thank you once again.'

It was over. The two Graces looked at each other, tears standing in the eyes of each. Grace lined up her class and set them walking back to their classroom, to sit on the carpet in a circle, ready to talk about what they had heard. But before leaving the hall, she walked quickly across to her guest and reached out her hand, which was, in turn, taken by Grazia.

'Thank you,' Grace murmured. 'Please can we talk? Would you like to come to tea?'

'Thank you, but no, I must rest. I will meet you at the church if you wish, which I need to visit before I leave – but a little later. Shall we say six o'clock?'

Still struggling to bring her emotions under control, Grace simply nodded.

Chapter 61

Grace's shadow stretched long before her in the late-afternoon sunshine, as she walked up the hill to the church after school. As she drew level with the lych-gate, she saw the tall, elegant figure of Grazia Romani bending to place a bunch of wild flowers on the grave of Charles and Catherine Brabazon. Grace walked quietly across the churchyard and stood silently by the side of the other woman.

'She was a truly remarkable woman, your mother.' Grazia spoke softly, resting her hand lightly on the newly-inscribed marble headstone. 'We had such fun together, constantly trying to make food we could eat; running the boring sewing bees for the Institution for Women …'

'Sorry, Signora Romani, I don't understand.'

'Grazia, please. During the years I spent here in the 1940's, the entire life of the village seemed to revolve around the Women's Institute, headed by a complete old battle-axe called Ginny Hartley. Dear Romani could never get his head around the concept and it became known to all in the Old Vicarage as the "Institution for Women".' She laughed and looked so like Grace that it was uncanny. 'Let us sit by the fountain, Grace, and talk. It would be good to hear your story and perhaps you would like to hear mine?'

⊰⊹⊱

They talked for hours, until the sun dipped below the far line of round-topped hills and the first stars came out. They relived their earlier lives and the total shock of finding themselves living in another time. Grazia tried to explain the searing beauty of her relationship with Romani, and Grace smiled gently as she told how she had grown to love Simon.

Both women had been silent for a long time, when Grazia murmured softly, 'I came back you know. I wrote as often as I could, and Catherine answered – often short, inconsequential, vague letters, but answers nevertheless. And then no more letters came and so I had to come back to find out for myself why this was.

'When I returned, the vicarage was shuttered and dead. There was no life anywhere. I still had my key, so let myself in – and it was as if Catherine had left everything in an instant. A thick layer of dust lay everywhere – on the cups and plates on the draining board, clearly just washed and left; a solitary paintbrush lying on the floor of her studio; and a half-finished painting on an easel.

'Everywhere in the house it was the same – things just left, often in chaos. Letters lay in dusty swathes by the front door – mine amongst them. I picked them up automatically and placed them on the desk in the cosy room at the back of the house, which we used to call the snug.'

'My father's study.'

'Yes, I thought it must have been – I found many of his sermons there. It was as if the spirit of the house had just disappeared and a shell was left. I searched everywhere, but there was no clue to its emptiness. I looked around one last time and was walking towards the kitchen door to leave, when the front door-bell rang – dull and harsh with lack of use. The sound echoed around the hall intrusively, emphasising how lifeless everything was. I opened the door with difficulty, because it had swollen, with damp presumably, and the last person I expected to see stood there before me – the Chair of the Women's Institute, Ginny Hartley – but so altered that I hardly recognised her. She had aged almost beyond recognition, and seemed diminished somehow. Her Amazonian figure had become frail and bent and her skin had a yellow, unhealthy colour. Her expression was unfathomable as she looked unblinkingly at me.

'"She has gone. There is nothing here for you now. When you left and took away Mr Romani, you ripped the heart out of the village. It was as if you took away our hope ..."

'Romani had taught me how to pity people rather than attack them and, looking at the shrunken, stooped figure, I found no words to retaliate, but instead laid my hand on her arm.

'"But where has Catherine gone?" I asked her. "Tell me where I can find her – please!"

'"Never!" declared my visitor with venom, snatching her arm away from my hand as slowly she turned away.

'And that was the recurring refrain of my brief stay all those years ago. No-one would tell me anything. Some people, including the vicar, refused to see me at all. In the end I had to return to my Romani and my life in Italy with the mystery unsolved.

'Such a strange thing,' Grazia breathed softly, pulling her wrap around her shoulders. 'If we were not here, together, knowing that this had happened, we would never believe it. For two lives which were heading nowhere to have been completely changed and fulfilled by this, this ...' she struggled to find the appropriate word, until Grace lent across and touched her lightly on the arm.

'Would "miracle" be the right way to express it?'

Grazia nodded, reaching her left hand down to trace the outline of the carving that was just visible in the evening light. Unaltered, even after more than half a century, it twisted around the fountain, linking the paeonies, daisies and roses of Grazia's wedding flowers long ago in a timeless dance of beauty, circling the sparkling water that still gushed freely from the earth. Even in the dim light of evening, the gold and brown stone in Grazia's ring glowed lustrously.

'What a beautiful ring, Grazia,' Grace observed.

'Ah yes, beautiful and unique,' sighed her companion sadly. 'It is Romani. I lost him earlier this summer – the day after our sixty-fifth wedding anniversary. He was determined to celebrate our anniversary one last time. Over the months I had noticed him gradually becoming quieter and more remote and every day he seemed to be garnering every gram of energy just to live! I teased him about this, as I always did, but all he did was to take me in his arms and say, "I want to be with you every second I can, my love, but my time is coming to an end. But I *will* celebrate with you the anniversary of the happiest day of my life once more. I am determined to do this." And, as always, he kissed my hand, folding my fingers over the palm, one by one, as he had done countless times before.'

Grazia unconsciously mimed the action she was describing, leaving her hand softly furled around the ring. 'On our last anniversary together we exchanged cards, as always, but Romani gave me another envelope "to open tomorrow". That night we sat in our flower-filled garden and talked of our life together: the unforgettable time in England during the war; the years of intense creativity when we moved to Italy; and the legacy of one of the most influential and individual fashion houses in the world, which we created together over more than half a century.

'"And now, my love, goodnight," Romani said to me. "I am tired. I promised I would be with you always and I have never broken my promises to you. Read what is in the envelope – tomorrow."

'When I awoke in the morning, turning to Romani as I always did first thing in the morning, I knew he had gone. He lay like a beautiful marble statue – skin pale, finely chiselled features, thick white hair.

'I knelt by our bedside and opened the envelope that he had given me the night before. In his slanting, highly-individual handwriting, I read:

"My love, I promised that I would be with you always. When we went together to Herculaneum, shortly after we arrived in Italy, and I saw those lovers fused together for all eternity, I decided how this could be. I have contacted someone who creates jewellery from human ashes. My last request is that my ashes should become a ring which you wear until you, too, leave this earth and we are able to be together again. You have been everything to me my love, the beauty of

the dawn and the mystery of night. You have been my inspiration, my energy, my life, my all.

> *Always remember how much I love you.*
> *Romani"'*

Both women sat until the last glimmer of light had died from the sky. Each was thinking how much she had learned of the other's character and how much liking and respect had grown between them in a few short hours. Eventually, Grace said, 'I must go. I need to tell Simon that we have talked and … and I am very hungry.'

Grazia smiled at Grace, stood up and embraced her gently.

'And perhaps you are "eating for two", as the women of the institution used to say?'

Grace nodded.

'God bless you. Enjoy the rest of my life. I will sit and rest a while here. Remember us, Grace.'

Curling her tall frame into the curved stone at the side of the fountain, Grazia Romani let the cool of the September evening wash over her, soothing her, and watched the sprinkle of lights flicker on across the fields and wooded lanes surrounding Quintin Parva.

Peace fell like a soft blanket across the gentle countryside and, for Grazia, it seemed that time had ceased to exist. She hovered on the boundary of past and present, feeling, seeing, hearing life more intensely than she had done since she had lost Romani.

Whether it was the whisper of the breeze in the grass and flowers surrounding the fountain, or perhaps something else, Grazia again heard the words: 'Close your eyes … Now open them, my love.'

Swiftly, with no sign of age, she stood, beautiful and striking to the last, and stretched out her hands to the figure she saw in front of her.

The owner of the Old Cider House contacted the police later that night, having checked with Doctor and Mrs Patterson that their guest was not with them. They soon found Grazia's body, sitting with her legs curled under her, like a girl, leaning back against the stone of the fountain, her right hand wrapped tightly around her left, a smile of complete joy on her face.

Chapter 62

Grace pushed the little pram along the village street, which was decked out in red and white bunting in honour of the Quintin Parva Summer Fête. Simon strolled by her side, stopping to chat to villagers and stall holders who were tucked into the areas of grass and the gaps between cottages throughout the village. Henry, on a long lead, galloped haphazardly about, seeking out the food stalls. Grace had sailed through her pregnancy which, pronounced Simon, had been 'textbook'. She had a labour which was free of pain relief and their daughter arrived on the exact due date – St George's Day, 23rd April, 2016.

Grace had arranged for a highly-respected supply teacher that Matthew used regularly to cover her maternity leave and, since there was seldom a day when she did not drop into her school, sometimes with her baby, sometimes by herself, neither children nor parents particularly noticed her absence.

'Just look at that cot quilt, Simon,' said Grace, fingering the pattern of pink and white octagonal patches proudly displayed on one of the stalls. 'It's exactly what I'm looking for!'

'I can refuse the two most precious women in the world absolutely nothing,' grinned Simon, reaching into his jacket for his wallet.

The whole of this part of Dorset seemed to be thronging the narrow lanes of Quintin Parva on this hot July day. There were jewellery makers, quilters, mead brewers, cheese makers and cake-bakers everywhere and everyone seemed in a generous, end of term, mood. Doctor and Mrs Patterson were very popular. They had taken so much responsibility within the village community, naturally and without any self-importance, and were consequently liked and respected. Soon they reached Rose Cottage, where Annie had been asked to serve cream teas, which she was doing with her usual calm capability, only a slight flush on her tanned face indicating the pace at which her scones and cakes were being served and consumed.

Annie waved cheerfully to them both and came across to cuddle their daughter. She was almost a grandmother figure, caring for the baby, when Grace unavoidably had to attend to school business, with just the right blend of love and inclusion: the pram went everywhere, into the vegetable garden, outside the kitchen door and along to the meetings of the WI in the village hall. Annie would brook no objection.

Chatting with villagers who were intently admiring Annie's immaculate rose beds, Grace glanced down towards the stream at the end of the garden. On a flat section of lawn was a colourful gazebo with a very professional sign outside, pronouncing:

Mishca Lawton,
Clairvoyant
Tarot Cards and Palm Readings.

'Do you mind if I go down there, Simon?' Grace asked.

'I would have thought you had experienced quite enough strange goings-on in your life, Grace …' Simon said quizzically, '… but, if you really want to, of course I don't mind!'

'I'm taking baby too.'

'All right, Grace. As I say, I can refuse you nothing.' Simon kissed his wife lightly on the forehead and watched her walk across the garden to the gazebo as Henry tried to drag him towards the cream teas. Tentatively, she drew aside the canvas flap and found an attractive woman sitting, sipping water, on the far side of a small table. The clairvoyant greeted her softly, smiling and extending her hand. 'What can I do for you today?'

'Oh, it's quite difficult to explain, but I have had a somewhat unusual life and I wondered whether you could tell if my baby has anything unexpected or exceptional about her, anything strange to be faced in her future …' responded Grace uncertainly.

'What a sweetheart!' smiled Mischa. 'And yes, there is certainly something exceptional about her: she has two auras, a blue one and a golden one.'

Grace sat down abruptly. 'Oh, no! I was once told that – by Alison Ingram. It was all part of the strange experience that I have had.'

'Ali Ingram! I know her well!'

'Surely knew her, Mischa,' interjected Grace gently.

'No … Know her. She is really happy.'

'Ah, I see.'

'Tell me about your auras.'

'Well, Alison said that she could see that I had two auras: a blue one surrounding me, but a separate aura, a golden one, as if surrounding another person, alongside my own.'

'Intriguing … But that is not what I see surrounding you now. You have a single aura, which is blue. And, as far as your gorgeous baby is concerned, she has two auras, certainly, but one is *inside* the other. The overarching aura is blue, the one held within it is golden. This child has a powerful, fully-integrated spirituality, never fear. By the way, what is her name?'

'Grazia. Grazia Angelo.'

'Grazia *Angela,* surely?'

'No, quite definitely, our daughter is called Grazia Angelo.'

Grace lightly stroked her baby daughter's soft, rounded cheek with the fingers of her right hand, causing the bright July sunlight to be reflected off the surfaces of the ring that she wore. The central square stone, brown flecked with gold, was steadily magnificent, whilst surrounding it dazzling blue stones perfected and completed the unforgettable design. The love that had lit up a lifetime continued to live in the ring as, around the steady magnificence of Romani, Grazia's passionate beauty danced and sparkled in the joy of the day.

About the Author

Alex lives in the Yorkshire Dales with her loyal labradors and husband who has the patience of a saint when it comes to her unconventional lifestyle. Alex has two highly individual grown-up daughters who are the inspiration for much of her work.

Before settling into country life and full-time writing, Alex enjoyed various careers in London, which she loves almost as much as the expanses of moorland in Yorkshire.

Alex grew up in the North of England, and, because her father, who was a well-known jazz musician, inspired her to try anything that life threw in her path, she enjoyed an eclectic childhood, before heading off to University to study English.

She is passionate about exploring the beauty the world has to offer and has been fortunate to be able to see many parts of it, inspiring her to regularly practise Tai Chi and Yoga with her like-minded friends.

Saving Graces is Alex's second novel, but there are more lined-up, so keep an eye open for updates, future books and events.

Find out more about Alex on her website: www.alexcharltonbooks.com

Or follow her on Twitter: @alexcharlton

CPSIA information can be obtained
at www.ICGtesting.com
Printed in the USA
BVHW071418160921
616891BV00003B/408